T0095043

THE LAST COURIER

THE LAST COURIER

A NOVEL

JOHN MARTIN

1SG USAR (Ret.)

iUniverse, Inc.
Bloomington

The Last Courier

Copyright © 2012 by John Martin.

All rights reserved. No part of this book may be used or reproduced by any means, graphic, electronic, or mechanical, including photocopying, recording, taping or by any information storage retrieval system without the written permission of the publisher except in the case of brief quotations embodied in critical articles and reviews.

This is a work of fiction. All of the characters, names, incidents, organizations, and dialogue in this novel are either the products of the author's imagination or are used fictitiously.

iUniverse books may be ordered through booksellers or by contacting:

iUniverse
1663 Liberty Drive
Bloomington, IN 47403
www.iuniverse.com
1-800-Authors (1-800-288-4677)

Because of the dynamic nature of the Internet, any web addresses or links contained in this book may have changed since publication and may no longer be valid. The views expressed in this work are solely those of the author and do not necessarily reflect the views of the publisher, and the publisher hereby disclaims any responsibility for them.

Any people depicted in stock imagery provided by Thinkstock are models, and such images are being used for illustrative purposes only.
Certain stock imagery © Thinkstock.

ISBN: 978-1-4759-6437-0 (sc)
ISBN: 978-1-4759-6439-4 (ebk)

Library of Congress Control Number: 2012922415

Printed in the United States of America

iUniverse rev. date: 12/03/2012

Where had he come from?

K HAN WAS SURPRISED TO BE
looking at the face he had first
seen so long ago at the roadblock
in Lashkar Gah, and then again when the infidel had put his hands
on him at the border crossing in Zaranj. Even though the mission had
been to locate and kill him and his friends, Khan never really expected
to be face to face with him again. The first man looked back and forth
at the two, trying to decide what was going on. At last something in the
dim recesses of his brain told him that the man he was supposed to be
watching and protecting was in trouble and he needed to do something.
He was trying to draw a nine millimeter pistol from under his shirt, a
weapon he was totally unfamiliar with; he carried it because it looked
"cool". It snagged on his shirt tail and the fabric tore as he yanked it
out. Khan also drew his small pistol that he had taken off the dead
woman in Vermont. He had at least familiarized himself with it and
could manipulate the controls. His first shots went wide, but his target
dropped to a crouch. He could see the soldier draw his own weapon
from under his blouse. The girl behind him screamed something and
threw her computer. It hit Darnel in the back, and he turned and raised
his gun at her. Nothing happened when he pulled the trigger, and he
realized he had not put a round in the chamber. Price popped up and
fired a quick shot at Khan, missing him. Darnel got his pistol ready
and fired one shot into the girl's chest, driving her back over her chair.
He then pivoted and fired several shots at Price, all going wild, but
not hitting anyone. Price lined up his sights and put two rounds into
Darnel, center of mass. Darnel staggered back and looked down at
the red stain on his shirt. He looked up in time for Price to put one
between the running lights.

John Martin

To all the Warriors

CHAPTER ONE

THE SHEIKH'S YOUNGEST WIFE WANTED fresh fruit, and he always indulged her. The old man could deny her nothing, but since he never left the compound anymore, it fell to the lower echelon of the staff to run the errands. Gamel had made the mistake of answering the call of nature at an inopportune moment. He was returning from the out building at the back of the compound when the bitch came down the stairs screaming for pomegranates. There was no one for him to delegate.

Leaving the compound in the middle of the night was always an exercise that left the security detail in a bad mood. The soldiers on the street weren't the best the Pakistani army had to offer. The one's who had to stay up all night never were. They made a big show of calling 'headquarters' to get permission for someone to leave. Gamel suspected they were arguing over a dead phone, just to screw with him. It never happened during the day when he left. The Pakistanis always deferred to the Sheikh's own security to regulate the comings and goings. They just stopped people who weren't on 'the list' and let others clear him. Someday, Gamel thought to himself, the war will be over and these dogs would realize who the real masters are. Pakistanis aren't Arabs, the true chosen ones of Allah. While they would be saved for believing, they still ranked after Arabs, Kurds and Palestinians. They could be in Paradise, but not in the best part.

He had to wake the dog of a merchant to get the fruit. This Pakistani was a particular pain in the ass when he was roused in the middle of the night, but he was the closest, and one of the few who would bother to come to the door. There was always a premium for the late night transactions, but the Sheikh, usually a niggardly man when it came to household expenses, allowed it, because he would deny nothing to his youngest wife. There was also the added indignation of having to deal in English, which Gamel had a very poor command of. The merchant could speak Urdu, or even Arabic, which Gamel preferred, but at night he insisted on English. Someday Allah would curse him and his family, and all of Pakistan for adopting the language of the infidels for their own.

He was completing his bargaining with this dog when he heard the helicopters. The two that passed overhead didn't sound like the usual ones that buzzed around the nearby military academy. These were muted, the beat of the rotors louder than the engine. He strained to see where they were heading, but was distracted by the sound of a louder aircraft circling in the distance. It was unusual. The Pakistani Air Force did not like to fly at night. Their equipment was not well maintained and their levels of training were not the best. The Sheikh would be furious if these Pakistani maneuvers kept him up all night. He was an important man, with many important tasks to accomplish.

As he was concluding his haggling he heard a 'pop' from down the street. He looked to see what it was when the lights went out. Power failures were a common occurrence in this neighborhood, which was why the Sheikh had a generator installed. He only hoped the Kuwaiti who lived in the guest house remembered how to start it. Up and down the street he could see flashlights come on and lanterns being lit. He strained to hear if the generator was coming on in his compound, but the helicopter sound was too close, it was blocking out any street sounds.

There was a crashing sound from the compound. Gamel saw a quick flash of flame over the wall, followed almost instantly by shooting. There were loud bursts of fire, mixed with softer 'pops'. The Pakistani guards looked through the grate in the gate. The security inside was asking them for help. The soldiers argued with one another, then took off running up the street. The gate swung part way open as a darkened figure stepped halfway out. An invisible hand seemed to punch the back of his head, tearing his scarf off as he fell forward. Gamel got to him as another face peered around the gate. A blackened face put his finger to his lip and shushed Gamel, then pushed the gate closed. There was the sound of another helicopter landing in the field across the street. More men swarmed out and made for the compound. He could see some of them splitting off to run down the walls of the compound. Not knowing what to do, Gamel half crawled into the small guard shack. There was shouting in both English and Arabic on both sides of the wall. The gate opened slightly, and men started running to it from both directions on the street. Gamel heard another person on the other side of the gate, pulling it open. A suppressed burst of fire pushed whoever it was up against the gate, and Gamel could hear him sliding down. There were painful moans coming through the opening. He crab crawled over and pushed it in slightly. There was something keeping it from opening more than a foot or so. Gamel looked in and saw the body laying face up. He recognized it as belonging to another of the Sheikhs men, one of his advisers, the only men who were allowed on the third floor of the house. He wasn't dead yet. His mouth was trying to form words and he was trying to hand Gamel something. He could only hear a pained mumble, what sounded like 'Yemen' and 'Awlaki'. Gamel took an oversized envelope from the bloody hand as bullets slapped into the body. More bullets hit the gate above his head. Gamel scurried back into the shack as the gate was pushed open and the men on the street rushed in. The last man fired a quiet burst into the man on the ground, dragged him into the compound and pulled the gate shut. Gamel didn't know what else to do, so he forced himself as far back into the little guard shack as possible. He waited there, hoping whoever was shooting inside didn't come back out.

There were shouts in Arabic, then more in another language: it was English, he recognized it from his dealings with the dog of a merchant. The Americans had come to kill the Sheikh. They had found Osama bin Laden.

Gamel stayed in the kiosk for what seemed like an eternity. He kept wondering where the Pakistanis were. The Americans were here, in the same city as one of their most important military bases, with a number of general officers living close by. He had seen them. They came to pay their respects to the Sheikh on a regular basis. Some even come to pray with him on Fridays. How could they not answer this invasion?

All the voices he could hear were in English, and there was soon no more shooting from the people inside. A louder helicopter came in and stayed for several minutes. Figures Gamel hadn't seen before ran from the sides of the compound and ran to the helicopter in the field across the road. This one took off to the west. There were more shouts, some closer to the gate. He could hear someone dragging the body out of the way, and the gate opened a little wider. A figure all in black looked out and swept the street with his rifle. He looked into the kiosk and again made a gesture with his finger to his lip, then pulled the body of the first man Gamel had seen killed back into the compound. The gate was slammed shut again, and the latch was closed. Flashes illuminated the grate. Gamel thought that the Americans were taking pictures of the bodies. He had heard the Americans liked to take pictures of their trophies. Pretty soon there was the noise from the helicopter leaving, and an explosion from where he had seen the first shot of flame at the beginning of the attack.

Everything became quiet. Gamel pulled himself out of the kiosk and tried the gate. Someone had secured it from the inside. Up and down the street sirens started blaring and flashing lights were racing towards Gamel. He still had the bloody envelope in his hand. He had forgotten all about it. He quickly stuffed it inside his shirt and started across the street. He found himself surrounded by Pakistani soldiers, all pointing their weapons at him. An officer grabbed him by the shirt and pulled him to the back of a truck.

Gamel lived for another 24 hours. He had only been interrogated by the Pakistanis for a few hours. They started by asking questions accompanied by slaps across the face. A Colonel was giving directions, but didn't seem to want to dirty his hands on the prisoner. After he had given up the envelope, the Colonel left and the routine changed to closed fist punches and the occasional baton on his knees or shoulders. No one was asking questions. They were joined by a well dressed Arab Gamel knew only by his title of 'Doctor'. He may not have been a doctor. He was one of the infrequent couriers who visited the Sheikh. There had only been two, and they were only referred to by their professions.

He noticed that when the Pakistanis turned over the envelope they had taken from Gamel, the only thing left in it was a small computer flash drive. Early on they had removed a very fat wad of US one hundred dollar bills and split them up. No mention of the money was made to the courier.

The courier proved himself to be an extremely efficient and cruel interrogator. He kept Gamel alive and in agony as he milked him for every bit of information he had. There were three concerns in his questions: did he know what was on the drive, how had he helped the Americans, and what was he supposed to do with the envelope? All Gamel could do was repeat the two words he had understood, 'Yemen' and 'Awlaki'. Once the 'Doctor' was satisfied that he would learn no more, he insured no one else would be able to use more effective methods. He cut Gamel's throat with a pocket knife.

The Doctor left the room without another glance at the body. The Pakistani Colonel was waiting for him. They spoke for a few seconds, long enough for the 'Doctor' to make certain there would be no record of his presence, or any trace of Gamel's body. The Pakistani gave him another piece of information. "After the Americans left we entered the compound to provide what assistance we could. We discovered that Osama's body had been taken by the Americans. Do you think they are going to put him on display somewhere?"

The 'Doctor' shook his head. The Americans may be able to make a bold move like striking into the heart of another country, but a bolder move like displaying a body as a trophy, as the Iraqis did in Fallujah, was beyond their political will. This was the fourth time that he was aware of that they had made a deep penetration raid; North Vietnam, Iran, Afghanistan in the early days, and now here. The military was formidable if left to its own devices. Fortunately, the American political leaders were too timid to use it to its full capabilities.

That seemed to conclude their business. Neither man had anything else to say. Satisfied, he wrapped a cape around his shoulders, patted the flash drive in his pocket and headed for the door. The Colonel called out a last warning, "The airport has been closed, my friend, and our airspace is about to be closed to all but our Air Force. You will have to travel overland. What will you do?"

"There are routes, and there are routes. I will find a way."

"May I suggest either north to Dushanbe, or south and east to Mumbai? It will limit your exposure, and it is a shorter journey before the borders are closed."

"Thank you for your consideration. I have stops to make along the way, and not all airports are as considerate as yours. I doubt the Indians are as sympathetic to my needs as one would like." Truly, since the attacks in Mumbai there had been even more security. He missed the old says, before the Americans and the drones had terrorized the friendly governments. Once, numbers of diplomatic passports were available and official planes were at his disposal. Now he was reduced to using a dwindling number of blank documents the forgers still had access to, and it was only a matter of time before the facial recognition technologies penetrated his disguises. He waved to the Colonel and went into the early morning light.

The courier ignored two important details once he was satisfied with his work. He didn't consider the Pakistani Security Agency, the ISI, would have had enough interest to copy the drive before they turned it over to him. He could imagine that now that bin Laden was gone they would want to wash their hands of anything to do with him. He had also taken their word that they had not used the battery of audio and video recording equipment to capture his image. They had, and the colonel was already making arrangements to sell the drive to his contact. The man was supposed to be a Russian, but the colonel believed he was really with the CIA. It didn't matter to him, the money, either Euros or Dollars, was just as good.

The 'Doctor' knew none of this. He had always expected that the people they had bought would stay bought. His car was waiting outside the gate. It was an older Mercedes, old enough to demand respect on these miserable streets, but not fancy enough to draw too much casual attention. It had been his mode of travel between Abbottabad and Karachi, and he would miss it, along with his driver. The man had been reliable and loyal, but once they got to the next safe house several hours away he would merely be a link that needed to be severed. He would become one more anonymous body no one would claim. As they drove off he turned the flash drive over in his fingers. The regular practice had been to encrypt any data just before the turnover, in the presence of the courier, with the decryption key hidden in a routine email to the intended recipient. It was done that way so any last minute files or instructions could be added, because once the key was sent, no record was kept. Only the recipient could unlock the secrets. The Doctor doubted that he been done this time, considering the sequence of events. He would have to check it when he had a safe opportunity. If it hadn't been coded, he would have to destroy it if he were compromised.

"Which way are we going?" The driver asked. "North? South?"

"Neither, my friend. I doubt the Pakistanis are enamored of us any more now that the Americans have paid them a visit. Head directly west. We will have to depend on whatever may be left of the Haqqani network." The Haqqanis were a Taliban off-shoot that specialized in spectacular, yet pointless attacks. "First we must stop at the flower stand." The flower stand had been one of his more secure safe houses, used only on the rarest of occasions. Since this would be the last time it would be used, it was disposable. "There are several details I must deal with before were leave."

From the safe house, Farouk al Assiz, his new identity according to his Qatari passport, walked several blocks to another, more ramshackle part of town. There he found a motor bike waiting for him. It looked like any of the thousands of others plying the roads of Pakistan, except this bike was meticulously maintained and carried a larger fuel tank, enough to get him to the tribal areas and the unregulated border with Afghanistan. It would be a two, possibly three day journey. The Pakistanis would have more roadblocks and checkpoints up now that the Americans had shown them what they thought of their sovereign status. It would cost most of his supply of Pakistani rupees to bribe the illiterate peasants that manned them. No matter. Farouk al Assiz despised Pakistan. It was nothing more than a colonial beggar, albeit one with a nuclear weapon. They never shook the vestiges of being part of the India of Great Britain. They kept the language, and even the unit of currency. They could not hold onto the lesser part of their country, East Pakistan, now known as Bangladesh. It was an abomination of an Islamic nation. He would be glad to never venture here again.

The trek to the border had indeed taken three days. The traffic at the roadblocks was slow moving, and his Qatari passport invited cursory searches that required rupees to avoid. There were several occasions where the road was closed for no reason, and remained that way for several hours. His final stop in the tribal area was at an unremarkable village that specialized in smuggling anything and everything in and out of Afghanistan. They had been doing it for years, since the days when they been a conduit for American supplies during the Russian occupation. After the withdrawal, the Taliban used them for one of their many routes for the lucrative opium trade. It was a convenient way station for al Qaeda agents trickling back and forth. The premium they were paid made them extremely reliable.

There was an old laptop computer in his quarters. There was no internet connection, no Wi-Fi, none of the capability to connect to the World Wide Web. It was intended to be so. He checked the fingernail polish that had been discretely applied to the screws and opened the battery compartment. It had not been tampered with, and there was no battery. After he was done it would be destroyed in a fire pit, and he would bring a replacement if he ever ventured this way again. It was a convenience to be used for viewing videos or checking computer disks that may have been sent to him with instructions, nothing more. Disposable cell phones were his preferred and only means of communication. He ran the power cord to a generator supplied outlet and powered up. He disliked the generator, but the local tribal elders distrusted solar panels. They viewed them as the work of Satan. He inserted the flash drive into a USB port and waited for the computer to recognize it. Once it did he called up the directory and selected a file to open. It was an unencrypted JPEG file containing several dozen photos. He selected the 'slide show' option and paged through them. After photos of several buildings he couldn't identify, but obviously were somewhere in the West, he paused at a picture of four American soldiers. They were walking abreast towards the camera. They were dirty and some were bloodied, and all were heavily armed, and each had a number above his head. In the background were some flames and smoke, maybe from a battle. The caption read 'The Wild Bunch'. It meant nothing to him. Other photos were numbered to the photo, giving close ups of each soldier. Some were captioned, but most were not. Other than the one group shot, the rest were individual pictures, some official looking, and others candid. The document files would give more information, but that would give him information he did not want to have. Looking at the photos was harmless. He flicked through them slowly, and came back to the group shot. The caption intrigued him. What was the 'Wild Bunch'? He removed the flash drive and shut down the computer. He thought for a moment about the Pakistani Colonel. Would an intelligence officer give up such a prize without making a copy? He would have to arrange a visit to the mans' home to check. Many of the ISI were on multiple payrolls. That one was no different. He used another of his dwindling supply of cell phones. When he was done it was put aside to join the computer in the fire. It was time for his next rebirth.

Farouk al Assiz, Qatari pilgrim, vanished from the face of the earth. He was replaced by Hosni Jabbar Mahoud, a Palestinian relief worker, the man he would be through Kandahar and Lashkar Gah. There, he would change identities again for the journey into Iran. He had been traveling in this manner for so long it was like putting on a clean shirt. It had helped him to remain anonymous through these long years. Now he would complete this one last mission for the cause and slip into obscurity. He smiled at the thought. There were caches of money, bullion and bearer bonds throughout the Middle East, South Asia and Europe. He knew most of them, because he had been responsible for placing them. He would establish his final identity in Sana'a, Yemen, transfer several hundred thousand dollars to bank accounts in Paris, Geneva and Venice, then leisurely travel the world and collect several millions more. Life would soon be good for him.

CHAPTER TWO

SERGEANT FIRST CLASS JONAH PRICE was in the process of re-evaluating some of his life's decisions for the third or fourth time today. His decision to volunteer to come to Afghanistan as an engineering NCO with the new Stryker Brigade may not have been his smartest move of the year. It was, sad to say, after ten years of war, led by a very inexperienced command group. That would be forgivable if they were willing to listen to the voices of experience, but they weren't. The Brigade Colonel, his staff, the battalion commanders and their staffs were all field grade and senior company grade officers who had somehow managed to avoid a combat arms deployment. The collective Sergeants Major were similarly blessed. They had suddenly realized that in the smaller post-war Army that was coming they would not be competitive if they hadn't at least been shot at. A lot of them spent too much time trying to get shot at and not hit, to the detriment of the people who were happy with a quiet day. His heavy equipment platoon had become a Brigade asset that was sent all over the Area of Operations doing what he considered to be these little shit jobs. Price was not a popular NCO in this Brigade. He was not one of their old familiar faces, and had a lot more combat experience than they were used to dealing with. He had been on the pointy end of the stick for his country for a very long time, and it showed every time he was able to express an opinion. The Brigade staff hated the fact that Price was usually right, and the younger company grade officers looked to him for guidance. The final straw had been during a pre-mission briefing from the Brigade operations officer. Price corrected the sand box mock-up of the objective based on his personal reconnaissance. There was a brief 'disagreement' about the details, until another officer produced an aerial photograph that showed the gully that Price had insisted was there. It was a high speed avenue of approach for any bad guys in the neighborhood, and it was exactly the route they used when they tried to ambush his work party. It was one thing to show up a Lieutenant Colonel, but when he called for questions at the end of his brief, many of them were directed at SFC Price. It was no way to win friends or influence people.

That led to a succession of odd jobs in out of the way places, usually where there were a few locals who weren't fond of the *infidel* help. His habit of sending heavy equipment rolling through poppy fields didn't help, but the NATO program for opium eradication kept him out of a court martial. There had been a brief attachment to a French Foreign Legion company that had truly been an eye opener. The Legionnaires liked their beer, wine and combat. They would use Price's equipment as bait and pounce on any Taliban who rose to the challenge. It was taking the fight to the enemy, but it was endangering his people. When he complained to the French commander, the response was "The Legion sends us to where men go to die." Price was very careful where he sent his people for the remainder of that assignment. He was pretty sure there had been a complaint to Brigade from his less than gracious hosts.

Today Price been tasked with repairing a blown culvert on a one lane goat path in the middle of nowhere. Close by was a small mud hut village a couple of hundred meters to the south. There had been children kicking a soccer ball around when they had arrived a few hours ago, but they were long since gone from sight. There were no kids hounding the Americans for their rations or their empty water bottles. That was not a good sign. When he first came to Afghanistan, Price would not have hesitated taking a squad through it to make sure the Taliban or any other rag heads with a gun or an RPG weren't lurking for them. That was then, and this was now. Rules of engagement had changed drastically, and some days it wasn't worth getting a JAG lawyer involved in the decision making process.

Down the road, a British explosive ordinance detachment was taking its' sweet time poking around the rubble of the culvert. Price had watched them suit up, poke around, come back, check some other equipment, then change who was wearing the suit. His own EOD guys had been detailed for a dog and pony show at the province government house, so he was dependent on the kindness of strangers. Price didn't mind working with the Brits. They were methodical, professional and cautious, three traits he was beginning to love, especially after dealing with the French. They just took so damn long at everything.

His driver was coming down the road with a message pad. The sound of a helicopter in the background told him what the message was. Somebody with no skin in the game wanted to know what the delay was, and the helicopter was carrying that somebody.

"I think its bad news, Sarge. That's Bulldozer Six coming for a visit." Bulldozer Six was the call sign the Brigade commander had adopted. Price didn't understand why he would pick that particular name. The commander seemed to have an instinctive dislike for engineers, and Price was rapidly becoming his least favorite.

"Yeah, yeah, I know. He's got that scraper promised out to level a sports field for the governor. This military shit is screwing up his brownie points." He turned to watch where the chopper was going to put down. He'd have to get a vehicle over to it so the 'Six' wouldn't have to walk far.

The cry of 'RPG' came from somewhere. Price turned to see the white trail of a rocket skim under the Blackhawk. It immediately pulled pitch and flew off. He followed the smoke back to the building on the corner of the mud village.

"Get that M240 cranked up!" he cried as he fired his M-4 in the direction of the village. An RPG was usually backed up by one or two riflemen, and he could hear the cracks of their AK-47s. Another rocket was snaking out, heading for the Brits. They were already trying to get below the road surface.

"40 mike mike! Get a 40 mike mike on that fucker," Price called for a grenade launcher. The closest one was with his driver, now prone about 25 yards away. He was returning fire with his rifle, oblivious to what Price was yelling. The M240 machine gun was starting to hammer the building where the RPG was located. The 7.62mm machine gun was a good weapon, but a .50 caliber Ma Deuce would had turned the

12

sun dried clay into dust already. Price swore to himself as he felt himself get up and start dashing across the field. He was firing his M-4 with one hand as he reached into a pouch for a grenade. He glanced over his shoulder and saw one of the Brits up and advancing to support him. They were the only two on their feet. The Brit had a grenade launcher on his rifle, and Price wondered why he didn't use it. Another quick glance and he knew why. The dumb son of a bitch had been in the middle of swapping out the blast suit. He wasn't wearing his harness. He seemed to realize this as he ejected his empty magazine and clawed for a fresh one and couldn't find it. He quickly wheeled and ran back to where his gear was hanging from the front of his truck. Price was alone now.

He reached the line of the huts and worked his way to the corner where the RPG had been. An AK barrel came out of a window ahead of him, so he slowed and cooked off the grenade in his hand before pitching it in. As soon as it went off he was moving again, taking out another grenade and pulling the pin. He crossed the gap to the last building and pitched in the grenade. When it blew it must have ignited another RPG warhead and it took out the front of the hut and drove him back towards the road. His head began ringing like a church bell. He shook it off and came up on one knee. There was another shooter out there somewhere. Under the dust cloud he could see feet moving his way. Just above them he could see flashes. They were long, not round, so he knew they weren't aimed at him. He raised his rifle and emptied his magazine. An AK dropped to the ground and the shooter fell backwards.

Everything got quiet, except for the ringing in his ears. He had a quick thought: they hadn't gotten permission to return fire. Bulldozer Six would be pissed at him again.

It was close to dark before he secured the scene and headed his equipment back to the Forward Operating Base, or FOB. The shooting had brought out the legal people, the tourists and the vultures. The legal people wanted statements from everyone, as well as trying to determine who might have taken pictures. NATO was real picky about pictures of bodies on the internet. After the statements came the cross-examinations. Who started shooting first? What did Price and his men do to antagonize the village? Why didn't he take any prisoners?

13

The most foolish question was how did he know the men he killed were insurgents?

"They were firing AKs and an RPG in our direction. As far as I could tell, they were trying to kill me, Sir."

"I don't need any of your smart assed answers, Sergeant."

"Yes, Sir, but it's the only one I've got right now. We'd been here for a couple of hours. They had plenty of time to ID us. Am I being charged with anything?"

"Not yet, Sergeant, you field troops seem to think anything goes when you're trying to pick up decorations, don't you?"

That rankled Price. He never knew a 'field troop', whatever the hell that was supposed to be, who looked for ways to get his ass shot at. "My guys have all the decorations they want, Captain. They earned every fucking one of them. All they want is to finish out their tour and go home with all their parts working. They don't need any make believe shit."

The Captain scowled. "What's that supposed to mean, Sergeant?"

Price gestured to the crowd by the village. One helicopter had disgorged a squad of headquarters pukes, every one of them with a camera. It seemed as though only the troops in the field who were getting their asses shot off were prohibited from taking pictures.

"How many of those guys are going to put in for a Combat Action Badge because they were in the neighborhood and they heard somebody shoot at somebody else?"

"You're on thin ice."

Fuck it, Price thought. The worse they can do is send me home. "And how many of those CABs will be approved by some other rear echelon asshole that'll slip his name into the pile to get one too?" Price was starting to hear rumors that now the war was winding down, some of the late comers were scrambling to get their chests filled with something besides 'I was there' ribbons. They would need them to avoid the reduction in force massacre that was coming.

The JAG officer didn't answer. He turned and stomped off. As he did he pulled a camera from his pocket and headed towards the bodies. There was the sound of a different sort of helicopter coming in. It was an old ex-Soviet Hind wearing Afghan National Army markings. The bird looked beat up, showing every one of the thirty plus years it had on its airframe. A couple of portly Afghan officers stepped out, along with a well fed civilian. Price knew that this was the shake down team from the provincial capitol. They would be counting every bullet hole, photographing every crumbling wall, and hoping for dead farm animals, or, even better, a body they could claim was an innocent civilian. Somewhere in Kabul there must be a government office charged with coming up with a price list, adjusted for inflation, for everything they could demand compensation for. It was always in the name of the people that the money was extorted, but in all his months in this bandit country he had never seem any damage repaired. Payments were never made in Afghani, the national currency. US dollars were the only medium accepted.

There would be a lot of cash changing hands before the day was out. Price went back to his people. The object of today's exercise had been to replace a culvert. It would go in fast, but it would go in today. There was no way he was coming back out here again. He gathered his equipment operators and told them what he wanted done.

Several days later Price was supposed to be enjoying a bit of down time back in the rear. It just didn't seem like down time because there was an awards ceremony scheduled for today. Price hated these things. Once in a while it was actually for deserving soldiers, the guys that pushed the sharp end of the stick out every day and got another one pushed back at them. They didn't do it for the medals, but Price made sure his guys were recognized when they earned them. He could usually find ways to avoid these things. He didn't like the attention when he was the recipient, and he didn't always agree with the awards some of the people were getting. Today would be a fine example of situations that made him uncomfortable. The awards NCO, an old infantry Sergeant who had lost a foot to an IED in a previous deployment, was of the same mind set as Price, and had shown him the roster of awardees.

His Platoon Leader had put him in for a Bronze Star for what was being called the culvert fight, in spite of the fact that Price had told him not to. His driver was getting an Army Achievement Medal, with a 'V' device, for valor. The kid deserved it. He had stayed exposed on the road trying to cover Price. The British soldier who had charged behind Price had been written up for one too, but his chain of command rejected it when they learned he had forgotten his gear. Bad form and good intentions in the British Army would not be rewarded. The JAG officer was also getting an award. They were giving him a Bronze Star for Achievement because of his "diligent processing of reparations to injured Afghani civilians." In some alternate universe twilight zone, that probably made sense. Price shot 'em up, and the JAG paid 'em off.

Since his was the highest combat award, Price was first. After the salutes, citation reading, and handshakes, the visiting General moved to the left. It was a solemn moment. Salutes were exchanged, the adjutant began to read out the citation, and Price began laughing. He didn't mean to, but he just couldn't help himself. It was infectious, spreading through the ranks and building in volume. The adjutant, not knowing what to do, started to speak louder. The General kept his composure, but he was glaring at Price. The object of all the attention, the JAG officer, red-faced and forgetting himself, turned to Price and muttered, "You son of a bitch!" Price could only reply "Now you know what they think of you too."

The General ordered Price off the field. He saluted, made a very precise facing movement, and marched off, followed by a ripple of applause from the ranks. Price knew his days in the Brigade were just about done, but somehow, it really didn't bother him.

The General never spoke to him again. He did, however, remind the Brigade Commander how tenuous his position was and how badly his Officer Efficiency Report could suffer if he did not deal with Sergeant First Class Jonah Price. The Colonel and his Command Sergeant Major spent thirty minutes in a tag team relay telling Price how his career was going to end badly. As far as ass chewing's went, Price considered them both to be amateurs. They overstated what they could do to him and basically substituted volume for substance. Orders had already been cut sending him to a Provincial Reconstruction Team located in some shithole city called Lashkar Gah. They tried to make it sound like the end of the earth, but Price had known NCOs who had served on PRTs in Iraq. There was actually a chance he would be doing something worthwhile. His duffel bag and ruck were packed and he caught the resupply chopper out later that afternoon. He would arrange transportation from wherever it dropped him off.

Two helicopter rides later he was deposited at his new home, 627th Provincial Reconstruction Team-Lashkar Gah. They were headquartered in what the locals would consider a rich man's villa on the edge of town, but what Price looked at as a dump. The walls had been reinforced Jersey barriers and oversized sand filled temporary walls. The watch towers were made of plywood and two by fours, with Kevlar panels overlaid. Not perfect, but better than the sheet metal he had seen some of the Afghani bases using. There was a dead zone cleared around the compound ringed with concertina wire deep enough to keep vehicles, and car bombs, away from the walls. The guards at the main (and only) gate seemed relatively alert, and were joined by a US element that appeared to be made up of a junior NCO and an enlisted man. There didn't seem to be much interaction between the two groups, but that could've just been the time of day. It was something Price, who spoke only a little Pashto or Urdu would keep an eye on.

He was ushered into his new Sergeant Major's office, prepared for the 'welcome to the 627th you fuck up, your ass is mine now' speech. He was surprised when SGM Carver offered him a cup of real brewed coffee and had him take a seat.

"Did you really laugh at a Captain getting the Bronze Star?" was the first question out of the box. Price explained what happened. Carver wasn't amused. "Price, I don't care what you wear on your chest. Any decoration awarded is a serious matter, an honor for the guy getting it. If you don't think he or she deserves it, make your feelings known before the ceremony, the proper way, understand?"

Price understood. "I would have been fine if they hadn't read his citation right after mine. It just made me think of the rag heads shooting at me, and this dick head running the risk of a paper cut. In fact, rumor had it that he was processing some casualty paperwork and got a paper cut. He tried to argue that if it hadn't been for enemy action, he would have never been in a position to be handling that document. He put in for a Purple Heart based on it being an indirect consequence of enemy action. I don't know if it was true or not."

"It won't happen again. I'm gonna try my damndest not to get shot at any more and I'll stay away from JAG officers and award ceremonies."

The Sergeant Major stared at him for a long moment, trying to figure him out. He gave up. "Your records say you've had a couple of concussions, including one pretty recently. How's that coming?"

"I'm good to go."

"Yeah, sure you are." The SGM made a call on his radio, asking a medic to come in. They discussed Price's concussion as if he wasn't there, then the medic flashed a light in his eyes and looked into his ears. He had him follow his fingertip on a series of figure eights. "What's the verdict?" Price asked.

The medic didn't waste time. "Well, you've still got some residual effects. Your reaction time is slow to stimuli. I'd say you've still got a few days or a week or so to let your brain stop rattling around."

The SGM thanked the medic and dismissed him. "Sergeant Price, I think we'll have you running the mobile biometric team for a while." Mobile biometrics. Price knew exactly what that meant: running road blocks and scanning faces and fingerprints of just about everybody that came through. It was boring work, with people who usually didn't want to cooperate, but with the right interpreter and Afghan soldiers, it wouldn't be too bad.

His interview with the SGM was over. "I'll take you in to see the Colonel now." LTC Davis was the PRT commander. "Then I'll take you to meet 'the Seagull', your interpreter."

"The Seagull? Why do you call him that?"

"He'll fight with you over your MRE's, go through your trash, and act like a rodent anytime he's near your stuff. He's also protected by law, just like the real ones."

Price spent the next several days on the roving road blocks. The US troops had grown casual, letting the Afghanis decide where and when to set up, and which vehicles to interdict. Price didn't like that. Sometimes it almost seemed pre-arranged, and heavy traffic would slow to a trickle or completely disappear. He quickly exerted his position as senior man, and, thanks to his partial command of the language, was able to convince the Afghanis to do it his way. At least he thought they were convinced. Seagull said they were, even though they looked sullen when Price would have them pull up their road block and move it several blocks. Price didn't care. The people that were being warned off were the very ones they needed to be checking. He was getting different traffic every day, and the biometrics were better. Lashkar Gah wasn't known as a hot spot of Taliban or al Qaeda activity, but you never knew when you'd get lucky.

Price didn't trust Seagull. There was something about the man that made him think of a kiss-ass subordinate who was just waiting to stab you in the back. There were a lot of Afghanis who worked for the coalition forces who were determined to make their country safe and better for their families. They were the ones who risked their lives just by being seen actively rooting out Taliban and foreign fighters. Seagull wasn't one of them. He spent most of his time trying to convince the Americans to set up in areas that didn't pose any threat. He was much too willing to vouch for military age males who stumbled across their checkpoints. Price thought it just wasn't possible for a guy who never left the wire on his own, or without any Americans around, could possibly know or be related to that many people in the area.

He also redefined the meaning of the title 'Seagull'. It was almost as if he could hear you thinking about your MREs. His hovering was almost intimidating to the younger troops, and some were willing to give up their meal rather than put up with his pestering. Price told his soldiers to identify anything they were eating as pork. If Seagull didn't want to learn to read English, he'd just have to take their word for it. It didn't stop him from begging the accessories that came packed in every meal. There was a time when combat rations came packed in cans instead of plastic pouches. It was inconvenient, but more fun to throw at someone who was pissing you off. Price decided that the next time he heard from Dave Sharp he would ask him to send him a couple of cans of Spam.

This particular day they had set up just on the outskirts, on the road that wandered generally to the west. A quick check of his map showed that eventually it led to a border crossing with Iran. Not the best indicator of insurgent traffic, but worth a gamble. Even Seagull looked nervous when they had set up and started checking vehicles. Price felt he might be on to something if the locals were worried. He remembered stories he heard when he was a very young soldier about South Vietnam, and how one good indicator of Viet Cong activity was the absence of civilians, or the reluctance of the Army of Viet Nam (ARVN) soldiers to go into the area. He warned his two American companions to stay alert.

About 1100 hours traffic started to pick up. There was one vehicle in line that the Afghans seemed to be acting deferential to the occupants. It might not mean anything, but Price started wandering over to the barrels that made the vehicles slow down and weave through the portable barriers. He pulled a bottle of water out of his cargo pocket and started to take a swallow as the car, a white Toyota, was almost up to him. He dropped the bottle and stepped in front of the car, bringing his M-4 carbine across his body for emphasis. The driver stepped on his brakes and looked over to the passenger sitting on the other side in the rear seat. Only important people left the front seat empty to sit in the back. Price gestured the driver out. He called Seagull over and had him go through the standard drill. ID papers were scanned, and inkless fingerprints were taken. Price took out the facial scanner and got a good clear picture of his features. The man was fidgety, and sullen, but cooperative.

"OK, Seagull, get the other one out here."

"He is not an Afghan, Sergeant Price. His name is Hosni Jabbar Mahoud. His driver tells me he is a Palestinian relief worker. We have no jurisdiction over him."

"Says who?" Price's radar was up now. "If he's in this country, we have jurisdiction."

"Sergeant . . ."

"Only the bad guys don't want to be scanned, Seagull. Get his ass out here, or I will, then you can go looking for another job." Price started to walk around the car. Seagull knew that his life depended on working for the Americans. He lived in their compound, ate their food and enjoyed their protection. Take that away and his life expectancy would be less than that of a swatted flea. He moved to cut Price off. He made a big show of arguing with the man who went by the name of Hosni Jabbar Mahoud, finally reaching in and pulling the man out. Price could speak to a Palestinian; he spoke enough Arabic to converse with the best of them. He decided to keep this to himself while Seagull alternated between pleading and ordering the man to cooperate. The Palestinian argued back. *"Do you know who I am? Is your life so worthless you would put your hands on one of your betters?"*

"Forgive me. The American forces me."

"The American forces nothing. You are no better that an apostate, an infidel for taking their coin. Don't try to put your hands on me again!" He started to get back in the car when Price kicked the door shut and prodded him with his carbine.

"I've got a Russian pistol in my pocket I'll be taking off your dead body if you don't start cooperating." Price said with a smile. He prodded with his muzzle again. The Palestinian started to say something, and stopped. His eyes fixed on Price's and stared. His mouth was moving, saying something unintelligible. Price got the feeling this rag head recognized him. He mentally ran through his limited data base of Arabs he had dealt with. This one drew a blank, but there was something there. The Palestinians hands went up and he indicated he was reaching into his robe for his passport. Price nodded and indicated he could go on. The passport was scanned, and Price personally finished the processing. His two American companions moved in closer to observe and provide cover. The Afghans seemed to shrink back out of the way. Once Price was satisfied with the data he motioned the Palestinian back into the car, and then waved the driver in too.

Two cars back, Hosni Jabbar Mahoud's two man security detail were debating what to do. They didn't know who their charge was, but they knew he was important, and their own lives were worthless compared to his. The passenger reached into a space under his seat and withdrew a grenade. He pulled the pin, stepped out of the car and ran towards the road block, shouting *"Allahu Akbar!"*

The Afghanis reacted slowly. Price already had his hand on the pistol grip of his carbine when he looked up to see who was yelling. His eyes immediately locked on the grenade in the upraised hand. He smoothly brought his weapon up, moved the safety switch with his thumb, and fired a long burst into the attackers' upper chest. The body flew back, dropping the grenade in front of him. Everyone but Price scrambled for cover. Price kept his weapon up, scanning the area, trusting to the inherent inaccuracy of the grenade as an area weapon. The shock wave hit him like a strong wind, and the ringing in his ears started again.

Afghan civilians fear suicide bombers and terror attacks, but like people the world over, once someone else has been the victim of the violence they become your typical tourist. Hosni Jabbar Mahoud took advantage of the confusion and directed his driver to pull away. Somewhere ahead was his other escort car, the one that should have kept him from getting screened here. Now that his face and his papers were part of an American data base it would be time to shave his beard and change his identity again. He was running out of clean passports to use. His escort car was pulled in at a roadside fruit stand, the guards looking back to the road block. His driver pulled in and he conferred with the escorts. It was decided he would continue on in their vehicle, a faded blue Hyundai. His old car and soon to be dead driver would be left behind for the infidels to find. Mahoud considered his good fortune that the trail vehicle was ready to perform their duty on his behalf. The two he was currently riding with would have to pay for their laxness, but not until they reached Zaranj on the Iranian border and he could pick up his next set of escorts who would guide him across the border. He looked back over his shoulder as the car drove off, now thinking about the American who had accosted him. Who was he, and how had his photo come to the Sheikh's attention? Perhaps the Iranian intelligence service could shed some light on it.

Afghan security was swarming the area, as well as a scratch force of Americans from the PRT compound. Price's head was pounding from the blast now, and all he wanted to do was sit somewhere out of the sun and get some aspirin. He knew he had been concussed, and this blast aggravated the hell out of it. He leaned into the back seat of his HUMMV and poured some water over his head, waiting for a medic to show up, when he noticed some civilian types in tan outfits and light weight body armor moving through the crowd, buttonholing likely looking suspects and doing biometrics on them. CIA, he thought. A day late and a dollar short if they were looking for anything here. One of them looked hard at Price and broke into a smile. Price recognized him too, but his fuzzy brain couldn't put a name to the face. He thought he remembered him from the 75th Rangers from before the start of the Iraq war.

"Hey, Price, what the fuck are you doing here directing traffic? We heard you got out and were screwing around with some National Guard outfit."

Price could read the name on his vest now, Cummings. He remembered Cummings from before the war. He remembered he didn't like him, but he couldn't remember why. "What are you doing here, Cummings? You're a little late."

"We've been here all along, Price. We've been following that Arab you were hassling. Did you see where he went?"

"No, I got a little distracted. Who was he?"

Cummings handed Price a stainless steel flask. "You look like you need this more than water right now."

Price sniffed it and pushed it back. "I'll pass. Somebody smells booze on me and I'll really be fucked. Tell me about the rag head. Who was he?"

The flask disappeared into a cargo pocket. "No idea. We've been following that gomer since Kandahar. CIA put us on to him, but we don't know why. We've pieced together some of his back story, but not much. He might be a courier. Rumor has it Paki Intel turned his picture over after the SEALs got bin Laden, but it's only a rumor. Guy you shot was his chase car. We took out the other guy. But you got the guys biometrics, didn't you?"

Price reached for the scanner that had been tied to his vest with an idiot cord. His fingers closed on jagged metal. He held it up for the other man to see. There was a grenade fragment sticking out of it. "Too bad, Price. We could have used that info."

Another tan clad soldier came up to them. Price didn't know this one. He reported that a Predator drone was up and checking the road to the west. There was a white Toyota that looked good parked about a mile up the road. They were going to check it out.

"Keep in touch, Price. You get tired of this traffic cop bullshit and we might have a home for you."

Price waved him off. His head was throbbing and the light was hurting his eyes. He hiked himself back and lay down on the gun platform. All he wanted to do was get some sleep. The scanner rolled off his chest and fell on the deck. He untied it from his vest and dropped it into a dump pouch. He'd worry about it later.

Some medics finally arrived and started checking over the US personnel before they went to the civilian casualties. Price had a cold thought that at least they couldn't blame him for this. It wasn't his grenade, so the JAG dickhead wouldn't be around passing out hundred dollar bills. One medic took one look at Price and called his partner over. Price could feel himself fading in and out and was having trouble focusing. The medics coaxed him out of the HUMMV and had him lie on a stretcher. Where the hell did that come from? Price wondered. The medic was yelling in his face, something about an IV. He felt a stab in his arm and his vision started to clear. There was a clear plastic bag hanging from the door handle of the truck.

"How're you doing, Sarge?"

"I'm OK" he tried to tell the medic. "Just a little bit of a headache. Got any aspirin?" He felt another prick in his other arm. He looked and saw a hypodermic needle being withdrawn. What the hell was that for?

"OK my ass, Sarge. You've got blood coming out of your nose and your eyes are all bloodshot. You're about as fucked up as you can get without having any extra holes, so just stay there. We've got a bird coming for you. I gave you something for the headache. It should be going away pretty soon."

He felt himself being lifted and put into an ambulance. The medic was right about the pain. It was slowly going away, and so were all his other feelings. It was a short bumpy ride to an open field where he could hear a Blackhawk coming in. He strained to look for it, but his eyes didn't seem to want to open. The rotor downdraft felt sharp against his face from the dust it was kicking up. The medic was yelling something unintelligible to the chopper crewman, and he felt the straps going across his legs and chest to keep him from sliding out. He hoped they'd be flying with the doors open. He always enjoyed a helicopter ride more when they left the doors open.

CHAPTER THREE

COMMAND SERGEANT MAJOR LUCAS GRANT was on leave and enjoying himself. The stool at the beach side bar of the Orangestad Caribbean Resort Hotel in Aruba had become his regular perch. From it he could make his forays into the water to cool off, or just sit there and enjoy the all-inclusive amenities (liquor included) and keep an eye on his traveling companions. Well, at least one of his companions. Sergeant First Class David Sharp and his companion, Sergeant Sheila Gordon, could look after themselves. Major Linda Bonneville was sunning herself down by the water's edge. She was the only piece of scenery he was interested in.

He would have preferred to be doing all this somewhere on the Mexican Pacific coast. It had long been his favorite vacation area, but that had ceased to be a travel destination for him and his friends. After they had cleaned out Mexican military drug cartel that had controlled a big chunk of the border area west of *Cuidad Juarez* by crossing the border, actually invading Mexico, and killing most of them, Grant and most of the members of the 289th Engineer Support group had been declared *persona non grata* by the Mexican government. Short of going to war, it was probably the best agreement the US government could make for them. They were now subject to arrest and prosecution if the ever set foot on Mexican soil again. There was still some negotiation over whether they would be referred to the International Criminal Court in The Hague, but a smart assed State Department geek had sort of promised that would not happen. It was ironic, therefore, that the US government had arranged for this trip to a Dutch territory. That was the reason Grant had acquired a .32 caliber automatic that resided in a zip lock bag in his cargo pocket. All his vacation clothes had cargo pockets, and no one gave them a second look. He would have preferred a .45 auto, but the .32 was easier to conceal. He didn't know if Sharp had picked up any fire power, but he was sure he had. Sharp was also a very cautious man.

Just before lunch a new face had appeared at the far end of the bar. Ordinarily that would be unusual, because mornings were usually check-out time for the tourists, and the new ones didn't show up from the airport until after lunch. He had been expecting something like this, but not as obvious as in the middle of the day without a crowd around. He had sensed that they were being watched for the past few days. There always seemed to be an extra tourist in the crowd, staying just far enough away to have his face obscured, but always snapping pictures in their direction, sometimes with a camera, sometimes with a phone. Always far enough away to be able to react and disappear if Grant moved towards him. If he had been dark skinned, or al least tanned, he could have been a local, but this guy was as white as a northern tourist in January. He kept a cell phone open on the bar next to his alcohol-free frozen lemonade. Grant was planning on getting his hands on it. If Sharp ever dragged his horny ass out of bed and came down they could double team him, otherwise, Grant would just wait for an opportunity.

Bonneville was coming up from the beach. Grant admired her figure, tanned as it was in a white bikini. She was, to say the least, well equipped, and men took notice when she walked by. A quick glance and Grant could see his drinking companion was also paying attention to her as she slowly came up the beach. He signaled to the bartender to get a drink ready for her so she wouldn't have to wait. She walked by without stopping, heading for the rest rooms. Grant waited until New Face was distracted, watching her pass by, then he made his move and picked up his phone. Grant slipped it in his pocket and was back on his stool before New Face turned back to his drink. He had taken a long swallow and looked back to the rest room before he looked at the bar and noticed his phone missing. Grant pretended to ignore him and sipped his drink, waiting to see what he would do.

The man looked around the bar, then down on the ground. He motioned to the bartender and asked if he had seen his phone. Grant had been a generous tipper for someone who was on an all inclusive package. He watched the bartender shrug and shake his head. He wasn't about to jeopardize his regular tips for some teetotaler. Tourists who don't drink don't tip. Grant looked over and smiled. New Face got up and came over.

"Can I have my phone back, Sergeant?"

Linda was coming back from the rest room. She heard the man ask for his phone and guessed Grant had something to do with it. "Lucas, are you making new friends again? Give him back his toy."

Grant pulled the phone out and opened it. "Why?"

"Why should you give him back his phone?"

"No, Sweetie, I want to know why he's keeping tabs on us."

"I'm not keeping tabs on you. I don't know who you are. I just came over for a drink."

"See? Let the man have his phone and get back to his drink, Luke. We're on vacation. Don't start any trouble. We are running out of countries to be thrown out of." That got the bartenders attention. This hotel did get the most interesting people.

"Why did he call me 'Sergeant'?"

Sharp and Gordon picked this time to appear. Sharp signaled the bartender for two drinks and sat down on the far side of New Face. "Who's calling you 'Sergeant', Boss? I thought we weren't going to play that Army shit on vacation." Grant was looking down at the phone, scrolling through the photos. "For a guy who doesn't know us, he seems to have a lot of photos of us. Some of them look like ID photos." He kept scrolling. "And he's been after us for a while. Linda, he really likes the way you dress for the beach." He scrolled through some more. "Sheila, it looks like he's been watching you go topless," he held up the screen for her to see. "Dave, you want copies? It looks like he's been sending them to his friends." He snapped the phone shut. The .32 came out of his pocket, still wrapped in the zip lock bag, but ready for action. "I'm a little sensitive. If you've been briefed on who we are, you'd understand." Sharp stood behind New Face and patted him down. "Nothing on him but this," he tossed a small wad of bills onto the bar, "not even a wallet."

"I got nothing to say."

"Unless you want to disappear like Jimmy Hoffa, you better start talking. Who are you working for?"

New Face remained quiet, looking down at the gun. "You won't use that."

Bonneville grabbed his arm. "Luke." Grant looked at her and grinned, then turned back to New Face.

"I guess you weren't briefed. OK, Dave, go get the Jeep. We're going to take a little trip to the north side of the island. Let's see if he's ready for martyrdom."

"What the fuck are you talking about? I'm not going anywhere."

Another voice came from behind him. "I don't know what disappoints me more, Sergeant Major Grant. Taking two days to spot a tail or trying to frighten my man like a little child. You're excused, Mister Smith. I'll handle them from here." Grant recognized the voice. It was the mysterious General Vaughn who had launched them on their Mexican incursion. Nothing good could come of him being here.

"Mister Smith? Is that as original as you could get? What do we owe the pleasure, Vaughn? You don't strike me as the vacation type."

"I'm not on vacation, Grant. This is business, although it is always nice to see Major Bonneville. And I will remind you that I'm a General." With that comment she wrapped her towel around he body. The first time she had met Vaughn, in Grant's hotel room in El Paso, she had almost been naked. She blushed at the memory.

"I didn't think you were a one star back in New Mexico. I haven't seen anything to change my mind." Grant picked up his drink and finished it, then signaled for the bartender. The man had disappeared.

"You'll be happy to hear that I'm a Major General now. That's two stars for you to try to ignore." He held out his hand. "Now give me my man's phone back, we need to go someplace and talk."

Grant tossed the phone to Sharp. "Get rid of the pictures."

Sharp laid the phone on the bar. He picked up an ornamental coconut and smashed it. Vaughn winced. "That was a very expensive piece of equipment. You could have just deleted them."

"Sharp is pretty much a technology barbarian. Too many buttons confuse him."

There was a passenger van waiting for them in front of the lobby. Grant held everyone up while he sent Linda Bonneville and Sheila Gordon up to their rooms to change. Vaughn argued, and Grant ignored him. He wasn't having Linda taken anywhere dressed in nothing but a bathing suit and a towel. They took their time, and when they returned Grant could tell Linda had taken a shower and put on some makeup. She probably grabbed their passports and some cash in case they had to run. The bag she had chosen was just the right size.

"I'll need to see that bag," Vaughn said as he reached for it. Grant grabbed his arm.

"No you don't. You didn't ask for my gun, you don't need to see what she's carrying."

Vaughn looked at the driver and shook his head. Wise move, Grant thought. If I picked up a toy of a gun, I'll bet Sharp did too, and Gordon grabbed it while she was in the room. Vaughn waved them into the van and climbed into the passenger seat. They were driven to another upscale hotel a short distance away. Grant asked why they couldn't have done this at their hotel. The answer surprised him.

"This is one of several properties the United States owns around the world that actually makes money on an annual basis. It's almost an embarrassment for the government. It gives us a secure base of operations. That means it has facilities, and the briefing you're about to get is very, very classified."

"You own the whole chain?" Sharp asked.

"Not me, the National Security Agency, but yes, the whole chain."

They were led into a large conference room. A buffet was laid on a side table. Sharp and Gordon made a bee line for it and filled their plates. Grant and Bonneville followed. If Vaughn was going to screw with their time, the least he could do was feed them. When everyone was comfortably seated around the table Vaughn spoke to a computer operator at the back of the room. A series of pictures was put up on the screen. Grant recognized them from news reports: it had been Osama bin Laden's compound in Pakistan. A voice from the back of the room started to describe each photo. Most were routine architectural plans peppered with the tactical details used to overcome or bypass them. The display stopped at an undistinguished middle aged man, either Eastern Mediterranean or Middle Eastern. He was well dressed, with a robe over his suit. It was followed by several others, in which he looked increasingly disheveled and tired, with a heavier growth of beard on his face.

Grant broke the silence. "OK, who is he?"

"Hold your questions for a bit. We want you to look at a few more, just to set the right atmosphere."

The next photo was of the same man standing with a US soldier. It looked like it was at a check point, and the soldier was taking biometric readings. Grant felt Sharp's elbow. He nudged him back. "I know. I see him." He whispered.

The next series of photos was disturbing. It started with the 'Wild Bunch' picture taken in Moldova that the troops had widely circulated among themselves after someone had discovered the tie-in with the movie of the same name. This copy had numbers on each figure. The next sequence was of each of each of them: Grant, Sharp, Price and First Sergeant Ralph Harrison, individually. There were some candid shots from different phases of the deployment that could have come from any number of web sites the troops liked to use. Then there was a series of Linda Bonneville, starting somewhere in Darfur. There were official Department of the Army file photos, candid snapshots from the operation in New Mexico, and what looked like surveillance photos taken after the 289th Engineers had returned to home station and deactivated. Price was missing from the line-up after New Mexico. He had stayed on active duty and deployed with another unit from New Mexico. Whoever had been doing the surveillance must have lost track of him. There were also some shots of the B-17, the 'Wicked Witch' that they had recovered in the Sudan. The restoration was coming along nicely. The parts that the General Services Administration had let them recover from the hanger in New Mexico had been put to good use. The plane was finally off the stands and jacks and was sitting on its own undercarriage. The last was a group shot of them waiting in Fort Bliss for their flight back to home station. That was the end of the slide show. The picture of the Arab went back up.

Vaughn stepped to the front of the room. "Any questions?"

Sharp started. "I can think of a bunch, but let's start small. How did they get the pictures of us?"

The best we can tell is that they were taken right off the internet, with a few exceptions. There's a mosque about a mile from the State

Reservation that's been asked to keep an eye on you. Before you ask, we have an informant inside.

"Who's the Arab?"

"The Arab is, or was, called Hosni Jabbar Mahoud. He is believed to be bin Laden's last courier. He was given a flash drive that may have been salvaged from his compound in Abbottabad. We don't know how it was overlooked, but it was in the hands of a servant that the Pakistani Inter-Service Intelligence Agency scooped up after the raid. The Colonel who retrieved it was playing both sides of the fence. He turned it over to the courier, but made a copy and sold it, this photo, and a copy of the interrogation of the servant to us."

"Where's this Pakistani now?" Grant asked.

"He's dead. Somebody shot up his car as he was leaving for work three days after the raid. We think al Qaeda didn't want to work with him any more. He might have been their link to the ISI, and they were disappointed in his performance when it came to protecting their boss."

"In any event, the rest of the pictures of him, up to the road block, were either obtained or taken by us. There was a suicide attack after the last picture was taken, and we lost him at that point. We haven't been able to locate that biometric reader yet. It nay have been damaged or lost in the attack. We think he's making his way to Iran and possibly Yemen. The car he was riding in was found about a mile down the road. His Palestinian passport was still on the seat. He must have had another escort car we didn't identify and he switched to it right after he got clear."

"Why Yemen?"

"His instructions seemed to be to deliver the data to Anwar al Awlaki. That bit we're not certain of. It was based on two words passed on third or fourth hand to us."

Sergeant Major Grant remained quiet. The briefing so far had been good, but pointless. If there were photos, there had to be documents. Vaughn hadn't discussed them yet. The fact that they were under some kind of surveillance back home meant they were the targets of an operation. Even if Vaughn wouldn't say it, they were targets. Grant was thinking that they were about to be used for bait.

"I have several questions." Grant finally said. "Let's start with documents. What did they say?"

"I didn't say anything about documents."

"I know you didn't, but I seriously doubt al Qaeda is just circulating our vacation album. There was a mission attached, some kind of operations order. What was it?"

Vaughn put his head down and conferred with a staffer at the head of the table. The staffer shrugged, nodded and shook his head. He handed Vaughn a folder, and Vaughn passed it to Grant. "Look at that later, and you'll know everything we do. It's a convoluted plan to bring weapons into Canada and across the border into northern New England. Some home town boys are supposed to meet them, get the weapons and kill all of you. It leaves a lot up to the imagination of the home grown jihadists. We are evaluating the plan to see if we can use it to shut down any network they have up north."

"Don't these idiots usually put a little more thought into their ops? 'Find these people and kill them' seems a little too minimalist, even for people who go around sticking Semtex into their diapers."

"Not really," Vaughn said. "We believe this may have been something one of the low level types was trying to run by the head man. More like a prospectus than a fully formed plan. We think that the fact that it was the only information that survived the SEALs pushed it off the back burner. If we can catch this Hosni Jabbar Mahoud before he gets into Iran, or before he hooks up with al Awlaki, there's no op."

"Have you told Harrison or Price yet?"

Vaughn nodded. "Harrison is being told as we speak. We'll brief Price as soon as we locate him. We have a projected time line, and, depending on travel time, we estimate there's a good four to six weeks before anything pops. Whatever happens, I thought that you would be the one calling the shots for your people. That seems to be how it's worked in the past. Harrison is busy standing up the new Engineer Battalion. You can decide how involved you want him to be."

Sharp perked up at the time line. "Four to six weeks? And you felt an absolute need to fuck with my vacation?" He looked at Grant. "Let's get out of here, Luke. This could have waited until we got home."

"Wait one on that." Grant had saved the best for last. "You can't leave out Price. What do you mean 'as soon as you locate him'? You can track an al Qaeda courier halfway around the world, but you can't find a US Army E-7 who never left government control? Other than that whole concept being totally fucked up on a whole bunch of levels, do you do realize how important he is to this whole thing?"

Vaughn looked like he was getting a little testy. Grant liked that. Testy people were off balance and often blurted out things they weren't supposed to. "Price isn't involved at this time. Our last information on him was that he's being evaluated for evacuation in Kandahar right now. He'll probably be on his way to Ramstein, then home in a few days."

"Shithead got himself shot again?" Sharp chimed in.

Vaughn shot him a scowl, and continued. "The good Sergeant has thus far avoided any gunshot wounds, although his last brigade commander would have gladly stood him up against a wall if he had the authority."

"How is he?" Bonneville asked.

"Sergeant Price is fine, Major, and I'm certain he'll be grateful for the concern. He's being evaluated for TBI, Traumatic Brain Injury. He's suffered several concussions, and the medics finally decided it wasn't in his best interest to stay in harm's way."

Grant insisted. "So you don't know where he is and haven't talked to him yet?"

"We haven't seen a need. As long as he's in the system he doesn't need to know. You can brief him in when he returns to the States."

Grant could understand the logic to that. Price had enough to worry about while he was recovering. Still, Vaughn seemed to be missing some important points here.

"Do you know where or when Price was injured?"

Vaughn said he didn't know. So Grant tried another tack. "You said you couldn't find the scanner in the last picture?"

"True. Unfortunately we haven't been able to identify the soldier who had it. There was an unconfirmed report that it was damaged in the grenade attack."

"You may not want to wait. I understand that TBI and concussions can affect short term memory, and you want to get into his head, especially if he's still in theater." He turned to the computer operator and asked him to put up the shot of the courier at the road block. Grant waved towards the screen. Vaughn looked at the screen, not comprehending what he was seeing.

"What am I missing here . . ." there was a pause, "Son of a bitch!"

"Yeah, in more ways than one. Price was the last person to talk to this guy. He's got all the information right there in his hand. He might still have it."

Price was sitting on the bus, waiting for the litter cases to be loaded first. There were only a few ambulatory casualties on the manifest, and they didn't require anywhere near the level of care some of the others did. More than one was a traumatic amputee from an IED. A few were traumatic brain injuries, or TBIs. They deserved every bit of comfort and priority they could get. There was only one over weight big mouth on the bus with his leg in a walking cast who was complaining about the wait. Even the nurses were tired of his whining. After another round of asking for pain medication and demanding he be given a litter and be carried onto the plane, a small blonde Captain come onboard and loudly told him to shut up or she'd arrange for him to be sent back to the field hospital to await a routine flight, which could take up to a week. The soldier protested that his priority was arranged and she couldn't change it.

"Your priority is 'Space Available'. The only reason you're here is because they got sick of your constant whining!" The Captain was really fired up about this guy. "Do you want them to know how you got here?" That quieted the soldier down, but only until the nurse left.

"She's got no right to talk to me like that. I was shot in a combat zone, and I'm gonna file a complaint with the Inspector General when I get to Germany!"

Price couldn't stand it any longer. He got off the bus and went to where the medics were waiting between litter loads. He recognized one who had treated him at the roadblock and waved him over. He asked what the story was with the cry baby. The medic tried to beg off, but Price insisted. "OK, Sarge. He was one of the medics in the post-op ward when he first got here. They caught him stealing meds from the patients. Instead of a court martial, they tried to transfer him out to a line outfit. The day his ride came for him he shot himself in the foot. They're going to hold his Court Martial in Germany"

Price thanked him and walked back to the bus. He sat down next to the self inflicted wound. When the soldier complained Price was crowding him, all eyes on the bus turned to see what was happening. Price leaned over closer and whispered in his ear. The soldiers face went white and he shrunk away from Price. As Price returned to his own seat, two soldiers asked what he had said. Price wouldn't tell them. Instead, he told them to take turns giving him dirty looks. That seemed to return peace to the bus.

Price was trying to get comfortable and maybe get a few winks in when a couple of HUMMVs pulled up. Two soldiers wearing Military Police brassards got out of the lead vehicle and approached the medics. The one Price had just been talking to pointed at the bus. The little Captain came over to find out what was going on. Whatever it was made her angry, and a brief argument took place. One of the soldiers gestured to the second vehicle, and an officer got out. Price could make out he was a full bull Colonel. He made short work of the Captain and strode over to the bus, the two MPs in tow. Price noticed he was walking with a slight limp.

Colonel Edgar T. Ashley was an infantry officer descended from a long line of infantry officers. There had been an Ashley serving in the United States Army all the way back to the Whiskey Rebellion. The generation before that was not spoken of. That particular dirty bastard had served in the King's Royal Americans during the Revolution. His only saving grace was that he did not survive the battle of Cowpens. Ashley had been a young Lieutenant during the first Gulf War, and had watched oil wells burning in Kuwait. He led security patrols as a new company commander in Mogadishu at the start of that adventure, and was a battalion commander on the 'Thunder Run' in the early days of the Iraq war that captured Baghdad International Airport. Just before he pinned on his eagles, a disgruntled ex-baathist police officer detonated a hand grenade during a police academy graduation. Ashley was the only American casualty, and it had cost him his left leg below the knee. It took over two years of rehabilitation and several different prosthetic legs before he finally found one that agreed with him and allowed him to remain on active duty. His only option for a billet in Afghanistan had been to accept an intelligence position. He jumped at the opportunity, and soon found he had a real talent for taking the odd and the insignificant pieces of information and making a story out of it. This assignment looked like a long shot when it came into his office. Ashley liked long shots.

Price looked back at the self inflicted wound and asked "You expecting company? Those MPs have gotta be here for you." The soldier looked petrified at the thought of being detained in Afghanistan instead of making it to Germany. He slumped down in his seat. The Colonel stepped on to the bus, and in his best parade ground voice, announced "Sergeant First Class Jonah Price, identify yourself!"

What the fuck is this all about, Price thought as he raised his hand.

"Come with me, Sergeant. You have something I want." Price had no idea what he had been talking about. All his government issue had been taken from him at the hospital and receipted. He had seen the form somewhere in the folder they gave him to keep all his medical paperwork copies in. The little Russian TT-33 pistol was the only souvenir he had left. He had amassed a nice collection, and was planning on getting them home with the unit gear when it rotated, but that plan went out the window when it was decided to evacuate him. He was sort of pissed at himself that the TT had been the gun he grabbed that morning. The 7.62x25mm round was effective if well placed, but it would be embarrassing taking it home. He had listened to CSM Grant berate Dave Sharp over his choice of that particular pistol. Grant was a .45 ACP man. There was a Norwegian Model 1912 Colt 11.45mm in his foot locker back at the PRT he was planning on giving to Grant when he got home. That was too bad, because it had been a damn nice gun.

"Where's your gear?"

"I'm wearing it, Sir. The Evac Hospital took everything else."

"Prove it." Prove it? That was different. Price thumbed through his forms until he came to the hand receipt. He showed it to the Colonel. "What are you looking for, Sir?" The Colonel wanted the biometric reader. Price pointed to the entry close to the bottom of the list. "It had a chunk of shrapnel in it. The supply specialist there thought it was junk. He's probably still got it on his shelf if he hasn't trashed it."

Ashley pulled out a phone and hit speed dial. Without any small talk he told whoever was on the other end to get to the hospital and find Sergeant Price's gear. "There's a hand held scanner in it, supposedly damaged. Get it, take it apart and strip the memory, then shoot it to my computer."

The other patients were starting to leave the bus and walk to the C-26J Spartan that had been configured as a hospital plane. "Colonel, my plane is leaving, can I go."

"You have anything on the bus?"

He held up a small bag. "This is all I've got."

"Put it in my vehicle. You'll catch another flight."

Two hours later Price was still waiting for the Colonel to tell him what was going on. Ashley kept checking his computer, muttering to himself. Other calls were coming in, and he was busy marking up a map and calling surveillance images on his screen. Finally, the information he wanted came through. He called Price over. There was a picture of the last civilian he had processed through the checkpoint. "Remember him?"

"Yeah, not a local guy. Claimed he was a Palestinian relief worker. Tried to give me some shit about not being under my jurisdiction. Did he make a complaint about me? Who is he?"

"Never mind. Why did you get involved with him?"

"He was a shit head. He was trying to throw his weight around with the Afghans. That's usually a good sign that he had something to hide. It pissed me off."

"Anything else?"

Price thought a couple of seconds. "Yeah, once he got out of the car he acted like he knew me. Knew me and didn't like me."

"Did he know you?"

"Colonel, there's a lot of people out there who know me and don't like me, and not all of them are rag heads. He could have been anybody from the last 20 years."

"Do you think you could recognize him if you saw him again?"

"Probably. We had a stare down going on for a bit. He lost. I don't think he wanted to smile for the birdie."

"You're going to help me find him. Come along. We have a Blackhawk waiting for us."

Ashley wouldn't give Price any more information about the Arab, but he did explain how they had tracked him. Someone had actually bothered to record plate numbers at the road block. Many of the plates were stolen, out of date or counterfeit, but that wasn't the point. If enough car/license plate combinations were recorded, they could track the anomalies better. This time, one of the anomalies paid off. The Afghan National Police had been running a checkpoint at the edge of Nimroz Province and just happened to log a blue Hyundai whose plates matched one that had passed through Prices' just ahead of the mystery Arab. About eight hours ago, the same car had been observed on the outskirts of a small town called Chehar Borjak. The occupants had been repairing a flat, and a passing dismounted patrol had casually recorded the car information, but did not process the occupants. Ashley was willing to gamble it was the same vehicle.

There was no way, given the distance involved, that the car could have reached Zaranj before dark, when a curfew was enforced at the Iranian border crossing. The border was fenced for a couple of miles north and south of Zaranj, but Price was experienced with border fences, especially in a high smuggling traffic area. Ashley was hoping the Arab wouldn't want to risk a night crossing in an unfamiliar area and would hole up until daylight and take his chances during the morning rush hour. The border crossing was a very sensitive area, and the Iranians were always looking for some way to provoke any Americans and draw them into an international incident. A film clip of a US soldier firing into Iranian territory would be ideal. The Quds Force, Iranian special forces, could round up the refugee women and children to provide a suitable number of 'innocent victims'.

Price didn't like Zaranj. This border town was worse than a lot he had been in. Everything he saw seemed to be a black market or a shakedown. In the rest of Afghanistan, merchants would hide illegal weapons or bales of opium when the Americans came by. They didn't do it here. The Afghans were sullen and defiant at the same time, the soldiers and police seemed to be afraid of everything that moved, and there were a shit load of Iranian nationals wandering through the streets. The American presence, what there was of it, kept to the east side of town to avoid incidents with the Iranians. Their rules of engagement prohibited them from anything but self defense, and they better be able to prove it was self defense. Morale sucked, and Price started to understand what it must have been like in the last days of Vietnam: the politicians were calling the shots.

Ashley and his MPs were fully suited up, with body armor and Kevlar. They managed to beg or borrow enough for Price to feel relatively safe, gave him a weapon and basic load of ammunition, and a lecture on where, when and how he could use them. As soon as they were out of the gate in a borrowed vehicle, Price loaded his weapon and stood up in the gun turret, charging the M240 in the Crew Remotely Operated Weapon System (CROWS), and checked the controls to make certain they were charged and operating. Ashley said nothing, but gestured to his soldiers to do the same. At an empty stretch of road Price touched off a short burst from the M240. There was an immediate radio call from the American base. Priced reached over Ashley's shoulder for the microphone. "May I?" Ashley handed it to them and Price responded that they hadn't heard anything. "Must have come from a different direction."

"You are a cautious and devious man, Sergeant Price." Ashley said with a smile.

"Yeah, hard to believe I keep getting my ass blown up on these little sight seeing trips people send me on."

"Let's not forget to add a 'Sir' to that once in a while, Sergeant Price. I do like to think having this bird on my chest counts for something once in a while."

"Yes, Sir," Price replied. "As long as we don't forget that the plane I almost got on last night is probably on the ground at Ramstein, and I should be on my fourth beer right about now."

"If we get the guy I'll get you a medal."

"I've got medals, Sir. I'd rather have the beer."

They got to the border crossing before the gates opened. The lines were already backed up for several hundred yards on either side of the border. The crossing must have been routine for most of the people, because everyone seemed cheerful, or maybe happy that they were getting out of Afghanistan. The mood changed subtlety when the HUMMV pulled up to the ANA Command Post. In what seemed to Price to be flawless Pashtu, Ashley explained to the Afghan Captain that they had been tasked by some headquarters to observe the operations for a while, and not to interfere. The Captain pointed out an imaginary line that the Americans were not to cross. It was the mutually agreed upon 'neutral zone' between Iran and Afghanistan. Price took it to mean that it was the area where they didn't fuck with each others nationals. He wondered if it would apply to Palestinians.

Promptly at 0700 the gates on both ends of a fenced in two lane road were opened and traffic started moving. Ashley gave Price his dark glasses and had him move to one of the jersey barriers that would give him a good view of west bound traffic.

By 1030 Price was wishing he either had his hydration pack or had gotten a couple more hours of sleep the night before. His attention was starting to wander when Colonel Ashley brought over a couple of cold drinks he had bought from a vendor. Price rolled the bottle across his face before he opened it.

"See anything that pops yet?"

"Not a fucking thing, Colonel. Think this guy might have a different route over the border?"

"I hope not. I've got a couple of drones tasked north and south of here, but we don't have the assets if we spot him."

"How about a Hellfire?" Hellfires were the missiles Predator drones carried that had been doing such a good job remotely killing the bad guys.

"Don't worry. I'll burn this bastard in a heartbeat if I have to, but I'd rather get him alive."

Price's curiosity was raised yet another notch. "Who is this guy, Colonel? Don't I at least get to know why he's fucking up my life?" Ashley didn't answer.

Price had taken off his dark glasses and pushed his helmet back when he cooled his face. The glasses were still dangling from a MOLLE strap when he noticed a tall man in a dirty robe doing a bad job of being nonchalant. He was with two other men, each carrying a basket of oranges, and they were carrying on an active conversation, each in turn trying not to look at him. Price nodded his head towards the group and put on his glasses.

"That's the son of a bitch."

Ashley turned to look as Price started to climb over the barrier. Ashley tried to hold him back. "Let the Afghans take him" and started shouting in Pashtu to the Afghan Captain. The tall man moved away from his companions as they moved to intercept the Afghan. Price vaulted the barrier and ran after him. The Afghan guards started shouting at Price. One fired his AK-47 into the air as a warning as another one ran to intercept him. Price had just grabbed the tall man and was bringing him to his knees when an Afghan soldier threw a body block at him and tried to knock him away. The tall man got to his feet and started running towards the Iranians with Price hot on his tail. The Iranians, alerted by the firing, were running towards the Afghan end of the crossing. The tall man reached them just as Price caught up with him again and brought him down with a flying tackle. One of the Iranians fired his weapon into the air, then stitched a trail of bullets to one side of Price and his almost prisoner. The other Iranian began beating Price with the butt of his weapon. More Iranians arrived and began pulling the tall man back to their side of the crossing. Other Afghans arrived and began pummeling Price and dragging him back to their side. Just before the lights went out for him, Price could see the tall man cross into Iranian territory.

He heard Colonel Ashley calling for a Quick Reaction Team to come to the border. It sounded close: he must have been whoever the hell it was fighting with the Afghans on top of him. He heard another burst of automatic weapons fire and he waited for the impact.

Then everything went black.

Chapter Four

EVERYTHING SOUNDED LIKE IT WAS under water. Price knew he was strapped to something semi-soft and he couldn't move his arms. There was a lot of activity that he couldn't see because everything was so black. Was this what it was like to be dead? He tried to raise his arms, but they seemed to be made out of lead. He pulled up a few more times before he realized he was restrained. Something was holding his head down too. Shit, he thought. This isn't good. He wondered if the last shooting he heard was the rag heads killing Colonel Ashley. That would explain his being tied up. The bastards gave, or sold, him to the Iranians. Won't they be surprised to find out the Army doesn't want him back. He heard himself laugh at the thought. That must have gotten someone's' attention, because he felt a hand on his wrist, maybe checking his pulse. He struggled to speak: "Make sure I'm still alive before you shoot me, you bastards!" He knew what he was trying to say, but the words didn't sound like it. Someone was shaking his shoulder now, calling his name.

"Sergeant Price? Can you hear me?" It sounded like a woman.

Another voice was in the background. "Is he alright? What's he trying to say?" It sounded like Ashley. They must have taken him prisoner too.

"Just babbling. He's a little fucked up, Colonel. I think he might have a skull fracture. He was bleeding pretty good when we picked him up." There was more noise. Was he in a helicopter? He tried to open his eyes.

As soon as he did it felt like someone was jamming ice picks into his skull. It sounded like a little girl was screaming. He realized it was him.

"That didn't sound good. Has he got any other injuries?"

"I can't find any, but there might be something internal. I can give him a little morphine, but it might not be good for him."

"Give me the fucking morphine!" He heard himself yell out. There was already a needle in his arm. An I.V.? He couldn't tell, but the pain started to fade, and he went to some happy place.

On the Iranian side of the border the guards were wondering what the hell they were going to do with this guy they had just snatched from the American. Their standing orders had been to provoke them at every opportunity, but nothing like this had ever come up before. The Americans made a habit of staying well back from Iranian territory. The ones they had met today must have been cowboys out looking for a little excitement. The man the Americans had been chasing was carrying an Iraqi passport made out to Ibn al Tariq, but the Officer in Charge of immigration control said it was a counterfeit passport, and the man was put into a holding cell until someone further up the chain of command made a decision. Iranian intelligence routinely issued false passports to terror groups they supported, but always with a special code so that they would be able to track them in areas that they had some control. All the while Ibn al Tariq kept talking about going to Tehran and meeting with some General in the Quds Regiment. The name he gave wasn't listed in any of their directories, and they had no intention of calling Tehran to ask for a nonexistent general officer.

District headquarters passed the buck up to the 11th Revolutionary Guards headquarters in Kerman, capitol of the next province over. Their instructions were short and brutal: interrogate him until he offers up something useful, and try not to kill him while you're doing it. The men of the Border Guard Service were glad that their "Advisor for Political and Religious Affairs", who went by the name of Massoud, was always willing to handle such a distasteful job. He believed everyone crossing the border was an apostate and deserved to be abused. Ibn al Tariq surprised them by being a strong man. He kept insisting he be taken to the unknown general for almost 24 hours. At that point a particularly vile method of torture revealed the flash drive he had kept wrapped in clear plastic and hidden in his anus. The method of extraction was very painful.

The Advisor, as he was known, because no one dared be familiar and call him Massoud, proudly displayed his trophy (once an unwilling aide had cleaned it up) and called Kerman. This was an important opportunity for an ambitious man. It would get him out of Zabol, this little shit hole of a border town. Perhaps it would elevate him to an assignment closer to one of the Ayatollahs, where his true talents could be revealed. He could barely contain his satisfaction when the duty officer at the 11th Revolutionary Guards told him to accompany the Iraqi pig and his espionage equipment to Kerman on the next available transport. Massoud wasted no time in arranging a truck and operator for the miserable two day drive. Zabol was too unimportant a post to have any helicopter assets assigned, and the 11th Revolutionary Guards was not in the habit of diverting one for the questionable benefit of the Border Guard Service.

Kerman, being a provincial capitol, was blessed with a more cosmopolitan population, civilized services, and a military base that accommodated the headquarters of a Revolutionary Guard training camp and administrative center. It was also blessed with an influential, if minor, Ayatollah who would observe the Iraqi spy once he arrived and render a religious as well as political verdict on his fate. The Ayatollah was a civilized and compassionate man, and insisted that the Iraqi, who had spent the past two days in the back of a truck, chained and regularly beaten, be treated according to the laws of hospitality before he underwent any further examination or interrogation. Ibn al Tariq was given the opportunity to bathe, received a cursory medical exam, and was permitted a meal before he was brought into the Ayatollahs' presence. While the cleric was waiting, he had his Revolutionary Guard aide de camp, an eager and religiously zealous sub-lieutenant, bring him a laptop computer (an instrument of the devil, but necessary to the new way of doing things) so he could review the contents of the spy device. Everyone agreed it had to be a spy device, because he had it secreted in such an unclean manner, and he hadn't offered its information to his benefactor at the border. A true soldier of Islam would have been grateful to the border guards for saving him from the hands of an American. To try and bluster his way by proclaiming the name of a nonexistent general was further proof of his perfidy.

He did not understand the meaning of the photos. Some were obviously candid, perhaps taken surreptitiously, and some appeared to be of an official nature. One made no sense at all to him, and he showed it to his aide de camp. "What is the meaning of this phrase? Who are the 'wild people'?"

"It says 'Wild Bunch', Holiness. I have seen this photo before, on the Internet. It is a group of Americans who had just massacred our Chechen brethren in Moldova some time ago. They seemed to consider it a bit of sport."

"The Internet, you say? You indulge in this devils invention for recreation?"

The aide hastened to explain. "It was not for recreation, Holiness. That is forbidden by Allah. It was part of my political education entitled 'Know Your Enemy'. These infidels are very vulgar and savage."

The Ayatollah nodded and paged through the documents. It appeared to be a series of proposals for a reprisal operation, along with suggestions for implementation and a brief memorandum for further study. Even by his unpracticed eye he could tell it was either in the very early stages, or very poorly conceived. The addressee on the memo caught his eye. "It seems our late brother Osama was not merely hiding with his whores. He was still actively pursuing means to strike at the great Satan." He indicated he was ready to see the Iraqi.

Ibn al Tariq looked marginally better when he came before the Ayatollah. He had been allowed a small basin in which to wash, and a fresh, if cheap robe, had been provided. A meager meal had been given to him, enough to take away some of the hunger pains, and a medic had given him a handful of aspirin. It was not the treatment he expected in his position as a courier for a great man, now a martyr, but he reminded himself that Iranians, although they considered themselves the saviors of Islam and the cutting edge of the revolution, were not Arabs, and as such were not true Muslims. The Prophet, bless his holy name, had been quite clear on that, a point ignored my most non-Arabs.

"Tell me your mission, Ibn al Tariq. What you carry does not seem to be worthy of the memory of Osama bin Laden." The Ayatollah turned the flash drive over slowly in his hands. It was a cursed piece of infidel technology.

"Holiness, I cannot explain what it contains. I am but a humble messenger. It was taken from the survivor of the bandit raid on my Sheikh. The instructions were very fragmentary. I am trying to carry out those instructions to the best of my ability." Tariq knew it would not serve him well to display the outrage he felt at his treatment.

"Why did you bring it to us? Is it your intent to involve us in this scheme?"

"No, Holiness. This was merely the path I was obliged to take. Air travel was forbidden to me due to events in Pakistan. I have come this way before, in a different guise and more favorable circumstances. I require the assistance of a devout warrior in your Quds organization."

"Yes, you have mentioned the Quds before, yet the man you identify does not exist."

"He was never a man, holiness, he is a code. A missive addressed to that name will be sufficient."

And so it was. The Ayatollah had a brief 'Do you know this man' message forwarded to Yazd. The message included a copy of Ibn al Tariq's passport and a time limit: if there was no answer in 12 hours, he would have the spy slaughtered. The Ayatollah like the word 'slaughtered' in describing a punishment. It struck more fear into the hearts of the apostates and the faithful alike. Allah was a powerful yet compassionate being, and it was important that all know he was capable of great savagery as well as mercy. Since he had no reasonable expectation of an answer, and looked forward to the beheading of this spy, who either worked for the Great Satan or the Zionists, he left instructions he was not to be disturbed and retired to his chambers.

In the fresh light of day the Ayatollah bathed, purified himself, and saw to his prayers. They were extra devout and pious this morning, as they should be when one is about to embark on the work of Allah. His military aide de camp was nowhere to be found this morning, and it was with an unholy amount of anger that he went to his office to seek him out. The aide was not there. He did not recognize the group that was present, only that one wore the striking blue beret he had heard was associated with a powerful arm of the intelligence service. This man was seated at his desk and speaking on the phone in low tones. The nerve of this interloper, he thought. The Ayatollah was not impressed. He was even less so when he was directed to bring the prisoner to a conference room.

"Who are you to order me? I represent the Grand Council, the supreme law of the land." The Ayatollah wore a black turban, signifying descent through some line of the prophets' family.

A thin figure in an unadorned uniform turned from his phone call and held up his hand. "Quiet, fool, and do as you are told and I will deal with you later."

"Did you not hear me? I am the representative of . . ."

The thin figure stood, leaned over the desk and delivered a back handed blow to the Ayatollah. "You are the representative of Allah in a very unimportant provincial mosque. You have violated the security of the State with your airs, your unsecure communications and you are wasting my time." He signaled two of his assistants who each took the cleric by an arm. "Find Ibn al Tariq. Put this idiot in his place. I will deal with him later."

The Ayatollah was struggling as they pulled him away. "You have no right to this!"

The thin man said one word. "Stop!" The escorts turned to face him, and, knowing what was coming, held their prisoner at arms length. The thin man drew a small pistol and pointed it at the Ayatollah. "I'll deal with him now," was all he said before he pulled the trigger.

The message to General Rafsanjani al Jin identified no one in the Iranian military. As far as was known, it did not identify anyone alive in Iran. It was a one time code, one of many, that called for a specific procedure if conditions were right. If they were not, the messenger was to be killed, the message destroyed, and all references to it expunged. The message to General Rafsanjani al Jin met the very minimum standards for such a message. It should not have come through official channels, which were widely believed to be monitored by the Americans. An emergency conference at the highest levels decided that since the one-page sheet of instructions did not specifically prohibit such communications, it would be accepted. It was the misfortune of the Ayatollah and his military aide de camp that they were outside any channels, accepted or extraordinary. Although General Rafsanjani al Jin did not exist, had never existed, and who would never have his name uttered again, it had been spoken. The tongues that did it would be silenced.

Ibn al Tariq was brought to the conference room. He was not permitted to speak unless spoken to, and was only allowed the briefest answers. His face was compared to the passport and his identity verified. The Iraqi passport had been issued by Iranian intelligence several years earlier, and had been periodically updated in their data bases. Fingerprints were taken, more photographs and a blood sample. None of this was necessary. It was only to make the subject of the interrogation believe he could hide nothing. Once a sufficient amount of time had passed, during which the fingerprint card, photos and blood sample were all discarded, tca was brought and the atmosphere became more relaxed. The thin man, who never revealed his name and was only addressed as 'Excellency' began a thorough debriefing, He began an almost minute by minute time line, from the moment the Doctor arrived in Abbottabad. It was very detailed, and the Doctor had been blessed with a very precise memory. Everything was covered, from what identity he had been using, who he had spoken to, his methods of transportation and exact times. Which routes were taken and why? There was a great deal of concern over the disposal of identity papers, vehicles, excess cash, weapons and clothing. Nothing escaped the inquisitor.

Once that matter had been disposed of, the subject turned to the data he was carrying. A laptop was called for, and once it was certain the unit could not be accessed from an external source, the flash drive was inserted. Each picture was brought up in turn, enlarged and examined. None made any sense to Ibn al Tariq. The chance meeting with the one identified as 'Price' at the road block was accepted as just that, a routine coincidence in the whirlpool of war. The second meeting at the border was not accepted as a coincidence. There had been a report of the incident, as all such incidents are reported, and the Iranians too had their surveillance photos.

The recording had been stop-action, owing to the lack of data storage at the crossing point, and seconds were missing between each photo. One of the thin man's staff was able to identify Colonel Edgar T. Ashley as a particularly tenacious counter-intelligence officer, and his dossier was called for and studied. It was agreed that if anyone knew anything, it had been Ashley, and not the soldier. The soldier had become an asset Ashley was exploiting, nothing more. It had been unfortunate that cooler heads had not prevailed at the Zaranj crossing. There was a brief opportunity for both Americans to have been neutralized or captured. Americans were notoriously slow to act when their people were seized, either officially or by Somali pirates. To be sure, they would eventually respond, but never with the swiftness one would expect from a military that considered itself so 'agile' in it's operations. A pity, because there would have been ample time to mine them for any information they possessed. Orders were given for both Ashley and Price to be located and killed.

"Do you want us to uncover any information they may have on our pilgrim?" one of the staff asked.

"No. Too often we make the mistake of spending resources to determine if a threat exists. Contradictions drag out the process, and opportunities are missed. Just assume they know something and eliminate the knowledge."

The debriefing continued for a number of hours. Everyone but the thin man appeared worn out by the process. He merely called for transportation to bring them to the airfield. He wanted to return to Yadz where he had more assets, and more time, to examine the documents. For some reason as yet unfathomable, four ordinary American soldiers had been identified to al Qaeda for special attention. By who? Why? A general or even a colonel like Ashley he could understand. It was probably nothing, but it would be worth dedicating a few days and some low level assets to finding out why, at least to satisfy his own curiosity.

The thin man travelled at night whenever possible. Also, whenever possible, his journeys began and ended under cover, to avoid the ever-present American spy satellites, or the increasingly effective drones they were so fond of. It was widely suspected that some of the so-called terrorist attacks the nuclear program had suffered were due to drones, either American or Zionist. The thin man was extremely secretive, even to his own people. He preferred no publicity. He did not attend public ceremonies or large prayer gatherings, although he was a devout Muslim. He worshipped in a small mosque near his headquarters, anonymously. His several trips to Mecca for the Hajj were all done under different identities. His reasons were very valid. He was believed to be the last surviving member of the Pahlavi family, the hated Shahs, left alive in Iran. A distant cousin, he had been a university student during the great Islamic revolution that brought the Ayatollah Khomeini back from France. He had occupied the American embassy, until his government gave in to fear of Ronald Reagan and released the prisoners. He distinguished himself on the front lines during the war with Iraq, surviving the children's offensives of Khomeini, where he sent unarmed twelve and thirteen year old boys against Iraqi machine guns with the promise of martyrdom. Mahmoud Pahlavi Khost was a child of the revolution, and he never stopped watching his back, because the revolution was not yet finished devouring its own.

His transport had been hangered while he was in Kerman, as was his practice. The flight to Yadz was brief, and he deplaned once they were in another hanger. His security detail was small, eschewing the large convoy others preferred, to avoid unwanted attention.

His efforts to avoid attention were exactly what called attention to himself. Many months previously a bored analyst in Langley, Virginia had noticed an anomaly while tracking aircraft heading to a military command post exercise in the city of Qom. All planes had parked lined up on the tarmac, as it developed, their distance from the main terminal was dictated by rank. One did not. A Canadian Bombardier commuter jet with a peculiar but distinctive stripe pattern on the dorsal axis of the plane, originally sold to Malaysia, was guided directly into a hangar some distance away. A small procession of vehicles proceeded out an access gate, and was painstakingly tracked to the site of the exercise. At the conclusion, the same number of vehicles was tracked back to the hanger, and while the other participants were posing for cameras, it flew quickly away. The pattern was seen to repeat itself frequently, and the aircraft was tagged for tracking. A Bombardier representative was paid handsomely to compromise the electronic systems of the plane so it was always visible to satellite. He had been unable to install surveillance equipment, so that was still an ongoing, but low priority project.

Once securely in his headquarters he turned the flash drive over to his technical analysts for study, ordering a set of everything printed, with translations to English, for his eyes only. Ibn al Tariq was dispatched to a guest house, actually a gilded bird cage, where he would await further developments.

The print outs were delivered to him within the hour.

General Khost was a meticulous organizer. The walls of his office were lined with white boards that would eventually contain every detail and every thought on the problem or operation he was working on. They were currently blank. The photos were attached to one, with grease pencil lines leading from the group photo to individual shots, with identifying data, when available, written underneath. Khost was multi-lingual, preferring to lay out his plans in the language of the area where an operation would be conducted. On a second board, each individual document and its translation were posted. That was also a standard procedure. Different eyes might detect nuances between original and translation that had been overlooked, disregarded, or misinterpreted. Each staff member was free to annotate the boards in his own color pen, and frequent conferences would discuss differences of opinion. The documents identified the source, time and location of each of the photos. As Khost read each he made more notations under the photo. The agency or group responsible for the information was also identified. It took three hours to transcribe all the information. Several times he had to pause and reorganize his boards. A casual reading of the documents would have revealed very little. They were uncoordinated and seemingly unrelated. Absent the photos, which might have been sent to a different desk for analysis, they were random reports about unrelated actions. His method had begun to reveal a relationship and a pattern. This was a very talented and dangerous group of men. They appeared fearless, but details revealed one of them was a very cautious planner, not willing to risk without an appropriate reward. There was a surprise in the documents he had not expected. An American female officer was mentioned several times, although she only appeared in the background of several of the photos. It called for another reorganization of information.

He went through the documents twice, discovering more information each time. When he finally looked at the clock on the wall he realized it was very late. He had missed evening prayers and his supper. The folder was closed and left on his desk. He would allow his staff to continue in the morning.

CHAPTER FIVE

KHOST ALLOWED HIS STAFF THE full day to see what else they could glean. That day stretched into two, then three. His people were very good. They had to be or they were gone. It was that simple. He felt no attachment to them, and he shared none of the credit. They worked for him, and after they left their reward would depend on how long they worked for him. Any analyst will lose his edge after time. How long it took would depend on the level of support he got from his co-workers. An ego could be a destructive force, and Khost would not tolerate them.

"We are ready to present our findings." They were always 'findings'. There were too many variables for conclusions.

"How much time should I allow?" Time was unimportant. He tried to limit them to get the pith of the information. The extraneous would come during the question and discussion session which would follow.

"No more than 2 hours, Excellency."

"Very well, I have some guests I would like present. Be prepared to begin at 13 hours." That would be 1 PM. His guests would be a coordinator of what were termed resistance groups and the other a strike planner, one who revised plans that would require Iranian assets. If there were anything that could be developed from the information, these would be the men who could tell him.

The brief began with a synopsis of each of the subjects, starting, surprisingly enough with the woman, who was the only officer in the group. The officer responsible gave a list of the qualifications of each, awards, their assignment history, and how they overlapped. Other than the woman, who was a recent addition, the four men had served together in various combinations for many years. The last assignment had been the only time they had all been present in the same unit at the same time, and even now they had all dispersed, although they did remain in the same regional command.

Personal failings were next. Those are always a weakness to be exploited. This group was no different. From the scanty information, they were opportunists, liars, blasphemers, fornicators: what one would expect from Americans. "These faults are well known among their peers and superiors, and do not seem to present any opportunities at this time." That comment interested Khost. He made note of it for later.

The next briefer gave the recent history of operations that was covered in the flash drive. It was an amazing recitation, even allowing for the exaggerations of the reporters who had been humiliated by them. In the Sudan they had force marched into the heart of Janjaweed territory, established an airbase and conducted offensive operations against the Janjaweed, the Sudanese Liberation Army, and the Sudanese National Army. A cultural relic had been stolen, the old bomber with a degenerate portrait on the nose, a base camp wiped out, and a city invaded to rescue unwilling guests of the Janjaweed. Once ordered out of the country they had conducted another successful forced march at night, overcoming and destroying a large ambush force on unfavorable ground. The strike planner looked at Khost with a raised eyebrow. Had he not known the reputation of this man and his quest for accuracy, he would have dismissed it as fantasy. Khost returned his stare. He knew what the man was thinking and could not blame him for skepticism.

"I found it difficult to believe too, Reza, but other sources in our own files confirmed it. An Arab named Ali Alawa Sharif had been responsible for the operation, and he failed miserably."

"I know this name. He had been well financed and he squandered his resources. A considerable sum went missing. He claimed the Americans took it."

"Did they?"

"The Americans are meticulous when it comes to captured assets. Look at Iraq, when they were uncovering huge caches of cash. The common soldier is not allowed to steal. That privilege is reserved for their superiors and politicians."

"Where is this Ali Alawa Sharif now?"

"The French have him, or had him, I should say. Their intelligence service recaptured him in Moldova and we have lost track of him."

"Recaptured?"

Reza explained. "He escaped the Sudan and made his way to Algiers. Our sources tell us that Algerian Intelligence recruited him to stir up resentment in the Muslim quarters of Marseilles, which he seemed to be successful at. The French caught him and tried to turn him to their purposes against the Russians in Moldova."

Khost held up his hand. "This is a briefing in a briefing. When we conclude can you have your people compare notes with mine? It seems compartmentalization has caught up with us again."

"It shall be done, Excellency." Khost signaled for the briefing to continue.

The story picked up in Germany, where the Americans were an embarrassment to NATO. Not knowing what to do with them, they were susceptible to Russian intrigues to get them to build a road as a form of humanitarian atonement for their actions. The road was needed by the Russians who had a facility in the area that recovered chemical weapons from abandoned stores in their former empire and forwarded them by air to depots in Siberia. The road was a back-up route they sorely needed because of the condition of the dirt runway they were using.

"Amazing," Khost interjected. "The stupidity of the Russians to invite Americans into a sensitive operation just to avoid spending a few Rubles."

The camp had also been used as a training school for Jihadist bomb makers the Russians encouraged against NATO.

"What happened to that camp?" It was an unexplored asset.

"Ali Alawa Sharif had been ordered to infiltrate the camp and gather information on the Russians for the French. He went rogue on them as soon as he could, and started to plan a vengeance operation against the Americans. He failed, and the French were able to seize him just as the Americans and Moldovan security were tracking him down. Somehow, the plane carrying the bomb makers was lost in a mid air explosion."

"The Americans?"

"Probably not. The Russians speculated that one of the graduates had brought some forbidden material with him on the plane."

"Now, back to this Ali Alawa Sharif. How was he captured?"

"He failed to take simple precautions. He felt secure in his surroundings."

"A simple manhunt," Reza offered, "and his plans were thwarted. The Americans seem to thrive on luck."

"If it had been the only operation," the briefer continued, "it would have been. Our Chechen brethren also knew of the facility, and were determined to take it. They attacked and destroyed a convoy that resulted in many chemical casualties among the local population and themselves. Another element tried to attack the camp, but was destroyed by the Americans and Moldovans. It was the aftermath of that battle that the photo captioned 'The Wild Bunch' was taken."

The briefer explained that it was a play on an old American cowboy movie, in which four aging bandits attack the Mexican army to rescue one of their accomplices. Khost mad a note to obtain a copy of the film. The analogy could be useful.

Reza again, "So the Americans were able to defeat the Janjaweed, yet again, through Ali Alawa Sharif, the Russians and the Chechens? They are building up an impressive list of enemies." Reza believed that a mans' greatness could be determined by the power of his enemies.

"The Americans, although the victors, were asked by the Moldovan government to leave the country. Publicly, they were sent back to America in disgrace. Privately, this man," he pointed to the photo of Command Sergeant Major Lucas Grant, "was given one of the armored vehicles that had been used in the fight."

"They gave him a tank?" Reza gasped.

"A small scout tank, an M-3, left over from the German war. It fit in a shipping container and was delivered to where they keep the stolen plane."

Reza was again moved to speak. "I shudder at the resources hey must have to be able to move people around the world as if they were post cards. The expense must have been enormous." The comment did not require a response.

Khost glanced at his watch. The timing seemed to be well paced.

"The Americans were assigned a meaningless task, re-grading several kilometers of dirt road and erecting barded wire along the international border with Mexico. In short order they managed to thwart an arms transfer we had planned and financed, disrupted numerous drug and illegal migrant infiltration routes and killed or wounded a number of the local Cartel members. Despite diligent supervision by their own government, which prohibited them from engaging in offensive operations, they also managed to discover the involvement of a Mexican Major, Apuesta, and his soldiers in the drug trade. He was trying to take over the area. The Americans conducted an invasion of Mexican territory, destroyed all the facilities, and killed Apuesta and most of his men. Their State Department has arranged reparations to the Mexican government. The American soldiers were returned to their home district and disbanded."

Khost found the drug trade to be distasteful but necessary to fund many of their activities. It also contributed to the internal destruction of the United States. He avoided it when he could. "So you see, Reza, they have added the Mexican government and army, the drug cartels, and one of our own agencies to their list of bitter enemies."

The briefer interrupted, "shall I continue with a listing of reporting agencies we have so far?"

"No," Khost replied. "More would only be adding to the obvious. Why don't we just skip ahead to the current situation of the subjects?"

A large map was unrolled. It had aerial photos attached with ribbons leading to specific locations. The overall area was centered on a small sized town. To the east was a small airport with aircraft hangers to the east side of the runway, and what was labeled a military installation to the north. Smaller labels identified each of the buildings as to their known or suspected function. A major highway intersected the map north to south, bordered by a river, with another road crossing east to west. On the northwest side of the intersection of those roads was another compound labeled 'heavy equipment park'. This had a single spur railroad line running behind it, bordered by an access road. The road and tracks led north to a large open area. This was border by the river to the east, residential areas to the north, and what appeared to be light manufacturing facilities to the west. Five smaller photos were scattered around the map, each keyed to a specific area. Each of those had a smaller picture of the occupant. One at the airfield was a hanger with an inset of an old four engine plane. Another inset showed a tank. According to the scale, about eight miles to the south was a pleasant looking home in the country. This had a picture of the American known as Grant. Northeast, set in a wooded lot, was a building identified with the woman, Bonneville. It seemed the most remote. A short distance from the two military installations was a brick apartment block. This was identified as 'Sharp'. Finally, across the street from Sharp, there was another cluster of brick apartments. This was identified as 'Harrison'.

Another aide passed out folders containing copies of the photos, as well as more detailed shots. Khost reminded everyone that none of the information could leave the room. That was accepted with a quiet murmur. The photo detail was stunning, and Reza commented on it. "The source of these photos?"

The briefer responded. "Google Earth, Excellency. They provide an asset to us that is well beyond our means. If there is cause to proceed with any operations we will conduct closer surveillance."

"And how will this be arranged?" Reza asked.

"There is a local mosque, as well as another in a neighboring city. We will use them as a cover as we utilize several of our itinerant assets. There are reports, unconfirmed as yet, that several of the young men from both of these mosques have attended training camps in Yemen with Anwar Al Awlaki and Lebanon with Hezbollah. There may be more in the camps now. We are hoping that the Coordinator of Resistance will be able to tell us more."

The 'Coordinator', another shadowy figure who preferred anonymity, had not spoken yet. He did now. "I can learn that information, but it may take some days. Some of my local representatives have a great deal of territory to be responsible for."

Khost reassured him. "That is understandable, my friend. As quickly as your means permit."

The briefer continued. "We have not yet begun to mine the internet for local information about the subjects. A preliminary search has revealed a number of sources for each, and it will be a matter of time to sift through to determine which are the subjects and which are merely cursed with a similar name."

"Yes, proceed with caution." The 'Coordinator' snorted. "It would be a pity to kill the wrong infidel by accident."

"It would be unwise to act on information based on a name alone. There may be a glimmer, a small nugget, in an unsuspected location that would open up many possibilities."

"Mahmoud, if you want to kill a man, kill him!" the 'Coordinator' said. "If bin Laden and all the rest had attempted more simple operations, and fewer of the complicated ones that seem to have failure built into them, he would have a penthouse in New York and a seat at the United Nations."

"It is not always that simple, my friend."

"Pah! Find some useful dupe eager for martyrdom, give him a gun and have him walk up to the target and shoot him in the face. If time permits, have him shoot as many more of the infidels before the security forces kill him. It will reap rewards in far greater proportion than the cost of a Glock and some extra magazines." The Coordinator's face was turning red. The man hated with a passion. "Look what that one man Hassan accomplished on an American military base! One man! Fifteen minutes! And we are still reaping the benefits."

Khost held up his hand. "I hear you. What you say is true, and it may be the solution if we agree to go ahead with an operation against these people. It is too early in the process to determine the execution. We must also know if there are any other benefits we would chose to reap at the same time. Your concerns are noted, and I assure you that you will have a seat in the planning council. I give you my word." That seemed to mollify the Coordinator, and he placed his hands on the table before picking up his glass and taking a long drink of water. Khost watched him for a long moment. The man was correct about direct action. It was always the simpler way. He failed to realize other results were often desired, whether or not the target was eliminated. The Coordinator nursed a burning hate that sometimes clouded his judgment. Khost hated too, but he always tried to have a specific reason for a specific hate. It was time to bring this session to an end. He waved his aides and briefers to their chairs and he took the central position behind the lectern.

"We have covered a lot today. You may feel free to arrange for yourself or a representative to come back at any time to review the information, but I must insist that none of it leave the room for now."

"All of this, obviously in a much simpler format, was contained on a computer flash drive rescued from the Pakistani compound of Osama bin Laden. The fact that it survived was a blessing from Allah. That we have it today is a greater blessing." He paused to look around the room. Every face was turned to him.

"The courier found his way to us. I do not believe that was the original intent, but he followed his instincts and realized that this information had to be protected and ultimately delivered to Anwar al Awlaki in the Yemeni tribal lands. This can still be done. We still have him as a guest of the Iranian Islamic Republic." He paused again to let the laughter die down.

"Awlaki is now a target. The Americans can devote more of their assets to finding and killing him. If they are successful before the information is delivered, what does the courier do? Destroy it? Return it to us? I do not have the answer."

"And what if it is delivered and plans are made before they kill him, which they most certainly will? Awlaki does not include us in the distribution chain of his plans. We cannot expect he will share his plans with our representative in his camp." His glass was empty. He signaled for another and everyone waited while the water was poured and Khost was able to take several swallows.

"We have several options. The simplest would be to destroy all this information, destroy the computer drive, and kill the courier. It would end the last legacy of Osama bin Laden and remove from us any temptation to act, one way or another."

"A second option would be to assist the courier in his delivery of the information. We can provide him with an identity, put him on a plane to Sana'a, and forget he ever existed. The problem would be where it was destined in the beginning, in the hands of Anwar al Awlaki out in the wilds of Yemen. I have no knowledge of Awlaki's dedication to bin Laden now that he is dead." He finished the glass. An aide approached with the pitcher, but he waved him off.

"There is a third option. These men are dangerous. They may stumble blindly into places they should not be, but they manage to always adapt to the situation and triumph. The list of our friends who they have materially damaged is long, and without a doubt will grow. We can act on the information simply and economically and eliminate these four threats to Islam."

"What will become of the courier" asked Reza. "Whatever we do, he is a liability because he knows we have been involved, if even on the periphery."

"Ibn al Tariq has few options left to him. There are a number of governments who would take him, if only to curry favor with the Americans. If we decide to proceed, he may be persuaded to be useful. Once a decision has been reached I will insure that he is not a liability."

"And the woman?" the Coordinator asked.

"She is a camp follower. A high ranking one, but a camp follower. She can die like the rest."

"No more questions. It is time for a preliminary decision."

The room unanimously chose option three. "Is the operation to have a name, Excellency?" Khost thought for a moment. Retribution would be the goal of this mission, for retribution it would be, but the infidel intelligence agencies were always alert to threatening code words and would spend resources looking further. While Khost was confident of his security, a dedicated search could always turn up incidental information he would not want them to have. The operation needed a name, so it would be a benign one. "Let us call it 'Operation Carnival', for with so many individual targets it will truly be a carnival of delights for our holy warriors."

Khost dispatched an aide to fetch Ibn al Tariq. It was time for him to come to a decision also.

"Ibn al Tariq, a decision has been reached by this committee. Are you prepared to continue your journey?"

Tariq was more than ready. He had realized that his quarters were no more than cell, slightly more opulent, but only slightly. His ultimate salvation did not lie within the borders of the Islamic Republic of Iran. "I am ready to do the will of Allah." He was not a deeply religious man. He practiced when necessary, but he had quickly come to understand that these people were zealots, and it was wise to humor them. Iranians were not Arabs. They were not the chosen, but they pretended to be. That made them dangerous.

He stood in front of the uniformed men, his mind turning over the events of the past few weeks as he half listened to their plan to complete bin Laden's last mission. Anwar al Awlaki might have a part, but that would be decided later.

He had gone from an unknown courier to a man on the run. He had been living on a generous allowance with ample opportunity to supplement it. There were bank accounts and safe deposit boxes scattered around Europe and the Middle East he had ready access to that would keep him comfortable in whatever life he chose. Much of that was gone now, the Iranians made a point of telling him where many of his caches were and how they had been frozen to be used for their needs. It was all gone because the Pakistanis, a nuclear power, could not defend their own airspace from a few helicopters and two dozen men, sailors no less. With all their resources they could not protect one man they knew was a target. He knew he could either participate in whatever these men had planned, or he would die in this wretched place.

Ibn al Tariq considered his options. There were still assets available to him, hidden even from the Iranians. There were organizations he could contact who would still help him in spite of what the Iranians said, Arab organizations who believed in their primacy in the Muslim world.

He would bide his time, await his opportunity, as he had always done in his previous life. All he had to do was cooperate. They could not watch him every moment. He could survive. *Insh' Allah*, he thought to himself, the will of god. Maybe he was a religious man after all. "I am a true son of Mohammed, bless his name. I have been a holy warrior against the infidel for many years. I am a loyal follower of Osama bin Laden, may he enjoy the fruits of paradise. He will be avenged!"

Days later, Ibn al Tariq would think back on this moment and smile. It had been a theatrical performance, one worthy of the mindless idiots who believed in the 72 virgins of martyrdom. The men looking at him had all smiled, except one, and nodded their heads, except one, the thin man. He did not believe, but it did not matter: the rest did. His opportunity would come.

Ibn al Tariq's living conditions changed almost immediately. He knew he was still a canary in a gilded cage, but the cage had more rooms and several acres of grounds. He could live with it for now. His training had commenced the following day. When General Khost had informed him of his need to learn some new skills and become proficient in weapons and explosives, Tariq imagined that he would be a middle aged man in an al Qaeda training video, dangling from a parallel ladder, jumping over a fire pit, crawling under logs and jogging in formation. He had often watched those videos on *al Jazeera* TV and wondered what the point was. Towards the end, bin Laden was actively seeking suicide warriors to blow themselves up with hordes of infidels. You rarely met hordes of infidels on a parallel ladder or in a fire pit.

Khost quickly explained what his regimen would be. They were rounding out his next identity, and he would need to learn his background, both personal and cultural. There was a Turkish *Sharia* lawyer currently undergoing treatment for cancer in Tehran. He bore a remarkable resemblance to Tariq, and even though his prognosis was poor, he was being encouraged to inform his small and distant family he was doing better. The man was doomed to die. Even if Allah himself, in his great mercy and wisdom, came down from paradise and cured him completely, he was doomed to die. He had been selected as a weapon in the struggle against the great Satan, or at least his identity had been selected.

"Will I need cosmetic surgery?"

Khost smiled. He produced a picture of the man who was on the large side. "There are enough similarities between you. We have used the same facial recognition program that the Turks use and the similarities are within eighty-five percent. His passport is close to expiration. At the proper time we will arrange for it to be renewed at the Turkish embassy. Detailed medical records will chart your remarkable recovery, complete with an enhanced photo record. You will present yourself as him, the comparison will be made, and a new identity will be yours."

"And if the Turks are not fooled?"

"Others have tried to obtain false passports in the past. The Turkish practice is to detain them and call our security services. If the plan fails we have a back-up plan, but I doubt it will be necessary."

From there his training progressed. He was drilled in his new identity, his life story, and the minutiae that surround a life. The Turk had carried a number of keepsakes with him, expecting to die here, and all of it had been carefully duplicated for Tariq to study. Once the Turk was no more, Tariq would have the originals, to include the forgotten scraps that hide in every wallet.

He received weapons training, but only to the level that he could identify the controls on most commonly used weapons and manipulate them. He was given frequent trips to an indoor range to practice his skills, but the goal was not to make him an Olympic shooter, but to give him the skills and the confidence to survive a close encounter.

His task was not to be the hunter. There had also been a quick course in bomb making and remote triggers. Others on whatever team was assembled for him would have the actual skills. Tariq was provided with an acquaintance with them so he could inspect their work.

There were classes in field craft, the skills of the spy in hostile territory. This was an easy class for him, because he had spent years perfecting the skills that kept him alive to this point. There were tricks and nuances he did pick up, and the simplistic codes he could devise in the field would be of a help controlling underlings of vastly different ability levels. And there were endless sessions of reading the Quran. He was to be a *Sharia* lawyer and he needed to be able to quote extensively. The most important lesson he learned though, was how to look pensive and ask, "May I consult the Holy Quran? I do not want to give my answer lightly."

As time progressed, Tariq received regular briefings on the activities of the young Muslims who would be his soldiers. The word had gone out to Iranian agents with the widely separated terrorist training camps to prepare young Muslims from America and Canada for their return. Tariq had been impressed with their numbers at first, but gradually the hot heads, the impulsive, and the overly zealous were weeded out. They were the unreliable who would be relegated to low level activities, or, the usual fate of the zealot, suicide bombing. He was drilled to remember the faces of the faithful who would become his weapons against the Great Satan. While he was learning these faces, he also studied the faces of those around him. Not the ones who gave him his training and his briefings, but the ones who hung back on the periphery. It was from these faces that his watchers would come from, and he knew that the Iranians would have people watching him, every step of the way. If he could identify them it would be easier to do what he had to while giving the appearance of obedience.

The camps in Yemen were especially fertile. Anwar al Awlaki had been popular among American immigrant Muslims because of his American birth and perceived persecution under the infidels. There were very few camps left in Iraq because even American Muslims were not trusted by the forces of Muqtada al Sadr, the broker of most insurgent action in the country. Pakistan had been fertile ground for many years, but the death of bin Laden had led to a crackdown on

American 'tourists' and 'students', usually a cover for jihadist training. Many had been relocated to Afghanistan, where the competent were used for intelligence gathering, and the incompetent had been used as cannon fodder.

Lebanon and Syria, with Hezbollah cooperating with Syrian intelligence in the common border region of the Bekka Valley, had been particularly fruitful. Hezbollah controlled a large portion of the Lebanese government. Identity documents, visas, schooling certificates and the like were routinely and officially produced. A Hezbollah prepared document had one of the better chances of evading immigration scrutiny. Syrian papers were also good, but the nascent uprising against the Bashir government was directing unwanted attention towards travelers from Damascus.

Lastly were Sudan and Somalia. They were lumped together because of the support Khartoum gave to the al Shabaab organization. Because of the piracy in the Red Sea there was increasing difficulty with transit from those camps, but it was an easy journey over the border to Kenya, and Nairobi and Mombasa were easy exit points.

The word had also gone out to the infiltrated mosques that were scattered across the US landscape. They were more numerous than could be hoped for, but it was still a pitifully small number. Many American Muslims were no better than apostates. There were two located in the same political subdivision known as a 'state', and each had willing brothers who would follow orders and act without question. They would be the intelligence gatherers, but they would not transmit their product back to Yadz. An Iranian operative, traveling on a student visa to study engineering, would compile the information. The quantity and quality of it would be transmitted back in the form of e-mails to his 'mother'. Chatty references about his new 'friends' would tell the tale. Ibn al Tariq would gather all this information when he finally entered Canada on his route into the US. He would be visiting several mosques in Montreal and Quebec before he crossed over into the United States through a little used border crossing in a place called 'Vermont'.

His training was coming to an end when the Turkish patient finally died. He had been clinging to life with a remarkable tenacity, and Tariq suspected he was assisted into paradise. At that moment Ibn al Tariq ceased to exist, and Mehmet Atta Khan was released from the hospital to begin his new life. The rebirth had an especially prophetic ring to it. Word had just been received of a great tragedy in the tribal lands of Yemen.

Anwar al Awlaki was enraged. This had become a common emotion for him since he had begun dealing directly with the Iranians. In the past they had been observers, bankers and sometimes advisors. The Iranians had intelligence assets and the power of a legitimate government behind them. They had been content to let bin Laden and Awlaki make their own plans, with gentle, if not insistent prodding from a succession of visitors. Since bin Laden's death, however, the Iranians had been trying to take a more active role in his operations. They had started to recruit some of his more promising acolytes, young Muslims from the United States who could travel in their own country with impunity. He had railed against the gradual erosion of his influence with the few who had willingly followed the Iranian pretenders, but the latest edict they had presented him was beyond the limits of his patience. Now they were simply removing the best and the brightest and forwarding them to only Allah knew where. He was losing his stature in the eyes of his organization, and it could not be allowed to continue.

He had called a conference of his chief lieutenants to decide on a plan of action to remove the Iranian influence. Their money had always been welcome, but it could be done without. Sympathy in the wake of bin Laden's assassination had loosened the purse strings in Saudi Arabia. There were ample funds to continue their *Jihad*.

He had opened the meeting, as was his custom, with prayers. At the conclusion, the assembled group remained seated on their prayer rugs as Awlaki outlined the problems and his proposed course of action. "As you see, the Iranians have no interest in our Jihad. They wish to use us to humble the United States, and cast us aside. They are, after all, not Arabs. They are very late comers to Jihad and do not understand their place in the eyes of Allah."

"So what is your plan?" This was from the Egyptian. He was a disagreeable man who worshipped Osama bin Laden as the thirteenth Imam. His death had made him even more sullen than before, and continually called for greater risks to be taken to avenge him. "Osama was my friend. At least the Iranians, may they be cursed, are planning a strike. We just sit here and talk."

Awlaki did not like this man. If it were not for his sources of funding and weapons, he would have suffered a 'training accident' a long time ago. "From what we could glean from our late friend," the Iranian representative had a tendency to boast about his 'privileged information' whenever he ran into resistance from Awlaki, "there is an operation afoot to eliminate some relatively minor players who have been involved in disrupting our operations. It is a very challenging operation, with much risk for very little reward. I have taken steps to modify it." Awlaki outlined his plans for the group. He had dispatched the American followers as he had been instructed, but had changed their mission parameters. Rather than an effort to kill four Americans at the cost of trained willing martyrs, the agents he had dispatched were imbued with a different philosophy. They were not to engage in suicide bombings. That was a waste of resources unless it was against a target like the World Trade Center. They were instead to follow the maxim of an American general whose life he had once seen in a movie. They were to make the other poor dumb son of a bitch die for his country. Awlaki sometimes reveled in his knowledge of American culture. He was a big fan of movies. He even understood the reference to the 'Wild Bunch', although it had been pointless trying to explain it to this group.

"The Americans have what they call a 'sting'," he told the gathering. "That is when you convince someone that what they are doing is in their own best interest, but it really is not. The Iranians think that by using our organization and people they will be furthering their own aims without exposing themselves. They content themselves with bluster while they act with proxies. It is my intention to change that."

The Egyptian again, "I fear you over reach Awlaki, and you will only succeed in turning the Iranians against us. Killing their agent was a mistake."

"The agent was unimportant, and his death while demonstrating the new trigger devices will bring pride to his family. It was more important to extract his knowledge, and turn it against our enemies, Iranian and American. Once their Quds have been implicated in killing American soldiers on American soil, the Americans will retaliate, unlike the aftermath of our brother Hassan's actions." He spoke of the Major who had done the killing at Fort Hood. "Once the Americans have struck back, Iran will be forced into action. Their first target will be the Straits of Hormuz, provoking a naval standoff. Then they will strike at Israel with their new missiles. Think of it, brothers, another major power, this one with missiles and a nuclear capability, at war with the Great Satan will enhance our abilities."

"And how is that to be accomplished?"

Awlaki held up his hand. There was a strange buzzing outside the cinder block building they were meeting in. It sounded like a swarm of honey bees leaving their nest. He had an image of the wall opposite him expanding and moving towards him.

An American drone had located Anwar al Awlaki and had killed him with one of the very effective and deadly Hellfire missiles. When General Khost learned of the strike he secretly reveled in it. Awlaki had always been a loose cannon who only paid lip service to the support he was receiving. There had been wisdom in keeping the operation out of Awlaki's hands. He had no way of knowing that, even in death, Awlaki had hijacked his operation just as it was beginning to bear fruit.

CHAPTER SIX

S ERGEANT SHARP LOOKED UP FROM his computer screen and scanned the tree line through his binoculars. He couldn't detect any movement, but the sensor array said they were there. He keyed his mike and signaled the flanking force to move in. They were stationed about a half a klick to the west, ready to roll up the enemy force. It was only the rehearsal portion of a field training exercise, but Sharp took them seriously. This was the latest class to go through the resident portion of the NCO academy, now known as the Warrior Leader Course, and some of the students would soon be leading men into harms way in Afghanistan or some other miserable place. They needed to be well prepared.

While he was monitoring the radios, he scanned all the terrain. There was a persistent blip to the east, in the direction of the river. Any troop over there was way out of position and in the fading light could end up blundering into the river. He tapped a few keys to call up a sub-menu that would give him an accurate headcount. As far as he could tell, all the infiltrating force was accounted for. The flank force was too far in the other direction for it to be one of them. It either had to be an animal wandering through the woods, or another anomaly. There had been several so far this week.

Sharp had decided to combine portions of his sniper stalking course and a shake out of the new 'Scorpion' ground sensor system. It wasn't so much a new piece of equipment as a new item of issue to the National Guard. This set, considering the well used condition, had already been deployed somewhere in a combat zone. It had been battle damaged and returned to the States for an overhaul. A fresh coat of paint couldn't hide the abuse it had suffered. It was now marked 'Non-deployable-For Training Use Only', meaning it wasn't 100%, so it got bundled off to his school. It was no big deal. At least they had one, and while he was trying to write a lesson plan on it, it would be put to good use. So far he had liked what he had seen of the system. He was reasonably well informed that anomalies didn't happen in the deployed sets, but even this, with all its glitches, was far ahead of the system they had used to monitor foot traffic on the Mexican border.

"Eddie, I've got another anomaly over by the river," he gave the GPS coordinates. "Go check it out." Sharp usually didn't like to use the GPS system in training. He preferred map and compass, but the troops needed to get used to the GPS, so he gradually introduced it. Students still had to pass the old land navigation course.

"I'm on it, Sarge." Eddie Robinson was a good kid. He had come a long way since CSM Grant had caught him and his twin brother screwing over the system with 3 hour lunch breaks. He had managed to get himself wounded and decorated, and so had his brother. They survived all that only to come home and have Edwin Robinson take a wrong step while unloading a trailer when they came home. He was still undergoing rehab for a shattered hip. Robinson took one of the spare radios and jogged off through the woods. Robinson loved these field exercises, and had memorized a complex system of trails so he could better observe, critique, and, when called for, harass the students. Sharp was glad he had been able to take him on as an assistant instructor. Once he was promoted to the proper grade in a few years, he would make an excellent instructor.

That detail being taken care of, Sharp turned his attention back to his screen. It showed that the attacking platoon was out of the tree line and crossing the field. A quick check with his binoculars told him that most of the class hadn't mastered the stalk, and they would be weeded out if any of them applied for his anticipated sniper school. He had found a local gun club with a one thousand yard rifle range that was adequate for his needs, but there was a small problem of contracting for it. Nobody wanted to pay the fees or the insurance the club was requiring.

Off to his left he could see the flanking force moving in slightly to the rear of the assault line. The pop of blank ammunition told him the battle had been joined, and the beeping of the MILES (Multiple Integrated Laser Engagement System) announced that one side was taking heavy casualties. He let the scenario play out before putting up a red pen flare to announce the end of the exercise. The attacking force had been badly outmaneuvered, and the after action report (AAR) would not be kind to the Sergeant whose turn it had been to be the platoon leader. It was only a rehearsal. He would have another chance.

He called his facilitators and told them to bring everyone back to the assembly area for the AAR. Then he called Robinson to check on the anomaly. He should have been back by now. Robinson answered in a whisper. "Sarge, we got any players out here with an AK?"

"Negative on the AK." That was strange. They did have AK-47s they used for familiarization, and sometimes for Opposing Forces play, but none of them had been authorized for this exercise. "What uniform is he wearing?" There were several camouflage patterns available to them for training, Woodland BDU, three color desert camo, chocolate chip camo, digital ACU and the new multicam uniform. Sharp like to keep the AK users in chocolate chip so they would look like Afghan National Army.

"I don't know. It looks like he's been in a paintball fight."

Sharp zoomed in on his computer and could see where the two were. He told Robinson to keep an eye on him but not spook him, just in case he was a poacher trying to jack an out of season deer. He reckoned his route to intercept, told the rest of his team to pack up, and headed out. Sharp estimated he was within fifty yards when he heard a burst of AK fire. Definitely AK, he had heard it often enough. "Robinson!"

"Shit, he's shooting at me!" It was no whisper. Sharp could hear him above the firing.

"Get down, Eddie, I'm almost there." Another burst gave him his new heading. He was closer than he thought. He peered around a tree and could see a figure in splattered fatigues searching the area through his rifle sights. Sharp called Robinson to give him a distraction, and as soon as the rifleman turned away Sharp was on him. He raised the muzzle with his right hand while he drove his elbow into the man's face. That dropped him like a rock. He called out to Robinson, "I got him, Eddie. You OK?"

"I'm good, I'm coming in." There was a crashing through the brush and Robinson entered the little clearing. The back of his uniform was wet. "Motherfucker shot my hydration pack! It's brand new!" Then he looked at the prone figure Sharp was securing with a length of Para cord. "What the fuck is he wearing?" I've never seen red cammies before." The uniform had a red dappled pattern to it.

"It's called 'alpenflage'. The Swiss used to use it."

"So Switzerland is invading us now?"

"I doubt he's Swiss, Eddie." He paused and held up his hand. There was another sound in the background, this one a dull thumping, like a lawn mower engine on a low idle. "How far are we from the river?"

"Couple of hundred yards maybe, why?"

"I think our friend has a friend. Finish tying this mutt up, search him and get on the radio and let everyone know the situation's under control. Don't say anything else. If they ask too many questions just go off the air. I'll be back in a few minutes. Have them send a vehicle for us." He pulled a spare magazine from the prisoners pocket and handed Robinson the AK. He took his own pistol out of a stuff sack and racked a round into the chamber. It was a Chinese copy of the TT-33. Sharp was glad Grant wasn't here.

He made his way through the woods, homing in on the motor. As he got closer he could hear someone thrashing around in the brush. He swung around the sound until he came to the river bank a few yards downstream from a small aluminum boat, the kind you'd use for fishing on a small pond. It had been beached, and a small outboard motor was tilted out of the water, idling. Whoever was there didn't want to have to waste time trying to pull start it if they needed to beat a hasty retreat. In the fading light he looked towards the sounds in the tree line. A figure dressed in the same pattern 'alpenflage' suddenly emerged, pulling up his pants. The moron had decided to answer the call of nature while his buddy was banging away with his AK. The boat driver saw Sharp and reacted by grabbing the pistol grip of an AK he had slung over his shoulder. In his haste to bring the weapon up he grabbed the trigger and stitched a line of dust clouds across the ground towards Sharp. Sharp reacted by jumping into the woods and crawling behind a tree. The boat driver gained control of his weapon and was firing short bursts into the brush. In between, Sharp could hear him grunt as he pushed the boat back into the water and revved the engine as he was lowering it into the water. Sharp chanced a quick glance around the tree and saw the boat heeling over as the driver pivoted the outboard to steer it. The driver took another quick burst at the shore, emptying the magazine. Sharp took two quick shots. He wasn't certain if he hit anything, but the AK went spinning into the water. The driver was now hunched over, twisting the throttle for all he was worth trying to escape upriver. Sharp squeezed off a few more shots as the range widened, knowing he wasn't going to hit anything. He watched the boat fade upstream, and then he stepped into the river to retrieve the rifle. The water was barely up to his knees.

Robinson was standing guard over the prisoner when Sharp got back. He was now sitting up, trussed like a bag of laundry. "You OK, Sarge?" Robinson asked.

"I'm fine, Eddie. This idiot's buddy was an even worse shot than him." Sharp picked a fresh magazine out of the pile of junk Robinson had emptied from the prisoners pockets and slipped it in his rifle. He squatted down in front of the prisoner, shining a flashlight in his face. "All right, Mustafa, just who the fuck do you think you are?" he asked. The prisoner responded by spitting at him. Sharp leaned back and gave him a backhand across the face. "I guess Mustafa isn't going to answer any questions here. Let's get him back." He signaled Robinson to grab him by the upper arm and they none too gently dragged to where their ride was waiting. On the ride to the assembly area he called the State Duty Officer. Since 9/11 there was always an officer, usually a junior company grade type, available by phone. He reached a female second lieutenant, and without giving her a chance to ask too many questions he identified himself, gave her a quick situation report, and told her to call the State Police and whatever Federal office she had on speed dial. "State Police? Not local?" was all she asked.

"This is State property. The locals don't have jurisdiction. And with the automatic weapons, I think the feds have a piece of the action too."

It took awhile for the State's finest to arrive. Even with GPS coordinates they had trouble finding the location in the dark. The prisoner was a dark skinned youth; Sharp figured he was Somali or Sudanese, from somewhere in that section of Africa. He wouldn't answer any questions, but did manage to shout out a few epithets in what sounded like Arabic. The state police weren't impressed. They had dealt with tough guys before. This one was no different from the average street punk. He knew they wouldn't hurt him now that he was secured, so he felt he had a license to act tough. They'd love him in prison, literally. Sharp filled them in on everything he knew, including the boat heading upstream. He did mention shooting at him, but no one asked to see his weapon. It didn't seem like a wise thing to offer it up. One cop raised his eyebrows and made a radio call, requesting someone check out local boat landings. After they took a cursory statement from Robinson they went through the property he had collected. Then they rechecked his pockets. He didn't have any ID, only had a few dollars in currency, two more spare magazines and a cell phone. Sharp had already called the only number that was preprogrammed. An Arabic sounding voice had answered and quickly hung up when Sharp asked who he was. The cops noted that and inventoried it all. Sharp demanded a receipt for the weapons, just so nobody could claim they had never seen them. They were commercial model AKs, probably made from imported parts with a US made receiver and barrel. They seemed to be popular. The one special capability it had, full auto fire, was not a standard feature. Automatic weapons were tightly regulated, expensive to buy, and required a lengthy background check and licensing process before a buyer could take possession. This one had obviously been illegally converted, a simpler process than one might think. Once the police were done they untied the prisoner, slipped him into handcuffs and put him in the back of their cruiser. "The feds are going to meet us at the Safety building in about a half hour. You two," pointing at Sharp and Robinson, "better meet us up there."

"I've gotta report to my higher ups first. We'll be there as soon as they let us go."

They watched the police drive off, and Sharp assembled his troops and gave them a quick debriefing. He needed to know if any of them had seen anything at all out in the training area. None of them had, so Sharp directed them to report back to their billets at the NCO Academy, clean and secure their weapons and gear, and each and every one of them was to write out their own AAR about the day, including anything they had seen with the prisoner. He put an NCO in charge and promised to see them in a few hours.

"Who do we have to report to, Sergeant Sharp?" Robinson asked.

"Nobody that I can think of yet, son, but I think I better let CSM Grant know the flag just went up." Robinson had no idea what he was talking about, but he did know one thing. "I'll bet the CSM is gonna be pissed at you when he finds out you're still using that little Russian gun." Grant's dislike of the small caliber pistols Sharp was fond of was legendary among veterans of the 289th Engineer Support Command.

"The CSM won't be if he doesn't find out."

They waited for an hour for Grant to arrive at the NCO Academy. While they were waiting the State Duty Officer called twice saying that the Federal agents were waiting impatiently for them at the Safety Building. Sharp acknowledged both times, repeating he was waiting for the CSM. During the second call, the young second lieutenant tried to flex her gold bars and order Sharp to report to the feds. Sharp replied that if he was going to be ordered, he wanted to exercise his right to speak to a Judge Advocate General, and have a JAG officer present during the interview. That flustered the lieutenant enough, that she said she would try to have one meet him

"We have a right to a JAG, Sarge?"

"I don't have any idea, Eddie. I don't think we did anything wrong, but if Sergeant Major Grant doesn't want us to go, we won't. You should be safe; you're only the victim here. I'm the one who shot at the other guy."

A voice boomed from the doorway, "What did you shoot at him with, that little fucking pistol I keep telling you to get rid of?" Grant had finally arrived. He had Major Bonneville with him. Neither was in uniform. Sharp had the feeling he had screwed up their evening and Grant wasn't happy about it. The Major had a legal pad with her. She sent Robinson out of the room and asked Sergeant Sharp to tell his story. He repeated everything he had told Grant over the phone, leaving nothing out. Once he was done, she had Sergeant Robinson come back in and tell his side. Sometime during the process the Duty Officer called and said she was having trouble locating a JAG, but she had spoken to General Cabot, who ordered them to 'get their sorry asses over to talk to the feds'. Grant informed him that there was an attorney now present who was also a military officer, so she better relay that to Cabot.

"I don't think the General wants to have a discussion on this, Sergeant Major. He was pretty adamant about them going."

"They'll go, Lieutenant, just as soon as their attorney is ready. If you speak to the General again, let him know that."

Bonneville was wrapping up her interviews. "I didn't know you were a lawyer, Ma'am" Sharp said.

"I already had a good job I liked when I finished law school. I wasn't in any hurry to give it up." Sharp looked at Grant with a worried look. Bonneville saw it and reassured him. "You haven't been charged with anything. Right now, the feds just want to talk to you." Turning to Grant, "Sergeant Major, I think it would be best if the initial interview was done here. I think it's best if we control the environment, not to mention that it all happened on a military reservation and they're both active duty soldiers. A JAG would have to approve any transfer of custody."

Sharp defended Robinson. "He didn't do anything but get shot at. Anything else he did was in following a lawful order."

"David," Bonneville smiled, "if this all goes south, someone else will decide if any order you gave was 'lawful' or not. When they get here you both just do what I tell you."

The two feds, one was FBI and the other was ATF, didn't arrive for another hour. When they came they had the two AKs Sharp had given to the State Police. Robinson had fallen asleep in an overstuffed chair, and Sharp was starting to mainline black coffee. The FBI agent, Rawlings, was pleasant enough. He asked to speak to Bonneville and Grant privately. He and Simmons, from ATF, had already been called by 'someone higher up the food chain' about the case. Some one from Homeland Security would be taking over. They would content themselves with the information the State Police had provided them and wait for further developments.

"Do you know who you spoke to?" Grant asked.

"Some guy named Vaughn. Know him? He said he had dealt with you before."

Grant knew him. He had put a call into an old number he had left over from Aruba trying to reach him. The voice at the end of the line told him it was a wrong number, but it looked like Vaughn got the word anyway.

They spoke to Sharp on the way out to let him know he was off the hook for now. Sharp asked about the kid the police were holding.

"That kid's long gone. Some slick lawyer showed up. Said he knew the kid from the local mosque and wanted to help."

Grant asked "How did he hear about it? The kid call him?"

"No idea. The kid never asked for his call, just sat there and smiled a lot. The lawyer talked to him for a few minutes then they gave a cock and bull story about how he had been fishing on the river. When he went to take a piss in the woods he found a rifle there. He said he knew there were soldiers around and thought one of them lost it. He was trying to return it when 'somebody', I guess that would be you, jumped him and beat him up."

Sharp laughed. "How did he explain shooting at Robinson?"

"Oh, he blamed you for that. He said it went off after you grabbed it."

"What about his buddy and the other gun?" Bonneville asked.

"He explained that too. He said he was all alone. One of the soldiers who jumped him had the second rifle."

Sharp asked about his fishing gear. "When I went to the river there was another guy and a boat. I didn't see any fishing pole. How did he get so far into the training area?"

ATF Simmons just shrugged. "He said he walked in. Left the gear on the bank, As far as he knows it's still there." Before Sharp could ask anything else FBI Rawlins put up his hand, "Look, Sergeant, once we heard from Vaughn it's not our call anymore. The State Police kicked the kid loose, and now it's just a funny story for the back page of the newspaper. We're done here."

"What about those?" Grant asked. Pointing at the rifles they had left on the table.

Simmons took a copy of the receipt Sharp had gotten out of his pocket and put it with the rifles. "As far as I'm concerned, everybody says these belong to the Army. You're the Army, so I'm giving them to you."

"Want a receipt?"

"Not a chance, pal. I don't know what's going on, and I don't think I want to. This is probably going to come back and bite somebody in the ass, and when it does I don't want my name anywhere near it."

They all sat around in silence for a few minutes after the feds left. Sharp was the first one to break the silence. "Feel that?"

"Feel what," Grant asked.

"The feeling of Vaughn fucking us again. And without a kiss, I might add." Looking over to Linda Bonneville he added, "No offense, Ma'am."

She answered him, "None taken, and quite calling me 'Ma'am', it makes me sound old." Grant was absently staring at a large scale map of the training area posted on the wall. He slowly realized what he was looking at and stood to get a closer look. He started to trace a line with his finger until he came to a spot where he tapped his index finger against the wall. Sharp looked over and asked, "Whatcha got, Luke?"

"I'm not sure. Are you up for a quick trip back out there?"

Bonneville tried to nix the idea. "Are you sure that's a good idea? It's still a crime scene."

"Nobody said we couldn't, besides, I don't think any one is giving this a second look now."

"What do you hope to find?"

"Linda, at this point I'd rather keep that to myself. Dave, give her your truck keys." He gave her a quick kiss on the cheek. "I'll let you know more when I do."

She waved her arm at Robinson sleeping in the next room. "And what about him?"

Grant answered. "Wake him up. Have him get these rifles into the arms room." He picked up the copy of the receipt and scrawled 'Hold for ATF' and signed it illegibly. "Make sure he keeps them separate from the authorized stuff. I don't want anybody taking them out for a training exercise."

They parked at an all night gas station, giving the clerk a twenty dollar bill to not have them towed. It was a couple of hundred meters up the street from a dirt access road that led into the northern end of the training area. From the looks of the ground, there had been several vehicles up and down the road recently. A steel gate located a hundred meters in was supposed to be chained and locked. They found the lock cut and the barrier pushed out of the way. The moon was up and there was plenty of illumination. Grant signaled Sharp to take the other side of the road and drew his pistol, an Argentine Colt M1911 clone.

Sharp was carrying an identical weapon Grant had kept in his truck console. He had made Sharp leave the little Chinese TT-33 locked in his office. On the ride here he had once again given Sharp the lecture on the ballistic performance of the .45 ACP round compared to the little 7.62x25mm.

Grant's map study had shown him that there were only a few places that a boat could be transported to the river bank that weren't public access. The two gunmen had obviously come in broad daylight in distinctive pattern camouflage and carrying automatic rifles. It was pretty clear they didn't use one of the public boat ramps. The area was pretty developed up river from the training area, so the options were narrowed even more. This was the best bet, and the forced gate added to the odds.

The brush was fairly dense on either side of the road, keeping whoever came down here trail bound. They heard a vehicle coming before they saw it, and just barely managed to step into the brush. A small car drove by, and Grant managed to read the plate number, writing it down on his hand. Once the engine noises faded they stepped back into the road, but they could hear other sounds coming from the further on. As they rounded the last bend before they came to the river, they saw the area was illuminated by a set of headlights. There were several figures working at loading the boat onto the back of a light colored, probably white, Toyota pickup. Lying on the ground at the edge of the light, Grant could make out a body on the ground. He couldn't tell if it was dead or just unconscious.

"Want to take them, Luke?" Grant shook his head. Whispering instructions to Sharp, they both stepped into the brush and moved closer. Both the men loading the boat looked East African, like the skinny one Sharp had caught. They were both wet to the waist, as if they had to go into the river to retrieve the boat and the body. Grant caught pieces of the conversation, and he was surprised it was in English. One kept asking the other what they were going to do. The response was that the 'Imam' would know what to do. The body was wrapped in a blue tarp and bungeed to the truck bed next to the boat. Grant angled himself so he could read the plate number on this vehicle too. When they drove off Sharp noticed they had left the outboard motor and the fuel can. He put on a pair of leather gloves before he picked it up to examine it. There was a bullet hole near the bottom. He proudly pointed it out to Grant. Grant ignored it. He was building a roster of potential enemies in his head, and the fucking list kept getting longer. He just added three more unknowns to his list.

"Why'd you let them go, Luke? We could have taken them."

"Yeah, and then we would have owned that body, too. You want to explain shooting a local kid with an unauthorized weapon? Remember the story the other one told. This one's family would probably swear he was a life long fisherman too. Dump that little fucking pea shooter and let them explain the corpse. You never saw him, and the other kid has to start making up stories."

"But . . ."

"But nothing. You didn't see him. Period. End of story. You went looking and found the other rifle. That's all you have to remember. Anything else you say only digs a hole we may not be able to get you out of. Let them make up the stories, and we can just point out how they change."

Sharp nodded, even though he didn't quite understand. He kicked at the outboard motor. "Why'd they leave this?" he asked.

"They probably though it was as dead as their buddy. Or they didn't want to try to explain a bullet hole." Grant walked around the area with his flashlight looking for anything else they may have left. Once he was satisfied there was nothing he told Sharp it was time to go. "Drag that piece of crap out of sight and let's get out of here."

Back at the truck Grant sprung for some coffee and they sat and drank it before pulling out. "What do we do next, Luke?"

Grant wasn't sure. This seemed almost too random to be part of what Vaughn had briefed them on. There was no way a lone gunman could have picked Sharp out of a group of soldiers on a training exercise. Hell, there was no way he could have even been certain Sharp would have been present. Still, it was Vaughn who had called off the dogs, so he might have thought it was connected.

"Those geniuses aren't the ones calling the shots. We've got to figure out who these people are. I know they're Muslims, because they were talking about an Imam, but there's gotta be more to it than that if we're going to go up against a bunch of locals."

"Think it might come to that?"

"I don't know, Dave. I want to talk to Vaughn before we make any plans. I'd like to get one of those 'get out of jail' cards he gave us for

Mexico. And I'd like to get Price back here. We're gonna need someone who can speak Arabic if we're gonna be visiting a mosque."

"Won't they know who he is? I mean, they've got his picture too."

"I don't plan on going for prayers."

Sharp nodded. "Price is going to be here next weekend. They just transferred him to the VA, and he's going into outpatient status on Friday. I told him he could stay with me until he gets settled."

CHAPTER SEVEN

EHMET ATTA KHAN'S JOURNEY BEGAN with a cramped flight from Tehran to Istanbul. It was considered necessary to maintain the fiction that the dead man was still alive. Entry and exit stamps on passports are carefully scrutinized by some intelligence agencies. A copy of his medical records was carefully included in his baggage, just in case.

There were several days to be wasted in Istanbul. Again to create the fiction that he had returned from a successful bout of treatment and had basked in the bosom of his family before continuing with his long anticipated lecture tour of Canada and the northeastern United States. Local doctors, Muslim doctors, in the host cities were already prepared to pronounce him too exhausted from his treatments to make some of his appearances. After all, Ibn al Tariq may have quite different opinions about *sharia* than Mehmet Atta Khan.

Once Khan was presented with his itinerary he groaned. He was unfamiliar with the accommodations arranged in Quebec and Montreal, but they sounded cheap. He had already done some research on the internet about his host cities, and these were not the names that were touted as the places to stay. The American hotels had better sounding names, most of them major chains, but they had qualifiers in the name such as 'Express' or 'Family' that warned him they would have less than four or five stars.

The flight arrangements were equally execrable. Every leg had been booked as an economy class seat. Could this be how a *sharia* lawyer would travel? The documents provided him did not indicate a miserly man, but there it was. A midnight flight on Turkish International from *Kemal Ataturk International* to *Charles deGaulle* in Paris would be torture. Having made this flight in the past on a connection from Bahrain, he knew there was a better scheduled flight on Air France. There was a six hour layover, (six hours!) waiting for a connecting flight on Lufthansa to *Schipool* in Amsterdam, with an overnight wait until he could board an Air Canada to Quebec. Whatever his handlers had in mind, he would be spending the night in the comfort of the *Amsterdam Ramada International* rather than a plastic seat in the terminal. He would insist. That would be more in keeping with the needs of a recently ill man.

The layover in Paris could be beneficial to him. If he could get a few moments unobserved, he could visit the *Banc International de Genève* which maintained a 24 hour branch office at *Charles deGaulle.* He knew because he had used it several times in the past. In casual conversation he had discovered it was an unpopular assignment and had a frequent turn over of staff, so there should be no one there who had the remotest possibility of remembering him from another life. There was an account there which held a great deal of money that was accessible only by account number and password, no identification necessary. It was one of the few places left where such a service could be obtained, and it had branches in Quebec and New York. While there he would arrange for limited access to Mehmet Atta Khan. Unlimited would only raise eyebrows. It would be enough for him to live comfortably until he could make more of such arrangements. There were other Mideast banks with international offices who would allow almost anonymous transfers. Mehmet Atta Khan would have a comfortable source of funds until he could get to another bank in Copenhagen and access his safe deposit box, where several complete identities awaited him. That bank had moved into the realm of biometrics, and he could access the box without an identification card. He merely had to pass a retinal scan. His years as a courier had given him access to amazing amounts of cash, valuables and identity documents, and he had been very meticulous in arranging safe storage for much of it in anticipation of the end of *Jihad*. It had not ended as he had anticipated, but he had also never anticipated enjoying the delights of the seventy-two virgins. That was the dream of the useful idiots. His mental inventory told him that, unless the Iranians were lying to him, they had missed a considerable amount of his cached resources.

His travel, as poorly as it was planned, met his expectations for shabby treatment; no leg room and lousy cabin service. The big surprise, and it was a surprise, was that there didn't appear to be any security agents on his flight from Tehran or Istanbul. He made it a point to be one of the last to board so he could do his own screening. There was a suspicious face in *Charles deGaulle*, but if it was following him it kept a discreet distance and he was able to slip into the bank to complete his arrangements. He was mildly surprised when the clerk offered to arrange an Automatic Teller card linked to the master account. Khan considered it, and decided that since it was a very discreet account that had had no activity since it was opened, it probably wasn't monitored by the western intelligence agencies. Even if it was, all the better, for he had no intention of putting his safety in peril, and if it looked like there was any risk, he planned to find a way to turn himself in. He would trade any information he had for a guarantee he would not be sent to Guantanamo. A temporary life in a CIA safe house was preferable to any alternative. If the mission, this half baked plan to kill individual unimportant American soldiers was successful and he could make a safe escape, he would retire to northern Europe and enjoy the cold climate with his hidden wealth.

There was no one he could identify waiting for him in Amsterdam, not that it would have changed his plans. He checked to make certain his baggage was checked through to Quebec, and stopped at a cash machine to test his new card. With 500 fresh, crisp Euros in his pocket, enough for a room, amenities and cabs, he walked outside to the taxi queue caught a ride to the hotel. A decent meal and a comfortable bed would do wonders for his back and his attitude on the next leg of his journey.

He awoke early, as was his custom, took another long shower and enjoyed a room service breakfast while still in a hotel robe. His financial arrangements had been completed in splendid anonymity, and he didn't care if the entire Iranian Security Service was accompanying him on the plane.

He was almost pleased when a man approached him in the departure lounge and identified himself as his security detail. It had been decided that a distraction should be available if there were any problems with Canadian passport control. Khan decided to play the stern supervisor and demanded to know why he had taken so long to make himself know.

"My apologies, Mehmet Atta Khan, a momentary lapse in Istanbul caused me to go to the wrong gate. Before I realized my error I had missed your flight, and have been trying to catch up ever since."

"My security should be your only concern. There is no need for anyone to believe we are travelling together. Now loudly apologize for mistaking me for someone you were once acquainted with and go away. If you do your job properly I need never see you again!"

The man was sheepish as he moved off. Another of the many useful idiots. Khan was pleased with himself that he had been able to cow the man so easily. He gathered his bag and coat and went to the check in stand. Now that he had established his displeasure, he saw no reason to stay in coach. He inquired if his seat could be upgraded to first class. If there were ever any question from his Iranian handlers, he could claim the expense was caused by the ineptitude of the security man. He felt it best to distance himself as much as possible from a man who could easily jeopardize his identity.

The weather in Quebec was surprisingly comfortable given the time of year. Khan's scheduled called for a lecture at a local mosque the next morning, so when he was met outside of baggage claim by a bright eyed young man in robes, who was driving a luxury model Mercedes Benz, he feigned illness. A prominent doctor who prayed at the mosque had previously been informed there would be a man, a recent cancer patient, who must be ordered to rest after his long journey. A true believer, the doctor saw no reason to doubt the Imam, so when he was called he fussed and clucked, as all good doctors do, and pronounced the visitor to be suffering from mild exhaustion and dehydration. He would re-examine him in the morning, but it would be best if the *sharia* lawyer merely moderated the planned discussion instead of being an active participant. Khan offered his apologies and put up a feeble resistance. In the end, he offered to retrace his steps to Quebec before he left for home and conduct a proper lecture appearance. He fretted about his need to go to Montreal immediately afterward, and asked about the possibility of being well enough to drive. The doctor, who had not planned beyond his initial diagnosis, stammered and paced, trying to display the wisdom of the prophet. He was saved by the intervention of the Imam who volunteered the services of the bright eyed young man in robes to drive him to his next appointment in the luxury Mercedes Benz. It could not have been easier.

Montreal was a large, cosmopolitan city that suited Mehmet Atta Khan. The hotel he was to stay at was far beneath his requirements, so he called a cab and was taken to a more upscale establishment closer to the heart of the city. Once ensconced in his room he made arrangements to meet with the contact the Iranians had established. He was ostensibly a low level economic attaché at the Lebanese embassy. In reality he was a senior member of Hezbollah. Now that they had a large bloc in the Lebanese government, it had been easy to place their people in embassies and consulates around the world. They were less visible than their Iranian counterparts who sometimes operated less than a block away.

They arranged to meet in a tea house near the central city market, more a tourist area than a true market, although they did sell produce and meats at inflated prices. There was some irritating Middle Eastern music playing in the background, enough to provide white noise to defeat listening devices or curious neighbors. They exchanged the small talk of old friends who hadn't seen each other in a while. Khan learned of his new friend's children and their success in the local schools, and Khan shared his recent ordeal with cancer treatment. There was much clucking of the tongue and reassuring comments about how well he looked. As they parted, Khan was surprised when he wasn't given any information. He was ready to write the meeting off as a dry run when his contact mentioned he would be out of the office for a few days, but if Khan needed to reach him there was a number. He handed him the business card of a car rental company. There was already a note written on the back. Khan could read part of what it said, and the contact wrote more. Khan was experienced enough in field craft to know not to read it here. He slipped the card into his pocket and bade his friend good bye. He finished his tea slowly, and went to the men's room to wash his hands. Only then did he read the message. It contained his new instructions.

Khan parked his rented Lexus in the underground garage. He did not believe he had been followed. The instructions on the card directed him to rent a vehicle, asking for one registered in the United States. The agent, a devout Canadian Muslim who was content with following instructions from the Imam, was especially pleased that the car he had been holding for a special 'guest' had been claimed. Many renters did not want the hassle of having foreign plates on their car. It made them an object of attention to the local police. Similarly, renters did not want to pay the extra expense of renting a vehicle to cross the border with, anticipating extra scrutiny and delays at the border crossing. It was simpler, and almost as cheap, to fly to the US. That meant that if the vehicle remained unused for any length of time, the agent would be required to pay some one an exorbitant fee to return it to a US agency. He would then be out the income that would normally be generated by a rental, his inventory would have one less vehicle to rent out, and he would be out the expense of hiring a driver. Mister Khan saved him all that trouble and did not hesitate to pay the premium rental rate. Added to the bonus he had been paid to attach a small flash drive to the key ring, it had indeed been a profitable transaction.

Khan plugged the drive into his laptop and began scrolling through the documents and photos. Some were duplicates of images he had already seen, and some were new. There was a fresh set of photos that attached a face to a name that had only appeared once in previous briefings, a woman doctor named Carson. One of them was very interesting on several levels. It had been taken through a telephoto lens of good quality. It was of the back of a large house, showing a hot tub on a concrete patio. The woman was standing beside it holding a phone to her ear. She was wearing a very skimpy bathing suit that barely covered her considerable attributes. Documents described her role in the assault on the hideout of Ali Alawa Sharif, a Sudanese Arab, in Moldova. Someone was casting a wide net to avenge old injustices.

The last document was troubling to him. Some of the young jihadists who had returned from camps in Yemen were acting against orders and were actively planning their own operations against the targets. So far they had achieved no results except to get one of their own killed (his death had been concealed from the authorities) and to lose two weapons. The worst was that one of the jihadists had been briefly detained by the local police before a clever lawyer was able to concoct a plausible story. No reason was given for this breach of discipline, unless they had decided to avenge the death of Anwar Al Awlaki on their own. Khan was instructed to take them to task and restore discipline to the operation.

That evening Khan took a late dinner in the hotel restaurant. They had an excellent Chilean sea bass and some rather fine French wines. He had several glasses with his dinner and had the sommelier hold it in the cellar for the following evening. In spite of Islamic prohibitions on alcohol, something he rarely followed when he was in a western country, he went to the bar and ordered a large Brandy. He sipped his drink, savoring the aroma as the glass warmed to the heat of his hand, and noticed a striking young woman seated at the bar. He legs were crossed and the skirt was slit just enough to give a tantalizing glimpse of thigh. She looked like a Berber from the mountain regions of Algeria, women noted for their beauty and sexual charms. Such was their notoriety that the French Foreign Legion had regularly recruited these women for their Mobile Field Brothels that followed the Legion around the world for most of their history. Berber whores had been present when the French lost Indochina at Dien Bien Phu. Khan wondered if this woman was following in the tradition as an entrepreneur. He caught her attention and signaled her over. A respectable woman, waiting for her husband or escort, would never have acknowledged him. She merely smiled, flashing more thigh as she got off her stool, and joined Khan at his table. She was definitely a working girl.

She willingly went up to Khan's room with him. Money was not discussed. She was affiliated with the bartender or the concierge, and there was probably a minimum acceptable figure. If she performed well, and there was no reason to doubt she would, Khan would not quibble. He had been without a woman since before the raid that killed bin Laden. She was very professional, and very adept. She drained him, aroused him again and toyed with his manhood until he fell asleep.

Khan woke alone in his bed. He looked around the room, but there was no sign of the Berber whore. The clock said it was nearing 2 AM. Strange, he though, there was no discussion of money. His next thought was for his wallet and credit cards, but they were all present on the bureau. This was more of a puzzle. Khan was not so self assured that he would think the woman came to him because she sensed his virility. She was too businesslike. There was a faint light coming from the small sitting room attached to his bedroom. He walked in and saw her sitting in the corner chair, still quite naked. Khan took a moment to enjoy the sight of her long legs reaching up to the dark patch of her womanhood. His eyes roamed to her magnificent breasts, with the dark aureoles circling her large nipples. How he had enjoyed toying with them. He felt himself getting aroused again. "My dear, you had me worried. I thought you had left." He walked closer, anticipating the pleasure her lips would bring. He stopped short. The way she was sitting was unnatural. Her head was tilted at a strange angle. He reached out to touch her.

"Mehmet Atta Khan, I did not think you were the type to enjoy sex with a dead woman, but if you insist, I will wait."

There was a man sitting on the couch behind him. He was holding a small gun on him. "Go ahead, pleasure yourself with her. That was her purpose, although I must admit I preferred her alive so she could respond to my attentions. Her lovemaking became more frenzied the more I hurt her. Have you ever noticed that in a woman?"

"You, and her, in here? I heard nothing."

"Of course you didn't. She was very good at what she did. You never noticed the trans-dermal sedative she attached to your buttocks." Khan reached down and felt the plastic square. He ripped it off. The man continued. "I needed to know if you had said anything to her in your moment of passion. In the end she begged for her life by offering herself to me. The pain aroused her and she begged for more. I do believe she was having an orgasm when I snapped her neck. A pity, really, the Berber whores are always the best."

Khan stumbled back, trying to hide his nakedness. "Who are you?"

The man smiled. "How rude of me. I am Ali Alawa Sharif. Your Iranian masters may have mentioned my name to you." Khan was familiar with the name. Much of this foolish mission was connected with his name, but how was he here? "You're supposed to be in a French prison, or dead."

"Yes, well, I can explain that. With all the changes in North Africa there were new priorities to be dealt with. I suddenly had value to both the French and the Algerians and they engaged in some complicated negotiations to exchange agents, information, opportunities and considerations, or something like that. I suddenly found myself on a plane to Yemen, of all places. It was a relief, because I had expected to go back to the Sudan, They plan to kill me very slowly there, but al Qaeda also had plans, so for more consideration, and a great deal of money and resources, I was also given an assignment."

Khan continued to shift his eyes between the gun and the dead girl. Even in her death sprawl she was quite beautiful, and he felt an involuntary reaction. Sharif noticed it and barked at him. "In the name of Allah, Khan! Go put on some pants. Necromancers will never find peace in paradise." Khan did as he was told. Sharif followed him and continued talking as he dressed. "My mission is similar to yours, with two minor changes. The Americans are to be killed, painfully and publicly if possible, but assuredly they are to be killed. Except the 'white whore'. She is to be mine to deal with."

Khan had heard the phrase before. It referred to one of the targets who was reported to be fond of flaunting her body. It had so inflamed the lust of a Janjaweed leader that his desire for her clouded his judgment, even though he had dubbed her a whore. "Do you mean the doctor who was added to the list?"

Alawa thought for a moment and shook his head. "No, the one who is referred to as the 'white whore' is a staff officer. The doctor whose picture now graces your computer is probably a whore also, judging by her manner of dress, but she was elevated to the target list because it was discovered that she was responsible for identifying my body in Moldova. She cannot escape punishment after rendering such a service to the infidels."

"What will you do with her?"

"The doctor? She will just die. I offer her to you as compensation for your Berber. As far as the other whore, the one called Bonneville, she will die eventually, but so much has been made of her charms, I am interested in exploring them. I hope that I can dispatch her in a manner similar to the Berber whore. Fitting end, don't you think?" Khan thought the man was a sadistic madman.

"What is the other alteration?"

Sharif broke into a broad grin, "That is even simpler to accomplish. In the end, the Americans are to know it was the work of the Iranians, all the planning, the personnel and the support."

"How are we to do that?"

"It's not for you to worry about for now. I have already made the arrangements. Your next step, after you dispose of the whore's body, is to pick me up on the other side of the United States border. I have already arranged my crossing; you will just have to provide the transportation to our destination. I understand you have a Lexus. A fine vehicle for our needs."

"Where am I to meet you? I am unfamiliar with the border area."

Sharif handed him a map. A route from Montreal to a border crossing near the New York-Vermont border was marked in red ink. South of the border in what looked like New York State a town had been circled. Khan strained his eyes to read the small print. Khan pulled the map back and folded it before handing it to him. "The village you are to meet me in is called 'Rousses Point'. It's only a short drive from Canada, and if you ask the border guards they will direct you to a coffee shop in the center of town.

"Cross over in two days." He looked at his watch. "Since it's already morning that would be tomorrow. When you arrive I would suggest you have a good meal and enjoy some of the historic sites near the village market place. I believe they call it the village common. I will meet you there at noon."

"How am I to dispose of the body?"

Sharif grinned again. This time it was accompanied by a hearty laugh. "A man of your means and abilities, Mehmet Atta Khan, should have no trouble with such a minor detail as that. If you start now you should be finished in time to have a hearty breakfast."

Sharif went to the door and turned. Khan noticed a small satchel in his hand. Sharif smiled again. It was beginning to be an annoying habit. "There is a laundry cart in an alcove at the end of the hall. If you hide the body in it, you can send it down to the parking garage in the service lift. I wouldn't advise riding down with it. Take the guest lift and meet it there. At this hour you should have all the privacy you desire. If anyone is present, just abandon it and go to your car until they leave. Do not abandon her body. She will undoubtedly be remembered, and so will the man she left with."

He looked at the body one last time. "She was a beautiful woman, Khan, you chose your whore well. Be content with the time you had with her. You really don't have time to satisfy your lust with her again, but if you must, be quick about it.

"I will see you in two days in Rousses Point. Don't be late."

"And if I am, Sharif?"

He held up the satchel. "Her clothing is in here, along with a soiled pair of your drawers. There will be no difficulty identifying your DNA. There is also one of your credit cards with an excellent fingerprint impression, just in case you have managed to avoid inclusion in any of the genetic registers the infidels have grown so fond of. Betray me at your own peril."

Mehmet Atta Khan stared at the body for a long time before he galvanized himself to take action. He finished dressing, packed his belongings and retrieved the laundry cart, exactly where Sharif said it would be. He left it in the hall outside his door. He did not recall ever seeing a cart brought into a hotel room, so it would look strange if someone were to see one coming out. There had been a smock draped over the side of the cart. He put it on to complete the illusion.

Hotels in cold climates always have spare blankets. Khan took one and wrapped the Berber girl in it. He curved her body to fit in the cart. There was an annoying squeak from one of the wheels now that there was weight on it. Khan hoped it wouldn't attract any attention from the sleeping guests. The service elevator was waiting for him, the door open and the 'Stop' button engaged. Sharif must have been helping him. He stripped off the smock and pushed the button for his level of the parking garage after he recovered his suit case. The guest elevator was conveniently located around the corner. Khan's eyes searched the ceiling and walls for signs of surveillance cameras. He didn't see any, but that meant nothing. They could be hidden anywhere.

In the garage there were cars parked on either side of the service elevator. He looked to see where the closest vacant space was and lifted the body out and placed it behind the car adjacent to it. He then retrieved his own vehicle and backed it into the slot. The body was quickly placed in the trunk and he sped off into the night, not knowing where he would dispose of the body. He drove until he came to a rundown looking industrial area. He searched for a manhole cover, not caring if it was for sewer, storm drain or utilities. He knew subterranean pipes in areas like these housed rats, and the rats would feast on the fresh body, hopefully rendering it unidentifiable before it was discovered. The first one he located reeked as he removed the cover. It would be perfect for his needs. His next need would be to leave his hotel before the body was discovered or a review of any security footage revealed a strange hotel employee moving laundry from his room in the middle of the night.

There was a map in the center console of his Lexus. He traced a route from Montreal to the town Sharif had told him about, Rousses Point. There was a border crossing just to the north of it, on what appeared to be quiet road. The villages on either side did not have any points of interest listed. He checked his watch. If he varied his driving speed and his route, and stopped for a leisurely breakfast along the way, he could cross into the United States around mid-morning. He could always find some rural inn or motel to spend the next twenty-four hours before he met with Ali Alawa Sharif.

CHAPTER EIGHT

C OMMAND SERGEANT MAJOR
LUCAS GRANT didn't get very
many weekends off. As the CSM
to the State Adjutant General, there were always units to visit, seminars
to attend, and Employer Support functions he was required to attend.
His boss saw to it. Major General Alonzo Price Cabot had expected to
be elevated to three stars and be named Chief of the National Guard
Bureau, which was rumored to become a seat with the Joint Chiefs
of Staff. He had carefully and politically maneuvered one of his units
into the limelight by volunteering it for a humanitarian assignment to
Darfur. Nobody else wanted it because it was looked at as being at the
dirty end of a very long stick with ample opportunity for things to go
very wrong. Cabot thought he could work around the risks and load
the unit up with politically reliable officers and a core of experienced
NCOs who could train and lead. CSM Grant was just such an NCO,
and was in hot water with the Army and looking for a new job. Cabot
recruited him, gave him *carte blanche* to bring in some NCOs of proven
ability, and sat back to wait for the apple to fall into his lap.

The apple didn't fall, the sky did. The 289th Engineer Support
Command was in over its head from the moment it crossed the border
into Darfur. They were harassed by the Janjaweed rebels, challenged by
the Sudanese Liberation Army, and openly attacked by the Sudanese

Army. They were accused of wiping out a Janjaweed camp when they rescued some UN hostages, and shot up a district capitol, Al Fashir, to save a congressman who later claimed he didn't need saving.

After that, they got involved in another shooting war in Eastern Europe, where all they had to do was build a few crummy miles of dirt road. The icing on the cake was getting the congressman who didn't need rescuing in Darfur killed in Moldova. Then they couldn't even stay out of trouble in the United States. Another simple road building job turned into an invasion of Mexico!

Cabot couldn't understand why they weren't all in jail. Instead, they came home to a heroes welcome (sort of), and he had been informed (directed) to take no action against any of them. The only thing he could do, legally and officially, was to split them up. Grant had originally been slotted as the Regular Army Enlisted Advisor to his office. It had been his idea to make him the State CSM so he could send him to Darfur. Now it was coming back to bite him in the ass. One of his unindicted co-conspirators, Ralph Harrison, had come to them as an intelligence NCO and had somehow shot up the ranks until he was now the acting Sergeant Major of the 289th Engineer Battalion that was being formed out of the wreckage of the 289th Engineer Support Command a mile or so down the road from his headquarters. Sergeant First Class David Sharp had likewise enjoyed a remarkable rise after what had been a drunken retirement. He was now advising curriculum development at the joint Officer Candidate School/NCO Academy located a short walk from his office.

He had been spared the last of the group, another screw up named Jonah Price. Who the hell names their kid Jonah? Grant had rescued his sorry ass from the deck of a fishing boat well out to sea. He even had a Coast guard helicopter fly out and pick him up off the deck. His Army career had been checkered enough that it required Cabot's intercession to get him in to the National Guard at all, and even then Grant had asked for a determination to bring him in at a Sergeant, instead of his discharge rank as a Specialist. Somehow under Grant's guidance and protection, he had managed to shoot up to his previous rank of Sergeant First Class. Grant knew when and where to pull strings in the big Army. Price elected to join a Stryker brigade that was training up to go to Afghanistan. It looked like once he was back in boots he was reluctant to risk trying civilian life again. He had been wounded

94

several times before he left the 289th in New Mexico. He could at least have had the decency to get wounded seriously enough in Afghanistan to be medically retired. The bastard had just managed to do enough damage to himself to get assigned to this headquarters full time while he was going through the Wounded Warrior Program and follow-up treatment at the local VA hospital.

Cabot would never get his third star now. He would repay them by making their lives an administrative hell. Sooner or later, one or all of them would screw up enough to get a bad efficiency review and they could be forced out in the coming Reduction in Force.

CSM Grant understood what was going on, but Cabot was so far away from the tempo of combat operations that he didn't understand the simple fact that a peacetime, home based National Guard outfit could not compare with the conditions of deployment. Cabot could only spend so much time trying to make his life miserable, and all it amounted to was poorly scheduled make-work. Some days, what he was doing was only slightly removed from painting rocks. On the bright side, if being the target of the remnants of a world wide terrorist group could be called a bright side, word had come down, presumably from the mysterious General Vaughn that he had to be available to Homeland Security to help assess the threat.

That Somali kid who ended up naked in a dumpster behind a local shopping mall with a couple of Russian bullets in him had pissed everybody off. The working story, one that was actively promoted by the local mosque, was that the kid had been a victim of gang turf struggles. It gave them an excuse to build up a fiction that there was a lot of racism in the community directed at the small Muslim presence. Almost as an afterthought it was suggested that the recent return of the 289th after fighting Muslims and Mexicans led to a resurgence of xenophobia.

Grant was certain that it had been the kid Sharp had shot at on the river, since he had seen a body wrapped in the same kind of tarp at the boat landing. Grant used the opportunity, once and for all, to get rid of that miserable little Russian pistol. Grant personally took a chop saw to it and scattered the pieces in the river. It had been easy to come up with a receipt showing that Sharp had been carrying an issue M-9 pistol during the exercise. If his buddy the shooter and his lawyer hadn't concocted such an elaborate story that he had been a solitary innocent bystander, the heat would truly be on. As it was, the local mosque was now conducting a series of sermons about how Muslims could not expect justice in the same city as 'the murderers from Darfur and Moldova'. The Imams never offered an excuse for why this particular kid would be the victim, innocent or otherwise, of gang activity, and the police, who had denied any serious activity in the press just a matter of months ago, refused to identify which gang they had in mind. There was cross over in the investigation, and every so often a bright cop would wander on down to the State Reservation and ask about the other kid and the AK. He was always referred to the State Police, who referred them to the feds, who referred them to the kids' lawyer.

Everybody knew, or at least suspected, the true story, but nobody was talking about it. The general trend was to build up Islamic rage against the soldiers. After all, if they hadn't been applauded for their service where they were actively killing Muslims, local infidels would not have felt justified in killing an innocent young Muslim lad. The verbiage had slowly morphed so that '*infidel*' was a word heard more often. It had even begun to appear in graffiti, and some of the local liberal bleeding hearts were beginning to take their side. One letter to the editor in the local newspaper went as far to say she could understand if Muslim rage exploded in the community, and she could forgive it because of the history of oppression. The gang aspect of the story, even though it was a load of crap, was slipping from the public consciousness.

The portable hoist Grant was jockeying around was originally bought by Ralph Harrison, or at least by his wife Willa, to aid in the restoration of the B-17 the 'Wicked Witch'. Now that the rebuilt engines had been mounted on the wings, Grant was using it to disassemble his new toy, the M-3 Stuart tank, a gift of the Government of Moldova, or more accurately, a gift of Senior Sergeant Yvegniy Kosavich, who turned out to be a senior colonel in Moldovan State Security. After the Chechen attack on the Russian compound, Kosavich had reported one of his tanks destroyed by an RPG. Grant had commented "Too bad. I wanted to take that home." Kosavich had replied that he had another. Grant laughed it off until he was at Fort Bliss, when a Judge Advocate General officer had asked him why he was getting a tank. He didn't realize until he got home that the vehicle had come through complete and operational, with everything, including the weapons, licensed by the State Department. Three .30 caliber machine guns and a 37mm main gun were a lot of firepower to add to the guns they had gotten with the B-17. The guns and the breech block were stored in the reinforced concrete and steel vault Harrison's wife had installed to house the weapons from the B-17. There was a lot of complicated paperwork attached to all this shit.

'Operational' was a generous word to use when describing an under-maintained 70 year old light tank. It had enough life left to drive it from the shipping container to where it now rested, but not much more. The oil sump and the fuel tanks were full of sludge. The electrical system was breaking down, and the mechanical parts were full of rust hidden by grease and paint. The spark plugs and the fuel lines were fouled. If this had been one of the tanks they used to fight the Chechens, it was a miracle they won. He had decided to tear it down and work on it system by system. Thank god they were all simple to understand.

The turret had already been pulled and was sitting on a support frame. He was in the last stages of pulling the engine. It was smaller than one would expect for a tank power plant, and there had been plenty of space to work in the engine compartment once all the hatches and panels were removed. He swung it clear and settled it on an engine stand when he heard a vehicle pull up outside the hanger. People were always coming by to look at the Witch, so when there was a crew working on her, they left the doors open. There was a rope line that the tourists were not allowed to cross. Early on there had been a problem with people trying to take bits and pieces as souvenirs. This was a friendlier way to keep them separate from the plane.

Weekends and evenings were a different story entirely. If it was a holiday weekend, volunteers could usually be found to man the rope line and give the occasional close-up tour; otherwise the sign on the door said 'Closed' and they meant it. Security had tightened up some since the would-be *jihadists* had showed up, including a better alarm system and some video monitoring. At one time there had been a live internet stream of the plane, but that had gone by the wayside too, replaced by a feed to the security company. Now, the only stream was when the full restoration crew was working, and that was down to only a few days a week. Even aviation fanatics had lives to live outside of their hobby. The video feed was the first thing Grant had checked when he arrived. He made certain it was off. He also checked the outside security cameras. Those were on a continuous digital recording that was downloaded remotely every twenty four hours. Grant didn't like the idea of a camera being on him when he worked, so an arrangement had been worked out so that he could call in a code and shut down the interior cameras. They went on again when he left.

He paged through the monitor screens until he could see who had pulled in. He watched the visitor walk to the door and press the buzzer. He remotely opened the door and went back to his tank.

A female voice called to him. "Your toys keep getting bigger. How's a girl supposed to compete with that?" It was Major Sylvia Carson, or Doctor Sylvia Carson, depending on whether she was in uniform.

Grant waved her over as he finished bolting the engine to the stand. His plan had been to start tearing it down today. "That's something women never seem to understand about machines: bigger is always better."

"Are you working on this thing all alone? That's not very safe. What if you had an accident?"

'It's safer than it looks, Major, but you're right. There should be someone else her. Can you handle a wrench?"

She laughed and put her hands up. She was wearing shorts and a halter top. Not exactly the outfit suited for fighting with an oily engine block. "I'll pass. And what's with the 'Major'? Won't I ever break you of that habit?" Grant had started sleeping with Carson on a casual basis in Moldova. It had continued in New Mexico. She was in it strictly for the sex, and that suited Grant. He has also involved with Linda Bonneville.

"Old habits die hard. Besides, I start calling you Sylvia at the wrong time and people are going to wonder."

"Like your little Major? I heard you took her to Aruba a while back. I'm jealous. You still owe me a weekend somewhere like you promised in New Mexico." She moved closer. Grant could tell she wasn't wearing a bra. "Careful. I'm kind of greasy."

She stepped back. "Don't worry. I'm not here to jump you. Well, I was, but not now. Is that our tank?" She asked.

"Our tank?" The first time they had made love was inside one of these steel boxes in Yvegniy Kosavich's warehouse in Moldova. He was lifting her through the turret hatch when she stuck one of those big hard nipples in his face. He was surprised at how much space there actually was.

"Is that the one you stole my innocence in?" She walked over and ducked under the turret. "Yup. This is it."

"How can you tell? They all looked alike to me."

"I'm sentimental. I was looking at a data plate when you attacked my boobs. There was a funny scratch on it. It's this one all right." She squatted down under the turret. "What's the latest with our little friends? I haven't heard anything since I got that visit from General Vaughn and his gnome." Vaughn's aide wasn't really a misshapen gnome, but he was one of the ugliest people on the face of the earth. "I keep expecting an RPG to come through my window some night. The idea scares the shit out of me."

"Then you probably shouldn't worry about it, Major. There's no real reason to think you're even involved in all this. You came up in a report on the raid we did on Moldova. Why don't you try to forget about it?"

"Fat chance of that. I don't know how it was presented to you, but that Vaughn scares the hell out of me."

Grant knew it was a slim chance she'd forget about it. Hell, he didn't even believe what Vaughn was telling them. If the rag heads were watching them, they'd probably be watching anybody associated with what they had been doing. Vaughn believed they may have either accessed some of their after action reports, which should have been classified, or they heard from some of the participants on the other side. It could have been either one. The 'Wikileaks' scandal pretty much showed them how insecure classified documents were, but Grant had the nagging feeling that somehow, somewhere, there was somebody on the other side who had been feeding the new bad guys information. Some of the excerpts were in the stilted language of a formal translation.

Carson wasn't convinced. When Vaughn told her that her name had been mentioned in some of the intelligence documents, he had been serious. His promise of periodic updates was anticipated, but she doubted she'd hear anything unless she got it from Grant. "Can I at least count on you letting me know when any more information gets in?"

"Not a problem. I'll make sure you get included, but Vaughn doesn't keep us in the tightest loop."

"Maybe not, but there are other things a girl would like to hear about, like that thing with Sergeant Sharp on the reservation?" Grant figured she would have heard about it, so he gave her the full story, including the body in the dumpster.

She walked around the tank and didn't say anything. When she came back she asked "Is this thing ever going to run again?"

Grant welcomed the change in subject. "Sure is. This beast may be old, but she's simple enough. There's not one solid state circuit or computer module in it. Even the radios have tubes. It's just a matter of tearing it down, cleaning it up, and replacing a few pieces of steel."

"And that?" she asked pointing to the 'Witch', "is that ever going to fly again?"

"That I can't say. Ralph Harrison thinks it will. He's even getting a license to fly it when it's ready later."

"How much later?"

"Another couple of months, maybe a year. I try not to get too involved in it. Something about that plane sucks people in and won't let them go."

She looked at him and smiled. She walked over to the nose and reached up to touch the nose art. Grant made a mental comparison between the pin-up and Carson's profile. If she had longer hair she could have posed for it. "Can I get a tour? Your tank's no fun anymore now that it's all apart. This looks more interesting."

Grant went to the wash station and cleaned his hands. His coveralls were grease stained so he peeled out of them too, leaving him wearing jeans and a golf shirt. The restoration crew kept the 'Witch' spotless, even the engines, and he never got close to it with dirty hands. He was there the day the first engine had been hung on the wing and they test ran it. After they grinned like little kids and probably wet their pants, they scrubbed the damn thing down until it looked like it had just come out of the crate. Harrison told him they did that for each of the four big radials. There were two spare engines that had been scrounged from somewhere, plus a bunch of spare parts and cylinders. Harrison said that the restoration crew wanted to mount all the engines and test them, as well as the spare parts. Since some of the newest were at least fifty years old, it was probably a good, if not time consuming, idea.

There were four ways to get into a B-17 on the ground. A hatch under the nose was where you saw the pilots lift themselves up in all the good war movies. It wasn't the most convenient method of entry, and a step ladder stood under it. The next was the bomb bay. When the plane wasn't carrying a bomb load there was plenty of room to step up from a small wooden platform. A narrow catwalk connected the flight deck with the radio compartment aft and the flight deck forward. Walking through it in flight must have been quite an experience.

Further back, on the right, or starboard, side, the main crew entrance was just forward of the tail wings. It was a good size door to accommodate a crew member wearing all his flight gear and parachute. Just behind the tail wing was a smaller door for the tail gunner. It was more on an escape hatch than a normal entrance way. It saved him the trouble of trying to climb over the tail wheel. Part of the suspension jutted up into the fuselage, making it an awkward passage with a lot of hang-ups if he had to get out in a hurry. Grant had Major Carson go around to the crew entrance. "This way you'll get the grand tour."

The fuselage of a B-17 was remarkably small. Grant doubted that there were very many crewmen over five feet, eight inches tall. Carson walked at a slight stoop, careful not to bump her head on one of the ribs. Once past the waist gun positions she stopped at a large hole in the floor. "What was this for?"

Grant explained the ball turret, and explained how the gunner got into the position, and then it was lowered to hang under the plane. If there was any damage to the mechanism, the gunner was trapped. There was at least one instance of a ball turret gunner being trapped in a B-17 that had to make a belly landing. The gunner did not survive. Hopefully, he was facing backwards so he didn't have to watch the ground coming at him. He pointed out a waist gunner's position to where the ball turret stood on its own cradle. Next to it was a taller open work cylinder topped with another dome. That was the top turret, usually named by the flight engineer. Both assemblies were just easier to work on outside of the fuselage.

They move on into the radio operator's compartment. This was very small, with only a small table with the radio mounted on it and a stool fixed to the floor. The dorsal hatch was stowed in the open position, and Carson could stand with her head and shoulders outside of the plane. Grant sat on the stool and watched her move around. She was starting to put on a show for him. She reached in back and retied her halter so that the fabric pulled tight across her breasts, making her nipples stand out. Grant fixated on them briefly, until he noticed her looking down at him. "See something you like, Sergeant Major?" she asked seductively as she untied the halter and slipped it over her head. She had been sunning herself topless, no tan lines. Grant reached over and pulled her closer, taking first one, then the other hard little nipple between his teeth. She moaned softly and unsnapped her shorts and slid them over her hips. Grant joined her on the floor of the radio compartment.

They finished up in the Plexiglas nose of the bomber. There was a surprising amount of space there. Carson had led Grant naked through the bomb bay and through the crawl space under the cockpit leading to this, the Bombardier and Navigator's position. She giggled, repeating 'cockpit' over and over. After she had amused herself on top of Grant, one of her preferred positions, she asked if they could do it again once the plane was in flying condition. "Can you imagine what it would be like having sex standing in that hatch? Or watching the ground go by here? That would be absolutely erotic!"

Grant laughed. "Once this plane is airworthy, I doubt it'll ever get off the ground without six or eight people aboard. Are you that much of an exhibitionist?"

She pretended to frown, and then perked up. "I thought you said Sergeant Harrison was learning how to fly it? I'll bet you can convince him to give us a private flight."

Grant wasn't so sure. "Maybe I can talk Ralph into it, but his wife keeps the books, and this big mother will probably cost four or five thousand an hour to operate."

She lay back against the Plexiglas and smiled. "I'll go halves with you. It'll be worth it. Now go get our clothes before I have to have you again."

Once back outside the plane Carson was getting ready to leave. "Can I see you later?"

"What about your boy toy?"

"Don't try to be cute. What makes you think I have a boy toy?"

"I was with the General at your unit a couple of weeks ago on a 'show the flag' visit. He asked for you specifically. I think he likes the way you wear your scrubs." She picked up a rag and threw it at him.

"Anyway, your CO told him you were at some conference with your cardiac guy. I just put two and two together."

"You're keeping tabs on me. I like that, but don't worry about him. He's got another one of those conferences this weekend. Will you come over?"

"I started to tear down that engine. I'd like to get that finished."

"I get it," she said sharply. "When you're done doing whatever that is will you be going to see your little Major?"

"Stop calling her that. She's got her kids this weekend. I'm *persona non grata* at her house when the grand parents and the ex are around. Birthdays and grand parents. I don't mix with civilized people. I thought you would have had enough of me for one day?"

"You're worried about keeping me happy. I like that."

"I'm not worried about it. I'm not as young as I used to be, so I just do my best. You'll let me know when it's not good enough for you. Besides, Dave Sharp is having a welcome home thing for Price tonight, so I'm heading there from here. He just got sprung from the Wounded Warrior Transition Unit at Walter Reed and he starts his out-patient next week." Damn it. I like Price too much to blow him off just to get laid, he thought to himself.

"How much later?"

Grant glanced at the wall clock. "I was planning to wrap up here about 5 or 6, and be there around 7."

"If you leave now we can have almost four hours, and more if you don't mind being a little late."

Grant thought about it. "Let me clean up and lock up. I'll be over in about 45 minutes." Yeah, Grant thought to himself again, as he did every time he was around Sylvia Carson, I'm going to hell. Another thought occurred to him, and I'll be the best laid guy when I get there.

"Make it 20 minutes," she said. "I'll help you with your shower. Then you can try out my new hot tub." That sealed the deal.

He was an hour late for Price's welcome home party. Carson's house was the only one on a country road. The road itself was an inconvenient shortcut for locals, and there wasn't much in the way of traffic. He did notice a white Toyota pickup truck parked on the opposite side of the road about 100 yards from her driveway. Since Sudan, where every *jihadi* seemed to have a white Toyota with a machine gun mounted in the bed, Grant always noticed them. It must have been a reflex that was now too ingrained to ignore. Grant had given the grounds a quick tactical analysis: easy to defend, but hard to get out of.

It was getting dark when he left. He noticed the same truck was still parked there. He couldn't see anyone sitting in it, so for no particular reason he turned in that direction and pulled up in front of it. There was no one in it. He walked around and checked the doors and looked in the cargo bed. It was empty. There was a note on the windshield that said they had run out of gas and would be back soon. Grant replaced the note and went back to his truck. He took out his cell phone and searched his preprogrammed numbers. Sylvia Carson was not one of them. He punched 411 to see if he could find it, but like a lot of people, she kept her number unlisted. He briefly considered going back to her house, to let her know to keep an eye on it but thought better of it. It had already taken all his will power to leave once. He knew he was weak. It was probably nothing. She had a pretty good security system, and he noticed she kept a pistol on her night stand. She had learned her lessons well hanging around Grant. He'd come back after the party to see if the truck was still there.

When he pulled into the parking lot at Sharp's condo unit, there were three Mediterranean looking young men sitting on a bench near the entrance. One of them had his cell phone out, and Grant got the impression they were taking his picture. He parked his truck in a visitors slot and walked directly across the grass to there the men were sitting. He had his phone out and for some reason decided to start snapping pictures. Before he could get too close they got up and walked away. Grant stood and watched where they were going, when a white Toyota pickup drove in to the end of the lot. The three men got in and the truck backed out and left. Grant snapped a few more shots of the truck, hoping he could use his computer to enlarge the pictures enough to read their plate number. There were enough cops in National Guard units that he knew, as well as an MP platoon attached to State headquarters. He would find out who they were. He also swore at himself for not taking the number from the truck at Major Carson's.

Sharp had a house full of people, so no one really noticed he was late except Jonah Price. He had been anxious to talk to Grant, and wanted to do so before the party got too loud or he got too drunk. Grant looked at the beer in his hand.

"Should you be drinking that?" He asked.

"Luke, this is only the third beer I've had tonight. It's only the third one in over two months too. I'm not taking any of their drugs, and I'll be sober when I get back on Monday."

"Make sure of that. Where's Sharp? I need to talk to him."

Price pointed across the room and Grant waved to get his attention. Sharp had had a few, but he was still pretty sober. Grant brought him outside to a little garden patio he had overlooking the parking lot. At least with trees planted around the perimeter it wasn't a totally depressing industrial look. Sharp was curious. "That's a party in there, Sergeant Major. Can't business wait until Monday? I really don't think I've fucked up anything in the past week."

Grant told him about the white Toyota, without telling him where he first saw it. He asked Sharp if he had been aware of it in the neighborhood. Sharp wasn't, but walked to the edge of his terrace and looked out over the lot. There were no white Toyotas parked there, but further down, close to the dumpsters, which was always a nice sight from your terrace, was an older maroon one. As they watched, the white Toyota Grant had seen before pulled in, stopped behind the maroon one, and the three men got out. They got into the truck and both vehicles left.

"Well, that was timely," Sharp said.

"Yeah, too timely. It looks like we're being watched. You have any weapons here?"

Sharp feigned a look of pain. "Of course I do. You taught me well."

"Is it a real gun? Not another one of those small caliber toys you're fond of?" Sharp had a liking for small, easy to conceal pistols. His favorite had been a Tokarev TT-33 in 7.62 x 25mm. Grant distrusted small calibers, and put his faith in the .45 ACP round and a 1911A1. He had frequently berated Sharp in the field for carrying his small gun.

"You chopped up my best one. The rest I just keep in the gun case. I've still got the .45 you gave me. Was it one of the guns I picked up from the Border Patrol?"

"Yeah, it was. Make sure you keep it. How about spare magazines and ammo?"

Now Sharp looked sheepish. "Only one magazine. I'll go out and get some spares and ammo in the morning."

"Dickhead. I've got some in the truck."

They went through the party and out to Grant's truck. He handed Sharp a box of hardball ammo and two loaded magazines from his console. Sharp got the impression there were several more. "You can buy your own holster and mag pouch." Once back inside Price came over to join them. "Got time for me now?"

"Always time for you, Jonah. Now, what were you saying about drugs?"

"They've been trying to get me to take something for 'mood swings', but they're the only ones that see them."

"They?"

"Well, not they as much as one doctor. She's some kind of new-ager that thinks anybody who goes to war willingly is already damaged and needs to be cleansed of the psychic images."

Dave Sharp chimed in. "Can you believe that bull shit, Luke? Price was telling me about that when he got here. Can we do something about it? We all know Price is fucked up, but he was like that before the Army got him."

"Can you refuse treatment?"

"Some of us have been doing that on the day ward. She gives us a ration of shit and writes us up as 'hostile' and suffering acute PTSD. She's getting a reputation for handling the worst cases, so the VA people all think she's special. The only way out is to take her pills, but the guys who have tried them say they're like hell itself, and every one of them said they only made them feel worse. She claimed it was the only way to unmask our 'true symptoms' so we can start getting well. I think she's trying to fuck us up even more."

"Price, I thought you had multiple concussions and a mild fracture." Harrison asked. "How did you end up on a PTSD ward?"

"Hold that thought." Grant's first beer was empty and he went for another one. Willa Harrison was sitting by the kitchen bar. Grant was surprised to see her. She lived a couple of hours away, and Harrison usually went to see her. She gave Grant an icy smile and a cold greeting. "Now all the boys are together again. Aren't we lucky?"

'It's good to see you too, Willa. You've been doing a hell of a job handling our money. I want to thank you for that."

"It makes Ralph happy, so I do it. When are you going to take your claws out of him?"

"Willa, I had nothing to do with Ralph staying in. General Cabot offered him the new unit and the Sergeant Major slot. He's going to get the star in the wreath," a Command Sergeant Major had a star surrounded by a wreath in the center of his stripes, "and that's what he wanted. You moving over to the seacoast to punish him isn't helping."

She turned away from him. Fuck it, Grant thought. She's done our money laundering and set up our off-shore accounts. Whatever happens, she's in it as deep as we are. He looked back to the small circle of friends. They were all looking at him, waiting for him to come back. He waved his beer and walked over. Price picked up where he had left off. "When I had my exit interview at Walter Reed they asked me how I got my head cracked. I told them about the guy we were chasing and how he knew me. That got me some funny looks."

"The Arab knew you?" Sharp snorted. "That sounds pretty stupid to me too."

Grant cut him off. "How'd he know you? You meet him somewhere before?" Grant didn't like where this story was going.

""I must have. I only remember seeing him once before, but the son of a bitch seemed to know who I was then, so we must have met before, but I'll be damned if I can remember where. The only other Arabs I met in 'Stan was the *jihadis*, but they were usually dead at the end of the conversation."

"*Jihadis*?" Sharp asked. "You didn't meet any other people over there?"

"Sure, lots of them, but Afghans ain't Arabs."

"I did not know that!"

"Shut up, Dave. Price, when was the first time you met this guy? Are you sure he was an Arab?"

"Absolutely, Boss. He was carrying a Palestinian passport and spoke in a pure Saudi dialect. He didn't know I could understand him and he was chewing out his driver. I threatened to toss a Tokarev on the ground after I wasted him. That got him to cooperate."

"Where did that happen?"

"At the road block where I got the concussion that almost got me evacuated the first time. I've been wondering who the fuck he was. The rag head that pulled the grenade was one of his escorts; at least that's what the spooks who were following him said. That Intel Colonel, Ashley, pulled me off the bus just before I got on the plane to go chasing after him. He was supposed to tell me about him when he got the chance, but he never got the chance. I saw him starting across the border and I figured he was important enough to go after. That's when the Iranians cracked my skull and it all went dark. I've been wondering about him ever since."

Grant held up his hand. "Don't talk about him any more. That little detail about him recognizing you hasn't been in any of the briefings. When they briefed you about all this shit they should have asked you about him."

"Jesus, Boss, they might have. I was still so fucked up when they talked to me I was hearing church bells all the time. Who is he?"

Sharp started to speak, but Grant cut him off. "No. Not now. Let's wait until after all these people are gone, so I want all of you to stay relatively sober." A thought occurred to him. "Ralph, I get the feeling your wife is going to want to leave pretty soon and she'll want you with her."

"Yeah, she really doesn't like you guys."

"We can deal with it," Price said.

"We'll have to. Ralph, I'll talk to you now out on the terrace. You two go back to entertaining the guests."

"People are gonna talk if you two aren't sociable."

"Tell him some Sergeant Major business came up." Turning back to Harrison, "it might be nothing, but we better make some plans. I've gotta get several things done first thing tomorrow. I'll make some calls, but it's Sunday, so nothing will probably happen until Monday. I've got to get hold of Vaughn."

Price interrupted. "Your buddy from New Mexico?"

"One and the same. I'll have him get somebody with enough juice to get you sprung from that Wounded Warrior Transition Unit. If you weren't talking about the man who never was supposed to be you wouldn't be there now."

The gathering lasted until midnight. Harrison and his wife had left shortly after Grant had told him about the observers. Harrison hadn't noticed anything, but admitted he hadn't been watching. "After they got Awlaki with a Predator I got the word that the threat level on us had gone down. My condo is pretty pricey. Someone would notice a strange vehicle full of strangers hanging around. It's a pretty tight condo association."

"Well, stay on your toes. Does Willa know about any of this?"

"Are you kidding? I've got enough problems just staying in the Guard. This extended active duty is really wearing on her. The only plus I can think of is that she blames you for it and prays for your solo ride into Valhalla. Well, almost solo. She won't mind too much if you take Sharp and Price with you."

Sharp and Price, almost as expected, drank more than Grant would have like. Sharp and Sheila Gordon retired to the master suite, while Price was still sitting on the couch with a good looking older woman. It took Grant a moment to recognize her as one of the instructors at the NCO academy. She looked totally different with her long hair down. Grant made a mental note that it was a good thing Price had met someone closer to his own age. Maybe he could pick up a little stability that way. He wished Sharp would find someone older too. Gordon was probably a nice girl, but she still had a wild streak about her, and David Sharp was a tad too old to be trying to keep up. Perhaps he could settle her down, but Grant doubted it.

As he left he took a slow walk around the parking lot, staying in the shadows as much as he could to see if there were any more watchers. He was also checking for more of the small trucks. One part of his brain told him everything was a coincidence, just normal Saturday night activities he was reading too much into. Another part was screaming that this was an organized effort. He looked over and under his truck before he got in and sat there with the engine idling for a few minutes. He had not had much to drink, but he still felt his reactions to all this were slowing down. As he pulled out of the parking lot some deeper instinct told him to turn east. Linda Bonneville's house was a fifteen or twenty minute drive, depending on lights and traffic. At this hour, it should be towards the lower end. She wasn't expecting him, and had given him strict instructions to stay away while her mother and other family members were present for the weekend. It was, after all, her son's birthday and she half expected her ex-husband to appear. His recent good behavior, and the insistence of her mother, had convinced her to let the restraining order she had against him lapse, for the benefit of the children. She did not want a confrontation between him and Lucas Grant. There was no question as to who the winner would be, but her family seemed to be firmly on her ex-husband's side, and they were already being pains in the ass about him.

Grant cruised north on the rural highway, looking for the turn off to her cul-de-sac. The road looked like another driveway at night, and the street sign was obscured by foliage. Linda had told him the neighborhood preferred it that way. It made it easier to identify strange traffic. As expected, Grant drove right past it. The tip off was a large truck tire half buried in the ground at the entrance to a construction company parking lot. That was the signal for southbound traffic to watch for the turn, and a convenient turn around point out of traffic for the rest of the slow learners. He pulled in and made his turn, noticing a dark vehicle parked towards the back of the lot. There was no reason a truck shouldn't be parked here, but it was a coincidence he wasn't prepared to ignore. He parked his truck on the opposite side, getting as close to the tree line as possible. He took his Colt, a spare magazine and a flashlight out of the console, making a mental note that he really needed to draw a set of Night Vision Glasses to keep on hand. As the State CSM he could probably get away with holding on to a serial numbered piece of equipment, claiming it was for impromptu visits to units in the field conducting night training.

There was still enough light from the setting moon to see a path that angled in the general direction of the cul-de-sac. He followed it for about fifty yards, coming out on the edge of the road. He stayed in the tree line until he could orient himself to the neighborhood. He had never seen it from this perspective before. He estimated he was two to three hundred meters from Linda's house. Skulking in this neighborhood was bound to draw more attention than someone boldly walking down the road, so he boldly stepped out and walked down the road. He could hear car doors closing, and as he got nearer to the source it appeared to be the last guests leaving a neighborhood house party a short distance down the road and across the street from Linda's. Saturday night was shaping up to be a big social night. One vehicle, an oversized truck like he was fond of driving, made a u-turn with its high beams on headed away from him. As it did he thought he saw a reflection in the woods at the edge of the road. The activity on the street would mask his movements enough to get him closer, so he stepped across the street and squeezed between the parked cars and the trees. There was a large oak on the edge of the property, and a short cleared distance to a semi-sunken driveway. If he squinted, he could barely make out a dim light. At the same time, he could hear a chirping to his left. He leaned out from the tree, and towards the back of the house he could see another dim light. Who ever these wanna-be ninjas were they were using their cell phones. Grant decided he wanted one of them.

Linda Bonneville was finishing up removing the debris of a child's birthday party. Her family, true to form, had used just about every dish and glass in the house, left empty bottles scattered around, and left without offering to help clean up. It was typical of them, aggravated by the fact her ex had shown up and had spent an hour criticizing her before she had had enough and asked him to leave. Her mother took the ex-husband's side, and Linda had to remind him and her that the local police department had experience escorting him from the property, and, because of his history, had expressed a willingness to do it again. The ex left, but the bad feelings remained until, one by one, the family had retired for the night. She cursed herself for letting the kids talk her into having them spend the night.

The dishwasher was loaded, and she noticed that the party across the way had died down too and she could hear the sounds of people leaving and driving off. She decided on one more glass of wine to sooth the frayed nerves before she went to bed. As she passed the open sliding door to the deck, she noticed a strange glow in the woods. A fire fly, perhaps? She was too tired to care, and poured a glass of cabernet, emptying her last bottle. She made a mental note to go to the wine shop in the morning to pick up some more. She also noticed most of the other liquor bottles on the counter were empty or near so. She guessed all the beer was gone too. Her family never brought booze when they came to visit, but they always managed to drink more than their share. She settled onto the couch and brought her feet up. It sounded like some of the party goers were having a scuffle out on the street. She got back up to close the slider.

Grant, despite his size and his age, was still very stealthy in wooded terrain. He had fixed the location of the phone and moved to it. Whoever was using it kept turning and moving, giving him occasional flashes to reorient himself by. After a few minutes he was on the other side of a large tree from the ninja. He was speaking in low tones, but it was unmistakably Arabic. This was not good. He waited for a pause in the conversation, then reached around the tree and grabbed the Arab by the face, slamming the back of his head into the tree. There was a sick thud and a groan, and the dead weight slid to the ground. Grant picked up the phone and listened. The other end had gone silent. He used his pocket knife to slice the unconscious figures shirt into strips, and hastily bound and gagged him with it. By now, the other ninja was moving across the yard. Grant closed the phone and put it in his pocket. He watched to see where the ninja was going.

He could see Linda Bonneville sitting on her sofa, wine glass in hand. The dark figure was working his way slowly up the steps to the deck. Something got Bonneville's attention and she put down her glass. She reached into a drawer on the end table and punched in a code. When she walked to the door she had a pistol in her hand. Good for her, Grant thought, it was the Colt automatic he had given her. Too bad she didn't think to turn off the interior light. The glare on the door would distort her view.

The ninja saw her coming to the door, and he could see the gun in her hand. He threw himself sideways and crawled under the stairs. Bonneville put her hand over her eyes to shield the glare and tried to look out. Not seeing anything she went back to her wine glass, leaving the gun on the arm of the sofa. After she finished her drink she placed the gun back in its lock box and shut off the light. The ninja waited a moment to make sure she wasn't coming back, and then half ran, half crawled to where he thought his partner was.

"Jamal," he was speaking in English "I told you we should have brought the weapon. The bitch has a gun. We'll have to come back another night. We could have had her whole family! What a strike that would have been." He waited for an answer. Peering around the tree he could see a dark form on the ground. "Jamal. Get up! We must leave! I told you, the bitch has a gun!" He was looking back to the darkened house when Grant reached around and clipped him on the side of his head with the barrel of his gun. Trying to render someone unconscious with a blow to the head with a hard steel object is not as simple as it looks on TV and in the movies. The skull has a tendency to collapse unexpectedly under blunt force. Grant was relieved when the figure still seemed to be breathing evenly. This one got the knife to the shirt treatment and was trussed up like his partner. He now had two phones, and two bags of Arab he didn't know what to do with. He looked at the house. He could see Linda standing in the window of her upstairs bedroom, straining to see into the back yard through the reflection on the glass. She gave up and walked away, shutting off the light. Only then did he stop to consider his problem. He had two unknown Arabic ninjas tied up, unconscious on the ground. Now what to do with them? He shrugged and checked each for a wallet. Using a scrap of cloth to avoid fingerprints, he removed the license and any loose papers from the wallets, leaving any cash or credit cards. Then he heaved one up over his shoulder and grabbed the other by his waist band. He lugged them out into the street and considered his options. Traffic was still leaving the other party, and he waited for his opportunity and dragged them across the pavement. Staying just to the tree line, he dumped them both at the edge of the yard. There was a freshly planted tree supported by wires. He cut these and used them to reinforce the bindings on his prisoners. That done, he carried them, still unconscious, one by one to the back of the house. There was a child's swing set a short distance from the house, just outside the light circle from the tiki torches on the rear deck. He draped each one across a swing set. Once he was satisfied with his handiwork he retraced his steps to the street, where he crossed over again and returned to his truck. Before leaving, he took his knife and slashed all four tires of the other truck. If he was wrong he could always send a couple of hundred dollars anonymously to the owner.

As he drove off he used one of the ninja phones to call 911. "I'd like to report a prowler at . . ."

Almost at the same moment two Arab youths parked their white Toyota truck on the side of the road miles away. As they got out, one left a note under the windshield wiper claiming they had overheated and would return in the morning with fresh coolant to repair the problem. The other drew a commercial model AK-47 from under his seat, along with a Chinese made chest pouch for extra magazines. Contrary to popular belief, fully automatic weapons were not available for purchase at every gun shop and gun show in the United States. They were tightly regulated and permits for them were very time consuming to obtain. The Mideast training camps instead trained them on how to obtain the necessary parts to convert a semi-automatic version into a fully functional military grade weapon. It only required three parts to complete: a so-called auto sear, a reconfigured spring, and a pivot pin.

A simple plastic template, the size of a credit card, located the one hole they had to drill through the sheet metal receiver. The entire process could be accomplished in less than ten minutes.

They argued briefly over who would carry the weapon, not because they wanted it, but because whoever carried it would have to wait his turn while the other savored the spoils of their mission first. The target was the woman military doctor, and she was to be defiled and abused before she was slaughtered to send a message to all about the price of resisting the Islamic Revolution. She was one of two American whores who would experience the retribution of zealous young *jihadists*, and they considered themselves fortunate for their selection for this mission. This one was by far the more attractive of the two. During the drive here they had discussed what they would do to her, and how long it would take. They justified their impure thoughts with declarations that the *fatwa* called for it.

They had scouted the area the previous afternoon, but there was another person in the house, the big American that everyone knew was constantly armed. They had nothing more than a knife between them at the time, so they had made their way back to where the truck had been parked, planning on a return visit after dark. They had met up with others of their group in the city, only to discover the big American had left their target alone. They decided to obtain a weapon from the cache that was kept at the mosque, just in case the big American returned. The team that would be targeting the woman known as 'the white whore' scoffed at their timidity, welcoming the opportunity to face what they termed an old man. They would content themselves with a large bladed knife.

The trees surrounding the doctor's home looked different in the dark, and rather than return to the truck for flashlights, they decided to stay inside the tree line and make their way to the driveway of the house. From there they could make their way to the rear of the house, staying under cover, where a stone patio separated the large French doors from a combination pool and hot tub. The approach would be hidden until they were a mere fifty meters or so from the house. The area was partially lit, making the last distance exposed but not difficult.

They could see their target dimly illuminated, reclining in the hot tub, occasionally taking a drink from a large wine glass. The two *jihadists* agreed that she would be easier to deal with in a wine befuddled state.

Sylvia Carson drained the last of her wine and searched for the bottle to refill her glass. As a doctor she knew that there were warnings about using alcohol in conjunction with a session in a hot tub, but she didn't care. She enjoyed the sensation of the wine accented by the stimulation of the air jets. The only thing that would make it better would be to have a man with her. The bottle was near at hand, but empty. She sighed at the thought, and decided on a quick dip in the pool before she went in for the night. She stepped from the spa and walked barefoot to the edge of the pool, the recessed lighting around the edges casting a glow on her body as she stood there.

In the trees, the two Arabs stood frozen as the woman stepped out of the tub and walked to the edge of the pool. Even from that distance, with the poor lighting, they could see she was naked. The whore was only encouraging the justice they were about to mete out. They stepped out of their cover and moved to a grouping of lawn chairs.

As she stepped into the pool, Carson noticed a movement at the edge of the light. Something, or someone, had come out of the woods and was hiding behind some chaise lounge chairs she had placed for maximum sun exposure. Prowlers had never been much of a problem around here, simply because of the out of the way location, and she automatically thought of the discussion she had with Sergeant Major Grant about the threat level, or lack of it. She quickly swam to the ladder on the far side and climbed out. A towel was draped over a chair near the spa. She wrapped herself with it and walked to the house. In the reflection in the French door she could see what could have been two figures moving closer, pausing by a small utility bin where she kept pool supplies. She closed the French door behind her and walked to the bar. She withdrew another bottle of wine from its rack and leaned over the bar to retrieve a cork screw. She also took a five shot .38 special from a holster affixed under the bar and placed it next to her glass. A small mirror behind the liquor bottles gave her a view to the doors, but the interior light reflected back, washing out any view of the outdoors. She opened the wine and poured herself a glass, focusing on the door handle.

The one with the gun was still upset he would not be first with the woman. As they passed the pool and spa he elbowed his way ahead of his companion, reaching the doors to the house first. He could see inside, and directly across the room from him she stood with her back to him, wrapped only in the towel. He promised himself that, with the weapon, he would be the first to taste the fruits of their victory. He raised the AK to his waist and opened the door.

Sylvia Carson was waiting for the door to open. She took a sip of the wine as she thumbed back the hammer on the .38 special. She had spent many hours in the woods behind the house where she had set up a small target range. At seven yards, about the distance from the bar to the door, she could group all her shots in the center of mass on a silhouette target, or center of the face if she was so inclined. As the door swung open she turned around, one hand holding her glass, the other on the bar, partially concealing the revolver. An Arabic looking youth stepped through the door; she could make out another figure behind him. The one in the doorway was carrying an AK-47, its muzzle pointing just off to her right. She half turned in that direction, reaching across to put the glass on the bar. As she did so she brushed the edge of the towel, loosening it.

The Arab in the doorway stood frozen as the towel dropped to the floor. His companion was trying to push past him, wanting to get a better look for himself. The whore was saying something to them.

"See anything you like, boys?" She lifted the .38 and squeezed two rounds off, putting one in the chest and the other in the forehead. The chest shot penetrated the body and hit the second Arab in the arm. He staggered back and turned to run. The first Arab reflexively squeezed the trigger as he fell backwards, stitching a line of holes up the bar to Sylvia Carson's left, shattering the mirror and finally bringing down plaster from the ceiling. She stood frozen for a moment, and sank down to sit on the floor, surveying the scene around her. She had several thoughts as she reached up to get her wine glass, now full of loose plaster. The first was to cover herself before she checked the body and called the police. The second was how she was going to make Lucas Grant pay for not spending the night.

General Mahmoud Pahlavi Khost was sitting in his office, idly scanning intelligence reports from various operations around the region and the world. There had been a disquieting number of negative setbacks over the past week, and he suspected the involvement of an American or a Zionist mole somewhere in his organization. It had to be more than coincidental that so many well placed operatives had been uncovered. His most troubling report had been about the disappearance

116

of the Coordinator of Islamic Resistance in the Western Hemisphere. He had been advised that he was too old and unschooled in field craft to undertake a visit to Libya prior to visiting the delegations in Ottawa, Canada and at the United Nations. It was a mission best left to the shadowy people who train and practice deception in their everyday lives, not a man who had joined the Ayatollah Khomeini during his exile in France. There were rumblings in his own staff that the 'Coordinator' was an Israeli mole who had lived a remarkable cover story for over forty years, and was now going home to Tel Aviv to bask in the glory.

Khost refused to believe it. There had to be another explanation.

A knock on his door ended his pondering. The aid placed another report on his desk and quickly backed out. This was not a good time to be in the General's presence. Khost scanned the report, picking out highlights, determining if it merited his attention. Then he went back and read it over carefully. Here was a glimmer of information that provided a hint to the truth. The 'Coordinator' had left Benghazi and flown on to Stockholm, where he connected with an SAS flight to Canada. His passport had been verified as being scanned by immigration control in Benghazi and Ottawa. The mystery was why he had not made the required checks with local embassies as was required. The last line of the message was puzzling. 'There has been a discrepancy' had been annotated in red ink. There was no indication of what the 'discrepancy' might be. He pushed his intercom button and uncharacteristically shouted for his intelligence chief to report. In the outer office there were audible sighs of relief from the staff members who had not been summoned.

"What is this 'discrepancy' you speak of? Wasn't his not reporting a 'discrepancy' enough?"

The intelligence Colonel squared himself and presented the information as simply and as quickly as possible. General Khost, unlike other senior officers, had never been known to indulge in summary execution of the bearer of bad tidings. A swift transfer to some miserable posting and an end to a promising career were always possible, but never an execution. Even liars or those who falsified reports could expect a chance with revolutionary justice. That could end in a death sentence, but at least it took longer.

"The 'Coordinator' was reported in Benghazi as planned, Excellency. He took his meetings as scheduled and was scheduled to leave on a late night flight. For some reason, he did not report as expected, and he did not take his scheduled flight. He went out twenty four hours later."

"Why was this not reported at the time? This paper says he processed through immigration controls normally."

The Colonel maintained his composure. The fault could be placed elsewhere, and he was about to do it. "There was a report. Excellency, but it was made to his office. His deputy received it in a timely fashion, but delayed forwarding it. He believed it was an oversight in the communications center and ordered a search for the message to begin there. Unfortunately, instead of following it up he left the office for prayers. He took ill at the mosque and had his driver bring him home, where he rested for two days. By then the second report from Stockholm and the third from Ottawa had been missed, and the trail had already grown cold."

Khost was glaring at the Colonel. He could tell by the man's demeanor that there was more to the story. He beckoned for the information with his upturned hand.

"Our people in Benghazi reported another individual had entered the country from Algeria. It was reported he had been repatriated from France in a prisoner exchange. This wasn't given the priority it deserved, and the information and documents were sent under a routine heading. The man is known to us, it was Ali Alawa Sharif. We are sponsoring $20,000 worth of the reward for his recapture after his massive bungling of the attacks on the Americans in Sudan."

"The Americans we currently have Mehmet Atta Khan leading an operation to kill? And his presence was not deemed important enough to inform us?"

"Sharif has been considered of low importance after the events of the past several months, Excellency. He was downgraded from a priority report to routine after we learned the French might have recaptured him in Moldova. He was overlooked in the current planning." The Colonel was inwardly pleased at that. General Khost had been the one designating priorities and back checking every aspect of the operation. If nothing else, General Khost would not foist the oversight onto the backs of the innocent. He had too much professionalism about him, and he was influential enough in the government to have some insulation from political fallout. "We are only now receiving data that indicates it was Sharif that replaced the 'Coordinator' during the missing twenty four hours in Benghazi. We had trouble obtaining the graphics from surveillance at the several airports. It seems to have been deliberate. There are forces working to protect Sharif."

Khost grunted and thanked the Colonel. There was nothing more that could be done about the situation here. It was time to initiate the contingency plan that had been put in place weeks ago. "Make the call to New York. I think it would be wise that the package we forwarded now be placed in Mehmet Atta Khan's hands." When the mission was first conceived, the thought that all lines of communication to the principal in the field could be severed was considered too remote to be contemplated. General Khost, however, felt nothing should be left to chance. He had been a member of the first army units that occupied the site known as 'Desert One' after the Americans disastrous attempt at rescuing the US Embassy personnel in 1980. The Americans, with all their technology and resources, had no contingencies other than to leave their casualties on the field and run. It was a bitter blow to their national pride, and a lesson for future operations on foreign soil. They could have learned much from the Jews who planned and executed the Entebbe raid.

The package consisted of a preprogrammed disposable cell phone and a set of identity papers. The phone had but three numbers: the Coordinator, the United Nations mission, and General Khosts' headquarters. The level of calamity would dictate which number was to be used, and the phone was to be destroyed.

"How long before we know the message was delivered?"

"I'm not certain, Excellency. The contacts should be made quickly, even with the time differences. It will be a matter of where the package is in relation to Mehmet Atta Khan."

CHAPTER NINE

MEHMET ATTA KHAN DROVE THROUGH the night until he came to a truck stop fifteen miles from the US-Canadian border just before sun rise. He was tired and hungry, and he needed a shower. The truck stop offered all that and more, looking more like a small department store once he entered from the parking lot. He first went to the clothing department and bought fresh linens and some casual golf shirts. Next he went to a small kiosk that advertised eight minute hot private showers for twenty Canadian dollars. It seemed exorbitant to him, but decided that if he had been driving an oversized tractor trailer cross country with few amenities, it was probably a cheap price to pay for the luxury.

After his quick shower, and it was quick, one doesn't realize how time passes until it is limited, he dressed in some of his new clothes and roamed the rest of the facility. He gathered some newspapers, knowing that if the Berber had been discovered it was too soon to appear in the news. His main interest was world news. International activities had a tendency to heighten border security, and he wanted to plan his crossing in the most benign manner. Over his breakfast of steak and eggs he scanned the papers and was relieved to discover that the world had granted him a quiet evening. He requested a refill of his cup. Coffee in Canada was brewed differently than Europe or the Middle

East. It had a richer flavor with none of the bitterness, and there were no grounds floating in his cup.

It appeared that many of the truckers had spent the night in this rest area. He was unaware of the requirement for the drivers to keep log books on their activities and were limited to a certain number of hours per day they could operate their vehicles and considered it to be a requirement, that truck crossings, like in many parts of the world, were closed during hours of darkness. He decided he would make his crossing in the midst of the heavier traffic. A small, unobtrusive vehicle would not attract much attention at a busy crossing. He searched the shops for 'window dressing', items that would enhance his innocent appearance. A selection of shirts and stuffed animals caught his eye. The decorated bears seemed a bit much, but the shirts would appear as understated souvenirs bought by a busy father. Before he got to the check out kiosk he noticed a display of snack foods. He picked up some bottled water and a large bag of fried pork rinds. A half eaten bag on the front seat would help allay suspicions that he could be a Muslim. A display of religious artifacts added a set of Christian rosary beads to dangle from the rear view mirror. It was well known that Turkey was a secular state that counted many Christians in its population. When he got to his car he arranged his souvenir shirts on the back seat to appear as they had fallen from the bag. The beads were wrapped around the mirror in such a way that they hung almost to the dash. He also ripped open the bag of pork rinds and dumped half of them on the ground. A few loose ones were strewn on the seat and the bag crumpled. His little tableau was complete.

Crossing the border was not as simple as he hoped, although it did seem that he was passed through without undue notice. The US border guard had waved him over to an inspection area under a marquee. There, a team went through his paperwork and examined the contents of his vehicle. One officer picked up his bag of pork rinds. "I've never tried this brand before. How do these taste?" He spoke with what could be considered a 'southern' accent.

Khan had prepared for small talk, just in case. "They aren't bad, but I had hoped for more of a bacon flavor. Try one and see."

The guard put the bag back on the seat. "Thanks, but it's against the rules. It takes a Texan to make a good pork rind."

"Texas? You are a long way from home." The guard looked at his passport again. "So are you. I don't recall many Turks coming through here before."

Khan was prepared for questions about his new identity. "Perhaps you will see more after I get home and tell my friends about the greenery and the marvelous climate. It's such a difference from where my family comes from." There was a call from the rear of the vehicle as the rest of the team closed the trunk, signaling they were through. The Texan handed back his papers and welcomed him to the United States.

It was a short drive from the border crossing to Rousses Point. On the way he pulled into a rest area that contained plastic toilet stalls and a large metal trash receptacle. The pork rinds, rosary and souvenir shirts were disposed of and he continued his way south. He drove around the town for a while, familiarizing himself with the layout and the road network. Once he was satisfied he could find his way around he stopped at another small roadside shop for a sweet and another coffee. He found himself growing to like the type of brew they used. As he paid for his snack he noticed a tourist map of the area by the cashier's station. He idly picked one up and looked it over as he enjoyed his coffee and Danish pastry. The map was done in a cartoonish fashion, and he quickly realized it was purposely done to highlight businesses that had paid for the privilege of being caricatured. The border was decorated with representations of business cards mixed with coupons for discounts. He traced his finger to the west, along what appeared to be a sparsely populated route, until he came to an image of a hotel with a familiar name. He would need a place to stay overnight until his meeting with Ali Alawa Sharif at noon the next day.

Sharif was sitting in the coffee shop he had specified when Mehmet Atta Khan arrived. He barely looked at Khan when he sat down, his attention focused on three people sitting at a table in a park across the street. Other than being dark skinned, they were unremarkable. Khan began to ask about them, but Sharif held up his hand to quiet him. "Watch and learn, my friend. You are about to learn an important lesson in dedication and loyalty."

As they watched a police car parked on the street between the park and the café. Two more were seen angling in from the far side. One bore the markings of the New York State Police. "Who are they?" Khan asked.

"They are unimportant. Merely three of the useful idiots much of our organizations are comprised of. Their task today is to protect the Coordinator of Islamic Resistance in the Western Hemisphere. He is here to arrange a massive attack on the American political infrastructure, and those three are eager to be a part of history."

Khan had met a man called 'the Coordinator' in Iran. He doubted he would be found in a back water town like Rousses Point, and he said so. Sharif just smiled and redirected his attention to the park. The police, there were six officers, were converging on the group at the table. One looked towards the café, and Khan saw Sharif give a nod. The youth stood up and raised his arms above his head. "That one is Jamal. He was a student in Khartoum when he felt the call to serve Allah. I first met him in Darfur. He escaped after the Americans overcame our ambush and ended up in Libya. He was one of my first converts when I began my new life." Khan and Sharif watched as the other two followed, and with chants of '*Allahu Akbar*', then each ran towards a pair of officers. The smile on Sharif's face grew wider, his fists clenched on the table. Khan looked around the café, but no one else seemed to be paying attention to the tableau unfolding in the park. The three each reached their targeted pair of officers at roughly the same time. As the youths were wrestled to the ground Sharif took a cell phone from his coat pocket. It was already on and a number was queued up. He hit the send button and slipped the phone back into his pocket. Khan's attention was drawn to that movement as the park erupted in three load but flash less explosions. He looked to the noise and saw small clouds of smoke above bodies and body parts tumbling across the ground as the plate glass window cracked and collapsed. There were screams as the crowd started to evacuate the café. Sharif took Khan by the arm and guided him out the door. "Which way to your car?" Khan pointed to the right and was pulled in that direction.

Khan had expected to cross the Rousses Point Bridge into Vermont. He was more than a little surprised when Sharif directed him to drive south, staying on the New York side of Lake Champlain. Once they were several miles out of town, and they had stopped passing police and rescue vehicles heading north, Sharif explained how his fortune had become linked with Khan's.

"I was working for joint Syrian and Iranian intelligence agency several years ago. One of their clients had been the Janjaweed in

Southern Darfur. One particular band was led by a chief called al Saif. The man had managed to place an American politician on his payroll, which was considered to be quite impressive. Unfortunately, he was a brutal thug who enjoyed watching his men rape and kill the African farmers. Saif's taste ran more to young girls, the younger the better, but that was the custom in his tribe. He was on the verge of cleansing the area around a small district capitol called al Fashir."

"I've heard of it," Khan interrupted," wasn't it the site of a battle with the Americans?"

"Yes it was, but you are getting ahead of the story. Saif and his men were cleansing the area of the Africans. All that remained was a group calling itself the Sudanese Liberation Front, or some such drivel. They were led by an American drug dealer who had fled his country. They would have been an easy target, except that at the same time the Americans appeared on the scene and al Saif's taste in women suddenly matured. He had heard of an American woman soldier who had been observed cavorting naked at a French base in Chad. Saif fixated on the idea of having her for himself, and when he met her at a United Nations sponsored conference in al Fashir, he lost his focus. He launched an attack on the conference not knowing the Americans had left because of other activities by his men. It was very successful, but all his hostages were essentially worthless for ransom. While Saif was planning another action he was called away to Tehran. While he was there, his camp was located by the Americans and destroyed."

"The entire camp? I heard there was less than a company of Americans in Darfur. How did they manage such a surprise?"

"When Saif left on his trip he had given the hostages to his men for sport. They considered that sport to be more important than security. They paid the price. While his men were dying, Saif passed through Baghdad and on to Syria, where arrangements were made for him to come into possession of several chemical weapons to use against any or all of his enemies."

Sharif continued, "When he was transiting back through Libya I was assigned to him as an advisor. I had specific instructions on the use of the new weapons. The Iranians saw an opportunity to embarrass the Americans, but Saif still wanted the white woman, and he modified his plans accordingly. The result was that I was ordered to eliminate him, which I did.

"There was an international outcry over the increased violence in Darfur and the government in Khartoum, never one to commit to any course of action fully, ordered the Americans out instead of destroying them at a very isolated base. I was tasked with attacking them on their march out, but several of the soldiers were able to thwart a very well laid ambush.

"My usefulness to the Syrians, the Iranians, the Sudanese and the Libyans came to an end. I found myself with a price on my head, so I made my way to Algeria. The Algerians weren't interested in collecting any bounties, but they saw a use for me in France. I was tasked with stirring up the Muslim population to destabilize the government."

"The riots I read about were your doing?" Khan asked.

"Yes they were. I was very proud of the results of my efforts."

"You interrupted what could have been a very pleasant vacation for me. The increased security caused me to leave France before I was ready."

Sharif snorted in derision. "Oh, the trials of the well paid courier. When I found you in Montreal I could tell you were still laboring under great hardships."

Khan did not respond. He had not suffered very many hardships in his tasks until recently.

"May I continue? French counter-intelligence managed to find me, and they attempted to use me for their own purposes. They wanted me to go to Moldova to interfere with the Americans in what they thought should be their sphere of influence, and they were the very same Americans as the ones who had bested me in Darfur. Allah was smiling on me that day. The Russians were conducting a training camp for fighters against the Americans in Iraq and Afghanistan, and they were stockpiling more chemical weapons! I soon escaped my French overseers and made contact with a Chechen group to conduct my own attacks. These very same Americans thwarted me yet again, but the result was another embarrassment for the Americans.

"The French were very upset that I had escaped their control in Moldova, and had made some arrangement with State Security to get me back. Since they were also working with the Americans to kill or capture me, it was a simple matter for the Moldovans to deceive the Americans with a false body. No one had anticipated the Americans bringing a doctor to take DNA samples, or the French killing a visiting

American politician, so the ruse only lasted a short while. It was doubly unfortunate since the politician was the one al Saif had controlled, now firmly ensconced on al Qaeda's payroll."

"An American politician? He was working for the Sheik? I wouldn't have believed it!"

"You can believe it, Mehmet Atta Khan. This great experiment in American democracy seems to attract a very venal sort of character. He was only one of several, although he had been the most influential.

"Unfortunately, I was recaptured by the French. The Moldovans saw fit to give me to them rather than let the Americans take me. Luckily, I was able to gather as much information about the Americans and pass it to Osama bin Laden, your employer, by several different conduits before my world started to end again. I was obviously successful, because here we are.

"I was brought back to Paris, where the French proceeded to punish me for my transgressions. I was fortunate that much of the upper echelons of French Intelligence are made up of politically connected dilettantes. Their punishment consisted of poor food, worse music, and the occasional beating such as you would administer to a misbehaving child. Had it been their Colonial Parachute troops or the Foreign Legion I would have died slowly, but I would have died.

"They soon tired of me, and when an opportunity arose to exchange me for a low level consular agent in Algiers who had a predilection for male prostitutes, it was quickly arranged. You see, the Algerians also wanted me dead, but one of their agents had the misfortune of running afoul of the new Libyan government, and, since I had worked closely with the Gaddafi regime in the past, they believed the Libyans would be happy to have me as a sacrificial goat, for you see the Algerians were eager to curry favor with the largest military in Northwest Africa. The Libyans were happy to have me, but for a different reason. It seems the Iranians had tried to meddle in their revolution on both sides, and they were found out. Libyan Intelligence also played both sides of the revolution, only they were more successful. They saw an opportunity to take a measure of revenge on the Iranian who coordinated the actions and perhaps embarrass Iran at the same time."

"Is that the 'coordinator' those youths were supposed to be protecting?"

"Please Mehmet Atta Khan, don't get ahead of me. I have not had the opportunity to tell this story to anyone, and I may not again." Sharif paused to light a cigarette. He rolled the window part way down and blew a cloud of grey smoke out. "Where was I? Oh, yes, the 'coordinator'. He had come into Tripoli under an Omani passport and had been arrested by the new intelligence service. It soon came to light that he was to recruit some foreign fighters, Americans, who had passed through Iranian funded camps and were still in Libya. They were to be repatriated back to their home country with new instructions. The Libyans helped me assume his Omani identity, provided me with additional resources, and introduced me to my new collection of warriors. Can you imagine my surprise when I was given his dossier and realized he was directing the very same operation I had passed on to your master? I selected fifteen of the most promising and gave them their new orders. Those three you saw, my personal guards, were to run interference for me on my journey into the United States. It was a remarkably uneventful trip."

"Was there a need for their sacrifice?"

"A need? No. They had outlived their usefulness."

"What about their new mission? Won't you need them to carry that out?"

"Their only mission is to die as noisily and publicly as possible. Each of them is carrying some little trinket that will link them back to the Iranians. None of it is too obvious to the unpracticed eye. One of them has no more than some Iranian currency in his wallet. Another has a stub to a movie theater in Tehran. The hints are subtle, but they paint a broad picture. They are serving their purpose in death. Five are now dead, two, I am informed, have been arrested by village police officers. There are only eight left to carry out my purpose."

"You said they provided additional resources. Are they to help the mission?"

Sharif laughed again. He did this frequently, and Khan found it to be an annoying habit, perhaps even one that indicated a psychological problem. "At the time I'm certain the Libyans thought they were furthering the mission, but my plans did not require their extra assets. My lifestyle, however, did require the large infusions of money and the new identities they made available. I am still under a *fatwa* of death from several groups, including the one you used to represent."

Khan let that last bit pass. He knew nothing of *fatwas*, and had no interest in carrying one out. "You have other identity papers. Are any of them to be made available to me?"

"Of course, Mehmet Atta," he used a more familiar form of address, "the real coordinator was carrying documents to help you in the aftermath of your mission. I will make them available at the appropriate moment. For now, concentrate on the mission at hand."

The mission at hand seemed to be in jeopardy with Sharif's handling of his holy warriors. He had already squandered half of them, and seemed to have little interest in the success or failure of the remainder. "And the American soldiers we are supposed to kill? Who is to carry out that duty? Surely you don't expect me to do it."

"Of course not, Mehmet Atta Khan, I do not expect you to do any more than your original instructions. All of them have been briefed on the vague parameters of their mission and are eager to do their duty. I have informed them that they may take limited actions depending on the certainty of success, but the major operation is not to commence until you give them the word."

"The other seven, did they not take heed of the phrase 'certainty of success'?"

"The parameters they were given were very generous, and the willing mind sometimes does not consider the certainty of anything. They are serving their purpose of misdirection. Should they happen to be effective it will be a blessing, but the real warriors do not even know they are involved yet, and once they are, even the Americans will not be able to grasp the magnitude of the threat. They have spent years and much capital bringing them to the United States, supporting them, housing them and educating them. They have brought their own seeds of destruction into their garden. I will instruct them personally."

Khan was fascinated by this revelation. Al Qaeda and other terror organizations had spent many years and much money trying to bring warriors into the United States. He had never heard that the Americans were actively assisting in this endeavor. "Who are these mighty warriors, Ali Alawa Sharif? How did you come to know of them?"

Sharif lit another cigarette and chuckled. "Everyone knows of them, and everyone discounts them once they are removed from the battlefield. They have been a potent force in Black Africa for years. You are only now beginning to realize their worth in Afghanistan. I have personally selected and trained many while I was in the Chad and Sudan. They are capable killers, and many of them enjoy the way of life. They are a volatile force waiting to explode."

"I ask you again, who are these mighty warriors?"

Sharif let out a mighty laugh, even louder than his usual. "They are the child warriors of Africa. Sudan and Nigeria have been especially productive in training them. American missionaries, in their zeal to cure the ills of Black Africans, have been 'rescuing' these young warriors and importing them into the United States for years. They seem to have a belief that once removed from the influences of drugs, alcohol and violence they will revert back to their docile, child like state. In actuality, they become the perfect infiltrator, lying dormant until they are given an infusion of their old familiar drugs and a new mission. The group I have in mind has been very active in criminal activities in the area we will be going to."

"Criminal elements are always difficult to control, Ali Alawa. Osama discovered this early on when he was looking for martyrs to attack the United States. Even the ones most imbued with Islamic *Jihadist* spirit frequently succumb to their more base nature. He decided that their faults made them more of a liability and were best eliminated."

"All too true, my friend." Khan did not like this man referring to him as a friend. "The Janjaweed also discovered this to be true, but when you are trying to spread terror for the sake of spreading terror, a criminal will not have the scruples of a pious man."

"But a pious man will be more willing to give himself to Allah. The selfish man will ultimately think only of himself."

That laugh again. "Sometimes, Mehmet Atta Khan, the secret to forging a true warrior of Allah is not to let the warrior know he is giving himself to Allah. Let him think he is doing it for the spoils and he will take amazing risks."

Khan turned to watch the road in silence. He had come to the realization that this man was going to betray him. "What of the agent planted deeply within their own ranks? Is he also to be one of my weapons?"

"I was not aware that you knew of this agent. I can see that the 'Coordinator' may have been better trained to resist interrogation than I had thought." Sharif thought about this for a moment. The 'Coordinator' had spoken of the agent who would reveal himself at the appropriate time. It was a cryptic remark that even the professional, and quite cruel, Libyan interrogators were not able to penetrate. The final response had been that the agent had been briefed and would act only in the extreme. He was too valuable to reveal himself for anything less than total disaster. "This agent must remain a mystery, even to us. I am hoping that he will be the proverbial *Jin* who will appear at the providential time if the situation requires, otherwise, he is to be an asset of Iranian intelligence, and not one of ours."

CHAPTER TEN

MEHMET ATTA KHAN AND ALI Alawa Sharif drove south from Rouses Point, staying off the main roads and following secondary routes along the shore of Lake Champlain. On the outskirts of Plattsburgh Sharif gave instructions to pull into a roadside picnic area. There was another car waiting for them. The driver got out and gave Khan specific instructions on where and how to drop off his rental car, and how to exit the airport. "There are three major intersections you will be going through. At the third one you will see a large Wal-Mart store. Ask the driver to let you off there. Do not enter the parking lot; there are too many security cameras. Instead walk to your right for two city blocks after you exit the bus and wait. I will pick you up there."

Khan did as he was told. There was an outdoor café at his rendezvous point, so he decided to stop for an iced tea. He was enjoying the solitude when he saw his new driver stop at the curb. Khan ignored him as he finished his tea slowly. These people were risking his safety by improvising a very dangerous and unsupported operation. This madman was planning to use children as weapons! As little sympathy he had for any American, the thought of using a child was abhorrent to him. It was one thing for a young adult to decide that martyrdom through suicide was his chosen profession. A child didn't have the intellect to decide for himself.

They had inconvenienced him enough, and he would enjoy his tea while he worked on a plan to get away from them safely. He briefly toyed with the idea of just finding a police station and turning himself in. He quickly erased that thought from his list of options. As a courier for Osama bin Laden he would have much information in his memory the CIA and other intelligence agencies would like to mine. Khan would have no problem giving up everything he knew, except for the money and other assets. What he believed though was that any offer of full disclosure he could make would be greeted with skepticism, and that skepticism would get him sent to Guantanamo Bay or some other black site, and he knew there were many. Guantanamo, despite the public outcry, was not the worst fate a prisoner of the United States could encounter. Khan needed to find an agency who would guarantee him civilized treatment in a country safe house, where he could lead a civilized life while he divulged his information, without having to dread water boarding. He believed if he was careful, it could be done. He finished his tea and walked slowly to the curb. There was a billboard on the side of the building across the street. It pictured several uniformed men and women in front of an American flag. Under it was the slogan:

"WE SUPPORT OUR TROOPS"

Khan smiled to himself as her read the slogan. The way this mission was going, he could become a supporter too.

The driver said nothing as Khan got in the car, but he was obviously put out by having to wait. He pulled away from the curb faster than he should have, cutting off another driver, who laid on his horn. "You can be as upset with me as you desire, my friend, but don't jeopardize the mission by being childish. If you are going to insist on driving like this you can let me out. I will find another mode of transportation."

The driver glared angrily at him. Khan placed him as a Hispanic, probably Mexican or Puerto Rican. He had the look of a thug about him. There were symbols tattooed on the back of his hands that had no meaning to Khan. His neck was festooned with snakes and lightning bolts, and there were tears permanently marking his cheeks. Khan decided to engage him in conversation to see if he was a true believer or just a street criminal Sharif had hired. "Does your body art glorify Allah?"

The question caught the man off guard. "What?"

"The designs on your hands and neck, were they placed there to glorify Allah?"

"I don't know what you mean."

He was a hired thug, nothing more. "Let me ask instead, are you a Muslim?"

"No."

"Then how did you come to be involved with this enterprise?"

"Some of my brothers worked with you people," 'you people' came out like it left a bad taste in his mouth, "further on south, trying to bring some of our product and your weapons into the country. The *soldados norte americanos* intercepted them and killed many of my *amigos*. In my country that cannot go unpunished. Your friend contacted my people and asked for assistance. He offers to pay well and supply us with intelligence and weapons. The routes from Mexico are very long and vulnerable. Anything he can provide us from Canada is preferred."

Khan doubted that Sharif had any smuggling routes coming into the US from Canada. If he hadn't gotten support and a false identity from the Libyans he would still be Benghazi looking for a sponsor. He seemed to be adept at convincing people to help with his dirty work. "Are you to assist us with our targets, the Americans?"

"That wasn't part of the deal. We agreed to move you people," the same bad taste was there, "along the way. I get you to your next ride, that's all I do."

"And what about Sharif?"

"You mean your *amigo*? He's in another car somewhere. Thanks to that little show you put on," he meant the bombing, "we had to change our plans. Originally we were going to take you across the lake to Burlington on the ferry instead of doing all this fucking driving. Now they got their security up and we've gotta do this the hard way. That means almost six hours in this car driving around the lake. This is going to cost extra."

"Do you have the means to protect me if we run into a problem?"

The driver laughed. "I got the means alright. I got a Glock under the seat and another one in the glove box, but I ain't here to protect you.

133

We run into any problems, you're just a hitch hiker I picked up on the road. I got enough problems. I don't need to go back to Dannemora."

"Where?"

"Dannemora. It's a prison not too far from here. I already did six years. I ain't going back."

"Then would you mind if I looked at the extra gun?"

"Go ahead. You paid for it."

Khan took the gun from the glove box. It was an older, well worn Glock 17 with two spare magazines in an open topped pouch. He released the magazine, as his Iranian instructors had shown him to do, and checked the chamber. It was unloaded. He reinserted the magazine and worked the slide. "Hey," the driver said sharply, "you know what you're doing with that thing?"

Khan nodded. "Don't you worry, my friend. Remember, we are trained terrorists who do this for a living. Now, keep alert for a comfort station. I have had too much tea today and my bladder cries out for relief."

They crossed into Vermont as the sun was setting, some seventy five miles south of Burlington. Conversation had long dried up between him and the driver, so Khan had amused himself by studying the travel map he had found in a pouch on the door. It was unexpected when the car pulled into a roadside sandwich shop. "Are you hungry?" Khan asked.

"Yeah, but this is where you change rides. Get something to eat if you want, I've gotta make a couple of phone calls first." Khan walked into the shop as his driver paced the parking lot with his cell phone stuck to his ear. The holster that came with his Glock was an inside-the-waistband type, and concealed the pistol well. The wind breaker he wore over it did not show any bulges, but he had decided to forego the magazine pouch and drop the spares in his inside jacket pocket. There were few looks as he seated himself at the counter and picked up a menu. A well worn looking woman in a stained pink smock asked if he wanted something to drink. He opted for coffee. When she returned with it he ordered a simple hamburger, not trusting some of the titles to sandwiches listed.

"Want anything on that?" He asked for tomato, lettuce and onion. The vegetables in this country were always fresh and full of flavor. "How about bacon?" He was unprepared for the question. Was this a test? Was the waitress an agent who was seeking out infiltrators? He thought not, but decided to try it. Pork was forbidden to Muslims, but so was alcohol and hiring prostitutes. When his sandwich arrived the aroma pleased him. So did the taste of the forbidden meat. He understood why it was so popular with the *infidels*. The taste was marvelous.

His driver came in and sat next to him. When the waitress came back he just indicated he would have the same as Khan. The waitress shrugged and called the order to someone in the back. As soon as they were alone again the driver told him that his next ride was waiting for him in the parking lot. "You better hurry. She doesn't like being kept waiting any more than I do. Your bag has already been transferred"

"My friend, you need to understand that haste draws attention. Were I to leave my meal abruptly it would be noticed. If it is noticed, it is remembered, and if it is remembered it can be reported. I intend to enjoy my sandwich, possibly have another cup of coffee, and leave a modest tip. I suggest you do the same. Can you call your friend?" He nodded. "Good. Tell her to come in and have a snack before the long drive. You can tell her to leave it unlocked so if I finish before her you can tell me what car she is driving and I can wait in the parking lot." Whatever else happens, Khan decided, he would rid himself of these amateurs as soon as he could. The map from the car, now in his pocket, showed that Burlington was a fair sized metropolitan area. There was an airport, and that would mean long term parking and car rental kiosks. A body hidden in a trunk could avoid detection for a day or two, depending on how well it was wrapped and how quickly it decayed.

No woman came in to the café while Khan was eating. He did as he told his driver he would. He enjoyed his meal, had another cup of coffee, and left a modest tip. He enjoyed the coffee so much that he ordered another to take with him. He was certain they would be driving well into the night. The car was a green Subaru of indeterminate age. Khan sighed as he approached it. He expected his female driver would be like the car, of an indeterminate age and possibly a disposition to match the color. He was right on both counts. He was surprised to see that this woman was wearing a *hajib* and was not another of the vulgar, flashy types he had seen on the road. This woman was speaking on her phone when he sat down. She signaled him, rather rudely, to remain silent until her conversation was over. It was in Farsi, but all he could understand was the occasional non-committal phrase. When she was done she took a manila envelope from under her seat and passed it to Khan. He opened it and looked at the phone. He tossed it to the seat and scanned the documents. It was another identity. He sighed and placed them in his pocket. He was comfortable as Mehmet Atta Khan and would miss the persona. He would study the new identity later. He picked up the phone and looked at the driver questioningly. "I already have a phone that hasn't been used," it was an airport disposable, "what am I to do with another?"

"The instructions are to call number three."

"And?" he asked.

"That is all I was told, it was all I wished to know."

Khan flipped the phone open and punched the power button. Nothing happened: the battery was dead. "Do you have a charger I can use?" She fished one out of the console and handed it over, but the plug wouldn't fit. Strange, he thought, for he always believed phone chargers were universal. It was the first time he had ever encountered this problem. He instructed her to drive and look for an electronics store or a suitable retailer who might have a selection of chargers. It was almost a half an hour before they came to a shopping center that had a suitable store. As they drove in he glanced at the lights in the parking area. Every one of them seemed to be topped with a surveillance camera. He glanced into the back seat to see if there was anything he could use. A loud green baseball cap bearing the image of a leprechaun would have to do. For the first time he also noticed a child's car seat and some plush toys. He would soon be leaving another motherless child in the world. He directed her to park close to the entrance and watch for him to come out. He wanted to limit his exposure to the cameras. Inside, he quickly found the electronics section and pawed through a rack of chargers. He did not realize there was such a variety. A helpful young woman in a blue smock examined his phone, and after declaring it 'the oldest one she had ever seen', selected one, opened the package and checked the fit. "Do you need one for your vehicle too?" Khan looked at the adapter. This one was equipped with a two prong wall plug. "Actually, I just need one for the car." She took it back and selected another one. Satisfied, she took him to a cash register and collected nine dollars and ninety nine cents, the price on the package, plus an additional six percent for what she termed 'sales tax'. He thought it to be the equivalent of the 'Value Added Tax' he was used to paying in Europe and Canada. A sales tax was a more honest term for it. There was nothing added to the value by taxing it.

Back in the car he struggled with the plastic case until his driver took out a knife and made a neat slash across the side of the package. Khan grunted his thanks as he took out the unit, connected it to his phone and searched for the cigarette lighter. It was below the dash in a recess partially stuffed with fast food wrappers. He turned on the phone, gave it a few seconds to cycle, and then called up the preprogrammed numbers. He didn't recognize any of them, although number three, the one he was to call, had the country code for Iran. His masters were calling him, possibly to remind him he was on a short leash. They didn't realize that the leash had been severed thousands of miles ago when Ali Alawa Sharif had assumed the identity of the 'Coordinator' back in Benghazi. He debated with himself whether he should call, and if he did, should he warn them about Sharif. He briefly debated not calling, just rolling down the window and throwing the phone to the side of the road. He could sense the driver watching him. She was half turned, part of her attention on the road, the rest on him. Her left hand was hidden from view in the folds of her sweater, maybe holding on to a gun. His own weapon was tucked into his waist at the small of his back. If there was going to be a gun fight, she had the advantage. He decided to make the call. If he was unhappy with the communication, he could feign compliance until an opportune moment presented itself to dispose of this woman.

The conversation had been brief: whoever he spoke to had been waiting for his call. There were no pleasantries, just a series of questions requesting his status, location and current traveling companion. He was asked several questions regarding any contact with the 'Coordinator' and any instructions he may have been given. Khan decided to pretend he had not been diverted from the operation specifics and gave the appropriate answers. There were instructions for him to access a prearranged email account to retrieve mission updates, and then came the dire warning. The 'Coordinator' had been compromised, and he was to ignore any instructions he may receive that would be considered to be contrary to the original plans. Khan expressed an appropriate level of surprise and asked how this had happened. His instructions were simply that the 'Coordinator' he was dealing with was an imposter, and should he have any additional contact with him he was to take steps to eliminate him, He was asked if he understood his instructions. Once he had acknowledged that he had, he was told to destroy the phone immediately, and the connection went dead.

He told his driver to pull over to the side of the road. "I have been instructed to destroy the phone. Do you have tools in the car?"

"Can't you just step on it on the side of the road?"

"I would prefer to make certain none of its data can be retrieved. What tools do you have?" She told him there were only the tire changing tools in the trunk. He told her to get them. He glanced up and down the road, looking for traffic. When he saw none he decided this would be his best opportunity. He walked to the back of the car where the driver was struggling with the spare tire to get at the lug wrench that was underneath. He slipped the Glock from its hiding place and snapped off the safety. The driver heard the click and tried to react, but she was off balance and couldn't turn fast enough. Khan fired one shot at close range into the side of her head. Her body fell into the trunk, only her legs sticking out from the hips down. The *hajib* contained most of the splatter from her skull. He felt for a pulse on her ankle. There was a faint one, but he doubted she could survive a bullet to the temple. Just to be safe, he fired another round into the back of her head, angling the muzzle so that the exit wound, if there was one, would go into the spare tire and not the gas tank. He quickly searched her for any items he could use. There was some cash in her pocket, another cell phone, and a small caliber automatic pistol, a typical woman's gun of 7.65mm caliber. He then arranged the body so that there would be space for the trash in the back seat. He did not want to be remembered as a family man driving a green car. Satisfied with his handiwork he took the plush animals, the family debris and the car seat out and tried to stuff them into the trunk. The car seat wouldn't fit and would be tossed into the brush. Before he closed the trunk he searched under the front seat for her hand bag and any identification she might have. He found a counterfeit designer bag wedged under the seat. He briefly considered taking her credit cards, but decided to leave them. Perhaps someone finding the bag by the side of the road would use them, adding more confusion to the affair. He heaved the seat into the brush and left the hand bag by the side of the road. Then he consulted his map and continued his journey to Burlington.

He stopped for a leisurely meal on the way, and didn't arrive in Burlington until well after dark, all the better to dispose of an anonymous car with a body in the trunk. He was disoriented by a poorly marked highway interchange, and didn't realize where he was until he saw a sign announcing the exit for St. Albans. A quick recheck of his map told him where he was, and he reversed direction. The route from the north was better marked, or at least easier to understand, and he was walking to the terminal shortly after midnight. He decided to take a shuttle to one of the better known hotels and relax for the night, or perhaps two. He was tired of the journey and the complications that kept piling up. If this were a well run operation, someone, some where would have realized that the initial objectives could not be met and any continued action would result in the loss of valuable assets and operatives. From the start this had not been a well run operation, and it had started to unravel as soon as his watcher missed the flight in Turkey. There were too many random elements in play, from the missing 'Coordinator' to Sharif assuming control. It was chaos, and as Khan enjoyed his shower it struck him: chaos was the plan. Chaos suited everyone involved. The Americans would be looking for shadows all over the world if even one of the targets was successfully hit. The trails led all over the world, and he was certain a reasonably competent intelligence agency, once it understood the basic facts, could not help but to follow them back to wherever they led. A casual comment in the presence of a listening device, a scrap of paper left on an unsecured desk or an anonymous informant with an innocuous bit of gossip could be the key.

Chaos. It was the ideal outcome for all involved. He mentally listed the countries involved. He had travelled from Pakistan across the Middle East to Turkey. Sharif had travelled from France to Algeria to Libya. Both of them had flown across Europe with several stops. They had operated in Canada, and now the United States, with assistance from an unknown Mexican drug cartel. Attention was pointed everywhere and nowhere. The diplomats would have migraines trying to speak to each other politely.

He toweled himself off and considered ordering something to eat. He hadn't eaten in over six hours now, and his stomach was growling. The room service menu said they offered a 24 hour kitchen, although after midnight it was limited to cold sandwiches and salads. He opted for a cold roast beef platter and a garden salad. He considered coffee, but elected tea instead. He didn't want the caffeine to rob him of what little sleep he could get before check out time. He would decide if he was going to spend another night here in the morning.

The knock on the door was welcome. Khan opened it to be greeted by vision he had hoped to never see again. Ali Alawa Sharif was standing there, gun in hand. He was smiling.

"How did you find me?"

Sharif threw what looked like a cheap toy cell phone at him. Khan looked at it, then at Sharif. "I don't understand. What is this?"

Sharif closed the door and motioned for Khan to sit on the bed. The he took a seat in the swivel chair at the desk. "A child's toy, really. In this country mothers like to keep their children on an electronic tether. They give them these little phones so they can feel important, but they are really a tracking device that can be located with a few clicks of a computer mouse. The mate to this one was placed in your bag when you changed cars yesterday. I found this one in the car at the airport." He looked over towards the bathroom. "The woman was not particularly attractive, but I can understand if you felt a need to satisfy your urges with her. Your last romantic interlude was rather rudely interrupted. Is she in there?" He motioned with the barrel of his gun.

"I left her in the trunk of the car. I found her to be unnecessary."

Sharif laughed. "A poor choice on your part. She was the only one in the transportation link who truly believed she was still working for the Iranians, but you are showing initiative. Perhaps you will be able to kill the Americans, as you are supposed to. Get dressed. We have a different place to stay tonight."

Khan tried to delay. "I have food coming."

"Excellent. I could use some refreshment. Very well, you get dressed and we'll wait for the food." He motioned to the bag on the stand at the foot of the bed. "I suggest you give me your gun first."

"I said nothing about having a gun. I broke the bitch's neck."

"Commendable, Mehmet Atta Khan, very commendable. You are a man of talents I had not suspected. You do need to practice your lying though. Your driver told me he gave you a Glock." Khan shrugged and slid the bag over with his foot. Sharif rummaged around and came up with the pistol and the spare magazines. The Glock went into his waistband. The spare magazines were removed from their pouch and went into his pocket. "Again you impress me, Mehmet Atta Khan. Most people would not have thought to carry spare ammunition already loaded in magazines. I cannot tell you how many times I've encountered supposedly trained people who have a gun and a box of bullets. They never stop to think they might have to reload in a hurry. It's a mistake they seldom live long enough to repeat." He was interrupted by a knock on the door. "Who is it?"

"Room service, Sir."

Sharif motioned with the gun. "I'll wait in the other room, Mehmet Atta. Just sign the check and leave a generous tip. You don't want him remembering the miser in room 324."

The waiter deposited the tray on the desk, seeming to not notice anything in the room. Khan signed the check and added another ten dollars for a gratuity. The man thanked him and turned to leave, stepping on the empty magazine pouch. He bent over and picked it up and handed it to Khan. "This was on the floor, Sir." Khan thanked him and ushered him to the door.

Sharif stepped out of the bathroom, gun still in his hand. "What was on the floor?"

Khan thought fast and took a comb from his pocket. "Only this. I think he was hinting for a larger gratuity." Sharif looked at it and grunted. He waved Khan back to the bed and cut the sandwich in half with one hand and slipped the knife in his pocket. "I don't want you to feel tempted, Mehmet Atta. Now, let's enjoy our meal and make haste. We are expected at my safe house, and you have an appointment in the afternoon."

"An appointment? With whom?"

"His identity is unimportant for now. Consider him to be an intermediary for the next step of your task."

They spent the night in a motor home parked in a campground several miles east of Burlington. Sharif's contact was another unpleasant burly man who complained about being woken up so late. Sharif quickly silenced him with several harsh words and a slap across the face. Khan watched this in puzzlement, for such an insult anywhere in the Muslim world would have been instantly answered with more violence. These American, or in this case, Mexican gangsters seemed to have little or no self respect.

The Winnebago was not in the best condition. The interior was shabby, with much of the woodwork marred or broken. The plumbing facilities were heavily stained, and there was a general odor of mold and rotted food. Air conditioning, if there ever was any, no longer functioned, and torn screens let all manner of insects in.

And the Mexican snored like the low roll of thunder. All in all, it made for an unpleasant night.

Morning came, and the Mexican was dispatched to a nearby restaurant to purchase breakfast. The stove and coffee maker in the motor home were broken, which came as no surprise to Khan. The two men sat outside at a rough hewn picnic table while waiting for their food. Khan surveyed the surrounding area with distaste. It was one thing to pass through the poverty and squalor of some of the battlefield countries of the Middle East, but this was not what he had expected in the United States. The campground was essentially an outdoor refugee camp. There was a mix of tents, tarps and broken down campers scattered about. The people were lethargic, and there were no children visible. Sharif ignored all this and spent his time in low tones on his phone. He was obviously not worried about electronic eavesdropping by the American intelligence services.

Whatever his contacts on the other end were saying, it appeared to anger Sharif. He moved off to the other side of the motor home to continue his conversations. Khan had lost interest anyway. All he wanted to do was find a way to lose Sharif and this succession of hired thugs. Khan's mission had bee to locate and kill several American service members. Reduced to its simplest elements, there were supposed to be helpers at his destination to carry out the deed. He was unsure what mischief Sharif had caused in the plans, but it was obviously catastrophic to a well ordered operation. He had perverted the plans somehow that Khan could not even comprehend what was going to happen. All he knew was that whoever his contacts were supposed to be in the target area, he would no longer have control of them.

He began to fantasize about his life once he was free of these people and could access the hidden funds across Europe and the Middle East. He knew there were clean identity documents he could use to live a life beyond suspicion. It would be his reward for faithfully serving a lost cause for so long.

The Mexican returned with their food and spread it out on the table. Khan and Sharif both had a Styrofoam package of something that resembled runny scrambled eggs, a biscuit that was supposed to be potato, a small cup of fruit and some of the worst coffee Khan had ever tasted. He had once had to survive on American rations for a few days. Even their instant coffee had been better than this.

The Mexican, however, seemed to have selected their meals deliberately so that he could showcase his. He had a similar Styrofoam container, but his contained plump looking crepes, or pancakes as they were called here, real eggs, rich syrup, and several fat slices of bacon. Khan remembered the bacon that he had on his sandwich the day before. He salivated involuntarily. *Halal* be damned, from now on he was adding bacon to his diet.

They had just finished eating when another vehicle arrived. This one, like all the others he had to endure recently, was Asian built and too small to be comfortable. The driver, a good sized African, greeted Sharif with a bow and a sincere *Salaam Alaikum*. It would be another long leg of his journey with a compulsive bead counter who would want to stop for prayer. He noticed that Sharif had dispensed with his morning prayers. His on again off again devotion to his faith was irritating.

Sharif spoke with the newcomer in low tones by the car. A map was produced and a route was traced with very little discussion. It seemed to please Sharif, and when they were done the driver returned to the vehicle and Sharif came to the picnic table. "Gather whatever belongings you have, Mehmet Atta Khan. Our driver is here to carry us on the last portion of our journey." Khan had very little to take with him. Ever since he had been taken by Sharif in Montreal, and he did consider himself to be under some form of captivity, his personal belongings had been continuously diminishing. If there had been some sort of pursuit or imminent threat it would not have mattered, but their frequent movements through an ever diminishing quality of accommodations was demeaning to a man who was used to a more cosmopolitan existence outside of Afghanistan or Pakistan. He exited the Winnebago with his meager possessions as Sharif was watching the Mexican point out locations and a route on an unfolded travel map spread across the hood of their next vehicle. He shuddered inwardly at the thought of another series of detours. The final destination would be a welcome sight, and he could begin to plan his new life once they were there.

The map was folded and the Mexican gave a quick bow to Sharif and brushed past him into the Winnebago. "*What was that all about?*" he asked in Arabic.

"Merely setting up our next rendezvous," Sharif responded in English. "There is no need for guile, our companions can be trusted. Once our holy assignment has been completed we will meet up with him for the last leg of our journey, our escape."

Khan looked back at the travel trailer with disgust. "This is a mere hovel on wheels. I doubt it could leave this place under its own power, never mind drive a few miles. Surely we can do better."

The Mexican overheard the comment and interrupted. "You don't have to worry about my wheels. It may not look pretty, but the engine and mechanicals are all first class. But I ain't taking this anywhere on any long ass trips. That wasn't part of the deal."

"He speaks the truth, Mehmet Atta. Here in this caravan park it blends in with the rest of the refuse. On the road everyone who saw it would remember it. It is far too obvious a vehicle. He will take the car we arrived in. I trust you have new license tags for it?"

"I have, but there's going to be expenses. It needs a new tire on the back and you've got a tail light out. I've got to fix that before I hit the road or it'll attract state troopers like a donut shop. Plus, I'm gonna need gas and I'll want to do an oil change."

"How much will you need?" Sharif asked. The Mexican did some calculations in his head. "I've gotta go about three hundred miles using back roads, maybe a little more, a lot of it up and down hill. Better give me three hundred just to be safe." Sharif took a wad of cash from his pocket and peeled off more than the amount asked for. The Mexican smiled and said "I'll see you tomorrow" and went back in the Winnebago.

"He's stealing from you. Ali Alawa. I doubt very much of that money will be spent on the vehicle."

"I know it won't, but that is not the purpose. He is motivated by greed, and he believes I will give him more money at out destination. It guarantees his arrival."

Sharif called the driver over and directed him to a small store across the road from the campground. He handed him some money for cold drinks, ice and a Styrofoam cooler and sent him inside. Khan took the opportunity to again protest the Mexican.

"Relax Mehmet Atta. Only two people ever expect us to see that abomination again, and neither one of them is sitting with us. He is a ruse, and at an appropriate time a call will be placed to the authorities directing them to his next location, which will be somewhat distant from the route we will be traveling."

"And our driver?"

"He will serve as another ruse. Once we have found our targets he will have an appointment with 72 virgins in paradise."

"Do you think the Americans might start to notice the trail of bodies you have been leaving?"

Sharif was not worried at all. "For all their vaunted technological superiority and organization, the Americans are worse than our fighters when it comes to sharing information. They jealously guard every nugget of information as if it were gold and would rather a crime go unsolved than to give credit to another agency. They refuse to learn from their past experiences, and we will continue to exploit it."

CHAPTER ELEVEN

G RANT HAD SPENT HIS SUNDAY morning calling just about every duty officer he could find at the Pentagon, the National Security Agency and the Central Intelligence Agency. He was truly surprised at how many numbers he could find by dialing 411. He was even more surprised at how many operators would forward him without any hesitation, even though the usual response was that no one had ever heard of the man he was calling. Grant was beginning to suspect there was a 'whacko' call line he was getting referred to. How many nut cases called these agencies on a regular basis to either pass on their own particular conspiracy theories, or just tried to waste their time? It had to be hundreds, if not thousands a day, so he was more than a little surprised when his phone rang and the caller was identified as unknown. That was different. It was usually displayed as 'blocked'.

"What's new, Sergeant Major?" It was Vaughn. You've managed to aggravate quite a few people on a slow weekend."

"How did you know I was calling?"

"Well, for one thing, you left your name all over the Metro area. And another might be the remarkable caller ID system we have here. It boggles the mind. What kind of trouble are you in?"

"How do you know there's trouble?"

"It's either the two the police found near Major Bonneville's house early this morning or the prowler Major Carson shot last night."

The shooting was news to Grant. "I hadn't heard about the shooting. I should have anticipated it." He went on to explain what he had been seeing the last 24 hours. Vaughn was mostly quiet, only interjecting an occasional "Hmm" into the conversation. When Grant was finished he asked what Vaughn knew.

"Not over this line. Let's just say there are certain names and addresses that are programmed to pop-up if they come to any kind of attention. Where are you now"?

Grant told him he was at home.

"That would be too far out of the way for my purposes. Round up the other miscreants and meet me where you keep all those relics", Grant knew he meant the hanger. "I have someone to pick up and I'll be there in about 2 hours. Have some lunch while you're waiting."

"What about Bonneville and Carson?"

"I'll contact them. Doctor Carson is still tied up with the police. Since her prowler was armed with an automatic weapon when he surprised her in her spa, there's not going to be any legal problems. I just have to figure out some way to explain the Arab connection. She's already mentioned that to them, and I need to keep it out of the papers. I may have to involve Simmons and Rawlins again." Simmons and Rawlins were the agents from the ATF and FBI who had almost investigated the shooting on the Military Reservation before Vaughn had the chance to call them off.

"And Major Bonneville?"

"Major Bonneville is blissfully unaware that the two prowlers arrested in her neighborhood last night had anything to do with her. I would prefer that the local authorities not tie the two incidents together yet."

Two hours later, Sharp and Price both brought company to the hanger, Gordon, and the other woman Grant had seen the night before. Price introduced her as Mary Magdalene. That wasn't real name. She was actually Sergeant First Class Mary Sullivan Connaught, a former Catholic nun who joined the Army after 9/11. Mary Magdalene had been her name in the convent. It became her semi-official name when some of her former sisters saw her when she was having lunch out with several other instructors. The name stuck, and she really didn't mind it. It was, after all, a part of who she was. How she ever got mixed up with Sharp and Price would be a fascinating story after a couple of drinks. She was a cultural awareness instructor at the NCO academy. This had the potential for being a problem. He called Price aside to ask him how much he had told her.

"Not much, Luke. She just knows were having some problems left over from the deployment. She'll be okay. She heard all about what happened to Sharp and Robinson, hell, everybody has. She's interested in what's going on, and she's a specialist on the subject. She can help us out."

"How's she gonna help, Jonah? I don't give a fuck about making nice to them or not offending their sensibilities. They want to kill us, and I'm not going to let that happen." Grant glanced over to where Mary Magdalene was staring at them, her head cocked like she could hear what they were saying. Price insisted. "You already let Sharp tell Sheila Gordon about it."

"I didn't let him, and that was a fucking mistake. I don't intend to repeat it." She had come over so quietly that Grant didn't know she was there until she touched him on the shoulder.

"Sergeant Major?" Grant snapped his head around, feeling a little whiplash. "If you're worried about me, don't. I have a clearance and I know what's going on. Everybody in Troop Command," the working title for State Headquarters, "has been wondering when the next attack is going to come."

"Everybody? What exactly constitutes everybody?"

"General Cabot has briefed most of the senior staff on the problem. He wants everyone to be aware and ready to help if they need to be."

That was fucking great, Grant thought. Vaughn shouldn't have said anything to Cabot, and Cabot should have known better than to open his mouth. He must still have dreams of a third star and thinks a counter terror operation in his own back yard is the way to get it. Grant decided to let her stay. Now that he knew about her it would be easier to keep track of her. Besides, Gordon had already heard part of the story while they were in Aruba, and Sharp never could keep a secret. He probably kept her up to date on everything.

It was funny, the thought occurred to him, that he had managed to not be involved in at least one of those briefings at headquarters. It would seem like General Cabot was trying to cut him out of the loop. That made less sense than anything else he could think of.

Harrison's wife had other plans for him that afternoon, and wouldn't call Ralph to the phone. Grant let it go. She was going home either that evening or in the morning, so Grant would catch up with him later. An unmarked corporate jet was making its approach when two more vehicles pulled up to the overhead doors on the street side of the building. Bonneville and Carson both got out. They hadn't seen each other since the unit returned from Fort Bliss, and they exchanged pleasantries. Both women were dressed for the weather, and Grant mentally compared them. Sylvia Carson was wearing slightly more than she had on the last time she was in the hanger, probably out of deference to the situation she found herself in after shooting the intruder. Grant waited for them to join the group. Linda Bonneville greeted him with a kiss and a hug. Behind her, Sylvia Carson had a wry smile on her face. This could be a problem if she ever decides she wants to play the woman scorned, Grant thought. He made a point of asking Carson how she was holding up. "I think I'll be able to cope, Sergeant Major."

"Well, if there's anything you think we can do to help, just say the word." Grant realized that was a mistake as soon as he said it. "I may just take you up on that, Sergeant Major." If no one else saw the flash in her eyes when she said that, Grant sure did. He decided he better change the subject and get away from the one on one interaction with her.

He decided to give everyone a quick recap of what was going on. He started with the situation with Sharp and the Arab with the AK-47 and the law enforcement response to it. He included what they had seen at the boat landing, including the wrapped body, and how it had been found in a dumpster in another part of town. There was a question, from Mary Magdalene. "I thought the police were telling everyone that it was due to gang activity in the area."

"That was the story, but rag head and his friends all know what really happened. That's why they ramped up the rhetoric about the Army being responsible for tensions in the area."

"Calling them 'rag heads' isn't going to endear you to them." Grant thought about that statement for a moment. He could let it pass, or he could deal with it here and now and let her decide if she still wanted to be a part of Price and his friends. "Sergeant Connaught, I appreciate your position, but we're not in a class room or in front of a formation right now." She started to speak, but Grant held up his hand. "I don't want to hear the cultural sensitivity talk. Save it for them. Those fucking people," the cursing was deliberate, "have decided to target us. They had to seek us out, research who we are, and conduct surveillance on us. They've tried to kill Sergeant Sharp and last night after watching us at his home, they attempted to kill Major Carson." He left out the part about seeing the Toyota parked on her street. "And I might as well tell you now, Linda, that two of them were looking around your back yard last night." That was news to her. "I heard about the prowlers across the street. They didn't have anything to do with me."

"Correction: they were found in your yard. I didn't know what else to do with them, so I dropped them on your neighbor's swing set. I didn't want to disturb you and your family."

"What were you doing in my back yard?" She seemed indignant.

"I was looking for a green Toyota that had been watching us at Sharp's place. I went down there on a hunch.'

As an afterthought he added, "By the way, keeping that pistol handy is a good idea. It looks like they're ramping up their activities." He could tell by the look on her face and the way she was tensing up that she was pissed about what had happened. Grant could only guess what she was more pissed about, that he didn't let her know what was going on when it happened, or that it happened while her family was present. He'd have to deal with it later. "I probably should have said something last night to let you know. I knew your family was there and I didn't want to upset things any more than I had to. It won't happen again." He could tell by the look she gave him that he was damn right it wouldn't happen again. He turned his attention back to Mary Magdalene. "If they don't like being called rag heads, that's too fucking bad. Stop trying to kill us, and maybe I'll give them a little cultural understanding. If that attitude is too much for you, feel free to leave now and report me to the Equal Opportunity Officer."

"Jeez, Luke, go easy on her. She just got here. She doesn't know us all that well yet."

"Price, we've been down a lot of roads together. You should've known better. If you want to drag her in to this, make sure she has her eyes wide open." He turned back to Mary Magdalene again. "We're playing for keeps here, no rules, no time outs. If you don't want to play, leave now."

Grant watched her for a moment. She returned his stare without saying a word. He turned his attention to the jet that was taxiing to the front of the hanger. It was still rolling when the door swung down and Vaughn appeared in the opening, resplendent in his blue uniform. There was another figure in multicam behind him. Priced recognized him. "That's Ashley, the guy who was tracking the Arab."

Sharp needled him. "He pulled you off an air conditioned bus in the middle of the night and had you doing his dirty work for him by daybreak? I've gotta meet this guy."

Price responded with an upraised middle finger, then pulled it down quickly and glanced over to see if Mary Magdalene had noticed. Grant had never known Price to worry about what someone might think of him. After the little speech he had just made, this was an interesting new development as Vaughn walked in. If he hadn't been looking at her, he would have never noticed the almost imperceptible smile, accompanied by the slight nod of Mary Magdalene's head. He was at just the right angle that he could see a similar smile and nod from Vaughn to her, with an added twitch of his hand in her direction. They knew each other, Grant was certain of it. Those were signs of recognition. How the hell did Vaughn get her in place so fast?"

Vaughn tried to act like he wasn't happy when he saw a new face in the group. "Grant, can't you keep a fucking secret? How many more people do you plan to drag into this?"

Grant didn't respond to the bait. Instead, he lowered his voice. "It's good to see you too. I hope you're happy your little friend joined our group."

"That's 'Good to see you too, Sir.' Try a little military courtesy." It took him a moment to grasp what Grant had said to him. "What do you mean by that crack?"

"Just what I said, Vaughn, Sergeant Connaught is one of yours, isn't she?"

Vaughn was just staring at him, searching for an answer. That convinced Grant, and he said so. "All you had to do was deny it, and I noticed you didn't. Get her out of here."

"You're on thin ice, Sergeant Major, trying to tell me how to run my operation."

"Would you care to fill us in on your 'operation'? So far all you've done is put us on a bull's eye and get a couple of kids killed. That doesn't seem like much of an operation to me, and if you can't trust us with a little more information, we may not want to play with you any more."

"You keep trying to fuck with me, Grant, and you're going to find out whose dick is bigger. Next time you open your mouth to me it better have a 'Sir' somewhere in the sentence, or you're going to find your ass up on charges of insubordination. Is that clear?" Grant still didn't think Vaughn was really in the Army, but made a half-hearted wave with his hand that approximated a salute. "I'll keep that in mind, Sir. I see you have a new friend. What happened to the one you had in New Mexico? You send him to Guantanamo because he knew too much?"

"Never mind being a smart ass. Captain Connaught, you can wait on the plane. We'll make arrangements to pick up your gear later." There were several surprised looks that Mary Magdalene was actually an officer. She stood up and walked out without a word. Price looked like someone had slapped him. "Now that we've settled that, and where's Harrison?"

"Harrison has other problems to deal with today. I can let him know anything important later."

Vaughn took a look around the room, mentally inventorying who was there. He locked on to Major Bonneville. He remembered the first time he had met her. She was in an adjoining room at the Guest House at Fort Bliss when Vaughn was briefing Grant on the New Mexico situation. She though Grant was still alone when she came into the room, clad only in some very revealing underwear. She ran out as soon as she realized there were other people there, but Vaughn enjoyed the memory. "Very nice to see you again, Major Bonneville." She didn't respond.

Vaughn made a signal to a group of men outside the hanger. They brought in a large screen TV and some computer equipment. While they were fussing with it to get everything on line, Vaughn walked to the center of the group. Without introducing Ashley he began his briefing, although not in the format he had originally planned. He needed Grant and company too much. "Ladies and Gentlemen, I hadn't planned on telling you this until much later, but it seems that events have accelerated.

"Several hours ago, three suspected terrorists blew themselves up in upstate New York, not far from the Canadian border. An anonymous call had alerted police to their presence, and had claimed that they were carrying weapons. When the police responded, they rushed the cops and detonated themselves."

"Were there any friendly casualties?" Grant asked.

"No, there weren't. For some reason they didn't try to get close before they set their explosives off and it seems there was very little in the way of fragmentation material. Agents on the scene are trying to determine why it happened that way."

"How does that affect us? That's a couple of hours drive from here, and it really seems like they're just wasting talent for no good reason."

"That's correct, Major Bonneville. It does seem like a waste of talent, so we started to backtrack. The three had a history of repeated border crossings over the past week. They all had valid ID, and it's a popular crossing for tax-free cigarette shopping on the Indian Reservation and trips up to the Canadian casinos, so nobody gave them a second look. We took a look back, using their ID information, to see if there was anyone else in their group. There didn't seem to be, until this face popped up, with the others immediately before or after him. They seemed to be acting as escorts, although no one picked up on it at the time." He directed them to the flat screen, where a familiar face appeared. "I believe you are familiar with this man." They were. Most of them had seen Ali Alawa Sharif at least once in Sudan or Moldova.

"How the hell did he get here? I thought he was dead."

"Hold your questions until later, Sergeant Major, my time on the ground here is limited." He signaled the computer operator, and another series of photos appeared. "It seems that Sharif is now traveling on an Omani passport under quasi-diplomatic status. The only problem we have is that he's not the man who originally left Oman. That individual disappeared while he was in Libya, and Sharif took his place. The passport is an absolutely beautiful forgery. We know that because the visa to enter Canada and the United States says so." Vaughn explained how intelligence agencies, trying to move people through friendly countries with problematic identification, had taken up the practice of coding visas to tell immigration control officers to ignore the passport. The bar code on the passport may flag an individual, but the visa code would over ride it.

"As we were tracking back, another familiar face appeared." Up went a photo of Mehmet Atta Khan. "I'm sure you recognize your old friend, Sergeant Price. He also came into the country through the same crossing. We know they are together now, because of this," there was a photo of the two Arabs sitting in a coffee shop. "This was taken by the store security camera in Rousses Point just before the suicide bombers blew up. It was found in a routine collection of security footage. We have descriptions and plate numbers of both rental vehicles they were traveling in at the time, but we have lost them for now. Sharif turned his in at a satellite office in Rousses Point and we think he continued with Khan. The bombers vehicles were all found at the scene of the blast."

Grant interrupted. It was nice to know where these men were, but he really would prefer to know where they are. "What about now? Don't most rental cars have GPS on them so the company can keep track of where they go?"

"Yes they do, Sergeant Major, and we know exactly where this car is. It was turned in at the Plattsburgh municipal airport a short while ago. Khan dropped it off, got on a shuttle bus, and rode off the airport grounds. When we interviewed the driver he said the man just asked him to let him off at a traffic light on the way to downtown. He didn't think anything of it. We're reviewing footage from traffic cams to see if anyone picked him up."

He looked around the room. "I'll take some questions now."

"Was Sharif with him when he dropped off the car?"

"No. We don't know where he was at the time."

"Rental agencies don't like cash transactions. Can you track their credit cards?"

"We're not amateurs, Sergeant Sharp. We're trolling Canadian sources to see if there was any activity at hotels, restaurants or ATMs. Canada will cooperate up to a point, and then we have to get creative. We're at the creative stage now." Vaughn looked at his watch. "Time to go. Colonel Ashley and Captain Connaught will be setting up a command post at the State Headquarters. There should be some vehicles arriving for them shortly. Ashley will be your liaison and pass on any new information to you. Major Bonneville, do you think you can arrange transportation? Colonel Ashley is expected."

"Will do, Sir." Bonneville didn't like Vaughn, but she wasn't as certain as Grant that he wasn't a real General. He may be a total ass, but he could still wreck her career.

A voice came from the back of the group. "Did I miss anything?" It was Ralph Harrison. Grant was surprised. He hadn't expected to see him until the following morning. "Ralph, what the hell are you doing here? I thought Willa had plans for you."

"Oh yeah, she did, but after your call she decided there was nothing I would want to do more than 'play soldier' as she put it. I guess I shouldn't have told her everything that was going on. She grabbed her suitcase and headed out the door."

"She's not leaving you, is she?"

"Nah, we're joined at the hip until death. She just really doesn't like you guys. Her happiest day is going to be when I finally get out of the 'green machine' and settle down. She thought she had that once, remember?"

"Yeah, maybe you shouldn't have told her, but at least she's out of the line of fire now."

Harrison motioned Grant to the rear of the group. "While you're all in here smokin' and jokin', I guess nobody's watching what's going on out on the street." Grant stepped over to the front door and leaned around the curtain. "Notice anything familiar out there?"

Grant did. There was another one of those fucking white Toyota trucks parked across the street. It might have even been the same truck he had seen the night before. "What the hell are they doing here?" Grant asked no one in particular. He could see two men sitting in the cab.

"Whatcha' got, Boss?" Price asked, looking over his shoulder. "Company." Grant answered. Looks like the bad guys heard we were here." He turned around to look at Vaughn. "Looks like they might have better Intel than we have, General. What are you going to do about it?"

Harrison pulled everyone away from the door. "Whatever he does will be a day late and a dollar short. I've already taken care of it." All faces turned to look at him. He held up his Smartphone. They were so busy watching the hanger they didn't pay attention to the homeless guy picking up cans next to their truck."

"Homeless guy?"

"It's amazing what a homeless guy will let you do with his shopping cart for fifty bucks. I found one who'd let me pick up cans for him." He paused and gave a little grin. "And somebody owes me fifty bucks

155

for my old phone. I duct taped it in their wheel well. I can track them on this." He pushed a few buttons and a small map appeared. When they crowded close they could see a blip that represented the truck out front. "I figured if they can watch us, we can keep an eye on them too. I'm kind of curious where they go to compare notes."

"You're pretty smart for an old man," Price said.

"Old man my ass, you're just jealous you couldn't figure out how to turn the tables on them. Always remember that old age and treachery will overcome youth and skill every time."

Vaughn had a quick conference with Ashley and Connaught, and then signaled for Grant to walk out to the Gulfstream with him. "Sergeant Major, I know you don't like me, and I don't much care." Grant started to interrupt, but Vaughn cut him off. "Hear me out before you decide to commit professional and personal suicide." He paused to let that sink in. "Do you remember back in New Mexico how we were running drones just about every chance we got?"

"I remember. They were one of our best assets. Why?"

"You weren't the only one with that asset. My guys were running them every night. There was a watering hole that looked promising as a rest stop for the smugglers. It was just a little north of that airstrip you people deactivated, and it was the only surface water in the area. We never got any bad guy activity, but we did get this," he took a small picture from his inside pocket. Grant recognized the people in the picture. "I thought you might like a souvenir of that interlude, so I took the liberty of having one made." Grant was trying to decide whether he should just punch Vaughn and be done with it. He took another small picture out. Grant recognized the people in that one too. "We got some more activity not too long after that, and I could never quite figure out who the other woman was. Now that I see Major Carson up close again, I can only compliment you on your choice of women, and the way you live on the edge." Vaughn paused to let the second picture sink in. "You keep those, Sergeant Major. I can get more. Just remember that if you keep trying to fuck with me, I can ruin three careers, and believe me, I'm just enough of a son of a bitch to do it."

"We're not done, Vaughn."

"We are for now, Sergeant Major, and the next time we meet I expect a little military courtesy. Now snap me the kind of salute a senior NCO would give to a visiting General Officer and I'll be on my way."

Grant stared at him for a second and turned away. He didn't look back until the Gulfstream had taxied to the end of the runway. Harrison noticed the look on his face. "Trouble, Luke?"

"Always with that guy, but I'll deal with it. What do you have in mind?"

Harrison's plan was simple. Send Price out in his truck to harass the Arabs and see if he could spook them into running. He could follow them for just long enough, and then let them go to make them think they lost him. While that was going on, Sharp could use the phone App to track them to where ever they hid out. Meanwhile, he and Grant would stay behind and work out living arrangements for everyone. It was pretty obvious that for the time being there would be a security problem with everyone staying at their own homes alone. Harrison suggested everyone start doubling up. There were a number of possible combinations, so after Price and Sharp were off Grant called everyone together to sort them out. Bonneville said she had to arrange for her kids to go with the grandparents for a while, and then she offered her guest room to Major Carson. Harrison put in an objection to that, saying the two women probably wouldn't be any more vulnerable than the rest of them, but living alone together would attract more attention from the bad guys. Grant agreed, although he knew better. "You've got a big place out in the country, Luke. I'd swear to Christ you picked it for its fields of fire. They're better off with you than any place else," Harrison said. Bonneville agreed, saying she'd be over after she made arrangements. Carson tried to be coy, and did a bad job of it. "I guess that's ok, but I'll need some help securing my house. There's a small problem with a shot out back door." She had a smile on her face as she looked at Grant. "Oh, relax, Sergeant Major, it'll only be for a night or two. As soon as my boy friend gets back from his conference I'll go stay with him. It won't be as exciting, but I don't think anybody will come crashing in there with a machine gun."

"We can only hope," was Grant's reply.

"I think the SGM can handle fixing the door," Harrison said, dismissing the problem. "Now for the rest of us," Harrison had already agreed that Price could bunk with him. Gordon would have preferred Bonneville, remembering how it had been with them. She thought that with the proper application of some good wine or liquor she could rekindle the old feelings in her, but since Linda had already decided on Grant's place, Gordon was looking forward to Sharp moving in, something she had been angling for him to do for a couple of weeks.

"Good," Harrison proclaimed. He had done what he did best, bringing order to chaos. "Everybody do what you have to before dark. I'll let Sharp and Price know when they get back."

Bonneville walked to her car with Grant. "I've been trying to get you to try living together ever since we got back. Now you'll get to see what it's like. Think you can handle it?"

Grant said he could. "Just remember two things: there's another house guest who'll be living down the hall, and my refrigerator isn't exactly stocked for civilized people."

"Not a problem. I can put on a robe when I leave the bedroom, and you can give me some cash for groceries. Better yet, give me your credit card."

"My credit card?"

"Of course! It's your house, and I expect you to be a good host to us ladies, right, Sylvia?"

Carson was standing next to them. "He better be, but to be on the safe side I'll bring some good wine from my house." Bonneville got into her car and drove off with a wave and a cheerful "See you in a couple of hours!" When she was out of sight, Carson slipped her arm through Grants. "I think you better drive. We only have a couple of hours, and I don't want to waste them in separate cars."

When Price pulled out the gate he could see the two men in the truck perk up. He could hear the grind of their starter as they anticipated following him, and were surprised when he pulled up right to their bumper. They sat stunned for a few seconds, not knowing what to do before the passenger started to shout something and the driver put the vehicle in reverse to give himself room to get around Price. Price anticipated their reaction and was ready to move up as they reversed. That unsettled them even more, so the driver smashed on his accelerator and backed into another parked car. The sound brought a resident out from the backyard, shouting at the white Toyota. The two men panicked again and sped off. Price decided to play the part of the innocent bystander and offered to follow them to get their plate number. The owner shouted "Hell, yeah!" and Price made a u-turn to follow. He already had a plate number, so he'd just come back later. The white Toyota was stopped at a set of lights a little bit ahead. Price could see Sharp parked on the side of the road. He had anticipated the two driving this way. He pulled up close to their rear end and laid on his horn. The Toyota jumped ahead and ignored the red light. It was fortunate that there was no cross traffic. Price played his part and waited at the lights while Sharp took up the tail. Price would follow and keep in contact by phone.

The Toyota led Sharp on an almost direct route to the down town area. Traffic continued to be light, so Sharp gave them some running space. Price called for a location, and Sharp directed him down a few side streets to where he anticipated the Toyota would run to. Instead of going in that direction, though, they made an unexpected turn. Sharp knew the area and gave Price another intercept point. When he got to the corner they had turned, Sharp carefully followed, just in case they had seen him and were preparing an ambush. You never knew what was going to happen when you dealt with amateurs. He drove slowly down the street, not seeing the truck again. He met Price at the end of the block.

"They go by you?"

"Nope, not a thing. Where'd you see them last?" Sharp told him they had driven this way. The road was straight in either direction without any traffic. If they had come this way they would have been easily visible. They both pulled into a shopping mall parking lot and got out to assess the area. Price walked to the corner and carefully looked up the street. There was nothing except an alley about halfway up the block. He called Sharp over and asked if he thought they might have used the route to get around them. "Jeez, Price, I doubt it. These guys did too many stupid things to get that smart all of a sudden, besides, I don't think they spotted me." He looked at his phone. The App that Harrison had him download showed the blip to be stationary and not far away. They looked at each other, and almost on signal they both shrugged and walked up towards the alley. At the alley they slowly looked around the corner. Sharp instinctively looked upward to see if there were any threats from visible windows. Price looked down and could see that it wasn't a through road. It ended in a small parking lot about twenty yards away. He could also see the rear of a white truck body up against the fence at the far end.

"Got 'em."

"Know what else we've got?" Price shook his head. Sharp pointed to a sign on the wall just above their heads. It read:

DELIVERIES: 9 AM-3 PM
ISLAMIC COMMUNITY CENTER
AND MOSQUE
NO PARKING

"I never gave this place any thought. Come on. There's a coffee shop around the corner with outside tables. We can give Harrison and Grant a call and figure out what to do."

CHAPTER TWELVE

N ASEER RAISOULI WAS DESCENDED FROM a long line of proud Syrian merchants and clerics. His father's family had produced almost three centuries of Imams for the largest mosques in Damascus, Aleppo and Golan. His mother's family had been successful business people, dealing in produce and livestock before turning to precious metals. They would still be prominent in Syria if not for two calamitous events in his lifetime. The first was the Israeli occupation of the Golan Heights in 1967, leaving the family estates in ruins and in the middle of a huge defensive network the Syrians constructed to keep the Israelis from moving on to Damascus. The other was the ascendancy of Bashar al Assad to the presidency of Syria. After the death of the elder Assad the Raisouli family had backed another candidate, earning the vitriol of the young Bashar. After much difficulty they had fled to Lebanon, where life had prospered for a while until Hezbollah became a political force in the country, leading to another period of violent instability. Hezbollah wanted the entire southern tier of Lebanon to be an armed camp and a springboard for attacks on Israel. To that end there had been forced military training. Naseer had been forced to spend time in a camp learning the intricacies of the AK-47, the construction of explosive vests (which he considered to be an abomination), and endless lectures on *Jihad* and *sharia*. Some of his fellow students were so rabidly fanatical that he decided it was time to move on from Lebanon. As head of the family, Naseer cast his eyes about for a stable country to settle in. The United States was the obvious choice. In spite of the barbarian culture, they could prosper in the free market and practice their religion without having to worry about the sectarian bickering that raged in every Muslim country. Even after the madness of 9/11, the wars in Iraq and Afghanistan, and a faltering economy, life could still be considered good for his family and his congregation.

Naseer Raisouli was the Imam of a small mosque on Main Street. It always amused him to think that the name of the main street in the city was actually 'Main Street'. It displayed a quaint lack of imagination that made this a peaceful area to live in. After a number of years of worshiping in a store front mosque, his new jewelry business and his congregation had prospered to the point that during a crash in the real estate market they were able to buy an late 19th century building that offered rental spaces on the ground floor, and an upstairs auditorium well suited for a prayer room with several classrooms. There was even the added bonus of a turreted corner that looked out over the intersection, ideal for the call to prayer. That had been one of the few times he had dealt with the intolerance of his neighbors. They objected to the amplified call sounding out five times a day, seven days a week. There was a brief court hearing in which a compromise had been reached, although it was not totally satisfactory. Like the Christian churches with their bells, they could broadcast the call at mid-day on the Sabbath and other holy days.

Raisouli wanted to be a good neighbor, and he wanted his congregation to be at peace. He had become an active member of the local inter-church council and was actively working with some of the Christian relief agencies with the settlement of African refugees, both Christian and Muslim. Of particular interest to all concerned was the large population of what were known as 'child soldiers' from various parts of Africa. These children had been taken from their parents, given drugs and some weapons training, and turned loose on enemies of whatever Warlord controlled them. Often, their first victims were their own family members. The Warlords kept them under control by providing victims to kill and, for the older ones, women and girls to use and abuse as they wished. Any morality was numbed by generous rations of liquor or drugs. These were very troubled youths who required a lot of attention and resources.

They weren't the only ones who had been touched by violence. He ignored the periodic absences of young men when they slipped out of the country to 'study' or to go on religious pilgrimages. He knew their true destinations. He tried to be a moderating influence when these same young men returned radicalized and tried to encourage others to join them in *jihad*. The more radical of them had moved on to mosques in the bigger cities. Some had returned to the conflict zones to become martyrs. His biggest challenge had been his own son. The boy had fallen in with some of the more radical elements of the youth group his mosque sponsored. He knew their weekend camping trips far to the north were paramilitary in nature. His son assured him that his interest was only for the excitement and for the brotherhood he enjoyed. He was sincere, he told his father, in his interest in his education as an electrical engineer. Raisouli believed him because he wanted to believe him. He did not want to lose his son to extremists.

The trouble had been slow in coming, but he had watched its march. For a number of years he had been doing volunteer work at the local prison. There were many self-professed Muslims in the prison population, most of them black, and he was eager to work with them. Some were sincere, others were merely curious, but they were welcomed. There were some, however, who consider Islam to be a political movement, and they tried to radicalize the others. Raisouli tried his best to overcome the new wave, but his twice weekly visits could not compete with the intensity these radicals brought with them. When some of them were released on parole, they gravitated to the mosque, some for support, but some to use religious freedom as a shield from the prying eyes of their parole officers. These few troublemakers had worked for an assistant prayer leader who was more 'in touch' with their cultural needs. This prayer leader, also called an Imam, was a magnet for some of the younger members of the congregation. The problems had started recently. One youth was caught trespassing on the nearby military reservation. Shots had been fired, but a good lawyer and a simple story seemed to win over the day, but there may have been repercussions. Some days after the incident the body of another youth, one of his son's close friends, had been found dumped naked like so much trash. The police attributed it to gang activity, but Raisouli wasn't so sure. His son seemed more upset than usual for some days after the funeral. Pieces of conversation he overheard in his own house indicated that his son knew more about the death than he was saying. There was also talk blaming the recently returned soldiers for the rise in tensions. A good part of their service had been in doing battle with Muslim warriors, both in Africa and Eastern Europe. Their victories had been widely proclaimed, and they returned to a heroes welcome. That did not sit well with the more disaffected.

The past few days had been truly tragic. Two of the more radicalized youth had been involved in some kind of dispute in the countryside. They had been found trussed up like dirty laundry by the police after an anonymous tip. Before they had settled the issue in that town, there was an even bigger tragedy in the other direction. One of the young firebrands from the prison had gotten a weapon and broken into the home of a local doctor. She had killed him without remorse, and the evidence of the automatic weapon being fired by the ex-convict made the police declare it to be justified. When it was discovered that the doctor had been one of the soldiers who had actively participated in the battles overseas, some of his son's friends began calling for revenge. They did not call for *jihad*: they wanted revenge, and his son was agreeing with them. They were planning a demonstration the next day at the local National Guard training facility. They were going to disrupt access through the main gate and perform reconnaissance for later actions. Raisouli had been unable to talk them out of it. The influence of the new Imam was too strong.

He sat in his office staring out the window along Main Street, as he often did when he was wrestling with a personal problem or stuck on a point for his sermon to the faithful. He could normally ignore the ringing of the phone, but this caller was very insistent, letting it ring continuously. He reluctantly reached for it.

"May the blessings of Allah be upon you. How may I help you?" He always answered in the same way. He felt it would be a reassuring gesture to someone in need.

"It's been a long time, Naseer; I see you have prospered in your new land."

He vaguely remembered the voice. It called to him from a past he had buried and would prefer to leave that way. "Who is this please?"

There was a chuckle at the other end, a low, sinister sound that mocked anyone who heard it. He remembered the chuckle from his time in the training camp. He could picture the face, goading a trainee who was exhausted from the heat and the intensity of a particular exercise, but he could not remember the name. "Surely you remember the Bekka?"

He did. "It was a long time ago. I had hoped to forget those days. What do you want?"

"I want nothing, Naseer, only to tell you that your training from so long ago is about to bear fruit. Do you remember your lessons? We spent many enjoyable hours going over them."

"They may have been enjoyable to you. I am a man of peace. I have chosen to put all of that behind me. There is nothing from those days that will bear fruit. I ask that you not contact me again." He started to hang up the phone, but a stern voice from the door ordered him not to. Shabaab X, the ex-convict Imam, was standing there, pointing a rifle at him. A rifle! In his mosque! Naseer Raisouli felt the anger rising. "Listen to the man. He already told me what he wants you to do, so you better pay attention."

Naseer turned back to the phone. "You forgot that part of your training already, didn't you Naseer. Always have a way to back up your threats. Now you know I have resources even in your life, even if it is just a criminal." Naseer didn't answer. "There will be a man coming to your mosque in the next few days. His name is unimportant, but you must remember he is a rather influential man. Show him every courtesy." Naseer still didn't answer.

"Naseer Raisouli, you forget that proof exists that you trained with us in the camps. There is an envelope in my possession. If I have any reason to believe you are not a faithful Muslim, I will see that your time in your adopted land comes to an end. The infidels take a dim view of having trained fighters in their midst." There was a brief pause. "Now, do you understand what is required of you?"

"I understand. What else?"

"Nothing. That is all I require of you for now. There may be something else in the future, but that will do for now. Give the phone to your assistant."

Naseer handed the phone over and sat quietly, listening to the one-sided conversation. All he heard was a series of one word replies, all in the affirmative. There was a broad smile on his face when he ended with "*Allahu Akbar!*" and put the receiver down. Naseer stood up and faced the ex-con. "There is no place for weapons in the house of Allah. I want it removed at once."

"Imam Raisouli, you don't got no idea of what's about to happen here, so just keep your mouth shut and do what you're told." The gutter dialect he had slipped into was grating on his ears. The man had never spoken to him like this before. "We're gonna bring a world of shit down on the man, and you already a part of it. There's a small army of the faithful here ready to do what needs to be done to avenge our brothers and burn this bunch of *infidels* to the ground."

"Is my new guest to lead this *Jihad?*"

"He's a part of it, but only a part. He's got his thing to do, and we got ours." There was a commotion in the hall way outside his office. Two young men came in, one was his son. If they noticed the weapon in Shabaab X's hands they said nothing. Shabaab merely lowered it to his side casually.

"Imam! The soldiers, they saw us! One of them tried to follow us here!" Raisouli wasn't certain who they were speaking to, but Shabaab answered. "Are they here now?"

"No, Imam, we lost them by the airport, but we didn't know what to do. We hit another car getting away."

"Can anyone identify you?"

"I don't think so, Imam. My driving was very skillful." Shabaab knew they would have said their driving was 'skillful' if they had caused a six car accident in front of a police station. They all thought they were 'skillful' when they were dealing with *infidels*. "Very well, it's a small matter."

Only then did Raisouli's son acknowledge him. "We are striking a blow for Allah, father, just as it should be in the land of the *infidels*." Raisouli looked from his son to Shabaab and back again. "My son, think long and hard at the road you are about to go down. The American security services are very good, and you are twisting the tails of some very well trained men. Shabaab X may have convinced you that your friend's simple training in the camps is sufficient to defeat them, but all they know is how to build bombs and blow themselves up. And Shabaab, what training do you think he may have gotten inside a prison? They are not the places American movies would have you think they are. Let them go on alone, this is not the path to paradise."

Shabaab looked like he wanted to interrupt, but the boy spoke first. "Shabaab X has told us all about the groups in prison. The holy warriors have been placing political prisoners in jails for years, preparing the faithful these struggles. And you have no experience with the training in the camps. You are a merchant. Shabaab has spoken of them to us."

Raisouli didn't dare mention that he had been trained in a camp in the old country. It was not knowledge he wanted the boy to have. He remained silent. The boy turned back to Shabaab and asked for instructions. "Leave the truck where it is. Put my weapon with the others and wait for me outside. We'll go to the safe house by the park and come up with another plan." There was a boarding house that was frequented by foreign students to the local community college. As if to rub his influence in the face of Raisouli, he gave the boy and hug and said, "You did good today, son. There will be other opportunities." The boy nodded in respect and left the room. Shabaab now spoke to Raisouli. He wasn't as eloquent as he tried to pretend when he preached, but he had a directness that could cut when he wanted it to. "You see, Naseer," Raisouli did not like this informal mode of address from this criminal, "your son is one of my warriors. He knows what it takes to be a man and get into paradise. I'll make a good martyr out of him and his friends." He turned and walked out of the room laughing. Raisouli closed the door after he left. He needed to find a way to wean his son from the influences of this man. It was his own fault. He had let the ex-convicts have too much freedom in his mosque. He tried to welcome them, even though they were nothing more than the pug-nosed slaves the Prophet spoke about. Now he was reaping the harvest of his own attempts to be inclusive and welcome all worshippers. He stood in the window looking out over Main Street. He could feel the tears running down his cheeks. A thought struck him as he sat there. Shabaab had told his son to put the weapon with the others and wait outside. There were other weapons in the mosque? He wondered where they could be. He was familiar with most of the rooms in both the mosque and the community center, but he rarely ventured into the basement area. If there were weapons here he must get rid of them. If there were no weapons, Shabaab would not be able to carry out his plans, at least not until he replaced them. By then Raisouli might be able to come up with his own plan to dispose of Shabaab and his influence.

Down below, Price and Sharp were watching the front of the Mosque. It wasn't the best vantage point as they were very exposed to counter-surveillance, but they could see the front of the building as well as the alley way. It would do for now. They saw the two young men come out of the front door, look up and down the street. They loitered in front of the building for several minutes.

"What the hell do you think that's all about?" Price asked out loud, not rally expecting an answer. Sharp remained silent, trying to use the electronic zoom on his smart phone to get some clear pictures. The table was stable enough to use as a base to keep it from shaking, and it looked like he was getting some clear shots. Another, man came out and joined them. He was an older black man, not at all what you would expect two Arabs barely out of their teens to be hanging with. Sharp snapped another series of images for Ashley and Connaught. If they were going to set up local operations, maybe they could come up with the resources to identify all these people.

"They're moving off," Price said. "Think we should follow them?"

"I will. They probably got a good look at you. Go get the truck and wait for me to call. I'll see how far I can get after them on foot. It would be nice to see if they've got another address we can keep an eye on."

They split up and Sharp casually strolled down the street, staying on the opposite side, trying to blend in with the afternoon pedestrian traffic. There wasn't much, but probably enough to keep him relatively anonymous for a few blocks. Price headed down to where the two trucks were parked. On a hunch, when he went by the alley he walked down to where the white Toyota was parked. If there was anyone watching the alley they would have to lean out an upper story window to look down on him. If he didn't look up they probably wouldn't be able to recognize him. He looked over the truck to see if there was anything he could pick up. It was unlocked, and there was a manila folder full of papers on the seat. He stuffed that into his shirt front. Next he went to the door that led into the rear of the mosque. He tried it and found it wasn't locked. It opened onto a long hallway that ended in what looked like a larger room. There were several doors that led off from either side of the hall. He resisted the urge to go in and look around. He was alone, unarmed, and Sharp was counting on him to come if he called. He closed the door, first examining the lock, and returned to his truck. He was just in time for Sharp's call.

"You can come and get me," he gave his location. He hadn't gone very far. "I lost them. The fuckers had another car parked a couple of streets away." Price drove over to where he was. Sharp got into the truck scrolling through the images on his phone. "I got a couple of clear shots of the black dude, and a couple of the van they had. Nice clear shot of the license plate."

"Too bad we couldn't find out where they're going."

"Yeah, but you don't see too many unmarked red panel vans on the street anymore. If it wasn't stolen we might be able to find out where it's registered to. Let's head back."

Price drove back to where the other truck was parked. "Before we leave there's something I want to show you. I took a look down that alley while you were gone. The basement door was left open. Want to take a look?"

Sharp wasn't certain. Whoever those people were, they could be coming right back. "I don't think it's a good idea, Jonah. We've got no plan and no back up." Price took a pistol out of the glove box and slipped it into his waistband. He reached under the seat and took out a tire iron and a flashlight and started to walk away. "Well, I want to see what they got down there. Come on. We've gotten into more trouble with less of a plan before. Why change now?" Sharp couldn't argue with the logic. He grabbed his own gun, rummaged around for a light and followed.

Price gave him a quick description of what he had seen in the basement. "There's a corridor that ends in what looks like a big open storeroom. There are at least two doors on either side of the corridor, probably smaller store rooms. We owe it to ourselves to see what's in there."

"We owe it to ourselves to call Grant and let him know we're about to do something stupid."

"Sharp, you're turning into an old lady. You should have come back to Afghanistan with me."

They were in the alley and standing outside the door. Sharp did a quick scan overhead to make sure nobody was watching from an upper story while Price opened the door and stepped in. Sharp joined him. There were two doors off each side of the hall. "What's the tire iron for?" He asked.

Price pointed at the first door. "Padlocks. Don't touch anything, just in case they call the police later." He took out the iron and pried off the first hasp. As the door opened with a creak Sharp brought his gun up to watch the end of the hall. Price disappeared for a couple of long seconds and came back out. "Just books and shit piled up on shelves." He motioned to the door opposite where they repeated the routine. This one contained the buildings mechanical room, with the oil tank, heating system and electrical panel. The dust on everything meant that the room was rarely visited.

They hit pay dirt at the next room. There was a work bench on one side with several wooden cases stacked under it. They were marked in Cyrillic characters, but Price could read '7.62x39mm'. This was their ammunition supply. He called Sharp, who backed in. He swept the room with his light and gun. There was a light switch by the door that he flicked on. A rack of about ten AK-47 rifles lined the wall. Price hadn't looked in that direction yet. "We got their ammo, amigo."

"We got more than that. Look over here." Sharp picked up one of the rifles with a rag that was draped across the top of the rack. He gave it a quick inspection, then took off the receiver cover. The rifle had been converted to select fire capability. There were several empty spaces on the rack. Price joined him. "I'll bet I know where the missing ones are. We better figure out something to do with these. Give the Sergeant Major a call; he'll want to know about this."

A voice shouted at them from the doorway. "What are you doing in here?" Sharp and Price spun around and crouched down. Seeing the surprise in the man's eyes, and no weapon in his hand, Sharp took a couple of quick steps across the room and pulled the man in. When Price grabbed him and put him on his knees Sharp went to the door to see if there was anyone else. The hallway was empty. He came back into the room and dragged the man over to a low stool by the workbench. He could tell by the look on the man's face that he was as surprised as they were to see the rack of guns in the room. "Are you the police?"

"Don't worry about us, amigo. You're the one with some explaining to do."

So they weren't the police. Raisouli knew enough about procedures from television that the police needed a warrant to search and had to announce themselves. These men were bandits. "You defile this holy place with your weapons. I want them out of here immediately!" Sharp and Price gave each other a puzzled look. Who the hell was this guy, and who did he think they were? Price stood in front of him. "Who the fuck are you, pal?"

"Don't shame yourself any more with your profanity. I am Imam Naseer Raisouli, spiritual leader of this mosque, and . . ." he stopped in mid-sentence as he suddenly realized that the two men standing before him were definitely not Arabic, and probably weren't Muslim. He stared at the taller of the two for a moment, knowing he had seen the face somewhere before. Then he remembered where he had seen him. His son had pictures of a group of American soldiers on the wall in his room. He had looked at them several times, and had accepted his son's explanation that he was using them to study their uniforms and equipment. Price recognized the look and told Sharp. "That's the same look that guy at the road block in Afghanistan gave me. This son of a bitch knows you, Dave."

"Why does my son have your picture on his wall, and why are these guns here?"

"Is your son one of the boys who has been trying to hunt some of us?" Sharp asked.

"My son has fallen in with bad influences, but I don't think he is trying to hunt anyone."

Price spit on the floor. He knew enough about Islam that if this was a mosque and this guy was an Imam, he would get very angry at the insult. He did and Price pushed it as soon as the man started to rise. He grabbed him by the shoulder and swept his legs out from under him, bringing his face to within inches of the rifle rack. "Bad influences? I've already been shot at by some of these, so don't give me any sanctimonious bullshit. This is part of some *Jihad* plan to kill me and some of my friends, so you and your boy are already on my shit list. You better start talking to me."

Raisouli was truly frightened. Not for himself, because he had always known his past could someday catch up with him. He was afraid for his son. These men were armed, dangerous and very angry at finding these weapons here. They had already confronted the youths who gathered around Shabaab X. Raisouli tried to think of what he could do to save his son.

Sharp was getting a little worried too. As things were ramping up here he kept thinking that the group who had driven away in the red panel truck could be coming back for the white Toyota and these weapons. He was also thinking that, no matter what else went on, he and Price had broken into this place carrying pistols of questionable lineage, and were now holding this guy against his will and at gun point. Dead or jail were the two possibilities right now, and he needed a way out.

"You want to save your son's life, Naseer?"

Raisouli didn't expect the offer to come from this angry man. It could be a ruse, a deception crafted to trick him into revealing where his son was. He had to keep thinking; to try to stay ahead of these men, for there was no good outcome from what was happening here. "My son is precious to me. I would do whatever it takes to keep him safe." Sharp considered the possibilities and came to a quick decision. He looked at Price. "OK, no names. Go get the truck and make the call. Let the others know where we are and what's going on. Pick out a place for them to meet us, and then get right back here. I think Naseer here is going to help us load this shit up just to get it out of his house of God."

Price got his truck and made the call. When he returned to the alley Sharp and Raisouli had already stacked the weapons by the door and were in the process of carrying out the crates of ammo. Sharp had been talking constantly to him about the problems he could have if anyone discovered what had happened here. He kept stressing that the investigation, if there were any, would be done at Guantanamo Bay, and because of all the weapons his home, business and this mosque and community center would be forfeit. He would also lose his son, possibly forever. Raisouli had been telling himself the same story. He wanted to save his son and get him away from the influence of Shabaab X. When they were done carrying out boxes of magazines for the rifles Price asked him about the black man who had left with the young men. Raisouli told them. "He is a criminal who is trying to pollute the minds of our young men. If you think you can help me get him away from our youths I will gladly give him up." Price noted the address that Raisouli gave him from memory. "No promises, amigo, but if this Shabaab guy thinks he wants to try to fuck with us any more, we will have to convince him of the error of his ways."

"There is only one way to convince an animal it is wrong, and that is to slaughter it. Shabaab is an animal. He has introduced violence into our lives, and I think he is the one responsible for the deaths of some of our young men. Whatever you can do to stop him will be blessed by Allah."

"I don't think anyone's going to bless me, Naseer. I've got too many points on my license." The reference was lost on Raisouli. "You just need to remember what we talked about and keep your kid out of this. Bad things are going to happen, and I'll do what I have to for my friends, understand."

"I understand." Raisouli answered. He also knew he had to get his family out of harm's way. He watched as the two Americans drove off with Shabaab's cache of weapons and ammunition. There would be a terrible scene when he discovered it. He closed and latched the door and returned to his office. He noticed that of the three storage rooms off the hallway, three had their hasps ripped off. The fourth, closest to the small meeting room, was intact. The Americans must have been satisfied with their discovery, or they would have broken the lock on that door too.

Sitting in his office he tried to think of what he could do. It would be important that he bring his son back into the family fold before they fled to safety, otherwise the boy would have nothing to counter the influence of Shabaab. It was also important that he leave before the man known as Sharif could contact him or Shabaab again, or worse, appear on his door step. He would discuss a small vacation with his wife this very evening. She had been asking him to take some time off, and she was always able to convince the boy to come with them. He had a small cabin to the far north, close to the border with Quebec. It was only accessible over old logging roads during good weather. Heavy rains made some of the stream crossings impassable, and snow closed the roads until spring. He had been able to assume a fifty year lease of the property from a now defunct logging company during the first years of his successful business. He had no idea who currently owned the land, only that he periodically received vague letters from some holding company in the Grand Cayman Islands. His own lawyer told him they were of no consequence, merely the new owner exercising their claim. It was a pleasant place, closed in by old growth forest. Until the advent of the GPS system it had been difficult to find, even with a map. Sometimes he suspected that all the twists and turns in the old logging roads led him into Quebec several times. On one occasion, after a particularly violent thunderstorm, his vehicle GPS actually showed that he was several kilometers over the border. The Raisouli family used it as a summer retreat, and he could often be persuaded to allow its use religious retreats, although he now suspected some of those retreats may have actually been *jihadist* recruitment and training sessions.

Having decided on his plan of action he made several calls to his mosques council of elders. It was an informal group, made up of the more successful, but not necessarily older members of the mosque. He told them he was planning on a few days away, and would turn over some of the responsibilities to members of the council. They would meet in his office the following morning to decide on the apportionment of responsibilities. His wife could do the shopping for the trip while he was so occupied, as would be normal for a good Muslim woman. Once he was done, they would leave.

Price and Sharp rendezvoused with Grant and Harrison in a hotel parking lot several blocks away. They weren't really surprised to see Major Carson sitting in the cab of his truck. They figured that he didn't want to leave her sitting alone someplace now. That was like Gordon sitting in Harrison's vehicle. They had left her at the hanger when they took off after the Arabs. She may not have been a principal in all this, but there could always be a chance she had been identified as a member of the group and had thus been targeted.

Major Carson did not look happy, and she wasn't. She was about to have her way with Grant on the seat of his truck in her driveway when the call from Price came. That damn voice activation on the vehicle system was unexpected. If it had just been his phone ringing she could have kept his attention away from it.

Price and Sharp took turns explaining what had happened and how they got the weapons. Grant was concerned about the Imam.

"Do you think you can trust him?"

"Jeez, I don't know, Luke. He did give us the guns, even helped load them. I think we put the fear of God into him, but only time will tell."

"OK. I wanted to take a look at that place anyway. Ralph, what time is that dog and pony show at your place tomorrow?"

"1000 to 1130. General Cabot wants an organizational update before he presents the flag next month. I think he's in a hurry to get us stood up."

"Yeah, well we can keep one eye on that ball and keep Cabot happy. I'll try to head over to the mosque and have a few words with this Raisouli guy. He might have to disappear."

"We aren't in the third world now, Luke. Somebody might notice."

Grant looked into the back of the truck and groaned. The weapons were barely covered by a tarp held down with the ammo cases and boxes of magazines. "Not a good plan, Dave. Get these things covered better and get them to the armory. You get stopped by a cop and you'll never talk your way out of it."

"You sure you want them at the armory, Luke, and not the hanger? We might have a need for these sooner than later."

Grant shook his head. "I don't want any of this with the legal stuff. We can always dummy up a page for the property book and get some new Second Lieutenant to sign it. We've got more unauthorized shit all over that place, so a little more won't matter." He thought about it for a moment. "On second thought, put it with the other AKs we picked up. Tag them the same as the others with that ATF guy's name, Rawlins."

"Rawlins was the FBI guy I think. You might mean Simmons."

"I don't care who you use. Put them both down. If push comes to shove I'd rather they spend the next month explaining what the hell they are. State Police already know they took possession of the first two, so there's already a history.

"Make sure Ashley and Connaught know about these too. They might have some ideas. Now get out of here."

Harrison came over to stand by him as the two trucks drove off. "Keep an eye on them Ralph, and make sure everyone stays on their toes tonight. This is starting to snowball faster than we can make plans for."

"At least we got the weapons."

"True, but now somebody else knows that we know. They're going to have to improvise too. We need some people to keep an eye on the mosque for a few days. Can you line up some troops who could use a couple of days active duty pay?"

"I'm sure I can, but do you want to bring more people in on this? Getting real hard to keep a secret around here."

Grant agreed, "But I don't see much of a choice. The Arab told Sharp he recognized him from a picture on his kid's wall, and he probably hadn't been studying it like some of the others have. Look at Carson. Her face only shows up in the background on one of the files, and they managed to track her down. One of us starts spending a lot of time sitting across the street from that mosque and they'd spot us in a heartbeat." He paused to gather his thoughts. "All we need is a couple of sets of eyes to ID people in and out. We'll give them some images for a cell phone or lap top and have them call us if they see anything. I don't want them to act, just observe and report."

"OK, Luke. I'll make some calls tonight. I'll try to keep them off the books until it's all over so nobody gets any ideas. And I'll tell them to bring some civilian clothes with them. They've gotta report in uniform, but we can wing it from there."

Carson picked that time to step out of the truck and announce she was going into the lobby to find a cold drink machine. She didn't notice her discarded bra fall out onto the ground. "Anybody want anything?" She saw Grant and Harrison looking at her feet. She glanced down and saw the undergarment laying there. She picked it up and threw it on the seat with a casual "It's too hot to keep that on" and walked away. The two men watched her. She was dressed to be looked at, and they both obliged.

After the long minute it took her to walk across the parking lot Harrison let out a sigh and looked at his friend. "You're playing with fire with that one, Luke."

"Fire my ass! It's more like napalm. I'm going to hell, Ralph, and she's greasing the skids."

"As long as you know what you're doing, my friend. I hate to see you screw up a good thing you've got going with Major Bonneville. Someone like that doesn't come around too often, and you damn well know it."

"You're a good friend, Ralph. You can be a pain in the ass, but you're usually right. I'll see you tomorrow."

Grant waited in his truck waiting for Carson to return. She came out of the lobby carrying two drink bottles. Even from a distance, it was obvious she wasn't wearing her bra. Somehow, she had managed to pull her blouse tight across her chest. The thin, light material hid nothing. Several men stopped and stared at her as she walked past. Christ, Grant though, I've got to stop thinking with the small head. Grant didn't realize how hard he was staring at her until she was in the truck and spoke to him. "I like that look, Sergeant Major. See something you like?" She passed over the extra drink, and undid a couple of buttons on her blouse. "Why don't you get this truck moving, and I'll see if I can remember where I left off."

CHAPTER THIRTEEN

IRST SERGEANT HARRISON ARRANGED FOR six soldiers to report for duty the next day. It only took a couple of calls, and he had no refusals. Jobs had been hard enough to come by before the deployment to Africa: coming home as hometown heroes hadn't improved the job prospects. Once he had his people lined up he organized them into shifts of one and two people. The next morning he would have them dress in civilian clothes, and issue laptops and give them some pocket money so they could set up at the outdoor café across from the mosque. It wouldn't do to have anyone just sitting there watching foot traffic, so they would have to appear to be doing something. Even if the Arabs had lousy counter surveillance techniques, they would be quickly noticed. Harrison had checked the weather report for the next few days and saw that the weather would be closing in soon. He would have to come up with another plan if the skies opened up on them.

The morning, thankfully, was just a little overcast. Harrison was up early and had the coffee going before Price rolled out of bed. There were many days when Harrison would walk the two and a half miles to his office, but today wasn't one of them. He wanted to get in early and set up for his surveillance rotations. Traffic was light, as it usually was at this time, and he was rolling through the gate while the security guards were still changing shift. The contract security was a bone of contention with Harrison. Not one of them was a member of any of the Guard or Reserve units in the State, and he doubted if many of them were even veterans. It was one of the complaints Harrison made on a regular basis. He knew of too many unemployed and underemployed soldiers and veterans who should have had the jobs.

There was also the usual small group of protesters walking the sidewalk this morning. They had been a regular feature for sometime now. They carried their signs, chanted and occasionally prayed. On a normal day it was a predominantly Muslim group with a sprinkling of college students, bored housewives and other so-called peace groups. The Muslims were usually polite, didn't block the traffic, and were willing to chat with the soldiers that Harrison had bring out a five gallon jug of cold water. It was the others who tried to incite some kind of trouble. Today, he noticed, it was just the Muslims. It was probably too early for the rest to be out of bed.

In the meantime, Grant had reported in to work at his usual time. It had taken an extra cup of coffee to get jump started. Sylvia Carson had made it a point to wear him out as much as she could before she let him take her to his house for the night. She made a point of telling Linda Bonneville that her own paramour would be back the next morning and she would be staying with him. She and Bonneville spent the evening drinking way too much of the wine Carson had retrieved from her house, and Bonneville was hungry for some attention when she joined Grant in bed. It had been a long, pleasurable, but exhausting night, and Grant felt every year of his age. He was glad Carson was leaving today. He had the feeling she was listening in on their bedroom activities and doubted she would be a quiet house guest for long.

He always entered through the back gate, opposite the Aviation Maintenance Facility. Some mornings all the Blackhawk helicopters were rolled out and preparing for whatever training was scheduled. From time to time he would exercise his stripes and join in on a flight or two. It let the troops know he was interested in what they were doing, and secretly, it was good for Grant's morale.

Grant was working on Ashley and Connaught to come up with resources to identify and neutralize all the players in the mosque. Naseer Raisouli and his family had entered the country as refugees a long time ago. They had obtained permanent visas, never went through the motions to become citizens, and had basically been forgotten by the system. Decades ago there was a system for tracking foreigners in the country. Older people could still remember announcements every year identifying January as 'Alien Registration Month'. Every foreigner in the country was supposed to go to the nearest US Post Office and register or face deportation. In spite of the international threats over the last twenty years, the idea had never been resurrected.

Ashley was able to connect with the Parole Office about Shabaab X, but it was a futile effort. Whether it was overwork or apathy, the parole officer he spoke to didn't place a high priority on Shabaab's activities. He was meeting his requirement for bi-weekly visits and random drug tests. As long as he didn't violate his curfew, get caught around children (it was a surprise to learn he was a sex offender) or get arrested, there was nothing the Parole Department was going to do to interfere with his freedom. Ashley tried to protest citing the reports of the past weekend involving young men from the mosque, but the state employed functionary cut him off. "Look, Colonel, if you think he's a national security threat, call Homeland Security. They love to roll in on these guys and generate a few headlines. As far as I'm concerned, he's managed to become some kind of prayer leader at that place. I'm sure as hell not going to start harassing him over his religious practices. That's one big ass lawsuit the State would rather avoid. Unless you can figure out some way to get the people at the mosque to complain he's diddling the altar boys or chasing after the nuns, what he does in there is his business."

"I don't think the Muslims have nuns or altar boys." Ashley replied.

"You know what I mean. You get something on him I can use, let me know, otherwise, I've got a beast of a case load and Shabaab is way down on the food chain right now."

Grant tried to get Ashley to call Homeland Security, or failing that, ATF or FBI. Ashley nixed any of those. "Look, Sergeant Major, once General Vaughn got involved and waved off the alphabets, they have no intention of getting involved. They rather see him trip over his own dick first, that's just how bad the inter-agency hard feelings are. Besides, Sharp and Price took the guns out. There's no evidence now, except for what they're holding on to, and there's no chain of custody any prosecutor would touch."

"What about Homeland? This is a terror cell, pure and simple."

"Grant, it isn't simple anymore. Your guys should have never gone through that fucking door. Next time figure out some way to get probable cause and a warrant."

"Like a shootout on Main Street? Is that what it'll take?"

"That would be perfect, but do me a favor and try not to be the one who starts it." Ashley regretted saying it as soon as the words were out of his mouth. Grant and company didn't ask to be the targets of a *Jihadist* operation, any more than Ashley had asked to lose his leg. "I still know people outside of Vaughn's circle of influence. Let me see if I can call in a favor from one of the alphabet agencies and get something else going. Where will you be later?"

Grant had a dog and pony show to attend with General Cabot and told Ashley that he'd be out of touch but could probably take a text message. Grant hated texting, and rarely ever told anyone to text him. He preferred to have conversations, not thumb exercises.

Before he went to his office he swung by the motor pool to arrange for a vehicle for the day. As much as he preferred the comfort of his own vehicle, there were times when it just made more sense to let the government pay for the gas. Today would be one of those days, because after one of these meetings with Cabot he usually had to put on a lot of miles mending fences. Cabot was becoming what the Army called a 'toxic leader' with his meddling in the activation of the new 289th Engineer Battalion. Meddling was not Cabot's usual style, but the last unit he set up called the 289th was the one Grant had deployed with, and some of the unfavorable publicity had touched him. The staff of the last unit had been hand picked by him. He was making the same mistake this time, and Grant was certain that his choices for some of the key staff positions were just as bad. He was familiar with some of the names from Sudan, Moldova and New Mexico and he did not think they were up to the task. He had put forward some suggestions, but Cabot had shot them down. He blamed Grant for whatever had gone bad on deployment.

The Motor Sergeant was a sharp looking Staff Sergeant who seemed to run a squared away operation, unlike the first motor pool Grant had walked into when he got here. This NCO had a good handle on tool control and made sure all required Preventative Maintenance Checks and Services were done before any vehicle rolled out, no matter how important the driver thought he was. Grant never minded getting his hands dirty if it meant he wouldn't be stuck on the side of the road in the middle of nowhere, but the young SSG always managed to have a mechanic available to help. Grant appreciated the gesture and had arranged for a coffee maker and a refrigerator to be delivered to their break room.

Once in his office Grant collected the files he thought he would need for the meeting. Someone had already been in his office and had left a small folder of 'information copies' of recent memos. He read through them quickly and could see the hand of a concerned NCO trying to bring him up to speed. The General's staff had gotten into the habit of cutting him and Harrison out of the information loop. Not only did it make their job harder, but it was also interfering in what should have been NCO territory. Grant resolved that whatever else happened at this meeting, he would have to tackle this one head on. General Cabot could assign whatever officers he wanted to the new unit, but it was up to Grant and Harrison to make sure they were backed up by the most competent NCOs available. Anything less would be unfair to the new commanders, the new platoon leaders and the new enlisted troops who would probably find themselves on active duty on the other side of the world in less than a year. Grant scooped everything up and slipped it into the old aviator's helmet bag he used as a briefcase, and headed out the door.

He headed out the main gate of the reservation, the most direct route to Harrisons area. He noticed that the usual group of picketers was larger than usual today. He stopped to ask the contract security guard about it.

"The story's been on the radio this morning that one of your Majors shot an Arab kid the other night. They've been interviewing some guy named Shabaab X who's been saying its more racist attacks by the National Guard on innocent Muslims." Grant noticed the guard was black, and had made the statement in a voice dripping with sarcasm.

"You don't buy that, I take it?"

"Sergeant Major, I did two tours in Iran and one in Afghanistan before I realized I didn't like those people shooting at me. I've seen enough to know that this guy Shabaab is full of shit. Those people over there," he waved his hand at the small group gathered on the sidewalk, "they're bigger sheep than the morons who put up with the suicide bombers in their market places. They ever figure that out and things might get better over there."

"Is this going to be a problem for you?"

The guard shook his head. "The regulars are usually pretty well behaved. They even ask how come we don't put out cold water for them like they do down the road." He was talking about Harrison's facility. Grant had told him not to give the protesters anything. It only encouraged them. "If the crowd gets any bigger we're going to call in more people and put a foot patrol along the fence." Grant gave him a wave and drove off. He turned on his radio and scanned for a news channel. The story about Carson seemed to be getting a lot of air play. If it had been presented factually there wouldn't have been a problem, but this station seemed to be indulging in a lot of speculation. They seemed to be liberally quoting Shabaab X and it was obvious that all he wanted to do was get the crowd agitated. This was not what they needed in light of everything else going on.

The crowd at the 289th Engineer facility was slightly larger than the one at the other gate. They seemed to be a surly lot, and were slow to clear out of the roadway to let him pass. Grant told the gate guard to keep the way clear. Those people could protest all they wanted on the sidewalk, but the gate was to be kept clear for official business. The guard said that they were usually a good natured crowd, and repeated the story about the shooting. He promised to do his best without antagonizing anyone and making the situation worse. Grant didn't hold out high hopes for this one, and made a mental note to tell Ralph Harrison to call the security company for more help.

Sharif and Khan arrived in the city at mid-morning. It had taken just over three hours to drive from the rat-hole campground and travel park on the outskirts of Burlington, and they had discovered too late that the mattresses had been infested with bed bugs. Khans' legs and back were covered with small bites that would have driven him to despair had he not been responsible for driving the car. Sharif had made it clear he did not trust him completely, and until there was an opportunity for Khan to prove himself, he would remain under suspicion. Sharif rode in the rear seat and slept for most of the ride to New Hampshire. The new escort, who was never introduced, sat in front, a small pistol constantly in one hand, a string of worry beads in the other. Khan's attempts to engage him in conversation were repeatedly rebuffed, the last time with a string of profanities. Judging from the tattoos the man had on his hands and neck, Khan assumed he was an ex-convict like the first driver had been.

Sharif was awakened by a phone call shortly before they arrived in a city called Lebanon. Khan noted the irony out loud, but he was ignored. There seemed to be bad news from the caller, and Sharif gave a series of instructions in Arabic. There was a pause, and Sharif got even angrier. "Then put on someone who does speak the language of Allah!" He waited while an Arabic speaker was summoned. "It's a sad state of affairs, Mehmet Atta Khan when we have to rely on make believe Muslims to carry out our wishes." He had spoken in Arabic so the escort couldn't understand. Someone came on the line and Sharif delivered a series of rapid fire instructions, and whoever he was speaking to must have been giving one word responses. Finally there was a pause in his tirade as he listened to what was being said. He ended with a terse, "I will deal with him when I get there. Now give me back that idiot I was talking to before." There was another pause while the phone again changed hands. "Listen well, Shabaab X, for I will not repeat myself. The operation will go forward as planned. Your bungling will not allow the will of Allah to be thwarted, do you understand? Get the weapons and ammunition you have stolen back from your criminal friends. I will be at the rendezvous in approximately one hour. I expect everything will be in readiness by then." He snapped the phone shut angrily.

"Bad news, Sharif?" Khan asked in Arabic, assuming the escort was also ignorant of the language.

Sharif answered the same way. "A small thing. It seems there is an apostate at our destination that needs to be dealt with. Some of our weapons have disappeared because an Imam has forgotten his true faith."

"You said something about stolen. Is the Imam dealing with a criminal element? That type is always unreliable, and I dislike dealing with mercenaries."

"No, the Imam in question seems to have decided the life of his son is more important than his duty to Allah. He has moved the weapons we had stored in his mosque and hidden them from us. I will convince him to return them. The thievery was done by this one's friend", he pointed to the escort. "He is using his new found faith for his own profit. That too will have to be corrected."

They rode in silence for most of the next hour. Sharif was carefully studying road signs and consulting a travel map. "At the end of this highway there will be a parking area to the right. Drive in there and look for a red tradesman's vehicle. That will be our next vehicle."

In the lot the red van stood alone in the back section. There were two men standing next to it, a large black man with an ornate *kufi* and a nervous looking youth who appeared to be in his late teens or early twenties. There were none of the cadaverous people that seemed to inhabit most of the Middle East. The escort was familiar with the two, and greeted them with bear hugs and a peculiar little ritual that Khan took to be related to a hand shake. Sharif was introduced to Shabaab X as 'the Coordinator', and the title seemed to satisfy every one. Khan was simply 'our friend', which also seemed satisfactory. Sharif and Shabaab X walked off a little distance and engaged in an animated conversation. Khan could tell it was angry by the hand gestures, but he heard none of the words. The escort, who had been called Darnel by the boy, asked what the problem was.

"The storage rooms were broken into last night. All the weapons stored in the basement are gone. Shabaab thinks my father may have disposed of them after we left. They had angry words about the operation."

"All the weapons? Even the book bags?"

The boy shook his head. "No, the book bags were still there. That was the only room that hadn't been entered. Shabaab gave them to the young warriors this morning. They should be in place at the appointed time."

Sharif returned and divided up the party. Sharif and Shabaab would go on ahead to the mosque and 'discuss' the weapons situation with the boys father. Khan was to continue with Darnel and wait outside the mosque. Sharif explained. "There was supposed to be a culmination of all our efforts today. While the young warriors were dealing a blow against the infidel soldiers, Hassan," he must be the young man here, Khan thought, "and his group was to hunt down the primary targets and kill them. There have been missteps, though. He claims several of his companions became over eager and felt they could act earlier. All they succeeded in doing was alerting the targets to their peril. There has been a delay while more weapons are obtained. It is unfortunate that our ally here got greedy. There is another supply cache that has been prepared at Hassan's father's camp in the woods far to the north. It will take a day or two to retrieve them to make up the short fall, unless we can convince Imam Raisouli to reveal where he has hidden them. In the meantime Shabaab has already deployed the young warriors. I have decided to delay the second phase of the attack to gauge the infidel response. They may consider this the main effort and relax their vigilance at their homes." He suddenly looked at Khan and gave a strange, almost mystical smile. It was totally out of character. "The life of a holy warrior is never easy, is it, Mehmet Atta Khan? Allah is constantly testing our resolve." Khan had noticed that Sharif was making more religious references as the mission progressed. He decided it had to be a ruse for the benefit of the local cell, because Sharif was definitely not a religious man.

The red van left first with the boy Hassan in tow. Darnel waited a few minutes and motioned for the car keys. "It'll be easier if I just drive instead of trying to give you directions." It was a short drive into the city, where Darnel found a parking space across the street from the red van. Khan was looking around, searching for signs of a mosque, until Darnel pointed to a sign on a commercial building on the corner. It wasn't what Khan had expected. He continued to look about until he saw the open air café about a half a block behind them. "Come," Khan said getting out of the car, "I'll buy you a coffee and pastry. I'm hungry."

"We should wait here."

"Suit yourself. I'll be sitting at a table over there," he pointed to the café. "Come get me when it's time to leave." Darnel sat for a moment, not knowing what to do, then got out of the car and followed Khan. There were a number of empty tables and the waitress told them to sit wherever they like. Khan chose a table near the far corner. There was a young girl at the table behind them with an open computer and a cell phone pressed to her ear. She seemed oblivious to her surroundings.

The first shift of surveillance at the café spent an idle two hours reading a magazine, texting and drinking coffee. Her attention span had been such that she missed every one who entered or left the mosque. Naseer Raisouli had walked right past the café on his way to the mosque and she never noticed him. She missed the red van pulling into the alley, and she never noticed the young teenagers who entered the front door in a group. She might have noticed the red van leaving, for it drove past the front of the café, except that she had chosen that moment to visit the rest room. When her relief arrived, she had nothing to report. She had been a poor choice to conduct surveillance.

The second young woman, Freya Heath, was more alert, except that she got caught up in texting a friend to let her know she had managed to get a few days of active duty and would not be available to hang out. She had deployed as a mechanic with the 289th ESC, and had found full time jobs few and far between when she returned. College had been an attractive alternative with the education benefits paying a decent living stipend if you could live at home or share expenses with someone.

The red van was already parked in front of the mosque before she noticed it. She decided to study the pictures First Sergeant Harrison had loaded onto the lap top just in case she spotted anyone coming back out. She didn't notice the two men walk from a half a block away until they were already seated with their backs to her. She left the pictures up on her laptop and tried to call the First Sergeant. She could at least report the red van he had mentioned.

Shabaab and Sharif entered the mosque and had climbed the stairs to Raisouli's office. Raisouli thought nothing of the footsteps in the hall, for he was expecting the council elders to join him, although he would not be surprised if some came early. Raisouli was noted for his fine coffee and the pot was always on. He looked up when the door open and froze when he saw Shabaab and the man behind him. It was a face he remembered from his time in the camp in the Bekka, the man who had called and told him he was coming.

"You!"

"You seem surprised, Raisouli. Didn't I tell you I was coming? Don't tell me you thought I was joking!" He walked over and sat in an overstuffed chair to the side of the desk. "Shabaab tells me you have betrayed our holy warriors, Raisouli. Where are the weapons?"

Raisouli remained silent. His mid was racing with possibilities, but none of them seemed appropriate for the moment. "Let me tell you, Naseer Raisouli, you will tell me, and I will even let you choose the method of interrogation." He nodded to Shabaab, who left the room. "Your son is downstairs. When Shabaab returns with him I will begin my interrogation by introducing your son to my blade." Sharif withdrew a straight razor from an inner pocket.

"He can tell you nothing."

Sharif laughed his sinister laugh. "Naseer Raisouli, I don't expect him to tell me anything. Once you see the blood begin to flow from his body, you will tell me all I need to know."

"I will have nothing to say to you."

"I am prepared for that too. Your wife is already on the way here with one of Shabaab's companions," this wasn't true, but Raisouli had no way to contact her. "As soon as I am done with your son, your wife will feel my blade, and perhaps more. Believe me, Naseer Raisouli, you will tell me everything."

Raisouli had a look of horror in his eyes. This animal would hack up his family to get him to talk. "The weapons were taken by the American soldiers he has been hunting. You cannot retrieve them."

"Too simple, Raisouli, far too simple. How would they know the weapons were here? Did you call them and invite them to defile this holy place?" Raisouli noted that 'holy place' was spoken with a sneer in Sharif's voice.

"I did not have to contact them. They followed my son here last night and searched the basement. They found the weapons and took them with them."

"And you did not try to stop them?"

"Nothing good will come from continued violence. Enough of our young men have died already. I helped them carry the weapons to their vehicle."

Shabaab returned with Hassan. The boy looked from his father to Sharif, not understanding what was happening. Sharif put his arm around the boys shoulder. "Do you want to help the holy *jihad* against the infidels, Hassan?"

"Yes, of course, but I don't understand . . ."

"Hold out your hand, Hassan."

"No, my son, don't!"

The boy looked at his father with fear in his eyes as he held out his hand palm up. Sharif made a quick slash across his wrist. Blood spurted across the room and landed on his fathers' desk. The boy let out a scream and dropped to his knees, holding his wrist and pressing it into his body. Sharif looked at Raisouli and smiled. "The truth, if you please."

"I have told you the truth. The Americans were here and took your weapons."

"Do you believe him, Shabaab?"

The ex-convict shrugged. "Kind of late for him to be lying now."

Sharif agreed. He looked down at Hassan. "The boy will be a cripple now, Naseer Raisouli, this will be more merciful." He grabbed a handful of the boys' hair and pulled his head back. With a smooth stroke he pulled the straight razor across the neck and pushed the head sideways to direct the blood splatter away from him. Raisouli cried out in agony, rushing around the desk to his son's lifeless body. Sharif nodded at Shabaab, who stepped around the body and fired a single shot into the back of Raisouli's head.

The sound of the shot was muffled, but it was heard on the street. The young specialist had been trying to contact First Sergeant Harrison about the red van, but he wasn't answering his phone. She was muttering to herself while she tried to send a text message. Out of the corner of her eye she noticed a soldier get out of a truck at the curb. She waved breezily and called out "Hey, I know you!" Freya had cultivated the habit of making her voice pass through an octave when she said 'hey'. It caught the attention of most of the patrons in the café, including the two men seated in front of her. They turned to see what was going on. She smiled at them just as the slide show of images on her laptop displayed a close up of the man sitting in front of her.

Jonah Price had some time to kill while Sharp took care of some administrative duties at the NCO academy. He decided to run out and get some coffee and pastries. He thought about the café on Main Street, and didn't think it would be a problem if he popped in and out real quick. A random soldier going into a shop shouldn't attract much attention. Like Grant, he paid attention to the protesters outside the main gate. The crowd had increased since he had arrived a few hours ago. There were now two security guards in the shack, but the crowd still seemed peaceful. There was one idiot with a bull horn trying to incite the crowd, but he wasn't having much effect. He also noticed that some people had brought their children today. As far as he was concerned, that was usually a good sign. Mothers didn't like to bring kids to places where they could get into trouble or get hurt. Further on down the road he could look over and see the gate to the new Engineer compound. There seemed to be a pretty good sized crowd there, too. Odd, but the radio had been hammering about the kid that Major Carson had shot over the weekend, so it wasn't much of a surprise. The reporters were making the whole thing sound sinister, as if the kid got ambushed. There were very few references to the AK-47 the little jerk was carrying.

There was a parking place right in front of the café. Price hopped out and quick stepped up to the take-out counter. Someone at the far end of the sidewalk dining area waved and called to him. He recognized the distinctive sound of the greeting and searched for the source. He was looking at her between the turned heads of two men at the table in front of her. Suddenly, her expression changed to one of surprise. She was looking at the faces in front of her. She managed to blurt out his name, "Sergeant Price . . ." First one, then the other man turned to look at him. His eyes locked with the second man, an Arab. Then all hell broke loose.

Khan was surprised to be looking at the face he had first seen so long ago at the roadblock in Lashkar Gah, and then again when the infidel had put his hands on him at the border crossing in Zaranj. Even though the mission had been to locate and kill him and his friends, Khan never really expected to be face to face with him again. The first man looked back and forth at the two, trying to decide what was going on. At last something in the dim recesses of his brain told him that the man he was supposed to be watching and protecting was in trouble and he needed to do something. He was trying to draw a nine millimeter pistol from under his shirt, a weapon he was totally unfamiliar with, but carried it because it looked 'cool'. It snagged on his shirt tail and the fabric tore as yet yanked it out. Khan also drew his small pistol that he had taken off the dead woman in Vermont. He had at least familiarized himself with it and could manipulate the controls. His first shots went wide, but his target dropped to a crouch. He could see the soldier draw his own weapon from under his blouse. The girl behind him screamed something and threw her computer. It hit Darnel in the back, and he turned and raised his gun at her. Nothing happened when he pulled the trigger, and he realized he had not put a round in the chamber. Price popped up and fired a quick shot at Khan, missing him. Darnel got his pistol ready and fired one shot into the girl's chest, driving her back over her chair. He then pivoted and fired several shots at Price, all going wild, but not hitting anyone. Price lined up his sights and put two rounds into Darnel, center of mass. Darnel staggered back and looked down at the red stain on his shirt. He looked up in time for Price to put one between the running lights.

Khan grabbed the car keys that were on the table and emptied what was left of his magazine at Price, sprinting off to the street. One bullet struck Price on the side of his chest, cracking a rib as it passed under the skin and back out. Another hit him in the right leg. The impact knocked Price to the ground, and when he got to his knees Khan was far off, running down the street. He was running to a red van that was pulling away from the curb in front of the mosque. It made a u-turn after Khan got in the open side door. Price tried to line up his sights for a long shot, but there were too many people in the way. He needed to check on the girl who had been shot and call Grant, Sharp, Harrison or anybody. He reached into his pocket for his phone. The bullet that had hit him in the leg hadn't penetrated the skin, but it had shattered his phone. He swore to himself, and then went to check the girl. He could tell by looking at her that she was dead. He picked up the phone that had fallen off the table. The pre-programmed number of First Sergeant Harrison had been called up. He pushed the 'send' button. He didn't recognize the voice that answered after a few rings, but it was answered in a proper military fashion, so he delivered his message. "Tell the First Sergeant that SFC Price called. There's been a shooting near the mosque. I've been hit and I think one of his surveillance crew is dead. One of the bad guys is down too. I think my buddy from Afghanistan got away. Have him inform Command Sergeant Major Grant. They should be together somewhere in your facility."

There was a little bit of confusion in the van as it slowed for Khan. "What the fuck are you doing, man? Where's Darnel?" Shabaab shouted as Sharif pulled the sliding door shut.

"He's dead. One of the Americans recognized me. We were being watched from the restaurant."

Sharif was furious. "Fool! If you had remained where you were supposed to be you would not have been seen. How did this happen?" He had his gun in his hand, waving it at Khan.

"Put that away you fool. They had a girl watching the mosque. She had a computer and a phone with her and was making regular reports. She saw this vehicle and told her superiors. We had no choice but to take action."

Sharif lowered the gun. "How do you know she reported?"

"The one called Price came. They had us trapped between them. Darnel was able to shoot the girl before he was killed. I hit the man. I saw him go down."

Shabaab was shouting, "How do you know Darnel's dead? He might have just been wounded and you left him for the cops!"

"He was dead, and if he wasn't, he soon will be. The back of his head was destroyed."

Sharif shouted to both of them to be quiet. "Time is too short for this. I want to see the fruits of our planning, not listen to how incompetents jeopardize it. Take me to where I can view one of the attacks." Shabaab protested. "Too many people got a look at us when he came running over. We should have left him. I need to dump this and get another set of wheels."

"Is there something else we can use?" Sharif asked looking at his watch. The time of the attack was approaching. Shabaab said he had another car they could use. It was only a few minutes away. "Good," Sharif said. "It is almost time. I want to watch our young warriors destroy the infidels!"

It had been a contentious meeting with the staff of the new 289th Engineer Battalion. Sergeant Major Grant knew there was really nothing he could do about the officer assignments, and decided he wouldn't even bother arguing against them. General Cabot seemed to be determined to make the same mistakes with this unit as he had with its predecessor. He looked around the table at the assembled officers and felt sorry for Ralph Harrison. The new Commander had been named, but was currently two states away wrapping up his assignment to another National Guard staff. He had made some discrete inquiries with the NCO cadre, and had discovered he was well regarded as a staff officer, but had not commanded anything larger than a company in over ten years. Not necessarily a bad thing if he was getting a strong support staff.

He wasn't. His new Executive Officer would be Major Stanley Fisher, former acting S-3 (Operations and Training) of the 289th

Engineer Support Command. Fisher's only notable achievement was that he had allowed a classified lap top to be used by a Sergeant who was selling information to the Mexican Army in New Mexico. Somehow he had managed to avoid any responsibility in the investigation. The new S-3 would be Captain (Promotable) Roger Menklin. His last billet had been as the S-2 (Intelligence) of the same 289th ESC. If Sergeant First Class David Sharp hadn't been around, there would have been no intelligence coming out of the section. Grant had recommended Linda Bonneville for the XO slot. She had successfully commanded the 289th ESC on its raid into Mexico, and she had the respect of many of the soldiers and NCOs who would be staffing the Battalion. She, however, was passed over by Cabot. There would have been a problem with the incompetent officers being rated by her.

The argument actually started when the subject of NCOs finally came up. The Sergeant Major slot was a done deal. Harrison was at the top of the list and would be frocked as soon as the unit was activated. There were a number of Master Sergeants who wanted to move into First Sergeant billets, as well as a promotion list of promising SFCs. Grant felt that this was where the senior NCOs should come from. Fisher and Menklin had other ideas. They had a list of NCOs that they wanted for the senior slots. Grant had looked at the list and the personnel records of all of them. There were no stand outs among them, and, in the coming reduction in force (RIF), he could see where several of them would be invited to leave the service. Most had too much time in grade and too little NCO education. Not one of them had deployed in the past eight years, but several of them had managed to stay on active duty in a number of inconsequential positions. It was cronyism, pure and simple, and Grant was prepared with a name by name comparison of the two lists. It was easy to see where the qualified people were. Cabot was not really interested in the arguments, but he knew Grant was right. He thought he was acting with the wisdom of Solomon when he announced that he would take both lists and take half, the most qualified, from each list. Then he tasked Grant with making the decisions. Grant felt he could live with that, even though it would lead to more complaints in the future. He would pick the most qualified only after he eliminated the unqualified. It looked like only two could possibly be chosen from the 'crony' list, and he might even be able to keep them limited to staff positions, and not send any of them to the line companies.

They were getting ready to discuss arrangements for the activation ceremony when an aide came in with a message for General Cabot. She was instantly followed by First Sergeant Harrison's clerk carrying his personal cell phone. He had inadvertently left it on his desk before the meeting and the clerk finally decided to answer it, even though it was something Harrison frowned on. The messages, from different sources, were the same. Cabot announce that there had been a shooting involving military personnel in the down town area and ordered that a television be brought to the room so they could follow the news reports. While that was happening, Harrison took Grant aside and gave him a quick rundown on what his clerk had just told him. "Son of a bitch," was Grant's first response. "What the fuck was Price doing downtown? He should have known better!"

Major Fisher was watching from across the room, straining to hear what was being said. He caught enough to know that the two NCOs knew more about what was going on than anyone else in the room. "General Cabot? I believe the Sergeant Major and the First Sergeant may know something about all this." Grant shot Fisher a dirty look. Fisher had a smile under that stupid little mustache he wore.

Cabot looked at the two. "Well, do you know what's going on?"

Harrison spoke first. "Yes Sir. I had a team watching the Islamic Center downtown. It looks like they were involved in a shooting. Sergeant Price is wounded; one of my soldiers is dead, as is one of what Sergeant Price referred to as the bad guys."

Fisher was secretly bursting inside. These two bastards were running another illegal operation, and this time they got caught! It was the next best thing to taking them down himself. "General, this is just like when we were overseas. These two think they can get away with using the United States Army for their personal ends."

"That's enough, Major. I want to hear their side."

"General, there's an American soldier dead, and possibly an innocent civilian too. I think we need to call in the authorities."

"I said that's enough, Major! Do I need you to leave the room?" There was no response from Fisher. Cabot turned back to Grant. Harrison started to speak, but Cabot held up his hand. "I think I want to hear from CSM Grant right now. You are the brains behind this, aren't you, Grant?"

Grant wasn't going to throw his friend under the bus. "Yes sir, I had the First Sergeant set up surveillance on the mosque. I did not plan on things to happen this way."

Cabot made the motion with his hand that he wanted more information. Grant hesitated: there were too many unauthorized ears in the room. "Sir, I think I need to speak to you alone. This has to do with the situation with General Vaughn and Colonel Ashley." No one besides Cabot had heard those names before, but he had already been telling his staff at headquarters about the mysterious Arabs that Homeland Security claimed were in the country and targeting Grant and company. The cat was already out of the bag. "Is this about the mysterious Arabs that are looking for you, Grant?"

"Yeah, Price said he saw the one from Afghanistan again. The guy was one of the shooters at the restaurant." There was a rumble of thunder from somewhere outside the building. Those that had been in the war zones recognized it for what it was, an explosion. Most faces turned to the windows and looked to the east, in the general direction of the State Reservation on the hill. There was a black cloud rising above the intervening trees. Everyone ran to the windows for a better look. Before anyone could move or say anything, Grant looked down at the crowd in front of the building. Most were standing around, trying to determine what the noise was. Harrison pointed out several figures forcing their way through the crowd, away from the guard shack. There was one little figure, a child, who was running towards the shack. Grant saw he was wearing a back pack, and he was grasping something in his outstretched hand. He recognized it immediately. "Everybody down!" he shouted and started pulling officers away from the window. There were some curses as bodies stumbled back, but he had the windows cleared before there was another explosion, this one much closer, right outside the building, followed immediately by the windows blowing in from the outside.

Chapter Fourteen

Dave Sharp was wrapping up his class evaluations, hating every piece of paper ever invented in the world. Sharp was a good NCO, and excelled in all the skills that made him good, but he hated paperwork. The digital age may have arrived, but the Army still insisted on hard copies of documents and multiple information recipients. He pitied the poor new Lieutenants who had to back up all their work with Power Point presentations.

Sergeant Robinson had just gone past his office on his way to lunch. There was a break room down the hall where a television was usually kept tuned to a twenty-four hour news channel. During breaks and lunch it slipped over to a sports channel, but only during breaks and lunch. Sharp thought about joining him, but thought about the lousy selections in the vending machines. He preferred MREs to the microwave sandwiches that were available. He slid the last report into a folder and walked down the hall calling out to Robinson, "Hey, Eddie, fuck that vending machine crap. I'll buy you and Price a burger." Robinson didn't answer him, which was odd, because Robinson never turned down fast food, especially when it was on someone else's dime. Sharp walked into the room and saw Robinson staring at the television. "Sarge, you gotta see this!" He recognized it as the café down town that they had watched the mosque from the day before. It seemed to be taken from across the street, because there were a lot of emergency vehicles parked in front. The camera panned around and zoomed in on a body lying on the ground, covered by a table cloth, then swung over to another one a short distance away. He wondered if something had gone really wrong with the surveillance Ralph Harrison had lined up, or if somebody had just decided today was the day he'd do something incredibly stupid in broad daylight. "There's a uniform sitting next to the ambulance on the right, Sarge. I caught a quick look at it when I came in."

"A uniform? One of ours?" He thought for a moment and looked around the room. "Where's Sergeant Price?"

"He went out a while ago. He said he needed a good cup of coffee. Yours sucks." He watched as the camera panned around. He kept telling himself that Price wouldn't have been stupid enough to go down there today. He knew the Arabs would be spooky if there were any uniforms around. Finally it stopped on the back of the ambulance. The view was obscured by two EMTs who were working on someone sitting on a gurney. There was a camouflaged leg sticking out. Finally one of the EMTs moved and the camera zoomed in even more. Whoever it was had his shirt off, and there were bandages on his upper chest, but the soldier was sitting upright, so it couldn't have been serious. It looked like Major Bonneville was talking to him. Then the camera zoomed in some more and focused on the wounded man. Sharp could make out the face of his friend, Jonah Price. He was looking up, saying something to the Major. How the hell had Major Bonneville gotten there so fast? "That dumb son of a bitch! Come on, Eddie."

"Where we going, Sarge?"

"Engineer compound. I've gotta tell the CSM and First Sergeant before somebody surprises them with this." As they walked down the hall Sharp had another thought and retrieved his pistol from his desk. It was the loaner he got from Grant. Two spare magazines went into his pocket and they hurried to the parking lot.

Linda Bonneville had been downtown on business for her employer when she heard shots out in the street. From the fourth floor window overlooking Main Street, she could see people scrambling away from an outdoor café. She was familiar with the place because of its reputation for decadent pastries and some rather fine coffees. As the chairs stopped falling she was able to focus in on a figure clad in an Army multi-cam uniform kneeling over another inert figure. As the person raised his head to look around she recognized him as Jonah Price. She knew there was something going to happen in relation to the mosques just down the street, but Lucas Grant had not shared any of the details with her or Sylvia Carson the evening before. The way he put it, 'the less you know, the better off you are,' was one of his stock phrases when something he was doing had the potential to go wrong and he was trying to limit the responsibility. She excused herself from the growing crowd by the window and hurried to the scene. Police were starting to arrive and cordon the area off. She dug into her hand bag to find her military ID and waved it at the first cop she saw. "He's one of my soldiers, and I'm his lawyer." The officer didn't have anyone to buck the question up to, so he shrugged and let her pass while he looked for a witness to interview. Price was truly surprised to see her. "What are you doing here, Major? I thought this was a private party."

She put her hand on his, which was still holding his gun. "Put that away. Believe me, if I knew you were planning to shoot up the area I wouldn't be here." She gestured to the two bodies. "Who are they?"

"The little girl is one of First Sergeant Harrison's. I think her name is Heath. She was with us in Darfur. She might be one of the kids he's got watching the mosque. The other mutt is one of the bad guys. He was here with the Arab from Afghanistan."

"The one from your road block? I thought he was somewhere in upstate New York. What's he doing here?"

Before he could answer there was a medical team on site asking him how bad he was hurt. Price pulled open his blouse and showed them his entrance and exit wounds. The medics didn't make any comment when they saw the holstered pistol. They helped him stand and put him on a gurney and moved him over to the ambulance. There was another team of medics checking the other casualties. Price told them to cover her up. "She's one of the good guys. Don't let the ghouls get any pictures." He could see a news crew setting up outside the perimeter the police had established.

A detective came over to talk to Price. Witnesses had said the two 'Mediterranean looking' men had started shooting first, and that Price had acted in self defense. "They also said the girl threw her computer at them when they started shooting at you. Did you know her?"

Price told him who she was, but he didn't say anything about the surveillance. That would complicate things for the moment. Besides, he wasn't sure what exactly Harrison had set up, so he could only speculate. Bonneville looked at him with raised eyebrows but said nothing. There were a few more formalities, like asking Price for his gun and if he had a concealed carry permit. Fortunately, Grant had insisted all his NCOs get one before they had deployed to Darfur, and had suggested all the women get one too after they were briefed on the potential threat. The detective also asked him about the van people had seen the second shooter run to. It had been variously described as red, black, and yellow, as well as late model, older, foreign and domestic. Price went one step further. He gave them a make and model, the right color and a partial plate number. He could have told him who the driver was and where he lived, but didn't want to give the detective any more reason to wonder what was going on. The police could verify it easily enough.

There was another disturbance across the street, and the detective excused himself to see what was going on. An older man had run out of the mosque, followed by several other gray beards. He was waving his arms and shouting something in Arabic to the police. They were trying to calm him down and get him to speak English, to no avail. "What's he saying?" Bonneville asked. She knew Price could speak the language.

"Nothing good. He's saying that the Imam and his son are dead upstairs in the mosque. He keeps saying 'slaughtered', so it must be messy. That must be what the red van was doing, and these two guys were just keeping an eye out." He was about to tell her to let Grant know what was going on when there was a rumble of thunder in the distance. They both looked up at the cloudless sky. "That was an explosion," Price said. "You better let the CSM know something's going on." She turned and walked away to use her phone just as another explosion, this time closer, sounded.

Sharp pulled up to the exit and was surprised to see the gates closed on both sides. He was two cars back, and could see the driver arguing with the gate guard. There seemed to be about fifty people outside the gate, blocking the driveway. He couldn't make out the chanting, but he knew it wasn't good. He left Robinson in the truck and walked to the head of the line, intending to tell the guard to just route everyone out the aircraft maintenance gate on the other side. It was more remote with less passing traffic, thus less attractive for making a scene. He was rapping on the roof of the arguing driver's car when the crowd suddenly quieted down. He looked around and could see individual figures working their way back away from the gate. The rest of the crowd seemed to be staring at something. Sharp stepped forward to see what was going on. There was an Arab kid, maybe thirteen or fourteen, walking towards the gate. He was wearing a prayer cap, and had an oversized book bag. He had something connected to the bag in his outstretched hand.

Sharp knew what it was instantly. He ducked back behind the concrete forms that separated the shack from the street. "Bomb! Bomb! Get down! Get down!" He looked over his shoulder to see Robinson standing on the far side of the car. He barely had time to wave him down when the back pack exploded. Sharp felt a hot wave flood over him, and the barrier he was behind rocked slightly. There must have been a hell of a lot of explosives in that pack. The prefabricated aluminum and glass guard shack was twisted off its foundation and pretty much smashed. One guard, the one who had been arguing with the first driver, was moaning. He had been catapulted over the car, which was lying on its side. The second guard was laying some distance away. He must have stepped out of the shack just as the blast occurred. He had been blown off his feet and decapitated. Out in the driveway there was a black blast pattern around the spot where the kid had been standing. There was no body, and Sharp guessed that the parts of him that weren't atomized would be scattered all over the area. Down by the sidewalk there were a number of casualties, all protesters. The bastards didn't have the decency to tell their own people to get out of the way. They just ran off and let them take their chances. He was pulling his cell phone out to call 911 when there was another blast from somewhere in the distance. Looking in that direction, he could see the plume of black and gray smoke rising to the west. Robinson was by his side. "You OK, Sarge?"

"Yeah, Eddie, I'm fine." More soldiers were running out the gate to see what was going on and to help the injured. They were even moving among the protestors, doing what they could. Sharp made his 911 call and gave what information he could.

"Where do you think that second one was, Sarge?"

"That was down at the Engineer facility, Eddie. There's plenty of help here. We better get down there."

"That truck ain't going anywhere, Sarge. You got two flats and a stove in windshield. We better take my car." Before they could get very far a State Police car came from the aviation entrance, lights and siren going. The trooper skewed his car around and blocked the entrance. Once he got out of his car he ordered everyone to stay where they were. This was a crime scene, and no one could leave until they were interviewed. Sharp tried to argue with him that he had to get to the other site. The Trooper told him 'no'. "We've already got people heading to that location. They don't need another tourist. There's bad stuff happening all over town today so let's find out what's happening here. What did you see?"

Shabaab had switched vehicles with another resident of the apartment building he was staying at. The kid was happy as hell to have the van to use for a few days, and parked it behind the house so he could trick it out for a party wagon for the next day. Sharif and Khan helped Shabaab carry some duffel bags down and store them in the car, and then they all piled into the kid's Volvo and headed for a fast food joint that looked at one of the targets across an open parking lot. Enroute Sharif asked what was in the bags. There was ammunition, a couple of rifles and some emergency supplies. "If we're going up to that cabin we're gonna need some food and other crap. I already told your people to meet us up there tomorrow"

"Why tomorrow, why not tonight?"

"The original plan was for them to take out the rest of the targets tonight. Raisouli fucked that up when he got rid of the AKs we had at the mosque. Good thing he didn't find the back packs. I told them to lay low tonight. We don't want too many people driving around in the woods tonight."

"And then what?" Khan asked.

"It's quite simple, Mehmet Atta," Sharif answered. After a few days they will think we have all gone to ground and their diligence will wane. We can sit in our sanctuary, restore our strength, and plan for the successful completion of our mission."

Shabaab grinned into the mirror at Sharif. "Yeah, they won't expect us to be back so soon, but I want that doctor bitch. I'm gonna do her real slow."

"And you may have her, Shabaab X, I give her to you as a gift, and as your right for all your planning. Khan, would you like the one you met at the café?"

"I would prefer another target, Ali Alawa. That one, the one called Price, is cursed. I have been near him three times now, and each time I have come close to paradise. I do not want to tempt fate."

They never made it to the parking lot. The explosion was almost a quarter hour early and they were still several blocks away. Sharif had Shabaab turn around and go to the other target. That explosion came early too.

After the explosions Sharif ordered they be driven north. They had all they needed for now in the car, and he explained to Shabaab that there would be more supplies stockpiled at their destination. Khan was skeptical, not believing Sharif had any idea of what they would find at Raisouli's cabin, but he kept silent. Sharif had settled into a strange mood of self satisfaction as soon as they had traveled several miles. The further north they went, the more confident he seemed. Just over two hours later they travelled through a high mountain pass, Shabaab called it a 'notch', a term Khan was totally unfamiliar with. The land past it changed in to some gently rolling farm lands with just a hint of high ground along the horizon. Sharif had them turn off the highway and drive into a small town with a biblical sounding name. It was close to the supper hour, and he decided they should rest for a while. He consulted a small notebook that Khan had not noticed before. From it he gave directions for several turns until they came to a remote cottage surrounded by tall pines. The name on the mail box was obscured, but Sharif said it was the home of a Lebanese sleeper agent who would respond to a short series of meaningless phrases. Sharif seemed to have them written in his notebook. This must be more fruit from the interrogation and death of the 'coordinator' back in Libya. Sharif exited the car alone and told his companions to wait. The door was answered by a stout woman shrouded in a *hajib*. Evidently, Khan thought to himself, having a woman answer the door to strangers was not frowned upon by Muslims here. Sharif waited by the open door as the woman disappeared inside. Soon a man was standing there. After what seemed like a brief, pleasant conversation Sharif turned and waved his companions to join him. Inside he introduced their host. "This is Abdul Mutallab, a Lebanese. He owns a small jewelry store locally and has consented to entertain and feed us during our journey." There were short niceties and bows all around. Khan noticed that the Lebanese was more formal with Shabaab than with the rest of them. He seemed to instinctively recognize that the man was a criminal and would not be welcomed in his home if it were not for the stranger with one of the phrases he had to memorize so long ago and the Muslim custom of hospitality.

There had been a simple but nourishing meal, after which tea was offered under some fruit trees in a small orchard. There was small talk, but no real effort at learning anything about each other. Khan noticed that Sharif was constantly checking his watch, and while the host was absent asking his wife to make more tea, he asked what he was waiting for.

"Our Mexican friend is overdue. I had expected he would have been waiting for us. This is starting to put our schedule seriously behind. I had hoped to begin the next leg of our journey before dark. Now we will have to hope our next stop is as easy to find in the dark."

It was late afternoon before everyone had been released from their area of their respective incidents, as the police were calling them, but they still weren't free to go. Federal authorities had swooped in as soon as possible and started taking over the investigations. Everyone found themselves giving their statements two or three times. Price had a brief respite when the ambulance crew decided his wound needed more attention than they could give him on the spot. Major Bonneville had stayed with him. She had tried to call Grant several times but had trouble getting a signal. Finally, by the time Price had been treated she got a call from Grant. He figured she would have heard about the explosions and didn't want her to worry. He was surprised to hear she had been downtown and was now with Price. He told her that as soon as Price was settled in to come to the State Headquarters. "Use the aviation gate. You'll never get in the front way."

Price was through the Emergency Room and into a semi-private room for observation when the mass casualty influx started, and he was temporarily forgotten until one of the feds started looking for the soldier who was involved in the café shooting. By the time FBI Special Agent Rawlins went looking for him, Price had started to argue his way out of the hospital. Major Sylvia Carson, who had been called in because of her military trauma experience, heard Price's voice and came to his rescue. She decreed they needed space for the influx of trauma patients, and he could go home to recuperate. She gave him her car keys and sent him on his way. "I'll call the Sergeant Major when I need a ride out of here." The thought of her regular beau, the cardiac surgeon, was banished from her mind. She found all the confusion and excitement to be stimulating, and the thought of the danger she might be in gave her an involuntary shudder. The surgeon was settled, successful, and, when he wasn't taking his nurse on business trips, pretty reliable.

Grant was dangerous to be around, and it was turning her on more and more.

General Cabot had decided that if he had to wait he would prefer to do it at his own headquarters, and informed the investigators he was taking his people with him. There was little they could add to the narrative anyway, and the crowd of protestors would be a better source. Several of them were dead from the blast, and more were injured and adding to the confusion of the local emergency room. Many had fled the scene as soon as they could, and the feds were trying to collect any security camera data to see if they could identify the persons Grant said he had seen running away before the blast. One agent confided that they were having the same problems at the first blast site, and that several of the witnesses there had also claimed to have seen several men running away before the explosion. There was a reluctance to publicly identify the incidents as 'coordinated' in the press briefings, but privately that was the operative theory.

Grant was puzzled by the timing of the attacks. If they had waited a few minutes, they could have caught the lunch crowd streaming out of both sites. Even if the timing had been off so that the blasts were not simultaneous, there would have been enough traffic to make it worthwhile. Sharp was willing to offer an opinion. "Whoever was putting the first kid out there may have had his watch stop. He panicked and sent the kid out instead of waiting, and the second one took his cue from the first one."

"Mighty thin, Dave. That calls for either a lot of speculation or a real incompetent bunch of terrorists."

"Well, from what I've seen so far, I'll speculate they're not the sharpest tools in the drawer, but I'll bet at some point they're gonna get some adult supervision and get better at it."

So far no one had suggested any tie in with the incidents with Sharp, Bonneville or Carson. It was obvious that none of these investigators had been briefed by military intelligence or Homeland Security about the threat to the members of the 289th. Grant wondered if General Vaughn or Colonel Ashley would see fit to advise them. When he dropped their names to the Senior Agent he was given a non-committal brush off.

Back at the State Reservation he gathered everyone together in the room Ashley was set up in. Captain Connaught received a cool answer when she asked about the missing Sergeant Price. When she pressed for information Sharp tore into her. He didn't care for anyone leading on his friend for any reason, but especially not when he was trying to recover from multiple concussions. Sharp told her exactly what he thought of her using his friend so that she could spy on his friends. Everyone expected her to pull rank and shout Sharp down, or at least try to. It was more of a surprise when she started to tear up and ran from the room.

"That's carrying it a little too far," Sharp said as the door closed behind her.

"Let it go, Dave. She was only doing her job. Yell at Vaughn when he gets here if you want to." Grant told him.

Ashley insisted on hearing as much information as he could so he could formulate a report for General Vaughn. They cooperated to a point, but made him work for a lot of the information. One sticking point was what Price had been doing downtown to trigger the shooting. Major Bonneville provided what information she could, but it was all secondhand and she hadn't spent a lot of time quizzing Price due to his injuries. "Besides." She said, "we were interrupted when they came out of the mosque wailing that their Imam had been killed. By the time that little drama had played out, cops were running over there and Sergeant Price was whisked away by the ambulance. If you want any more information you'll have to go up to the hospital and ask Price yourself."

"Ask me what?" came a voice from the doorway. Price was standing there looking pale as a sheet still wearing his bloody uniform. The blood on his bandages looked fresh. Grant led him to a chair before he fell over. Sharp was the first one to talk to him. "Pricey, what the fuck are you doing here? You look like shit." Ashley tried to interrupt. "I need to speak to him."

"The hell you do, we need to get him back to the hospital." He turned to Price. "How did you get here?"

"I talked Doc Carson into letting me go. She even let me take her car, but she made me put a rubber sheet over the seat."

"Price, for Christ's sake look at you! You probably ripped open whatever they did to you up there and you can barely hold your head up. You belong in the hospital."

"Dave's right, Jonah," Grant added. "You should have stayed there. What the hell was Carson thinking?"

"Don't blame her, Luke. The place was a fucking zoo, and I thought I could do more good with you guys."

Sharp didn't let go. "Price, for the love of God will you use your head for a change? You need to be in the hospital and let them take care of you." Sharp was talking to an empty chair. Price had passed out and fell to the floor. Grant and Sharp stepped over him and rolled him over to his back. His wound was bleeding and Grant sent Robinson to look for a first aid kit and a stretcher. He knew there was one in the training aid room. When he returned Grant took two pressure bandages and did his best to cover the wounds. Then they placed him on the stretcher and carried him out and placed him in the bed of Grant's truck.

"Shouldn't we get an ambulance," Sharp asked?

"They're probably still busy. This'll be faster. Get in with him and don't let him flop around too much."

They made good time to the hospital. Not worrying about speed limits, stop signs or traffic signals. The police were too busy in other areas to be concerned with such minor matters anyway. Grant pulled up to the Emergency Room Ambulance door and backed up. A big security guard came out to tell him he had to move, but Grant ignored him. They dropped the tail gate and took the litter out and went through the automatic doors. The guard made the mistake of trying to block them. Sharp just hunched his shoulders and knocked him over. Sharp looked down at him. "Don't do that again," was all he said. Inside the Receiving area they put the stretcher on top of a gurney. Sharp saw Major Carson talking to a nurse and he angled the gurney towards her. When she saw him coming she got a look of surprise on her face. It turned to a smile when she saw Grant, and then one of concern when she saw the bloody bandages and recognized Price. "Oh my God!" she blurted out as she called for help to get him into an examining room.

"What the fuck is wrong with you, lady? You gave him your car?"

Grant pulled Sharp back and led him back to the door. "Price is in good hands now. Let's get out of here before we have any more problems." The security guard was on his feet and started to block their path. He saw the look on Sharp's face and stepped back.

Twenty minutes later Sylvia Carson came out of Price's examining room. He had been stabilized (again) and they had started IV fluids to stave off the signs of shock. They were waiting for a room to be assigned, and Carson gave specific orders that if he couldn't be placed in a private room, he was not to be placed with any of the casualties from the bombings. When asked why she explained that he had been shot by one of the people who had planned the bombings, and he deserved better. A nursing supervisor made note of the comment: she didn't like Carson anyway, so she'd be happy to report the remark to the equal opportunity people.

Carson looked around for Grant in the waiting room. He was gone. She told herself it probably wouldn't be a good idea to call for a ride now.

Grant headed his truck back down town. "What's next, Boss?" Sharp asked.

"I want to get a look inside that mosque. You and Price missed something yesterday, and I'll bet all those feds down there will miss it too?"

"Miss what?"

"I don't know, Dave. It seems like we're the only ones who know what this is all about, and if Vaughn or Ashley isn't going to tell anybody else they're just going to keep going around in circles trying to figure out what it all means. I want to drop a few hints."

The FBI and other alphabet agencies had lights set up so they could continue their investigation into the night. Grant parked his truck right by the police tape and told the local cop they were delivering some equipment for the Agent in Charge. The cop waved them through and pointed them towards the mosque.

"Why this guy, Luke? Can't we go to one of the other sites and talk to them?"

"This one was closer."

Grant stepped into the entrance of the mosque and asked for the lead agent. Before they could get an answer a voice called down from somewhere overhead. Grant looked up and saw Vaughn at the top of the stairs. He was in full uniform. "You saved me the trouble of calling for you, Sergeant Major. Come up here and help Agent Lindsay fill in the blanks. He doesn't believe a bunch of Sergeants could have fucked up his life so badly."

Grant and Sharp climbed the stairs. Vaughn directed them into the room where the bodies of Naseer Raisouli and his son still lay on the floor. The kid was on his back, looking up at the ceiling with wide, unbelieving eyes. Grant noted the slashed throat and the deep gash on the boy's right wrist. The older man was face down across his mid section. He had been shot in the side of the head, just behind the ear. "We think this was a case of cleaning up loose ends," Agent Lindsay opined. Vaughn looked at the two Sergeants. "What do you think?"

"Anything I have is second hand or speculation," Grant answered.

"How about you, Sergeant Sharp?"

Sharp recognized both of them. "I don't now who the kid is, but I saw him yesterday. He was one of the two watching the hanger." That was news to Vaughn. "I guess your buddy Ashley forgot to mention it to you."

"That would have been nice. Go on."

"Well, me and Price followed them here and saw them meet another guy, big, black . . ."

"Shabaab X." Grant offered. Vaughn just gave him an annoyed look.

". . . and saw them leave in a red panel van with him."

"Where did they go?"

"No idea. At the time I was on foot, and by the time Price caught up to me with some wheels they were long gone."

Grant took out a notebook and copied something. He ripped the page out and handed it to Vaughn. "He's a parolee. This is where the van is registered to."

Vaughn looked at it and passed it to Lindsay without a word. He then made a gesture for Sharp to continue.

"Me and Price came back here and checked out the basement, that's where we found the AK's."

"There are weapons in the building? Where?" Lindsay asked.

"They're gone now. When the older guy," Sharp pointed at the bodies," caught us poking around he helped us load about a dozen rifles, ammo and magazines. They're back at the NCO Academy arms room right now." He looked at Vaughn. "I guess Ashley didn't bother to mention that, either."

"I need to see those weapons," Lindsay demanded. Vaughn waved him off. "Don't worry about them, Agent. If these men have them they're as good as in custody of Homeland Security." He turned to look at Sharp. "What I want to know is why you didn't take the explosives too."

"We didn't find any explosives here. We only checked a couple of rooms in the basement. We got out of here once we secured the weapons. We didn't have any authority to be here and we thought we had done well enough with them."

"In for a penny, in for a pound, Sergeant Sharp. The last room in the basement has a couple of the back packs loaded with Semtex and a detonator. It looks like that's where they had the ones they used today stored."

"They had no way of knowing that, Vaughn."

"That's 'General Vaughn" Sergeant Major. I don't want to have to tell you again. And I wasn't making an accusation against Sharp, merely an observation. Just securing the weapons probably saved a lot of lives today. Witnesses all agree that several men ran from both sites just before the blasts. It's a pretty good bet that if they had AKs there would have been a lot more victims. You did good, Sergeant Sharp. I may have to recommend you and Sergeant Price for a commendation, unless I decide to Court Martial you all first."

Lindsay was getting insistent. "I want to see those weapons and get statements from him and this Sergeant Price!"

Vaughn turned on him with a snarl. "Lindsay, whether you like it or not, I'm calling the shots here, so fuck off. If you want to do something useful go find this guy Shabaab's parole officer, get his address, and secure it." He tried to protest. Vaughn ignored him and took out his phone. He tapped a few buttons and put the phone on speaker.

Agent Lindsay recognized the voice of his director when he answered. Vaughn didn't even bother to introduce himself, he just started right in. "Director, one of your agents here seems to want to keep his head stuck up his ass. Would you mind telling him, once and for all, what his place is on the food chain and who the predator is?"

The director obviously recognized Vaughn's voice, and he also apparently knew his place on the food chain. He asked Agent Lindsay one simple question: "Lindsay, do I have to explain this to you?"

"No, Sir, Mr. Director, I know what I have to do."

"Satisfied, General?"

"For now. I'll call if there are any more issues with your people."

Vaughn repeated his instructions to Lindsay, and added that he was to report to Colonel Ashley, who would assume the mantle of 'Incident Commander.' He was also to keep Grant informed of anything they found at the Shabaab address. He left the room without taking any questions.

"Your General is a son of a bitch."

"He's not mine, and I don't think he's a general. When are you going to Shabaab's?"

"As soon as I verify the address and get a warrant."

Grant wrote down his number and handed it to him. "Call me when you've got it set up. I want to be there."

"You think he'll be willing to talk to you?"

"I could care less about some wannabe tough guy. I want the guy he's traveling with."

"Who is he?"

"I really don't know, but he's been a pain in the ass ever since Sergeant Price met him in Afghanistan. Some of the important people seem to think he had something to do with Osama bin Laden. They probably didn't bother to tell you he's got a hit list they've been trying to work their way through for a couple of days now." He told the agent about the shooting at the training area with Sharp, as well as the prowlers at Bonneville's and the home invader that Carson killed. "They seem to be ramping up their efforts now that the new guy is here. I'm going to end it."

"We want to take them alive."

"I want him alive too, Agent Lindsay. He's been traveling with another rag head who doesn't like me. That one used to be important in the Janjaweed in Darfur before we screwed up his plans. I've missed a couple of chances to kill him. I'm not going to miss another."

Grant left the room with Sharp. He had seen and heard enough and had his own plans to make. Lindsay watched them go, wondering who the fuck were these people, and how did he get stuck with them?

Grant stopped Sharp outside the building. He looked around to make sure there were no unwelcome ears, and asked Sharp what he had.

"What do you mean, Luke?"

"When Vaughn was having that little cluster fuck on the phone you took something off the desk. What was it?"

Sharp took a folded map out of his cargo pocket. It was U.S. Geodetic Survey map folded up with the northern portion of New Hampshire above the Connecticut Lakes exposed. There was also a folded legal paper, a deed, attached to it. "Nobody was paying any attention to this, Luke, and I have a thing for maps. I thought it would make a good souvenir." Grant took it from him and looked at the area that was highlighted. A red line seemed to mark an old logging road running close to the border. There were GPS coordinates printed in green ink on the front of the deed. Grant did a quick translation to the coordinates on the paper map. "Souvenir my ass. This is pretty close to the border. Hell, it might even be in Canada."

"The deed says it belonged to the dead guy. I thought I might take a look at it after all this is over."

"Through a rifle scope?" Grant knew what his friend was thinking. This was probably the training camp for the local *Jihadists*. Sharp was planning his own revenge. "You won't be going alone." Grant looked at his watch. "I'll bet these guys are already on their way up there, but let's see what the feds come up with at this guy Shabaab's place, then we'll see what we can find up north."

"I can get some people together and try to get there ahead of him."

Grant shook his head. "No, they probably have an eight hour head start if they left right after the bombings. Even if their planning is as bad as it has been, they could have been there by dark. Even if they didn't, we don't need you stumbling around in the dark trying to find them. There are a lot of camps up in those old paper company tracts, and I'll bet most of them have some kind of a weapon. You go up there in face paint and body armor you could end up getting shot at by a friendly. Let's see if we can get Ashley to get a couple of drones up there to narrow things down."

CHAPTER FIFTEEN

T HE MEXICAN FINALLY ARRIVED AT the safe house before the sun went down. Sharif allowed Shabaab the pleasure of berating the man for his incompetence. Sharif had long ago come to realize the animosity between the criminals of both the black and the Hispanic community, and saw a value in keeping it alive. Shabaab came back with a disgusted look on his face. "This idiot stopped off on the way to arrange for his girlfriend to come up and join him at his RV. He had to find a place to wire her some money, and then he had to wait to make sure the dumb bitch picked it up all right. I'm gonna keep this son of a bitch on a short leash. He might have told her anything."

"Don't worry, my friend. I will let you deal with him when the time is right. For now, we need him and his vehicle to accompany us. There may be a need for a diversion, and a burning vehicle with a body in it seems to be a popular theme in American crime dramas. For now, prepare both vehicles for the next leg. Make certain your new found friend has sufficient fuel. I would hate to think that he sent his operational funds to some piece of fluff."

Shabaab didn't ask the Mexican to check. He took the keys and looked at the gauge himself. As Sharif suspected, the tank was almost empty. When the Mexican protested he needed more money, Shabaab pushed him down and searched his pockets. He still had a small wad of bills, and Shabaab took them. "I'll take care of your finances, amigo. You don't seem to understand what's going on here."

Khan intervened before the men started shooting at each other. Sharif joined and made a new division of forces. "I was planning to have our tardy friend follow us on the next leg, but now it would be best if he had a passenger. Khan, you ride with Shabaab, and I will follow." Sharif was pleased with the apparent dislike all his subordinates had developed for each other. This would keep them from forming any conspiracies against him.

Shabaab led the two car caravan into the woods and through a series of logging roads. Periodically he had to stop and check his map, and twice he got out of his car to find a better signal on his cell phone navigation system. Once he got it by standing on the roof. "There ain't much coverage up here, and the signal goes in and out, especially on this cheap ass phone."

"Can you find the cabin in the dark?" Sharif asked.

"I'll find it. It's just a matter of finding the right dirt road to bounce down. I came up here with Naseer Raisouli once and he got totally lost for a couple of hours. His phone is even cheaper than mine. He got so lost that to his dying day he swore that the cabin was in Canada."

"Are you certain it's not?"

"I'm pretty fucking sure. They cleared about fifty yards of trees and brush on either side of the line, and there are steel gates on all the roads except the ones that the border guards work at. I even heard they got some 'people sniffers' planted so they'll know if anyone is in the area. You'd know it if you crossed into Canada."

"'People sniffers'?" Khan asked.

"I think he means a seismic detector. The Americans have been enamored of them for many years."

Shabaab compared the coordinates he was getting on the GPS with his map. He muttered to himself as his fingers wandered across the paper. "I found it! We should have taken the last side road to the left."

"Road? That little trail about two miles back? That hardly qualifies as a road." Sharif said.

"These roads were originally made by oxen dragging timber and then heavy trucks in all kinds of weather. They were not made for cars.

It will be a rough ride, but it isn't too bad. I've made the trip a couple of times. We'll be there in less than a half hour."

"Where is the border from here?" Khan asked.

Shabaab looked at the map and turned around, pointing with his left hand. "Keep up this road for a couple of miles. There's a gate, then the clearing, and you're in Canada. There's a road just like it going up for a mile or so from the cabin. Before all the border security the lumber trucks used to cross over all the time. All anybody cared about back then was the money they got for the wood."

They got in their cars and turned around. Sure enough, just about two miles back they found the road. As Shabaab said, it was a rough ride, but Khan didn't consider it much worse than some of the mountain trails he had traveled in Tora Bora in the early days of the Afghan war. At least this place didn't have helicopters and drones looking for them, although with the tall trees and the canopy, he doubted they would be easy to find. The cabin was close, but the travel time seemed like an eternity due to the bouncing of the vehicles. As they pulled up to a small wooden shack everyone made a bee line for the trees to empty aching bladders. Sharif gave orders for their supplies to be unloaded and brought inside. He walked around the building and examined every facet of it, as well as the surrounding terrain. There was an out building, obviously the toilet facilities, and another small structure that looked like a dog house. He peered inside and found a generator. It was a compact model that didn't have much of a noise signature, and he wondered if it would power more than a few light bulbs. Shabaab caught up to him and explained it was for the several lights and to power the pump for the well, but only during cloudy weather and at night. He stepped back and pointed up at a small array of solar panels on the roof. That was what provided the main power. The small generator ran off propane tanks, and a small one would only keep it running for about 36 hours, but it was enough to give them a week of intermittent use. For a camp site, they were probably a good idea, but Sharif considered them a serious risk. Aerial observation could not possibly miss them, even if the pilot were not looking too hard.

There were several paths leading into the woods from the cabin. Strangely, they were all marked with signs telling what one would find if they ventured down them. One said 'Swimming'; another was 'Picnic Area", and the last said "Nature Trail'. Odd, Sharif thought. You would expect them to know what was down the path and not have a need to label it. He would have to ask Shabaab about them.

Inside the house was surprisingly neat and comfortable. There were two bedrooms in the back, off a main room that served as kitchen, dining room and living room. When Sharif stopped thinking of a vacation home and remembered that this was for people who wanted to enjoy nature without the discomfort of sleeping in a tent on the ground he began to recognize the appeal. He had to admit it was better than some of the tent camps he had endured in Darfur. At least the toilet was enclosed, even if it was a short distance away.

Khan was not convinced this was a good place to be. The trees were much too close and there were too few windows. It was an easy place to approach unseen and hard place to defend. He was also concerned the Americans already knew where they were. They would have investigated Raisouli's background and his holdings by now. Such a place had to be recorded somewhere.

Shabaab tried to reassure him with the history of the camp lease. Over the years the lumber companies had changed hands many times, and their rules on recording the lease holders for the camps varied. They were usually granted for long periods of time, and some were even taken out, divided into smaller holdings, and re-leased by brokers. It was not uncommon for a family to have one of these sites for twenty, forty or sixty years, pass the lease holding through a will, or assign it to someone else. There was also the question of improvements to the sites. Some were originally leased with out-buildings the lumber companies no longer needed. The rest were bare sites, with no 'amenities', as they were called. Over the years, much of the improvements were done illegally, without permits or records, and in the frequent comings and goings of the large land owners, no one kept track of who was doing what. Ownership, or tenancy, was a very changeable state.

Shabaab confided that he had anticipated the authorities would find out about Naseer Raisouli and his love of the outdoors. He had encouraged the belief that the property was actually in Canada, and had taken steps to misdirect Raisouli if he tried to locate it by either a map search or with a GPS. He had transposed several of the numbers of the coordinates that were recorded so that at least one axis would be correct. The other could be explained away as 'human error' or some such. Raisouli was willing to accept any explanation that confirmed his belief that he was in Canada.

"Then how did you find it, Shabaab? Aren't all the numbers copied wrong?"

"I'm smarter than that. I made sure that I kept the right numbers. I could see the potential for this place the first time I saw it. If those fools ever lighten up and open the borders up like they're supposed to, this will be one sweet set up for bringing merchandise over the border. I might even be willing to go into business with the Mexican here."

The Mexican didn't respond. He didn't like these Arabs or the *Negro*, but they paid well and he was willing to ignore them. He had also made it a point not to share his name with them. He considered their methods to be amateurish and certain to get them caught. That cluster fuck in Concord when they killed the old guy and his kid was all over the news as he was driving to meet them. It was sloppy and had no point. His own organization would have done it differently. The end result would have been the same, two dead bodies, but it would have sent more of a terror message to anyone foolish enough to get in their way. He lay down on the couch to nap until some kind of a dinner had been prepared. He was not about to cook for these *idiotas* too.

As expected, Lindsay called with details of the planned raid. They had established surveillance on the building, a six apartment flop house in a residential area of the city. There was some activity inside, but they weren't certain which unit belonged to Shabaab. The registered owner of the building was also a resident, and he had an Arabic name, so prudence dictated they not call him. The current plan was once they had the warrant in hand they would wait until just before daylight, when it would be safe to assume all the residents were asleep. Then they would swoop in and take down the entire building and secure all the occupants. The neighborhood was too densely packed to try to go in and evacuate the neighbors without tipping off the targets, so this was the best plan they could come up with. Grant told him that he and Sharp would meet them at his designated assembly area several blocks from the site of the raid. He also informed that they would be 'suitably dressed and equipped'. Lindsay didn't bother to ask what that meant. He knew they would show up in body armor and fully armed.

The assembly point was a small church community center that had seen better days. Grant and Sharp appeared in full body armor and carrying weapons. Lindsay laid out the plan and let the tactical commander explain the procedure. He made it a point to tell Grant and Sharp that, no matter what they were thinking, they would not take part in the entry. They would have to content themselves with watching from the sidelines. Sharp answered for both of them. "We didn't come here to play, but we've seen shit like this go bad really fast. Just consider us your back-up plan."

"I'll stick to my own back-up plan. You two stay out of the way."

The teams loaded into their vehicles and drove off to the target area by different routes. The idea was to approach from different direction, secure the perimeter, and then have the assault teams pull up to the front of the building and make a quick, forceful entry. The idea was to surprise all the occupants and take everybody down before they could gather their wits and weapons to resist. On paper it seemed like a good plan.

Grant was surprised to see FBI Agent Rawlins in the vehicle he was assigned to. He was there as an observer from the local office, and was not part of the large team that had responded to the 'incidents'. They nodded at each other, but didn't speak.

They were set up about half a block from the target building. While Grant watched through his binoculars with some professional interest as the perimeter teams made their way through the streets and back yards to isolate the area, Sharp was more interested in the surrounding buildings. He thought the feds were suffering from target fixation and ignoring potential trouble spots in the neighborhood. The assault commander chose to ignore him. Sharp studied each building intently, looking for something that could turn into a problem.

He thought he found something, and pointed it out to Grant. The next building down from the target was an almost identical structure, probably built at the same time by the same contractor. The first story had oversized windows. And the one facing the target building had a green banner hanging in it, with what looked like Arabic scrawl on it. Someone had pulled a corner of the banner back and quickly let it go. He pointed it out, but could tell that Grant hadn't seen it. He pointed it out again.

"You sure, Dave?"

"I'm sure. Somebody over there looked out and saw the feds going down that alley. We better let Lindsay know."

Grant was explaining what Sharp had seen to Rawlins, who had a radio and was monitoring what was going on. He nodded and called Lindsay. Before he got a reply, Sharp saw the banner pulled back again, and a rifle barrel was pushed out, breaking the window. Before he could say anything there was a burst of fire. An automatic rifle was shooting at the backs of the agents who were securing the area. At almost the same time, more rifle fire could be heard coming from the back of the house. The raid had failed before it got started.

The assault team was rolling up to the front of the building as the firing started. The shooter in the neighboring house switched his fire towards them. He was wide of the mark, but it forced the agents to take cover behind their vehicle, unable to return accurate fire. One agent had to be dragged back. It looked like he was hit in the leg.

Sharp didn't hesitate. Without a word he jacked a round into the chamber of his M16A2 rifle and sprinted down the street. Grant was ten steps behind him by the time he realized what Sharp was doing. The shooter didn't see Sharp until he was almost to the FBI van in the street. He must have been in the middle of a very slow magazine change, because Sharp closed the distance even more and fired a burst into him. There was no more fire from the window. Grant had run down on the far side of the van and grabbed one of the agents by his harness. "We've got that one, you guys get in there. The agent shook himself out of his daze and started barking orders to his team. Except for the wounded man, they were up and crashed the front door. The shooting had also stopped from the rear, but sounds of resistance were coming from inside now. There were some single shots, answered by bursts of automatic fire, then shouts of 'Get down, Get down!' Out back, the sentry who had fired on the rear security team had fired wildly and hit one agent across the back of his vest. The man in front of him had been armed with a Remington 870 shotgun loaded with breaching rounds. This was a compressed metal powder slug that would tear out hinges and locks and disintegrate without over-penetrating into the room. He had responded instinctively and returned fire. The frangible slug was terribly effective on the human body.

Sharp flattened himself against the wall under the window and waited for Grant to join him. He pointed to a trash can a few feet away, and Grant pulled it over. Sharp climbed on it, crouched under the window and reached up to pull the green banner down. It wasn't fastened very securely and came right out. Sharp popped up, his rifle thrust into the room, looking for his target. In the dim glow of a night light he could see a body sprawled on its back, feet towards the window. All he had on were his socks and a pair of boxer shorts. His chest was torn up by the 5.56mm NATO rounds Sharp had inserted into him. He used the hand guard of his rifle to brush away any broken glass left in the casing and climbed into the room. There was a sickly sweet smell of burning marijuana in the room. A lit joint was sitting in an ashtray by the bed. There was a figure on the bed hiding behind a sheet, just the top of the head visible. Grant was climbing in the window behind him as he grabbed the sheet and pulled it away. There was a dazed, naked girl cowering in the corner, trying to get as far away from Sharp as she could while trying to cover herself up. There was no identifying the sounds she was making. Grant came up along side him and told him the rest of the room was clear.

"What about her?" Sharp asked.

"Let her cover up with the sheet and bring her outside." He looked down at the smoking joint. "I'll bet she didn't count on getting this high tonight."

The agents went through the building room to room. There was some resistance, but in each case it was rapidly and violently dealt with. There was liberal use of flash-bang grenades to disorient anyone behind a locked door, and smoke filled the hallways. The last room on the top floor had been particularly challenging. Instead of the cheap hollow wooden door of the other apartments, this one was steel plated. One of the agents readied his shotgun with a breaching round when his partner stopped him. "Smell that?" There was a strong chemical odor in the hall. Both agents backed off and called for a battering ram to force the door.

While that was playing out, the remaining agents searched the rest of the building and cleared everyone out who was still ambulatory. Four of the occupants were dead in the hallways or in their rooms, the result of misguided attempts to resist. Each had been grasping a weapon when they died. Most of the occupants appeared to be young men of Mediterranean or African extraction. A couple more looked like your typical, older gang bangers. They were probably ex-convict acquaintances of Shabaab. Once the building had been cleared the agents who had entered the last room reappeared. The room on the top floor had been turned into a methamphetamine lab, and the agents were glad that all of the shooting had taken place on the first two floors.

When they saw the woman prisoner several agents were dispatched to secure the next building. There was no resistance and most of the occupants responded to voice commands before the agents had to resort to more violent methods. Another dozen young people were rounded up and brought outside. The decision was made to keep them separate from the drug house.

One of the youths from the first house, he admitted to being Syrian, soiled himself while he was kneeling in the street. He began crying. One of the older men started to curse him and told him to shut up. Sharp had turned the girl over to an FBI agent and walked over to the tough guy. "Can I have a few minutes with big mouth here before you haul him off?" There was no answer from the feds. The tough guy looked at Sharp and spit at him. "You can't do nothing' to me, mutha fucka. Just read me my rights and call my lawyer." Sharp kneeled down in front of him. He could tell the man was getting ready to spit again, so he lowered is rifle barrel and jammed it into his crotch, He could tell by the reaction that he had found the right spot. "Spit at me again and I might have an accident." The man's eyes grew round. Sharp could see every vein in them. "I need some information, and I think you might be the guy to tell me."

"I don't know nuthin'. And you wouldn't be so tough if my hands were free."

"Don't be so quick to judge. Maybe it would help if I did have that nice man with the badge take off your cuffs, then we could talk like civilized people." The idea of having his handcuffs removed suddenly didn't sound like a good idea.

"Where's Shabaab?" He leaned into his rifle a little harder. It had an immediate effect. Grant moved closer to shield what was happening. There was no answer, but Sharp could tell it was a struggle for the man to keep quiet. Grant flicked open his knife and passed it over Sharp's shoulder. "Here, this might work better." That was all it took. The man spilled his guts about Shabaab. He didn't know where he was, but he did know he had changed vehicles, and pointed out where the kid who swapped for the van lived. It was the kid with the dope and the AK that Sharp had killed. When Sharp and Grant were done with him they called an agent over to take custody of him. As soon as he was in federal custody and moving away he found his courage again. "You can't use any of that shit; you didn't give me my rights."

Sharp walked back over to him. Big mouth tried to scurry behind the agent that was leading him. Sharp grabbed him by the chin and turned his face to him. "I'm not a cop, dickhead. You don't have any rights with me. But if they set bail, I may pay it for you, just to find out how tough you really are." The man's eyes went wide again. As he walked away with Grant he was chuckling to himself. "You know. Luke, I kind of enjoyed that. I might just pay that fucker's bail." It was loud enough for everyone to hear.

FBI Agent Rawlins wanted to know what the prisoner had told Sharp. He didn't want to share the information, but Grant told him to. "If we're going after these guys we may need somebody with a badge around to run interference."

Sharp gave him the rundown. He started with the map he took from Raisouli's desk and added the information that he had just received that Shabaab and his new contacts were heading to a cabin somewhere up north. They were fuzzy on the details, but it seemed there were GPS coordinates that would lead the rest of the terror group to it. They were supposed to rendezvous over the next few days if they couldn't take any more action against the soldiers. The men who had run from the explosions were originally supposed to be armed with the AKs from the mosques basement and were supposed to finish off anyone who was left in the buildings. They had learned from the Fort Hood massacre that American soldiers, unlike their Middle East counterparts, did not normally travel armed. It was supposed to have been a 'target rich' environment. The loss of the weapons had altered that plan, but there were supposed to be more weapons available, and the plan would be adapted and refined when they all met at the cabin. Sharp showed the map and the coordinates to Rawlins.

"That's pretty close to the border," he commented.

"Close, hell," Sharp answered. "If those numbers are right those bastards are going to be hiding in Canada."

"We can always ask the Mounties to take a look at it for us."

Grant didn't like that idea. "If you just ask, they'll send a couple of cops to knock on the door, and they won't stand a chance. If you tell them to go in hard, we may never get the chance to find out who they really are. Can you hold off for a bit so we can try to track them down first?"

"I can't let you guys, go and invade Canada looking for them. Do you realize how much trouble that would cause?"

"We aren't looking to go into Canada with all guns blazing. All I want to do is find out where they're at, how many there are and maybe get a bug or two in there. If we get lucky we can find their routes across the border and get them when they come back to our side. Getting another country involved is not what we want to do."

Rawlins shook his head. "That'll never fly. My boss will want these guys taken down as soon as possible. I don't think he'll care who gets credit for it."

Grant looked at Rawlins, then over at Sharp. Sharp gave him a small grin and nodded his head. He and Grant were on the same page. Sharp said one word: "Vaughn."

"Absolutely," Grant replied. He turned to look back at Rawlins. "Your buddy Lindsay over there already got the word from General Vaughn that he was calling the shots, and I'm pretty sure he mentioned that we were part of the team. You better put your head together with his and decide who's going to wake Vaughn up at this ungodly hour of the morning and tell him you're fucking with his plans." Rawlins didn't answer. He had already had dealings with Vaughn after Sharp grabbed the two AKs at the training area. He had already been told what the food chain looked like. Grant felt he had the answer he was looking for. He sent Sharp off to find them a ride back to the assembly area. He was going to start waking people up early this morning. The object of all this attention was probably already across the border, and they needed to get into position and get some drones in the air, the small ones liked they used in Mexico, not the big assed Predators. Sharp regularly trained with them at the NCO Academy, writing the doctrine for their local use. He would need to get a couple of trustworthy operators involved in their plans.

Ashley was dead set against anything having to do with crossing the Canadian border. He threatened to have all their equipment impounded so they couldn't operate on their own. It was only the intervention of General Vaughn that silenced his objections, which Grant thought was a good thing, because Sharp had already loaded the equipment.

"Before you two go off and start another war, would you mind telling me exactly what you're planning on doing once you get up there?" Vaughn asked.

"Well," Sharp began, "first thing tomorrow morning I've got a couple of drone operators coming in. I'm going to find a good spot on the border, get set up, and start looking for the bastards."

"Then what? If they're in Canada there's not a hell of a lot you can do, and this time I can't authorize you to just ignore an international border. What exactly do you think you're going to say to the Royal Canadian Mounted Police? 'Hi! My name is David Sharp and I found some suspected terrorists living in a cabin in the woods with my little drones here. Hope you don't mind me violating your air space?' That's not going to endear you to their border people or our State Department."

"I don't plan on telling the Canucks anything. Once I find them I'm going to cross over and take care of them."

"All by yourself? That's a little bold, even for you."

"Don't worry about him, General." Vaughn turned around to see Harrison and Price had entered the room. Price was pretty well bandaged up, but he was standing on his own two feet. "Friends don't let friends go to Canada alone. There will be a few of us along to back him up." Grant could see Major Carson just outside the doorway. She must have been the one who brought him. Grant waved her in. The more witnesses the better.

Vaughn wasn't impressed with what he saw. "Three old men and a cripple aren't going to do much. Is that your best plan?"

"Listen, General, we're doing it," Grant said. You can come along for the ride or you can stand back and we'll tell you all about it later, but we're going." Grant paused to let that sink in for a moment. "And before you think you can stop us, think about this: we've been pretty fucking good about keeping your secrets. You owe us. This is what it's going to cost you."

"You think you can blackmail me into going along with this, Sergeant Major? That's a pretty bold statement from a man who just crossed the line into insubordination and is rapidly closing on mutiny.

I'll bury all of you so far in a hole that people will think you never existed."

"There are always witnesses left behind, Vaughn; a smart guy like you should realize that. We've got a dozen or more troops that went with us into Al Fashir, Moldova and Mexico ready and geared up to take another ride, and we told every one of them to make absolutely sure that their family and friends know exactly where they're going. I figure that'll make at least a hundred people you'll have to bury in that hole, and that's just guessing we stop at a reinforced squad. There might be more."

Vaughn thought about that, and went to confer with Ashley and Connaught. The four NCOs huddled across the room and watched them. "That was a big bluff, Luke," Harrison said. "He calls it and we've got nothing to fall back on. I don't think we'll have more than eight people counting us. What's your plan?"

"I had Sharp call Robinson and have him round up as many of the old shooters as he could. We should have a pretty good group by the time Sharp pulls out. I'm not bluffing anymore. They're over at the NCO Academy loading up enough gear for us to stay out for a few days."

"I've already been over there, Luke. You're going to be disappointed."

Vaughn finished his little conference and came back. "Okay, smart ass, I'm going to go along with this stupid idea, but with a couple of conditions. You don't agree to them and there are enough Marshals and agents locally to roll all of you up."

"Let's hear them," Grant said in a low voice. Conditions were not something he was ready to accept.

"First, I want an officer with you. You can get Bonneville if you want, or I'll send Colonel Ashley with you. Hell, you can even take the doctor there, but you aren't going up there unsupervised. You and your gang have a habit of going overboard. I want somebody there who can say no to you."

"You think I can say no to them?" Bonneville was in the room. Nobody had seen her come in. "Better yet, you think they'll listen to me? Then I'm your girl."

"He's setting you up, Linda."

"I know that." She replied. "But when does it stop? I know one of them has been after me since Darfur. They came to my house the other night, remember? My kids were there." Everyone was quiet listening to her. "It's got to stop now. I don't want to have to worry about some scumbag coming after my kids in school or in my house again." She turned on Vaughn. "I'll go with them. I'll even take the blame if something goes wrong. But at least they'll be doing something." Grant put his arms around her and kissed her forehead. "You got anything else, Vaughn?"

"Yeah, you use my drone operators. There's going to be a hard limit to how far north you can go. You've got coordinates, and I'll give you those and an extra klick to the north, no more."

"How about ground recon? Are you going to limit that too?"

"No. Even if those coordinates are wrong it can't be off more than a grid square. If you're stupid enough to go wandering around farther afield than that and get caught we'll just deny we know you. You have enough of a rogue operator reputation that we can probably write you off with an apology."

"What else?"

"I'd prefer you not take any US marked equipment, but there's so much surplus shit out there I probably couldn't back that up." He walked back to where Ashley was sitting behind his computer. "On second thought, I do want Ashley with you. I want you to run everything by him before you do it."

"We already agreed to Major Bonneville. I'm not giving him any veto power over what we do. No deal."

"Not a deal, Sergeant Major. You run it by him. I don't care if you take his advice or not. I just want somebody there who can tell you when you're out of your mind so I can have deniability. Take it or leave it."

"We'll take it." He turned to look at Ashley. "Colonel, since you'll be coming, can you be ready to roll at first light? I want to have a base camp set up and get the drones up for their first pass over the border before sundown."

Vaughn had a better idea. "As much as I hate you to think I'm helping you, there's a small border station not too far from where you want to look. It's only manned part time, and they'll be willing to let you use it. I don't know why, but those border guys like you after Mexico. It's got a small, one bird LZ there that can take a Blackhawk."

"You giving me air support?"

"Absolutely not. But I will make sure you have a Medevac bird tasked to you. You'll probably need it for the bullet magnet over there."

"I think he means you, Pricey," Sharp said.

Grant waved them off. "I'll take it, as long as it's dedicated to me. I don't want to have to go begging for it if we need it."

"Done." The conversation was over. He walked out of the room. Grant looked at his watch, then at each and every one in the room. "Finish loading, then get some sleep. We'll head out at 0500. If you don't have it by then, it ain't going." He asked Major Carson for a moment. "Is Price good to go this time? I don't want him to start leaking all over the place again."

"He won't leak unless he gets more holes in him. The last time was an accident. He didn't bother to tell me they hadn't put the stitches in, just temporary bandages." She pointed out the door at a duffel bag. "And General Vaughn wants me to be on stand-by with the Blackhawk."

"That's not a good idea."

"Vaughn offered me to you, so you might as well take advantage of having a doctor on hand. Besides, it gets cold up in the Great North Woods. You might want somebody to warm your sleeping bag for you. Your little Major might not always be handy."

CHAPTER SIXTEEN

E VERYBODY IN GRANT'S GROUP
WAS ready early the next morning.
Despite any concerns from Vaughn
or Ashley, everybody had packed US issue gear and supplies. Sharp had
raided the shipping containers of left-over deployment equipment and
had packed rations, weapons and ammo. His trusty M70 sniper rifle,
outdated as it was, found its way onto the back of his truck in a hard
case. Several of the volunteers that Sergeant Robinson had recruited also
brought their long range weapons. They were all souvenirs or trophies
from the Sudan. The border area was supposed to have a broad swath
cleared on both sides of the international line. If he had to, Sharp could
deploy his shooters and cover several kilometers of open area. It wasn't
the ideal density he would have liked, but it was all he had. If the Arabs
were out there, he did not intend to miss them. Everyone was of a
mind, like Major Bonneville, that this had gone on long enough. It was
going to end in the next few days.

One concession Grant did make to discretion was to veto the idea
of using any military vehicles. There was a distinct possibility that he
could dispatch a scouting team into Canada by legal means, and a
HUMMV would not be able to cross. There was also a chance that
there might be outlying camp sites or cabins that were also used by
the Arabs, and a military presence would stand out in the area like a

lighthouse. A minivan and three trucks with extended cabs were enough to carry everyone and their equipment without looking too obvious. There was a minimum of personal gear. Nobody was expecting to be lounging around the campfire.

Colonel Ashley had brought Mary Magdalene and two drone operators. Grant didn't like the idea of that entire group traveling together, so he split them up. The two operators would ride with Robinson, and Harrison and one of the shooters would take their place in Ashley's' van. Price had decided he wanted to ride with Mary Magdalene, so another arrangement was made, and they ended up riding with Sharp. There was one unhappy camper in the crowd, Major Carson. Since Vaughn had decided that she would travel with the helicopter she would not be going with the convoy. She would have to wait until the aviation unit took off later in the day. Grant gave a silent prayer of thanks for small favors. The choppers had been tasked with a mountain rescue training mission and would be staging out of a grass airstrip at a town called Colebrook, close to the Canadian border but further south than where they'd be operating. She had wanted to ride up in Grant's truck and made no bones about her disappointment. This wasn't his only problem, because at the last minute he learned that Sheila Gordon was coming too. That made three women in the travel group. He might have to use them if the tactical situation called for it. He didn't like the idea.

Ashley had a problem with the redistribution of his people. "I get the feeling you don't trust me, Sergeant Major. May I remind you that I've been trying to catch the courier since Afghanistan? Your Sergeant Price knows that better than anyone here."

"Look at it from my perspective, Colonel, you work for Vaughn and I don't know you. And other than telling us that this guy is carrying files on us and wants to kill us, we've gotten damn little information. You just called him a courier. A courier for who?"

Ashley gave him a puzzled look. "You don't know? I thought you had been told a long time ago. We believe he was the last courier Osama bin Laden dispatched before he was killed. Pakistani intelligence was pretty definite with their information, and for a change, we didn't have any reason to doubt them. The only two things we're not sure of is how the Iranians got involved, and where this Ali Alawa Sharif came from."

Grant found that funny, and the smile that crossed his face confused Ashley. "I knew about the bin Laden connection, but I would have thought you might know more about Sharif."

"You know something about this Sharif character? What should I know about him?" Grant gave him the condensed version of their history with Ali Alawa Sharif. They had had two serious incidents with him, along with several opportunities to kill him. "Our best shot had been in Moldova, but we hadn't counted on their Security Service people playing fast and loose with the French. I guess that's why they sent me the tank, sort of as a consolation prize."

"I wondered where that came from when I saw it in the hanger. Vaughn has a real problem with you having the B-17. He never said a word about the Stuart tank."

"Well, now you know, and that's the way we're going to play it for now. You work with us up on the border and we'll see."

Major Carson made her feelings known about the arrangements again. Under the guise of discussing Price's condition before she got a ride over to the aviation facility she pulled Grant aside and told him so. "I thought I was going to get to ride all the way up there with you. I don't think I like this arrangement."

""The decision to have you with the Medevac was Vaughn's, not mine."

"But you're not too unhappy with it, are you?"

"What the hell did you expect? Have you been listening to yourself? You've been pushing the envelope a little too much with all your comments. Even if you had been along for the ride, did you think I was going to put Linda in with Ashley just so you could see how much you could get away with? You're going, and in spite of my reservations it's probably a good thing because we might need a medic. It's not going to be a romantic getaway in the woods."

"I thought it was because you were going to try to get me jealous by having to wonder what you and the little Major were up to on that long ride. You know how hot that would make me? I just love jealous make up sex."

"You've got to stop referring to her like that. Somebody else is going to hear that and wonder what you've got against her. Too many questions might screw up this little arrangement you've got going."

"Well then, I'll make a deal with you. I'll be a good little girl and watch my mouth, but you have to promise me another one of those little 'night patrols' you took me on in New Mexico." She was referring to the visit to the little pond Gant took her on. "I don't even care if there's any water around this time."

"You do know that Vaughn has drone pictures of that?"

"I didn't know. Do you think he'd give me copies if I asked nicely?" With that she turned and walked away. Grant watched her walk up to Linda Bonneville and ask, rather loudly, if she and Sergeant Gordon were willing to assist her if needed. "All this organization and they managed not to include a single medic. If things go to hell, and they always seem to do with this group, I'm going to need someone I can count on."

"Of course I'll do what I can, but I'm pretty certain there are a couple of combat lifesavers in the group. I just hope we don't have to worry about that." Bonneville replied. The two women walked together to Grant's vehicle talking about the situation. As she passed Grant she gave one of her air kisses. Harrison saw it and commented. "Still playing with that napalm, Luke? That woman is definitely going to fry your ass one of these days."

"I know, Ralph, I know."

"As long as you think you know what you're doing, Luke."

The group got on the road ahead of schedule and headed north. New Hampshire has a limited number of routes to the Canadian border, and they traveled convoy style. To avoid more than casual interest, Grant gave orders for the vehicles to keep a lengthy interval, and to not be shy about turning off from time to time for coffee or rest breaks. Only his and the vehicle Ashley was in were to make a deliberate approach to the Border Patrol station in order to get organized and get the first drone in the air. The rest he just wanted on site by late afternoon. That didn't sit well with Sharp. "I'd like to get 'boots on the ground' and start taking a look at approaches as soon as I can. We can all be up there by noon, because there ain't one hell of a lot to do on the way."

"Okay, but I want you to stop and buy beer, soda, coolers, ice, junk food, and anything else a bunch of young guys would be taking on a camping trip. Keep the guns out of sight and for God's sake don't be calling each other by rank. People aren't stupid, even if they are civilians."

In the cabin in the woods no one woke early. It was as if they considered themselves in a secure environment with an army of loyal followers keeping watch. The Mexican was the first one up. It took a few moments for him to orient himself to his surroundings, wondering where the toilet was. Once he remembered, he stumbled out onto the porch and looked at the outhouse set back in the tree line. He considered walking to it, but decided against it in his bare feet. He walked to the corner of the porch and urinated off it. When he went inside he could hear stirrings in the other rooms. Before anyone could make an appearance he had found a coffee press and had started to boil water. He made enough for two cups, his usual ration at breakfast. It would have been just as easy for him to make a full pot, but he had no intention of doing anything more than driving for these people.

He was finishing off his first cup when Shabaab stumbled out of his room in his boxer shorts, barefoot. He sniffed the air and commented that the coffee smelled good, then he too went outside looking for the outhouse, and, like the Mexican, decided not to walk to it in his bare feet. He came back in he looked for the source of the coffee aroma. Seeing the coffee press he opened a cabinet looking for a mug. Before he could turn around the Mexican took the press and refilled his mug, emptying the press. Shabaab looked from the empty press to the Mexican and then back at the press again. He didn't feel like starting the day with an argument, so he just asked "How does this thing work?" The Mexican told him. As he was filling a pot with water to boil Sharif came out of his room. He could smell the coffee and saw the coffee press. "Make enough for all of us," he said to Shabaab, and walked out looking for the outhouse. He too decided against the long walk and went to the edge of the porch to urinate. Khan walked out behind him and looked at what he was doing in disgust. "That will soon attract insects and make the entire area small of urine. Is it too much to ask you walk a few steps?"

"You are right, Mehmet Atta, I apologize for my laziness, but I fear I am not the first to violate your hygiene standards. I will instruct everyone not to do this again." Khan grunted and walked to the outhouse. He was living with barbarians. The sooner he was rid of them, the better. He needed to get a good look at the map and begin to plan his escape into Canada. Even if the border were electronically monitored, there were no land mines or barbed wire fences to hinder his journey. All he had to do was evade any ground patrols long enough to reach a town with an Automatic Teller Machine and a bus station. A car rental agency would be better, but he would take whatever transportation he could find. He had a sense that there were small villages scattered along the border less than several miles away. There had to be a road network supporting them, so he doubted he would have to wander the woods for long. He had already tried to get a signal on his cell phone to activate the navigation feature, but it had been hopeless. There was a cheap compass hanging from a nail just inside the cabin door. He would make his escape the old fashioned way.

After coffee, and everyone fended for himself as far as breakfast went, Sharif presented his plans for the next few days. The bomb attacks did not seem to produce the desired results, and with the loss of the weapons stored at the mosque the follow-up attacks didn't occur. This was a setback of sorts, but it had been the first step in spreading fear in the small towns of America. He was confident that the cell that Shabaab had built up from the graduates of the camps and the willing young men who had joined them, like Raisouli's son, would celebrate their accomplishments and wait to be contacted for further actions. For the next few days they would remain here, allowing the hue and cry of the increased security and paranoia to die down. Shabaab indicated that there were other caches of supplies that could be used when the time was right. Sharif asked for a detailed list, and after he heard a few of the items he stopped Shabaab. "That is perfect, my friend. We will need more supplies than the meager larder here offers. You and I will find a place this afternoon to get them, and while we are there we will try to make contact with one of your trusted subordinates. A small action some distance to the south will divert attention from our original objective. Once they feel secure in their own homes again we will swoop down and slaughter them in their own beds."

"Do I still get the doctor?" Shabaab asked with a toothy grin.

"Of course you do, and I will settle accounts with the white whore who caused the downfall of al Saif!" He looked around the table at all the faces, stopping on Khan's. "Do you agree, my brother? The timing does not matter, as long as the objective is reached!"

Khan wasn't so sure, but he kept his own council. "You are correct, Ali Alawa Sharif. You have much more experience than I in these

233

matters, but your plan seems to be the correct one. Once they again feel secure, we can strike with impunity." He left unspoken that he would be far away when the time finally came. The trip for supplies would give him the opportunity to plan his escape route. He looked at the Mexican, who didn't seem very interested in Sharif's plans. Perhaps, Khan thought, there is an ally here I can use.

The first drone flight was up by mid afternoon. The tactical set they were using was designed for quick and easy deployment, and the operators Ashley had brought along knew their jobs well. Grant gave them the coordinates of the cabin that Sharp had picked up, and the bird was winging in that direction. "You do know, Sergeant Major, that we've got a hard limit as to how far we can go into Canadian airspace?"

"I know, Specialist. You just start a little to the north of those coordinates and work your search pattern back to the south. Even if the numbers are wrong, it's really hard to be off by more than a kilometer." One thousand meters was the size of the standard grid square on a map. Even the poorest map reader could usually locate his or her self to within a klick.

"Will do."

Shortly after the drone had climbed to altitude and crossed the border, Sharp arrived with the rest of the group. The two Border Patrol agents who had been manning the station had given Grant the keys, explained the layout and the patrol schedules along the border and went about their own business. They still had a routine to follow, which consisted of periodic trips along the border to check for activity. There was a sensor array planted, but it did not yet give 100% coverage, and, even if it did, there was a lot of animal traffic through the woods and across the border. Bear, moose and large deer weren't always discernable from human foot traffic. Sharp went looking for the agents to get more details about their duties. He had a hunch that, if he had to do a border crossing, he could use their activity to mask his. His hunch was right.

The agents told him that they were familiar with what had happened along the New Mexico border. There was an unofficial information channel in Immigration and Customs Enforcement that spread the word about the good, the bad and the stupid rather quickly. The289th and the Mexican army battle were considered one of the good things.

There was a large scale map in the office that Sharp could compare to his own Geodetic Survey map that most hunters used. If there was a military map of the area available he had not been able to find it in existing National Guard stocks. The map he was using came from a sporting goods store he had detoured to on the way up. The larger scale made it easy to transfer information, and he was surprised to see that there were a number of trails marked on both sides of the border. When he asked about this one of the agents told him that if they had a sense that the trail might be well used, they would find the time to back track several hundred meters. They had learned from long experience on the southern border that the bad guys tended to keep the immediate border area as clean as possible, but there was usually an assembly/rest area somewhere close by where they could reorganize for the crossing and keep an eye on Border Patrol activity. "If the smugglers are using any given area, they usually get to know our routines as well as we do, so we try to shake it up from time to time." Sharp discovered that the direct north-south route to his target passed through an area that was seeded with sensors. Not many, but enough to alert the monitoring station over in Vermont that there was activity in the area. Sometimes they would send their own helicopter to check, but usually it would be a routine trip by four-wheeler to the area. There was an interesting feature about five hundred meters to the west of the area. There was a road that angled sharply to the border area. Once it came into the cleared area, it followed what was the usual patrol route for four wheelers or all wheel drive vehicles. As it got closer to his line of latitude, there was a poorly defined turn around area, one of several that seemed to appear every few hundred meters. That was also explained as a Border Patrol creation so they could occasionally double back during their patrol runs if an area had seen more traffic than could be explained by wild life. Sharp decided to try to coordinate any crossing he made with a routine patrol, that way the activity would be reported as 'normal' and not raise any red flags. He also checked on Canadian law enforcement activity in the area. He was pleased to discover that the Canadians were more than willing to let the Americans take the lead in these out of the way areas. Their budget came nowhere close to what the United States routinely spent on remote crossing points that no legitimate traffic was using. That meant that, barring a drastic change in Canadian border policy or the onset of a major gun battle, Sharp could operate without worrying about friendly interference. He decided to press the Border agents on what they knew about the terrain just on the other side of the line, particularly in the area he was interested in. One of the agents compared his coordinates to the map and scoffed at the idea that he would find anything there. He doubted that anyone could have crossed the border in a vehicle anywhere in their patrol area without them knowing about it. The gates were all chained and alarmed and there were no bypasses. If they had crossed legally, there would be a record of it. The area only had limited access, so they would have been limited to what crossing they could have used. He told Sharp he was on a wild goose chase. "There's nothing in that area. If there was we'd hear noise, see lights, or smell smoke. In this area any human activity won't go unnoticed for long, even if it's on the Canadian side."

Sharp had his doubts about their information. The drone that was up had the capability for infra red as well as visual sensing. The first pass up the latitude line produced no hits, so Grant gave instructions for a gradually widening 'racetrack' course, using the northern limit Ashley was insisting on as the turning point. Each leg would move out an additional fifty yards from the base line on either side. The southern limit was set at a point one kilometer south of the border. The built in GPS navigation system made the turns easy to determine on the monitors.

There were several 'hits' as the drone followed its racetrack, indicating activity, or recent activity, in the area. Heavy overhead coverage didn't permit visual observation, but the infra red showed what seemed to be a parked vehicle and some kind of structure about fifteen hundred meters north. It had been just beyond the northern limit, and had been detected by the side looking sensor. The operator decided to check on it on his own, and didn't advise Ashley until after he confirmed his data. Ashley promptly relieved the operator of his duties and threatened disciplinary action, but Grant had re-entered the room just in time to see the data stream before Ashley had it scrubbed. There was a brief argument, but Grant prevailed. He reminded Ashley he was just supposed to 'advise' him of any action. He didn't have any veto power. He took the information and the coordinates to Sharp.

Shabaab and Sharif left just before noon to get supplies at a trading post some distance to the south. It was hoped that there would be reliable cell phone service at the post, but if there wasn't Shabaab recalled it had one of the few remaining pay phones in the North Country. The actual 'straight line' distance to be travelled wasn't great, but there was no 'straight line' they could follow. And the journey took a little over an hour one way. Sharif went into the store with a list while Shabaab tried to call his people in the south. It took several tries before he was able to contact one of them, and he was angry when he heard the report. He was told about the raid on his apartment house and the fight that followed. Most of his followers had either been killed or swept up by the authorities, and only four of them remained at large. This was a group that had resisted relocating to Shabaab's apartment house, and as a result they escaped detection, but only learned of the raid on the radio. The immediate area around the apartment house was still cordoned off, "And they are stopping and interrogating any black or brown skinned men who come close to the area." Shabaab asked where they were. He was told they were at yet another safe house, this one established by a Christian peace group who protested the heavy handed raid and was sheltering Arabic youths from the authorities.

"Do you have any supplies?"

"We have weapons and some explosives. We didn't know if we should take any action until we heard from you."

Shabaab told them to stay put for now. He told them he would decide on their next moves and call back within the hour. He went into the store to join Sharif and inform him of the developments. Sharif remained impassive as he listened to the report, his mind working over the possibilities. He told Shabaab to buy some ready made sandwiches and drinks and wait for him outside. He would complete his shopping and join him, and then they could make plans. Once Shabaab left Sharif went to the counter and asked about a package that may have been left addressed only to 'The Photographer'. The man behind the counter called for a woman to come relieve him while he went to fetch it from the back room.

The store functioned as an unofficial post office for the summer camping and hiking traffic. Much like post offices on the Appalachian Trail, they would get parcels of supplies and equipment beginning in the late spring and hold them until claimed. Sometimes the packages were never claimed, and the end of the season always saw a yard sale of sorts on unclaimed goods. There had been a question of legality in the early years, but the system had developed so that all parcels were addressed to the store, with a 'hold for' disclaimer somewhere other than the address block. That meant the parcels were property of the store, so no problems developed.

The store owners, an older couple who had been there for forty years, had seen all kinds of unprepared people come through their store. The big black man buying sandwiches and sodas looked out of place, but at least he was wearing jeans and sneakers. Not the best attire for hiking, but it was better than what the Mediterranean looking fellow was wearing. He had on a dress shirt and a pair of slacks, and what looked to be some very expensive and very uncomfortable dress shoes. Whatever he was doing in this part of the woods, he was definitely unprepared. As the wife rang up his purchases, the husband tried to engage the stranger in conversation when he brought out the parcel. It was smaller than normal, and since small usually meant valuable, he had been hoping it would have been one of the unclaimed parcels. Something of this size and weight had to be electronic, and therefore valuable. All he could get out of the man was that he was a 'nature photographer' and that he was 'on assignment' from a European animal rights magazine to try and photograph an albino moose. The package was an accessory for his camera that he did not need on his previous assignment, but did not want to risk damaging it by carrying it in his bag. The husband was skeptical, but tried to help him. "Well, friend, if you're looking for moose you should probably wander over to the swamps over by the Connecticut Lake. If you're going to find any white moose, that'll be the place."

The man was grateful for the information, and asked if he could point out the area on a map. The husband did, and commented on the strangers outfit. The stranger assured him that he had more than adequately prepared for his adventure, and had all his gear in his car. He paid for his purchases and started to leave the store. "What do you call those pastries?" he asked, pointing to a display.

"Bear claws. My wife makes them every morning." The man asked for one and took a bite. "These are delicious. You say your wife makes them every morning?"

"That's right. They're pretty popular with the regulars around here."

"Excellent. I may have to stop by again before I leave the area."

The husband and wife watched as he loaded his supplies in the trunk and joined the black man at a picnic table. "Now those two sure don't look like they belong together, do they, Artie?"

"Nope, they sure don't, and for a guy who says he's got the right gear to be up here, that trunk was awfully empty looking to me?"

"Think we should call somebody? There's been a lot of trouble down south. Those fellows might have had something to do with it."

Artie was reluctant to get involved in somebody else's business. Years of living up in the woods had isolated him from the troubles of the world, and getting involved in anything usually just complicated his life. "There's nobody to call, Hon, the State Police hardly ever come up this way, and you know the sheriff's at least an hour away."

"How about the Border Patrol? They might be interested."

"Those fellows are feds. They don't like to get involved in local business if they don't have to, but that one guy likes to stop here on his way up from seeing his girl friend on his day off. If comes by tonight I'll let him know."

Sharp planned his border crossing carefully. There would be enough daylight left by the time he got to the scene of the activity for a quick look, so he planned on getting as close as possible with a sniper team and hunkering down for the night. He could make an overnight assessment and decide on a course of action for day break. The agents came in handy when Sharp asked them to comment on his route. Local experience again paid off. They told him to just cross the border directly across from the station. There were no sensors and the terrain was flat and relatively underbrush free. He could stay in the tree line until he came to a large boulder, they called it a 'glacial erratic'. That would mark the approximate start of the sensor line and give him a hard land mark to use. They pointed it out on the map. They also told him that they made a late afternoon patrol for several miles in either direction, and if it would help they'd use the four wheelers. They had a louder noise signature and would help mask his approach.

"I thought you said there was nothing up there?"

"We did, but we'll give you the benefit of the doubt. It's not every day we get to help smuggle stuff the other way."

The going was easy for most of the way to the target site. The terrain was gentle and the forest was pretty open. The team moved slowly, stopping frequently to check for activity ahead. There were signs that there was a human presence somewhere close by, and it looked hostile. There were several trip wires scattered about connected to noise makers. They had been in place for some time, so Sharp had them deactivated before they went on. He was watching his GPS readout when one of his team held everyone up and called Sharp forward. The man had found another trip wire; only this one ran back to an old single barreled shotgun that was pointed at the trail. His other team member also made a discovery high up in the trees. There was a cloth solar panel rigged, with cables running down to a box mounted on the tree. The soldier recognized it for what it was. After disarming the shotgun Sharp moved over to look at it. He was directed to the back side of the tree and given the signal to be silent. There was another cable leading down to the ground and partially buried as it ran back into the woods. After scanning the area the soldier led Sharp back a ways and told him what it was. "It's the housing for a trail camera, Sarge, but this one looks modified. I think it's got a Web camera hooked up instead. The solar panel feeds it and the signal runs back to a computer somewhere."

"Good eyes, Eric, it looks like we may have found our Arabs. Let's get off the trail just in case they have more of those things." They moved into the woods single file for several yards, and the point man held them up again. The ground was sloping away into a small depression and on the rise on the far side there was a small surplus General Purpose tent set up. A bearded man dressed in mismatched camo sat on a folding lounge chair sunning himself. He had what looked to be a suppressed Mac-10 on his lap. Another man walked out of the tent, nudged him and gestured with his thumb. The one in the lounge chair grunted and got up and went in the tent. The newcomer took his place in the chair. This one was carrying an old triangular style handguard M-16A1.

Sharp felt a poke in his side, and his attention was directed into the depression. It stretched to the west for several hundred meters, and it was filled with identical green undergrowth. "It's a pot farm, Sarge! I guess even the Canucks like their weed. I don't think these are our guys."

"I think you're right. Let's get out of here. We can tell the ICE guys about this and they can decide if they want to let the Mounties know about it." They started to move back when the last man in line hissed. He pointed to his right, where a line of porters carrying bundles of the weed were approaching. They must have had another field close by and it was harvest time. The first one in the line of dope growers carried a shotgun and was joking with man behind him. The language sounded like French. The second man was laughing, and suddenly stopped. He was looking in exactly the right place to see Sharp, who was partially exposed on that side. He shouted a warning to the armed escort. He looked up and snapped off a shot from the hip. Sharp could hear the pellets passing through the brush just above him when one of his men returned fire. He was carrying a .308 caliber sniper rifle and the blast woke up the entire forest. The heavy round punched through the man with the shotgun and on into the porter right behind him. The rest of the line of porters dropped their loads and ran off, away from the shooting. There had been a couple of escorts bringing up the rear and they hurried forward, firing wildly into the trees and bushes, not knowing what their target was.

Sharp could hear shouts from behind as the two men at the tent came over to see who was threatening their harvest. The one with the Mac-10 had seen too many movies and was trying to sweep the hill with a one hand grip. The muzzle climb wasted the 30 round magazine, and he was fumbling with a magazine change when he was hit by a burst of AK fire from the hill. Sharp heard the firing and knew his trail man was dealing with the threat. In front, another .308 round had taken out another of the drug escorts, and Sharp lined up the sights of his AK on another one. His earpiece had come alive with a voice asking him what was going on, but he didn't think to answer. He took out his target and could see two more men taking cover behind some rather flimsy trees. He fired a burst at each one to make them keep their heads down and turned to see his trail man and the M16A1 carrier swapping shots. His man grunted and went limp as the M16A1 emptied his magazine. Sharp empted his magazine and eliminated the threat. Another .308 blast behind him announced the demise of another of the escorts with a shot right through the tree he was behind, and the final man decided he had had enough and threw out his weapon. He was yelling something in French.

The sniper called to Sharp. "What do I do with him, Sarge?"

"Keep an eye on him. Eric's down!' He crawled over to the injured man and rolled him over. The bullet that hit him had been a ricochet, striking a rock to his side and traveling under his light weight body armor through the arm hole. Before he could pull off the armor to check the wound there was a movement below him. One of the dope growers was staggering to his feet. He still had a weapon in his hand. Sharp's weapon was empty, so he picked up Eric's and dispatched him.

Eric had an open wound across his chest. It looked like the bullet had struck a rib and followed it around to the front. It was probably painful as hell, and it was bleeding heavily. The other man was still calling to Sharp. "Sarge!" He looked over and saw the last escort was walking towards them, his hands behind his head. He was babbling something and it looked like he was crying. "Don't let him get any closer!"

The radio was still crackling in his ear. He could hear Grant calling him.

"I've got one man down, and what looks like a prisoner." He spoke into his microphone. Just then there was another boom of the .308. The last escort was flung back into a sitting position against a tree. "He had another gun, Sarge!"

"Check the bodies then come here and help me." He spoke to Grant again. "Check that. No prisoners." He had torn open a pack of clotting agent and was pouring it on the wound. As soon as the pack was empty he took out a large field dressing and placed it over the wound, wrapping the tails around the casualty. Grant was still talking. "How bad is your casualty? Do you need a Dust-Off?"

"Negative. There's no LZ here. I'll get him to the border by the big rock. Have somebody pick us up there." The sniper came up and reported that all the bad guys were dead. He had no idea where the porters ran off to. With that, he stepped over Sharp and effortlessly lifted the wounded man up over his shoulder. Sharp pointed south and they headed off. He reported what had happened to Grant. "No Arabs here, Boss, just a bunch of dopers."

"Dopers?" Grant wondered what he meant. There had been an awful lot of shooting.

"Yeah, we found a bunch of Canadian pot farmers harvesting their crop. They must have thought we were poachers and they put up a fight. They lost."

They made good time getting back to the border. Grant had one of the Border Patrol trucks waiting by the glacial erratic. "The Blackhawk is inbound. I called as soon as the shooting started. Should be here in ten."

The wounded man was conscious by the time they got to the border station and claiming he was all right. Grant kept him in the bed of the truck as a precaution. The patient is usually the last person to give an accurate assessment of how bad a gun shot wound is. They could hear the Blackhawk approaching and Grant threw out a green smoke grenade out of habit. The LZ was already clearly marked. Carson hopped out with a medic in tow and climbed into the back of the truck to examine the patient. She probed the wound with her fingers and gave some quick instructions to the medic. Then she pulled Grant aside. "Miss me?"

"Not enough to get one of my men shot. How's he going to be?"

"He'll be fine. Cracked ribs, pretty good tissue damage. His scar will be the envy of all the macho men in the gym." She looked around. "Where's your little Major?"

"I told you not to call her that."

"Sorry, I forgot. But where is she. I have a message for her."

"She's inside with Sergeant Sharp getting a report on all this, why."

"She needs to grab her gear and get on the chopper. She's going back to Concord. Her mother had a heart attack shortly after you all left."

"Damn it!" Grant let out. "She doesn't need that on top of all this. I'll go tell her."

"You better let me do this, Sergeant Major. I've heard the medical report, and I can explain it to her better."

Carson went into the station to give the news to Bonneville. While she was gone the casualty had been transferred to a litter and secured in the helicopter. The pilot was sitting in his seat, looking at Grant, tapping the face of his watch. Grant put out his hands in an exaggerated shrug. This had all gotten out of his control pretty quick.

Carson came out of the station first. "We've got to go, but you need to make a decision. Ashley thinks he'll be in charge if Bonneville leaves. You need to tell him I'm taking her place."

"What good would that do? You'll be down in Colebrook with the Medevac."

"No I won't. I'll get this kid stabilized and in the hospital and I'll be back as soon as I can." Grant was slow to respond. "Think about it, Sergeant Major. You may think I'll be a pain in the ass, but Ashley really doesn't like the way you operate. He's chomping at the bit to take over."

243

"All right. Get back here as soon as you can." She ran off giving a wave over her shoulder. Somehow she had managed to look good in a flight suit.

Bonneville came out of the station without any gear. She ran over to Grant to give him a kiss good bye and to get him up to date. "Sheila Gordon is finishing up with Sergeant Sharp. I left her my lap top so she'll be able to send the report in on a classified channel. She'll be handling all the admin so you don't have to deal with Colonel Ashley and his people."

"What about your gear?"

"I left it here with Sheila. She'll pack it up for me and haul it out when you're done. There's nothing in it I'll need back home. Did Major Carson tell you what was happening?"

"Yeah, she said she'd come back up."

"Good, I don't have time to go over it all, so I'll brief her on the helicopter." She gave Grant another kiss. "Don't let anyone else get hurt while I'm gone, especially yourself." She put her hand on his cheek and turned to run to the chopper. As soon as she was on board the medic pulled the door shut and the pilot lifted off. He sensed Major Carson could be an unnecessary complication as he watched the Blackhawk fade into the distance, but he really didn't have a choice. One of the drone operators came out to get him. "Sergeant Major, one of the relief agents just showed up for duty. I think you ought to hear what he just told your Sergeant Sharp. You might be looking in the wrong place."

"What do you mean?"

"He said that a couple of store keepers south of here told him they had a couple of strange visitors this afternoon, two guys who looked totally out of place. You might want to hear about this."

Grant looked at her without a word and went into the station. Sharp was leaning over the large scale map with the agent. The agent was marking up the plexiglass cover with a grease pencil. Grant stood by silently to listen in. A pair of store keepers had two unusual customers this afternoon. They had acted like they weren't together at first. One of them, a big black guy, didn't say much, but the second, a Mediterranean looking type, claimed he was a nature photographer looking for albino moose. Grant asked if nature types and black hikers were unusual in the area. The agent said they weren't, except the shop keepers were old timers and knew when somebody didn't belong. "These two guys didn't belong."

Grant was considering this while Sharp looked at the coordinates he had and compared them to the grease lines on the map. "You know, Luke, if we stay on the same east-west axis, these north south coordinates can just have a couple of numbers transposed and you end up in this area here."

"Think that's a possibility, Dave?"

"Yeah, I do. If you just move two numbers around that gives you at least full grid square to hide in, and if you're really clever it can be as much as ten klicks. These guys could be five miles off in either direction."

"What about your pot farm?"

"Perfect cover. Anybody who's on the shady side of things would know about stuff like that. Remember, that Shabaab guy is an ex-con. He might know about shit like this, and it's a perfect way to fuck with a search party, just have them walk into a pot field protected by armed dopers. If we had been a legit operation you know damn well the powers that be would have called us off to figure out what went wrong."

Grant looked at the map and sent for one of the drone operators. He came out of the back room with Ashley. Grant told him what was going on and outlined his new plan. Ashley looked over at the drone operator and asked what he thought. "I just got here, Colonel, but it all makes sense to me. I say give it a go."

Ashley agreed and sent for Captain Connaught. She had been outside with Sergeant Price, who followed her in with a sheepish look on his face. It looked like they had been making up after he found out she was supposed to be watching them all. Good for Price. Ashley gave her a quick rundown while Grant kept checking his watch. Finally he looked at Grant and told him that they had discussed it long enough. He gave the drone operator a new search area and told him to get right on it.

"I'll have to break out the back-up unit, Sergeant Major. My primary bent a strut on landing. It'll take about an hour to repair it. I can have the new bird up in about twenty minutes."

"Get it done, soldier. I don't want to lose the target if it's out there."

"It's getting late, Grant. Maybe you should wait until first light so you don't make another mistake. I don't want you shooting up some tourist camp because you're in a hurry."

"Don't worry about us, Colonel. Sharp would have been out of that pot farm without anybody knowing it if they hadn't started shooting first. We'll ID our targets before we take any action."

Grant walked out of the room to find the coffee pot. Sharp followed him. "You know, Luke, you probably shouldn't try to antagonize Ashley as much as you do. He can still screw things up for us."

"Dave, don't go siding with him on this. He doesn't have any skin in the game. Those people are targeting us, not him. If we all walk away from this right now he gets to go to his next assignment. We have to keep looking over our shoulders. I'm not living like that."

"Don't you worry, Sergeant Major, I have no intention of taking his side. I want this to be over as much as you do." Grant thought he was being honest.

"All right, I'll back off of Ashley a bit. He starts complaining and Vaughn will probably start to butt in again."

CHAPTER SEVENTEEN

EHMET ATTA KHAN HEARD A buzzing in the sky but couldn't quite identify it. He stepped outside and searched the sky, wondering if it had anything to do with the brief outbreak of shooting he had heard some time earlier. It had been far off, how far he couldn't judge with all this greenery around, but far enough away that Shabaab and Sharif didn't seem too concerned.

"Relax, Mehmet Atta, relax. I can tell you that the shooting you heard had nothing to do with us. From the direction I would guess that it came from one of the many marijuana farms that dot both sides of the border up here. It may even have come from the one that Shabaab X has used as the location for this cabin. If we hear nothing on the radio tonight we will venture back to that little market again in the morning. The proprietors seem to be a wealth of knowledge for the area." He didn't add that his information was about to come from a new source. The package he had gotten at the trading post had contained a most interesting little device. In the age of the cellular phone, it was a small child's walkie-talkie with a cheap ear piece attached. He had never seen such a device, but could see its usefulness. The radio had a dial with ten settings, which were obviously frequencies. The note included in the parcel directed that it be set to the last digit of the day of the month. He assumed it was from the mole in the American organization. He marveled at the foresight that included that little store in the mission planning.

Khan said he felt it unwise to venture into the community again so soon. "I disagree. I have given orders for another action tonight. If Shabaab's men carry it out with sufficient zeal, it will be well reported on the evening news broadcasts. I will need to contact the warriors for a damage assessment and to give them their next assignment. If the Americans have decided to search the woods for us, the new attacks will redirect their attention to the south away from us. I plan a series of attacks on a daily basis stretching far to the south, each one more distant than the last. Soon they will be searching hundreds of miles away from our targets, and they will be lulled into a sense of safety and invulnerability. Then we will strike." His smile broadened again as if he was the only one who understood the joke. "But don't worry, Mehmet Atta, I will not be rash. I was able to converse with the shop keepers today, and they would surely remember me. Tomorrow I will send Shabaab with the Mexican, then the following day you and I will go."

"We can't keep calling him 'the Mexican'. Doesn't he have a name?"

"He prefers to remain anonymous. That is his right. I would prefer not getting too friendly with him anyway. He is merely the hired help at this stage. We can tolerate it for a few more days."

"I don't relish the thought of spending too many days in this hovel, Ali Alawa. I hope your plan moves with some alacrity."

"Bingo!" came the cry from the drone controller. I've got a target about eight kilometers due east on a line with the pot field. You were right, Sergeant Major, and they're on the American side of the border."

"Okay, orbit out of the area so they don't spot you and let's review the tapes." The operator told her assistant to take over the drone and hold it in its current orbit. Then she cued up the images and everyone clustered around her lap top monitor. She ran the file and played it back at half speed. All anyone could see was an endless tract of pine trees that was suddenly interrupted by a flash of light. "That's what tipped me off. I climbed for better altitude to get a look down and made a slow pass back over. This is what I got." She fast forwarded until they were looking down on a small cabin. From an angle it would have been almost completely obscured, but from up high there was a pretty good look at the clearing it was in. There were two men visible. She froze the frame and did several screen captures, making sure the grid coordinates were printed on each picture. Grant patted the operator on the shoulder and told her she had done good. "Now bring your bird home. Try not to overfly the cabin again. We don't want then to know we've found them."

There was the sound of the helicopter outside. Major Carson was returning earlier than Grant had anticipated. Carson had used her influence to have another helicopter meet them at the hospital and pick up Bonneville for her flight south. Once she was certain that the wounded soldier had been stabilized, she had the Blackhawk return her to the border station. They could bring her gear up on another run the following day.

Sharp took the pictures over to the large scale map. He located the site and started marking up trails and roads in the area, and transferring them to his own map. Grant could see the wheels turning in his head as he planned his next approach. Carson came in the room and asked what was going on. Grant gave her a quick briefing while Sharp continued to talk to himself. "Does he always do that?" Carson asked as she watched him. "Only when he's excited. That shoot out he had this morning got his blood up. He's pretty sure the Arabs set us up with the phony coordinates, but he thinks he might have figured out what they did. He really wants the bastards now." Sharp was eager to get started, but Grant slowed him down. "Don't get too far ahead of yourself. If you're sure we can task the drone to make a couple of high altitude passes and see what they come up with. We can't kick in every cabin door up here."

"You're right, Boss, but I've got a good feeling about this. Look at this picture. There's not a hell of a lot of detail, but you can tell one of these guys is black. That's got to be the Shabaab guy who did Raisouli and his kid. Let's get the NVGs out and do a recon tonight, just in case there's more there than we know about. We can have everybody else hold back until we're certain, and if it's them, we can take them out."" He pointed to a ridge line that was on the far side of the target area. "We can make a wide sweep to this point," he tapped the map, "and dismount with a team. It's less than a kilometer, and under pretty good cover. The vehicle can wait and they won't have a long walk back if we're wrong."

"Okay, we'll get started after the moon goes down." Grant said.

"Nobody's going anywhere," Ashley shouted as he came out of his make shift office. "There's been another bombing down south. Somebody walked into a fast food place and touched himself off. General Vaughn wants to close down this operation and get everybody back on the main target."

"We're pretty certain we've got our main target just a couple of klicks east of here, Colonel, we're going after them tonight."

"Negative, Sergeant Major. I intend to have everybody on the road and headed south within the hour. Get your gear packed." He directed his attention to the drone operators and told them to get their birds on the ground and packed up ASAP. The senior operator acknowledged and gave instructions to her assistant. She looked over and asked Grant, "Do you still want us to download all the data for you?"

"Forget that, soldier, I gave you an order."

The operator just looked at Grant and shrugged, but Grant noticed she hit a few keys on her control panel and something on the side started to flash. The operator looked at Ashley walking back to his room and flashed Grant a thumbs up. The data had been saved and downloaded for him.

Carson looked lost and asked Grant what he was going to do. "Exactly what we came here for, Major. Sergeant Sharp thinks one of the guys at that cabin might be one of the men we're looking for. We want to go out tonight and make sure."

"What about Ashley and Vaughn?"

"Remember what Vaughn said? Ashley is only here so we can run stuff by him. He's the adult supervision, but he's not in command. According to what I heard, it was either going to be Major Bonneville or you. Now that she's gone, I guess it's you."

"And you want me to tell that to Ashley? It'll cost you."

"I'm running a pretty big tab with you as it is. One more isn't going to matter now. Just don't try to collect right away. We might be a tad busy."

"OK, Sergeant Major. I'm going to hold you to that." There was a pause. "And in case you're worried about your little Major finding out, don't. I like our arrangement, and I intend to see it goes on for a while." She started to walk away towards Ashley's office but stopped and came back. "Maybe you better come along, just in case you need to remind him of the arrangement."

There was an argument with Ashley, as Grant had expected, but when he tried to call Vaughn to verify his orders, Vaughn was not available. "You son of a bitch. You're not going to be satisfied until you've got everything all screwed up here. Well, I've got Major Carson here, and I'm going to bring Captain Connaught in on it too. If anything goes wrong up here, it'll all be on your head, not mine."

Outside the room Carson smiled at Grant. "That went easier than I imagined. Are you worried about his threat?"

"Not in the least. I can be retired and out of the country before the ceiling comes down on me. How about you?"

"I've got bigger things to worry about than some Colonel threatening my career. Every one of them who's tried to get into my panties has made the same threat, and here I am number six on the Medical Corps Lieutenant Colonel list. Just remember our deal."

Sharp went about his planning while everyone packed up. He didn't have a lot to do, but with limited resources he wanted to cover all his contingencies. He was finished at about the same time Ashley had packed all his gear and people into the van. In what seemed to be a last ditch effort to change their mind, he came over and argued his point one last time. When Carson, with no prodding at all from Grant, stood firm on their decision, he tried another tack. "Well, Captain Connaught has volunteered to stay behind to keep an eye on things for me."

"I don't think that'll be necessary Colonel. I think I can rely on my NCOs to do the right thing."

"I doubt you can, Major, but it doesn't matter. Connaught is under my orders, so she's staying. I'm going to make you responsible for her well being and transportation back to Concord."

"Just tell her to stay out of the way. I understand she might be sweet on Sergeant Price, so he can look after her."

After Ashley was gone Grant assembled everyone in the parking lot. They would all be leaving the area too. He doubted that when Ashley finally made contact with Vaughn again that they would still have the support of the Border Patrol. "Better we set up someplace out of the way so we don't have to worry about screwing them up. They were good to us today."

Sharp stepped to the front with his map and started to give everyone their assignments. Mary Magdalene stayed in the back of the crowd, but she seemed to be taking a lot of notes. She kept fidgeting with something in her hands. Grant guessed it was a cell phone and she was still trying to get a signal up here. He turned away and forgot about it.

When Sharp was done Grant took him aside. "Are you up to this? You've had one long ass day so far."

"Let me get a power nap in, Boss, and I'll be fine. We've got a couple of hours before it gets dark. If you want, I'll sleep in the back of your truck and you can wake me when it's time to go."

"All right, but I'm making one change. Before you take everyone down into that clearing I'm going to do the recon. Let's make sure we know what we've got first."

"I was already planning to do that, Luke. I don't want to risk anybody down there if I don't have to."

"Negative. You stand down for this. You've had a long day and we need someone fresh for this."

"Who'll go with you?"

"I can go alone. I can travel faster."

"That's not a good idea, Sergeant Major." Robinson was speaking up for the first time. "If something goes wrong you'll have your ass stuck way out on that limb. I'll go with you."

"Thanks, Eddie. I'll take you up on that."

"I'll go with you too." Carson spoke up from the back of the room.

"That's not a good idea, Major. You don't know what the terrain will be like where I'm going, and the two of us can travel better on our own."

"Travel better my ass. I don't care how fast you can go. If something goes wrong there are still only two of you. Look what happened to Sergeant Sharp today. Even with the third man on his team it was still a close run thing. At the very least I want you to have a back-up team."

"And you think two teams won't get noticed if the bad guys are on their toes?"

"They might, but if you all are as good as you're supposed to be nobody will know."

"I'll take Harrison." He looked at his friend. "Ralph, are you up to playing back-up for me one more time?"

"I'll go anywhere you want, Luke, but are you sure this is the way you want to do it? Maybe we shouldn't take the chance of being seen and just let Sharp take them out in one swoop. Why risk having to make the approach twice?"

"What if we're wrong again? No offense, Dave, but I let you go after the first target we had. Look how that one ended. What if it's just a family on vacation? A couple of flash-bangs and we won't have the border to protect us."

"You're right, Boss," Sharp said. "No offense taken."

Harrison threw up his hands in surrender. "I don't like it, but I see your point. I guess I'm in."

"Don't worry, Ralph, I won't let anything happen to you. If it looks like its going south we'll bow out gracefully."

"Yeah, I can see it now: two old men prowling around after dark. That's another one of your good ideas I'll probably come to regret. No wonder my wife doesn't like you."

"You need a medic. I'm going too." Everyone turned to look at Major Carson.

Grant shook his head. "Bad idea. You're the commander now. Your place is with the main body."

She gave a sharp, unpleasant laugh. "You made a deal with Vaughn for adult supervision. Now that Bonneville is gone, I'm it, so I'm going."

Harrison chose this moment to chime in. "I hate to say it, Luke, but she may have a point. We can handle the bad guys, but it's a long, lonely trip in the dark back to where the assembly point is if you're leaking. Remember how bad Sharp was when you hauled him out of the ambush in Darfur. All the medics were busy working on me when I had my heart attack. She can come with me. I don't think I'll travel too fast for her to keep up, and once we're sure who's in the cabin I can show her the best place to set up an aid station. If we need it we'll have it, and if we don't it won't matter."

"You've got a bad habit of being right about all the wrong things, Ralph. All right, Major, you're in. See what kind of gear and clothes you can round up. Major Bonneville left her stuff behind, maybe there's something you can fit into."

"Don't look so pessimistic, Sergeant Major. You took me on that little outing in Moldova to identify the body of the guy who's still trying to kill you. Maybe this time we can get it right."

That seemed to settle the plan. Harrison could tell from the look on Grant's face that he didn't like it, but the First Sergeant didn't care. Grant kept forgetting that they were all getting old, and accidents happened. They had gambled and won too often not to expect the odds to turn.

"If we're doing it this way then we should get going while there's light." Grant told the assembled group. Meet back here in a half hour for a map briefing, then we'll go. Ralph, we'll take a full commo set each and my vehicle."

"Weapons?"

"We'll take side arms and the AMDs with us." They were the fold up Polish AKs with 13 inch barrels. They had absolutely no long range accuracy, but were handy for close in work if it had to be done. They were souvenirs of Mexico. "You and the Major do likewise. Just remember we're there to look around. We don't know how many or who might be in the cabin. Those two cars parked there might mean there's more company than we're ready for."

Grant led out in his truck. The maps had been annotated to show the most direct route on known trails. The Border Patrol had been helpful on that count. Some of the data printed on the maps was so far out of date that old roads were now tree stands. Not a lot of money had been spent on preparing updates for the northern border. The south got all the cash and fancy programs. Sharp waited ten minutes before he followed.

Major Carson had been in a good mood during the briefing and ever since. Grant had expected her to try to maneuver her way into going in the lead with Grant, but, to his surprise, had accepted the assignments without a murmur. She did smile at Grant once or twice when he looked at her. It was one of those wry little smiles that spoke volumes, but Grant was having trouble with the translation. He shook off any thoughts in that direction and resolved to keep his mind on the job at hand.

They did a commo check as soon as they were out of the parking lot. The radios were functioning as expected. Grant would have liked Carson to get a refresher on the AK style weapon she was carrying, but live fire at the border station would be out of the question. The Border Patrol had already monitored transmissions from the Canadian side, and there was a lot of traffic about a shoot out between two gangs over a marijuana farm. They had put out a request that the Americans keep an extra sharp watch for the gang that got away in case they tried to make it into the US. One of their number was wounded, "and it seems whoever treated him was carrying a military grade first aid kit."

Eight kilometers isn't all that far to drive, but in the woods roads tended to not go in the direction you needed, and the on the ground distance was closer to twenty, so it was closer to moon set than Grant had planned on. The last two kilometers were driven with the headlights out, using the excellent NVGs the United States military is supplied with. And, in spite of his dislike for GPS navigation, Grant had set his system for the location almost directly east of the cabin over a good sized ridge. He doubted whoever in the cabin would have thought to set a guard at the top.

The set-up would be simple. They would travel in two groups to the top of the ridge, Harrison and Carson trailing by about fifty meters. There they would spread out and survey the terrain for stray individuals before any move was made on the cabin. If everything was quiet, Harrison and Carson would remain on the military crest to provide immediate support while Grant and Robinson approached the cabin in a direct line. There was enough detail in the drone pictures to see an out building and the two parked cars. Robinson would position himself to cover those areas while Grant got closer to the cabin for a look inside. If the targets were there, Grant and Robinson would fade back into the tree line and call Sharp and his people. They would deploy to cover all approaches and make the actual assault and entry. It was a simple plan. The simple plans were usually the best. The goal was not to finesse the terrorists. The goal was to kill them.

Sharif was playing with the radio he had picked up at the store. The battery that had come packed with it was dead, so he had spent some time searching the cabin for a suitable power source. He was to the point of taping flashlight batteries together to get the proper voltage. Khan watched with interest. "Tell me again how you knew to ask for the package? This was not a destination I would have predicted at all."

Sharif tried to connect his battery contraption to the radio. He was many things, but good at manipulating small objects was not one of them. He put the radio aside, disgusted with his inability to master the problem. "Some of the many items of information I was able to get in Libya before the 'Coordinator' died were a series of telephone numbers to be called once entry was made into the United States. It was unspoken that the numbers were not to be called internationally, but it is well known that the Americans are sensitive about eavesdropping on their own citizens, so they concentrate on calls made from outside their borders. I have been dialing them periodically since Rousses Point and discovered most of them were no longer in service. A very few of them were to operatives who were awaiting instructions, which I was happy to give them, but one call was answered by a woman. She was not awaiting instructions, but instead had some. It was a very cryptic 'While you are in the north ask about a package for the photographer.'"

"That was all she said? I don't see how she could have guessed that any more than I did."

"Nonetheless, Mehmet Atta, that was her message. She also said that the number would not work again, and when I tried after I collected the radio there was no answer."

"Could it have been a trap set by the Americans?" Khan asked.

"I would doubt that," Sharif replied. "The Americans have had precious little success in infiltrating agents into Iranian State Security. The Israelis, on the other hand, have committed vast resources with more success than the Iranians would like to admit, but their relations with the Americans wax and wane, and they distrust the intelligence leaks the Americans plague themselves with." He picked up the radio and studied it some more. He was a proud man and reluctant to ask for assistance on such a simple project. He went around the cabin one more time, collecting spare batteries and bits of wire. Shabaab X watched from the couch with half closed eyes. There was a simple solution to what the Arab was trying to do, as it had been a common practice in prison when they were trying to power up an illegal cell phone that didn't have a charger or an external power cord. Everything he needed was visible in the room and within easy reach, but Shabaab enjoyed watching the frustration grow. Finally, Sharif threw up his hands and sputtered, "I am a leader and a warrior, not a tradesman! This cursed thing has information for me and I cannot get it."

Shabaab was laughing on the couch, which only added to Sharif's anger. There was a string of Arabic, which could only be profanities, to which Khan also chuckled. Shabaab got off the couch and held out his hands. "I can't believe you can't figure this out." He laid everything out on the small coffee table and called for some additional items, two rolls of paper towels and another flashlight. He explained what he was doing as he went, enjoying the moment as he demonstrated his talent. The radio was powered by a 9 volt battery. Sharif had been trying to wire several batteries together from spare flashlights, but he hadn't used enough to get the right power level. Shabaab explained that the small 'C' and 'D' cell batteries he had been using were only rated for one and a half volts each. Simple math told them they needed six batteries to make the nine volts. He repeated "simple math" several times just to rub it in. Then, he explained, there needed to be a good contact between the cells. He showed them how to do that by inserting them one by one into the paper towel rolls. Sharif sputtered that he was still going to have trouble making the connections, because the two different sized batteries wouldn't line up in the cardboard roll. As Shabaab was demonstrating how one wrapped each of the smaller batteries in paper towels until they were of a sufficient diameter to fit tightly, the Mexican got up and grabbed the last flashlight. "I need this for the little house before you drain all the power."

Grant stopped on the side of the road just shy of where the GPS indicated he should be. The last kilometer or so had been driven using the NVGs and the going had been slower than he anticipated, but he reckoned better late than early so that the targets would, hopefully, be asleep. He assembled everyone in the dark and led out, letting Robinson keep the pace count. When it seemed they had gone far enough, Grant had Harrison wait by the trail until he had covered the interval, then he signaled them to follow. The NVGs were performing exactly as he had anticipated, and the night was lit up with the unearthly green glow that let the United States Armed Forces rule the night. It was a slow climb, but not too difficult. Grant figured it was enough to make Harrison breath hard, but not put him into cardiac arrest. Besides, he was with Major Carson. She would take care of him and call for help if she needed any. At the top of the ridge the terrain opened up. There was precious little undergrowth ahead of them, and he could make out the cabin at the edge of his NVGs range. He gave a brief command into his microphone and waited for Harrison and Carson to join them. They took longer than anticipated, but Grant used the time to lay out the approach with Robinson. There was the faint hum of a gasoline engine from the far side of the cabin. Grant guessed that there was a small generator somewhere, probably under a lean-to powering the cabin lights. They would move to opposite ends of the clearing that the cabin was in. Robinson would take up position by the parked vehicles while

Grant circled the cabin trying to determine who was inside. There was light showing through the windows, so he didn't think he would have to deal with curtains or trying to maneuver the NVG goggles against the glass. The down side of that meant that whoever was inside was still up and about. He heard Harrison and Carson come up behind him. They lay down on either side of him, Carson pressing up closer than she needed to. Grant whispered his approach plan to them, and pointed out positions he wanted them to take. Once they acknowledged, Harrison moved right off to his spot about twenty meters to the right. Carson half rolled and pushed herself up against Grant, bringing her face close to his, she pushed his NVGs off his face and kissed him, and whispering into his ear "you owe me for this, and I intend to collect," and then she was gone.

Grant clicked his radio back on and called to Robinson. "You ready for this?"

"All set, Sergeant Major," and they both started their hunched over descent of the slope, moving one at a time from tree to tree until they were at the bottom. Grant looked over to the vehicles and could see Robinson in position. He could also see that the young soldier had his weapon up and ready. Grant brought his own AMD around and felt that the safety was still on. This would not be a good time for an accidental discharge. He started his slow approach across the open ground to the cabin, keeping his head swiveling across the entire face of the cabin. He avoided the small porch and flattened against the side wall, listening. He could hear some activity inside.

The first window he tried to look in was heavily curtained, and so was the second. If he had been able to see this side from the ridge he would have tried the other side first. He stepped away from the wall to avoid a jumble of tools and broken furniture and moved to the far side. He called to Robinson to let him know where he was.

A door that he hadn't anticipated suddenly opened, the light momentarily washing out his NVG. He flipped the goggles up as he stepped back around the corner, weapon up, and watched a figure walk across the clearing to a small out building that he hadn't seen before. From the size and location, he guessed it was an out house. The figure snapped on a flash light and did a cursory sweep of the area, briefly illuminating the nearest vehicle, then swinging back and stopping, the pool of light inches from Grant's feet. It was then focused on the out house and the figure disappeared inside. He could hear Robinson in his ear piece, asking if he was OK. He told him to shut up and hold his position. Grant decided to wait until the man returned to the cabin before moving from his position. He could hear grunting coming from the out house. It sounded like a bear shitting in the woods. He smiled at the thought. Years from now that would be one of the humorous details when this story was repeated over a few drinks.

The man finally came out, the flash light focused on the back door. Grant waited an extra minute, expecting someone else to come out to use the facilities. When no one did, he moved as quickly as he dared to the front corner, opposite Robinson. He bypassed a window that was partially illuminated. Another visitor to the out house might be able to see him in the glow. He stepped onto the porch slowly, trying to minimize any squeaking planks. He raised himself up to the window and looked in. There were four men clustered around a low table, fiddling with something. He could see the disassembled parts of several flashlights scattered about, and wads of paper towels. He could make out one of the faces at the far end of the group. It was the same face he had seen in Darfur and Moldova.

Once the Mexican was back in the cabin Shabaab called for the light and removed the batteries. He had everything else prepared, so it was a simple matter of attaching the wires to the contacts with several layers of tape and running the other ends to the battery contacts in the radio. Sharif was impressed, but he wasn't going to allow this pug-nosed slave to enjoy any superiority. He took the radio and switched it on, disconnecting the battery pack in doing so. He looked at it in disgust and passed it back to Shabaab, who did a quick repair and flicked the radio on. There was a burst of static as the volume was turned up, and then the sound settled down to a soft, throaty hum. The sound suddenly stopped, only to be replaced by the sound of what could have been car doors closing, then the muffled sound of voices. Shabaab looked at the radio and said, "That ain't good."

"What do you mean?" Sharif asked.

"Where ever that is it's got to be close. Those little radios don't have much more than a couple of mile range."

Grant got back to the tree line and joined Robinson. Together they began their move back up the hill to Harrison and Carson. As soon as Grant got there he gave Sharp the signal that he had located the targets. As they settled down to wait for the assault team to come up Grant gave a quick overview over the air. In response, he could hear Sharp giving directions to spread his meager forces out even more to cover both sides of the cabin. Grant could hear them before he could see them arrive on the top of the ridge. Sharp took a long look at the target and tweaked his instructions ever so slightly, and then they were all off. He was surprised to see Sheila Gordon there, since he thought she would be staying with Price. Carson and Harrison continued to wait at the top of the hill.

The teams were about halfway into position when there was a muffled shot from behind them. Grant instantly was on the radio asking Harrison what was going on. As he answered there was the sound of an engine starting from the same direction as the shot. "I don't know what it was, Luke, it sounded like it came from where we parked. Want me to go look?"

"Negative. Stay where you're at but keep an eye out behind you. See if you can get Price on the radio." Price had stayed with Captain Connaught at the vehicle park. He was to provide security there, but no one, not even Price, thought he was really in shape to go tramping through the woods at night. Since Connaught hadn't brought a weapon, the plan was he and Gordon would keep an eye on her and the vehicles.

"No answer from Price, Luke, but I can see headlights. One of the trucks is leaving."

At that moment, the lights in the cabin went out.

The four men in the cabin continued to stare at the radio as the voices faded. There was a faint carrier wave sound, and Sharif knew that meant that wherever the radio was, the transmit button had been fixed in the depressed position. He gave instructions for everyone to get weapons. Shabaab slid a foot locker from under the table and threw it open. He took out AK-47s and bandoleers of magazines and passed them out. Suddenly the radio came to life. There was the sound of a voice asking "What are you doing?" followed by a single gunshot. There was a pause of a few seconds, then the sound of an engine starting and being revved up.

"What does that mean, Sharif?" Khan asked. "I don't know. Shabaab, kill the lights. You, Mexican, see if there's anything outside." Then there was a voice on the radio that startled them all. It was a woman whose voice was just on the edge of cracking. "They're on the hill coming for you! Get out now! I'll meet you on the road!"

Sharif looked around with a puzzled expression, then the importance of what he heard finally set in. "Go, go to the cars! Get out now!" There was a mad dash to the doorway.

The assault teams were frozen as they all tried to understand what just happened. Sharp gave a command for everyone to take cover while he reassessed the situation. Suddenly the cabin door flew open and a man stepped out and blindly sprayed the tree line with an automatic weapon. Firing wildly from the hip may look sexy and exciting in a movie, but in real life a rifle caliber weapon firing at full automatic from the hip is very difficult to control. The first shot may be level, but everything that comes after follows the recoil and goes high. No one was hit in the initial burst.

Two more figures came running out and headed for the parked cars, but neither of them were firing so they didn't get immediate attention. They made it to the vehicles as the fourth man came out. This one stopped a few feet from the building and dropped into a kneeling position, trying to stay low. He covered the first man as he ran a few feet to a new position, then he was up and moving as the first man took up the firing again. It was a short burst, as his initial wild shooting had exhausted his magazine. The second man was calling out for him to take shorter bursts as the lights of one of the cars snapped on and locked him fully exposed in the open. He stood up to move as the car sped past him, but he wasn't quick enough. One of the shooters in the tree line was able to zero in on him with a controlled burst, throwing him back and down.

The other shooter had been hunched over, struggling with his magazine change when the car went by. He turned and tried to shoot at it, emptying his magazine, when another burst of fire caught him low in the legs. He went down, trying to turn himself around to shoot back. More bullets tore into his arm, causing his weapon to hang limply. He realized he would no longer be participating in the fight and tried to surrender. "Don't shoot! Don't shoot! I give up!" His calls came too late. Another burst of fire ripped into the ground in front of him. He watched the little geysers of the bullet impacts move closer and closer, until he couldn't see anything anymore.

The lack of return fire made the assault teams hold theirs. Sharp told them to hold their positions while he and Grant checked the building. Both men threw flash-bang grenades through the door before going in. Grant sprayed the interior and stepped out of the way to reload and follow Sharp in. With their NVGs they could see well enough to know that there was no one left inside. Grant grunted to remove the goggles as he flicked on a wall switch, illuminating the inside. He immediately went over to the coffee table, where the radio with the jury rigged battery pack still lay. The unit seemed to be undamaged, but he could hear the whine of an engine racing. Whoever it was still had the send button down.

He came out of the cabin with the radio in his hand. "Somebody get me a nine volt battery. This set-up isn't going to work long." While the troops were searching their packs and pockets he called to Harrison to find out what the shot had been from the vehicles. Harrison acknowledged and said he was on his way down to check, but he had a pretty good idea that one of the trucks was gone. "I can't get Price on the radio, and Connaught wasn't wired for one. Give me a minute."

Sharp wanted to follow the car that had sped off. He was searching through the pockets of the two dead terrorists looking for the keys. One of them had a pocketful of Mexican pesos. "I think I know where this one came from, Luke. It looks like maybe the Mexican army is trying to get in on this *jihad* business too." He handed the coins to Grant and kept searching. He came up with a set of keys and headed for the last car, a beat up Volvo. It started on the first try. Grant stopped him before he could leave. "You're not going alone." He looked around for who was closest. "Robinson! Get over here. You're going with Sergeant Sharp."

"Where to?"

"He'll tell you on the way." Robinson got into the car and Sharp sped off. He turned the headlights on and flicked on the high beams. He thought better of it and turned them off. He'd go back to using the NVGs. It would help pick up their lights in the dark.

Harrison was on the radio again. "Price is down. Looks like a single shot to the chest. His radio is gone, and so is Connaught."

"How is he?"

"Doc Carson is looking at him. He's still alive, but I think he's in a bad way. By the way, tell Sharp his truck is gone."

"Do you think she took it?"

"Looks like it, Luke. If she's with the bad guys they have one of our radios now. Better switch frequencies."

Grant swore to himself and did a quick survey of the scene. He had two dead bodies in the middle of nowhere and not enough transportation to get everybody and everything out. He searched through his packs for the satellite phone he had packed. The Medevac bird was an available asset and he intended to use it. He got an immediate answer and gave the coordinates of a field they had passed on there way here. Out of habit he had noted the location just in case he needed it. The voice on the far end of the phone gave an ETA of about fifteen minutes. Grant acknowledged and called to Harrison to have Carson load Price up on his truck and get him to the new LZ. "Take Gordon with you. You stay with Carson until they evacuate Price. Tell the chopper to take him to the nearest hospital, then get his ass back here. I want to try to use him to follow the other Arabs."

"Then what?"

"Then get back here. We'll start shuttling out of here to the LZ."

Robinson saw the glow of the fugitives' lights first. They were on a stretch of road that kept veering left and right, but the image in the NVGs made them look like a searchlight. The glow suddenly stopped and increased in intensity. "It looks like they stopped, Sarge. Think they hooked up with whoever took your truck?" They had heard the exchange between Grant and Harrison. "Might be, Eddie. I'm going to pull over a little before them and go the rest of the way on foot. You stay with the car and come up as soon as I call you." Sharp pulled to the side of the road, but he didn't open the door. Instead, he rolled the window down and squeezed out, that way he didn't turn on the interior lights. Robinson slid across the center console into the drivers' seat.

Sharp hadn't gotten very far when he heard voices ahead. A man was shouting something in Arabic, and a woman was answering in English, saying she had done her part. It sounded like Mary Magdalene. There was more shouting, this time in English that he couldn't make out, and a burst of automatic fire. He could see the long muzzle flash

263

through his NVGs. It had been directed up the road towards him. He doubted that the Arabs could see him. They must have been firing blindly for effect. He moved to the side of the road to continue under cover. There was a sudden increase in the sound of the engines and his truck appeared to block the road. The headlights were on the high beam setting and his roll bar lights were switched on. He flipped his NVGs off and looked over his shoulder. The car he had come in was caught in the bright illumination. Robinson had the presence of mind to drop the transmission into reverse and start backing up as fast as he could. There were two gouts of flame from either side of his truck chasing the car away. It swerved off the road and into the brush. He tried to pick out a target on the side of his truck and let loose a couple of rounds. There was no return fire, but he could see the glow of tail lights speeding away. Whoever had been there was gone now.

He headed back to check on Robinson, who wasn't answering his radio. The car was fully off the road and there was steam rising from under the hood. The windshield had also been shot out. He called to Robinson.

"Yeah, I'm here. The bastards hit me in the arm. I think they clipped my mike too."

Sharp pulled him out of the car and fished for a light. Robinson had taken a hit to the upper left arm. It didn't look too serious; at least the blood wasn't spurting out, just a slow ooze. He took a field dressing from one of his vest pockets and applied it. "Can you walk?" Robinson signaled that he could and struggled to his feet. Once he was steady Sharp led him down the road to his truck. He gave the area a quick once over to make certain there wasn't anyone left behind to ambush them, then flicked on his light to inspect the vehicle. There was a line of holes down the body on the driver's side, ending in a shredded tire. That seemed to be the only damage. He clicked his radio a few times to try to contact Grant. He finally realized that he must have switched frequencies and changed his settings. He gave a situation report and told him Robinson was hit and he had lost the Arabs. The car was out of commission, but he had his truck back and would rejoin him as soon as he changed the flat tire. There was an intersecting road going left to right just beyond his disabled truck. He had Robinson take a position so that he could cover all directions while he worked.

Robinson squatted in the brush and tried to ignore the throb in his arm. He was suddenly thirsty, and hoped that the cooler was still in the back of the truck with some bottled water. He stepped out from behind the bush and stumbled over something in the road. Lying on the dirt was a military headset radio. He guessed it was probably the one taken from Price. He checked it out and was surprised to discover that it was still intact. He switched to the alternate frequency and listened to the chatter from back at the cabin. He broke in to tell Grant he could stop worrying about the bad guys listening in on their commo.

Grant was developing an entirely new set of headaches back at the cabin. He was anxious to get the Blackhawk back so he could continue his pursuit. The Arabs shouldn't be too hard to track if he could just get into the air. At night they would have to travel with their headlights on, and they had a ways to go before they were out of the trees and onto paved roads. Carson had gone with Price to the hospital, so there was no need for the on board medic to have to delay giving a casualty briefing to the Emergency Room people. He finally tried calling Carson's cell phone with the satellite unit. She must have had service where ever she was. She picked up quickly and Grant asked her where the bird was.

"He's still sitting on the pad out here."

"Tell him to get his ass back here. We can still wrap this up tonight."

"He's not coming. As soon as we landed he got hold of Ashley somehow. He was ordered to wait until the Colonel could get here and ferry him to your location. The pilot told me Ashley asked if the LZ you picked out could take more than one helicopter at a time. When he said it could he was told to mark it for two more birds that should be here shortly. I tried to get more information, but that was it. You might want to try to call him directly. He won't answer my call."

Grant snapped off and dialed another number. He wasn't bothering with Ashley; he was going right to Vaughn. It went right to voice mail. Before he could try again he had an incoming call. It was Vaughn, and from the background noise, it sounded like he was on a helicopter.

"Grant, I'm inbound with my own team. Get that LZ marked for me. We should be there in ten to fifteen."

"Listen, Vaughn, while you're up in the air you can spot the Arabs. There can't be a hell of a lot of cars out in the woods at this time of night. They've only got about a half hour head start. As far as I know they've got Connaught with them. It looks like she's playing on their team now."

"I know all about that, Grant, so let me worry about it. Captain Connaught is exactly where I want her to be. We'll talk when I get there. Make sure you have transportation for me."

CHAPTER EIGHTEEN

I
T WAS A SOMBER GROUP that made the hours long drive back to Concord. Their world had been turned upside down, shaken apart, and, as far as they were concerned, discarded by the Green Machine. General Vaughn had arrived with a team of 'specialists' who proceeded to strip the site of every piece of paper and any item that looked like it may have intelligence or forensic value. The vehicles were commandeered to shuttle personnel and equipment between the cabin and the LZ, and Grant and his soldiers were relegated to sitting off to the side and watching. No one was providing any information to them, and any questions they asked were referred to Vaughn or Ashley, who had made a quick return to the scene once the firing stopped. Once Ashley was on site the process of interviewing everyone involved in the raid began in earnest. Grant had anticipated that and had instructed his people to offer as little as possible. The rule of thumb was that if they hadn't fired their weapon, they should deny having been in position to see anything, which was true for most of them. The terrorists had burst out of the cabin shooting before most of them had been in position, and the risk of inadvertently catching a 'friendly' in a cross fire had caused them to hold their fire. There was a general disbelief that so few people had fired their weapons, and even an examination of the cabin, vehicles and trees didn't convince the interrogators. They collected all

the weapons and magazines, empty and full, and searched the grounds for spent shell casings.

A State Police Crime Scene van arrived just after dawn along with a convoy of mysterious people who were all riding in General Services Administration vehicles. The State Police technicians assumed the posture of innocent bystanders as Vaughn gave instructions for his people to handle all evidence gathering and processing in the name of 'National Security'. The techs seemed to be more than willing to let someone else take the lead, and concentrated on keeping track of their equipment and supplies. Someone, after all, would have to pay to restock the van.

Grant, Sharp and Robinson all came under the most scrutiny, as they had fired most of the rounds. Sharp had to lead a small team to the cross roads where he had recovered his truck. Again it was a question of who shot at what and how many rounds were expended. Robinson was able to plead ignorance to most of the events. He had been hunched down trying to stay out of the line of fire. The Feds confiscated the shot up tire over Sharp's protest. The rim had been part of an expensive set of custom wheels he had installed, and he knew he would never see it again.

They were finally released at mid-morning. There was plenty of room in the vehicles for everyone to ride together. Grant called Carson to check on Price's condition. She told him he was out of surgery, but still in critical condition. She was in the process of arranging an air ambulance to take him to a better facility. She had gone right to the top, General Cabot, and demanded he release one of the Blackhawk UH-60s to transport him. "These people are good, but they don't have experience with his type of wound. I'll stay with him until I can get all the arrangements made."

"Would it do any good for us to come?"

"He wouldn't know you were here. He's so far under they're keeping him on a respirator, just in case. It would do my morale a world of good to see you, but you'd probably bring a crowd with you. Anyway, from where you're at it would take too long to get here. I should have one of the Blackhawks from Colebrook here in a little bit."

Grant gave the update to his passengers, and then passed the word to the other truck. The fact that Price was still hanging on was a good sign and lifted the spirits a little. Sharp had another piece of news:

"When we get close to Bethlehem, let me take the lead. I've got an address we might want to check out."

"What's that?"

"I cleaned out the glove box on the Volvo. There was a road map with a route highlighted and an address written on it. Might be another safe house they're using."

"You didn't give it to the Feds?"

"What did they give us? Besides, I figure this is personal enough that you'd want to look into it yourself. Are we going? Most of us still have side arms if there's any trouble."

Grant slowed to let Sharp take the lead. The exit came up quickly and they followed a number of side roads through and out of town. They seemed to be heading to a pillar of smoke. Grant called to Sharp to hold up. "I don't like the looks of the smoke up ahead. We'll leave everyone here and you and I will go on ahead." They found a small roadside general store to stop at. It would give everyone an opportunity to at least get some food. No one seemed to have eaten since the afternoon before. Grant and Sharp grabbed coffees and then headed out. As they got closer to the smoke there was a fire department tanker truck refilling from a pond. Grant pulled over to ask if they could get through. The fireman told him that it might be tight, but the fire was pretty much out and the road was passable.

"What happened up there?"

"Old Lebanese couple had a place up there. It looks like they had a kerosene heater blow up on them. Don't know why they were using it though; it wasn't that cold last night. They must have been getting ready for autumn. Too bad. They were nice people from what I hear."

Grant thanked the man and drove on. As they got closer to the scene there were emergency vehicles parked on both sides of the road. Grant slowed as they went by the house. Sharp pointed down the driveway at a small Japanese car visible near the side door. "That's the car the Arabs took off in last night. I can see a couple of bullet holes in the rear panel where one of the dead guys shot at them." At that moment a local cop walked up and told them to move on before he wrote them up for blocking an emergency vehicle. Grant nodded and drove off, looking for a place to turn around.

Back at the general store they got sandwiches and talked about the fire. There was a lot of speculation, but it seemed the most likely explanation was that this had been a safe house that the Arabs used, and once they were able to change vehicles it was no longer of any use to them. "It looks like they're cleaning up after themselves, Luke. Think this means they're getting out of the country?"

"I doubt it, Dave. Somebody put a lot of time and effort into trying to kill us, and so far all they've managed to do is whack Price. That's not much to show for all that. I think they'll try to clean up some of their mess and lie low for awhile and wait for things to die down."

"What do you think they're going to do about Mary Magdalene? She had to be the one who shot Price; there was no one else around."

"Yeah, that's the big question for me now. Vaughn said something about her being right where they wanted her. We already know she was supposed to be keeping tabs on us. I'm wondering if she was working both sides of the street here."

"You mean like a double agent?"

"Could be, Dave, could be. I'd like to get my hands on her before she can get back to Vaughn and Ashley. If she was just trying to get in with the Arabs, there were other ways to handle Price besides shooting him. He's smart enough to know how to go along with a simple plan."

They arrived back at the State Armory mid afternoon. It had been no surprise that a flight of Blackhawks had over flown them shortly after they left the town of Bethlehem. All the birds were lined up on the ramp at the aircraft maintenance facility. Vaughn's corporate jet was also parked there.

Grant told everyone they were released, but nobody went anywhere. They were all concerned about Sergeant Price, and they all wanted to know what was going to happen next. Grant promised that he would let them know as soon as he found out something, and he went inside to find General Vaughn. He had the answers that Grant wanted. He found him sitting in Cabot's office. They had been expecting him. General Cabot was not happy with the turn of events as Vaughn had described them, but Vaughn seemed to be the one calling the shots right now. Grant pressed him for an explanation about Captain Connaught.

"She was exactly what she said she was, Grant, a nun who wanted to do more after 9/11. Her problem was that she came from a family of dedicated political liberals, and they all believed they could change the world just by 'understanding' everyone else. She had a brother who thought he could build bridges with the *Jihadists* by sympathizing with them working from the inside. He found out fairly quickly that it didn't work.

"The moron was grabbed in Syria a couple of years ago by Hezbollah and turned over to their bosses the Iranians. They found out that he had a sister who was a serving officer in Afghanistan and they made contact with her. The deal was that she would do some low level work for them and she'd get to see her brother again. She found out pretty quick that once you did a little, they wanted a lot. That's when she turned herself in."

Grant followed along and knew what came next. "Naturally, since she was already working for them you saw an opportunity to use that against them didn't you?"

"Nobody said this was a friendly game, Sergeant Major. She became an asset, a very valuable one. She was able to identify agents and safe house all over the Middle East and parts of Europe. We've been able to use that information to monitor a lot of activity and roll up some pretty bad people without tipping our hand. When they contacted her about this operation to take out the 'Wild Bunch' from the 289th, we saw an opportunity to grab the one the Iranians call 'the Coordinator' and maybe even turn him. The other one, who we think was a courier for Osama bin Laden, was an unexpected bonus. There's a lot of information we want to milk out of him."

"Yeah, Vaughn," Grant responded, "and how long did it take for your whole idea to go south? You'd think that if you were going to use us as bait you would have been a little more forthcoming with information. Maybe Price wouldn't be holding on with his fingernails right now."

"I'm sorry about Price. I don't know what happened with Connaught. She was only to provide them with information that we wanted them to have. She was never supposed to take any direct action, or even get close enough to them to join them. We want to find her and get some answers."

"What about her brother? Could they have used him as more leverage to get her to up her cooperation? Or maybe you've got someone else in your house telling tales out of school."

"As far as we know her brother has been dead for some time. We haven't told her that yet. We were waiting for this assignment to run its course before we let her know."

"Maybe you should have let her know so she could make her own decisions. Right now it looks like the Iranians are pulling all the strings. Do you know where the Arabs are now?"

"We haven't been able to locate them. We've got an alert out for their car, but it hasn't turned up anywhere yet. If we hear anything I'll let you know,"

"I already found their car. They aren't using it anymore." Grant told them about the house fire and seeing the car in the yard. "They probably killed the Lebanese couple and took their car, then burned the bodies to cover it. If there's another body in the house it might be Mary Magdalene. It looks to me like they're starting to close the books."

"I'll check on that" Vaughn said. "In the meanwhile, you look like crap. Why don't you and your band of outlaws go home and get some sleep. I doubt our friends will be doing anything but trying to find another hiding place and lying low for a few days."

"Will one of you arrange for an air ambulance to get Price down here so he can get taken care of?"

"What's wrong with where he's at now? I heard it was a fine hospital." Cabot was already counting the beans and trying to cut his expenses. "Why don't you leave him there for a few days until he's stable?"

"Major Carson is still with him. She says the docs up there are good, but they aren't the ones Price needs. They've got some specialists down here that can get him back together again, and that's where I want him."

"Where you want him? That's a little presumptuous, don't you think?"

"The only thing I'm presuming right now is that he's my friend and he's in a hospital all fucked up because we were trying to take out a terror cell in our own back yard, and General Vaughn here didn't bother to tell us about a double agent. I'd say the least he can expect right now is a grateful country will fly him to the right hospital. I'd hate to have to make a stink about it."

Vaughn understood his meaning. "I believe you would, Sergeant Major." There was a pause. "General Cabot, as long as I still have operational control of your aviation assets, I'm going to authorize a medevac flight for Price." He turned back to Grant. We'll have him down here today. Is there anything else?"

There wasn't, and Grant walked out. He went back to where his soldiers were waiting and gave them the good word on Price. He told them there was nothing more they could do for the time being, so they should all go home and get some rest. He cautioned everyone to stay buddy'd up, just in case, and told them all to report back in the morning. "I'll have orders cut putting all of you on thirty days active duty, more if I can get it. Least I can do is make sure you're getting paid for all this."

Robinson spoke for all of them. "I'm already a full timer, Sergeant Major, but the per diem will help these guys out a lot. Can you get them ninety days instead? At least carry some of them over until they can get regular jobs. Times are tough out there." Grant promised he'd do what he could, and tasked Harrison with taking care of it. The group broke up after that. It had been a long few days for everyone. Finally, only Harrison, Sharp and Gordon were still there. He considered them for a moment, then asked, "You three all set until tomorrow, or do you need to come and bunk at my place?" They told him they were all set, but were more concerned about what he was going to do. "You always seem to be the odd man out, Luke. Why don't you come home with me tonight? You know Major Bonneville is probably going to be staying with her mother in the hospital. You probably could use some company."

"I'll be fine, Ralph. I'm gonna take a ride by the cardiac unit and see if there's anything she needs, then I think I'll wait around to make sure Price gets settled in."

Grant found Bonneville in the waiting area of the cardiac care unit. Her mother's condition was serious, but she was undergoing catheterization to put a couple of stents in her arteries. Harrison had had the same work done, and it seemed to be the cure for a lot of problems, but Bonneville was still worried. Grant sat with her for a few hours until her mother was out of surgery and back in her room. She asked about the raid on the cabin and how Price got hurt again. She was distressed to hear Mary Magdalene was responsible. "I was really starting to like her. She seemed genuine."

"Genuine? You do remember she was supposed to be keeping tabs on us for Vaughn?"

"I remember, but that's not what I meant. I got to talk to her a little and she seemed like she really didn't like doing it and she seemed to be developing a real attachment to Price."

"Some attachment. She shot him in the chest."

Grant didn't feel a need to be there when the old lady came out from under, so he said his goodbyes. "Where are you going to stay tonight?"

"The kids are at my sister's house, so if I don't stay here I'll be going over there."

"Sure you don't want to come over to my place? Be a lot quieter, and you look like you could use a little quiet time, some wine and a soak in the hot tub right about now." She smiled at him, put her hand on his cheek and said no. "As much as I'd like to, you look like you could use some quiet time too, and I don't think we'd get much of that with that combination. Let me get a rain check for after everything has quieted down."

Grant went outside and moved his truck over by the helipad. The security guard who had given him and Sharp a hard time a few nights ago came by, but when he saw who it was he decided that discretion was the better part of valor and left him alone. He knew there was a military helicopter on the way in and figured Grant was waiting for it. Grant didn't have long to wait. He could hear the bird before he could see it, and he got out to scan the sky to the north. The Blackhawk appeared in the distance and came in quickly. The pilot had done several tours in Iraq and Afghanistan and understood the need for speed when he was carrying a casualty. He came in hot and flared at the last second, making a smooth landing on the pad. A team from the emergency room was waiting and the transfer was quick. Major Carson had been riding with Price to keep an eye on him and hopped off when she saw Grant. She waved him over to join them as they pushed the gurney indoors. A nurse tried to block Grant from going into the examining room, but Carson overruled her. The nurses knew her as somewhat of a bitch and didn't argue. Carson gave a quick but thorough briefing to the new specialist, who she seemed to know well enough to call by his first name. He followed along on the chart that came with Price, and then gave a few orders and Price was on the move again, this time to the intensive care unit. Once he was gone Carson sat down in a plastic chair heavily and ran her hands through her hair. She looked at Grant and gave him a smile. "Somehow, I knew you'd be here. I expected the rest of the 289ᵗʰ to be standing there too. What happened to them?"

"I sent them home for the night. They've been through a lot. So have you. You look like you could use a drink or three."

"I most certainly can, but I'll settle for a cup of coffee. Let's go up to the cafeteria. What about your little Major? Will she be joining us?"

"I told you not to call her that. She's upstairs in the cardiac unit. Her mother came out of surgery a few hours ago. She's going to stay with her for a while, and then probably go see her kids at her sister's."

"You didn't invite her back to your place? Is chivalry dead, Sergeant Major, or did you have other plans?"

"I asked her, but she turned me down. She thought I could use the rest too."

Carson made a pouty face. "So I'm the back-up plan? I don't know if I should be insulted by that."

Before Grant answered he steered her to a booth and went and got two cups of coffee. When he came back he sat down across from her and slid her cup over. She had unzipped her flight suit. He didn't think she was wearing a bra underneath it. "I didn't know you were coming in with Price so I hadn't made any kind of plans. I was just going to go home, have a few drinks and sleep for a couple of hours."

"Good plan. I'll come with you."

"Not a good plan. Linda changes her mind and walks in on us, and I'm fucked in more ways than one."

"Then it's settled, you'll come with me." Grant looked at her and shook his head. She didn't skip a beat. "Look, at the very least I need a ride to my car, and you, Sergeant Major, are too much of a gentleman to leave me stranded here. I don't even have money for a cab. So you can take me to my car and I'll follow you home, or you can follow me home, or we can just save a lot of time and effort and you can just drive me home. I've had a long couple of days and I don't feel like taking my next shower alone." Grant knew she had outmaneuvered him. He just didn't have the will power to ignore the little head that was doing the thinking for him.

Carson didn't waste any time once they were in his truck. She folded the center console out of the way and quickly started to pay attention to him. It took all of Grant's concentration and self control to keep the truck on the road. He didn't notice the car that followed them out of the hospital parking lot. She was totally naked by the time he drove into her yard, and she wasn't in the mood to wait. She mounted him in the cab and quickly brought them both to an explosive climax. She was, as always, an energetic and passionate lover, and she knew how to get the most out of her partner. When they were done she led him by the hand, both naked now, around back to the hot tub where she proceeded to bring him to arousal again. When she was finished with him she sent him to the truck to get her clothes while she went in and got some towels and found something for them to eat. She was famished after her long day and her recent activity, and so was Grant. It wasn't quite dark yet, but the front yard was shielded from the road by shrubs and trees, so Grant didn't hesitate walking wet and naked to his truck. As he collected their garments he heard a vehicle on the road. It sounded like it was going by slowly, then stopped, turned around, and made another pass out front. It was probably nothing, but Grant folded the console back down and retrieved his pistol and a few spare magazines, just to be on the safe side. Something caught his eye sitting on the back seat. It was the duffel that Carson had brought with her. He reached back and took it out. The weight made him curious, so he looked inside. The folding stock AMD 65 and a chest pack of magazines were nestled under her personal gear. It looked like Vaughn's people didn't get all their weapons after all. Grant slung the duffel over his shoulder and carried everything back to the house.

He returned to the back yard and entered the house through the boarded up French doors. They were both wide open to let in the cool of the evening. There were a couple of towels tossed across the back of a chair, and he could hear her humming, in another room. "Wrap yourself in a towel and make us some drinks. I'm getting a cold plate for us. There's a wine cooler under the bar, and I think you'll find tequila you'll like back there."

He dried himself off and put on his trousers and undershirt, as sitting naked to eat wasn't his idea of comfort. He was too old to start living like a free spirit. He went to the bar and perused the stock. If nothing else, Sylvia Carson didn't skimp on her liquor supply. He poured himself a good *anejo* over ice and drank it down, then poured himself another before he checked the wine cooler. He picked out a cabernet, not because he knew much about what she liked in wine, but because it was there. He didn't think she would keep anything on ice in anticipation of guests dropping in: if it was there, she drank it. He uncorked the wine, picked out a glass, and brought it to the table.

She brought out a large try with salads and cold cuts on it, still wrapped in a towel. She wrinkled her nose at the sight of Grant dressed. "Going somewhere?"

"No, but I'm hungry and this is how I like to eat."

"Really? It's going to be awkward for the desert I have planned for you."

"I'll take my chances."

By the end of the meal she had let her towel slip so that it was just draped on the chair. Any self control Grant may have planned on tapping into vanished as she came over and sat in his lap, her tongue teasing his ear. "Do you want your desert here or upstairs?"

"Upstairs, by all means." He watched as she walked away from him and climbed the stairs. He took the duffel and almost as an after thought grabbed the bottles and glasses. She looked over her shoulder as she got to the top of the stairs and smiled. A little more booze and a lot more sex and Grant wouldn't be going anywhere until morning. That fit into her plans very nicely.

It was dark out when she finally gave him a break. The excitement of the past few days had turned her on, and Grant had been hard pressed to keep up with her. She reached over him, breasts dragging across his chest, to turn on a lamp by the bed. She got up and walked to the vanity where the bottles had been left and poured both of them another drink. When she came back to the bed she straddled his legs and sipped her wine, giving Grant the full view of her body. Grant appreciated it and took it all in. Sylvia Carson was a very fit and beautiful woman. Her only short coming was her demanding personality, which even carried over into the bedroom. She drank her wine down and put the glass on the floor, then she lowered her head and began to work on Grant again. He leaned back and sipped his drink, enjoying the attention. He was definitely going to hell. At least he was enjoying the trip.

He started to respond to her efforts and pulled her up so he could pay attention to her nipples and have her mount him. She began rocking back and forth, her eyes half closed and the tip of her tongue on her upper lip. They were both building to a climax together.

There was the sound of breaking glass from somewhere in the house. Grant took Carson by the hips and rolled her off to the side. She grabbed for him and tried to stay on him, but he was too strong for her. She hadn't heard the sound. He put his finger to his lips, and then pointed to the door. Her expression changed as she began to understand something else was going on. His pistol was on a chair across the room with his trousers. He got up and dressed quickly. He took the AMD out of the duffel and snapped in a magazine. Spare magazines got stuffed in his pockets. She pulled the sheet up and wrapped herself with it. Then she opened her nightstand and took out another one of he little .38 revolvers she favored. He told her to close the door behind him. "What are you going to do?"

"I'm not going to give them the chance to get up here. Whatever happens, don't come downstairs. Wait for me up here. If anyone comes to the door and you don't hear my voice, shoot until you're empty." He handed her the nine millimeter pistol that was also in the bag. "Then shoot some more."

He slipped out the door. She locked it behind him, and took some clothes out of the closet and dressed. Then she sat on the floor by the bed and waited.

Grant crept to the top of the stairs and paused, listening to the sounds below. He could make out what seemed to be two people trying to be stealthy, but not doing a very good job of it. They came into the room from the kitchen with flash lights and examined the remains of the meal on the table. They murmured back and forth, and one spoke louder than he should have. "The whore likes to bath naked outside."

The second one answered him. "Good, we will shoot carefully and save her for last. We will be entitled to a little reward after we kill the big one." They both slowly moved to the doors and stepped outside. Grant took the stairs two at a time to get behind them. The hot tub was easily seen from the door, but you would have to get close to see if anyone was in it at night if the underwater lights weren't on. He was hoping they would move away from the house so he could engage them in the open. They didn't oblige him. He was crossing the room when he heard them coming back in. He crouched behind a sofa and lifted the barrel of his rifle over the cushions. Now they were practicing dispersion techniques, and Grant cursed them for it. The first one was halfway to the stairs before the second one came in the door. He was the most observant and seen something in the glow of his partners light. He started to bring his rifle around when Grant decided enough was enough. He put a controlled burst into his torso and dropped down and pivoted to engage the second target. His AMD picked that precise time to jam, and Grant only got one shot off. The second man had turned around and was looking for the source of the firing. He could see his partner lying spread eagled on his back in the door way. He sensed a movement behind the sofa as Grant got his only shot off, and in the true style of an amateur fired a long, sweeping burst from the hip. If he had better control he might have hit something. The first rounds were level with Grant's head, and then recoil and muzzle climb took over. It gave Grant the time to drop his rifle and draw his .45 ACP. Before he could return fire though, there was the sound of another gun coming from the stairs. He glanced over and saw Sylvia Carson coming down, a pistol in each hand, firing into the back of the intruder. Barely audible above the blasts Grant could hear her screaming something. He shook himself back into action and rose up and started putting rounds into the intruder. He died with his finger on the trigger, emptying his magazine into the steps in front of Carson. She continued firing until both guns were empty and stood on the stairs looking at the body. Grant slowly got up and called to her, letting her know he was there. She came down the stairs and dropped the guns on the sofa and wrapped her arms around Grant. Grant led her over to the bar and poured them both a stiff drink. He turned on the lights and examined both bodies to see if he recognized either of them. They were strangers to him, but that didn't mean anything. He found the cell phone he had left on the table earlier in the evening and punched a few numbers into it. He didn't recognize the voice at the other end, but that seemed to be par for the course when he called Vaughn. The voice claimed the General was not available. Grant didn't care. He identified himself and made his report. "Well, you better tell him he is available. There's been another shooting at Major Carson's. I have two dead bad guys here, and I'd really rather not get the local police involved. He needs to clean this one up." The voice at the other end started to say something but Grant ignored it and closed his phone. No one spoke, and the house was quiet. He walked back to the bar and poured another drink. His cell phone started to buzz and he looked at the screen, half expecting it to be General Vaughn calling back. Instead, he saw that the caller was Linda Bonneville. He looked at Sylvia Carson and showed her the phone. She just waved her hand at it and took another sip of her drink. He punched a button to take the call.

"Luke, I think I just saw Captain Connaught at the hospital."

Chapter Nineteen

"Say that again, Linda? Where at the hospital did you see her?"

"I just left my mother's room and I'm heading to my sister's. That's where my kids are, and I saw her driving through the parking lot. I'm certain it was her. What do you think she's doing here, Luke?"

Grant knew exactly what it was: the Arab from Sudan had a fixation for her and he was using Mary Magdalene to track her down. "She's working with the Arabs, and she knows you're there with your mother. That makes you a soft target. Get someplace safe and stay there. I'll get hold of Vaughn and have him send a security detail to cover you."

"Will you come too?"

"First things first. Did you see anyone else with her?"

"I couldn't be sure, but I don't think so. Would she come after me alone?"

"The Iranians grabbed her brother a while back and she thinks they're still holding him. Grabbing you could be what she thinks is her chance to get him back. Get away from the building and wait for either me or the feds."

They both hung up and Grant redialed Vaughn's number. While he was waiting for an answer he told Carson to get any extra ammo she might have and reload her pistols. She was halfway up the stairs when

Vaughn answered. "I thought I'd hear from you again, Sergeant Major. Tell me what happened."

"That can wait. I just got a call from Major Bonneville. She says she spotted Connaught at the hospital. She's probably looking for the Major. I don't think she'd know Price was there yet. You need to get a team there ASAP."

"I'll handle that, Grant. Where are you right now?"

He briefly considered giving his location, but decided against it. That would only confuse the issue right now. He'd rather explain later. "I'm on my way to the hospital."

"What about Major Carson?"

So much for discretion. "I've got her with me."

"I worry about you, Grant, but I'll see you in a few minutes."

Grant folded his phone and stuck it in his pocket. Carson was coming back down the stairs. He saw she had shoes on now. He grabbed Carson by the hand before she could refill her drink and led her to his truck. "Where are we going? Your place this time I hope. My insurance company is going to be royally pissed when they see all this damage."

"Insurance probably doesn't cover a terrorist attack. You better hope Vaughn will pay for it. We're going to the hospital again."

She looked at him with her mouth open. "What the fuck is wrong with you? Do you think I want to get in the middle of you explaining to your little Major what I'm doing with you? I though you were the one who wanted to keep us far apart?"

He had already considered the eventual explanation, but that wasn't a concern right now. "I'll burn that bridge when I get to it. You're all the back-up I have right now. We're just going to try to grab Connaught before she can do any more damage. Linda couldn't tell me if the Arabs were with her, but if they are I want to end this tonight."

They drove in silence the rest of the way. As he pulled into the emergency room entrance he saw a gaggle of cars with blue and red lights flashing. Standing in front of the crowd was Rawlins, the FBI agent. Bonneville's car was parked there, but she was nowhere to be seen.

"What are you doing here, Grant? I thought you were somewhere up north invading Canada."

Grant ignored the comment and asked Rawlins where Bonneville was. "We've got her secured over by the helipad. I'll ask again: what are you doing here?" Grant ignored the question and told Rawlins what he knew. The agent returned the favor and let him know what the current plan was. "We identified a car belonging to a Lebanese couple that had been killed execution style parked in the upper lot. Your buddy Vaughn tumbled us on to that. The surveillance system they have here sucks, but we were able to see that she was the only one who got out of the car. We've got all the exits covered and we're trying to locate her now. This place must have paid someone to put all their cameras in exactly the wrong places. We're starting a floor to floor search, but it's going to take time."

Grant looked at Carson. "You know this place pretty good. How far apart is the cardiac unit from where Price is?"

She thought a moment and looked up at the building. She pointed to the wing directly above them. "The Cardiac Care Unit is right up there, on the fourth floor. Price is in Intensive Care on the same floor, probably a hundred feet apart at most."

He pulled her after him and dashed to the entrance. "I want you to show me." The agent at the door tried to stop them but Grant barreled through. He could hear Rawlins shouting after him to stop. Carson tried to get in front to lead but he stopped her. "Stay behind me. Just tell me where to go." She directed him to a stairwell and they began the climb to the fourth floor. Grant was starting to feel every bit of his age by the time he reached the last flight of stairs. Too much booze, too much driving, too much sex and not enough sleep in the past two days. He pushed the door open slightly and looked down the hall. Everything looked normal on the floor. The FBI had not wanted to start a panic by trying to evacuate everyone. Grant stepped out with Carson in tow. A nurse behind a desk looked at him and started to say something, but recognized Carson and greeted her. "Are you here to check on the soldier you brought in?" Carson said yes and asked for his room number. The nurse gave it and pointed down the hall. As they passed she said, "Oh, by the way, his wife is here. She just came by a little while ago and I think she's still in the room." Carson looked at Grant. "I didn't know he was married."

"He isn't!"

Grant started running down the hall. The door to Price's room was closed. He pressed up against it slightly and it moved. Connaught had not locked it. He pushed a little harder and could see the privacy curtain pulled across the room. The image of shadows on the fabric weren't there: another movie myth. He edged into the room slowly. He pushed Carson back, but she had her gun out and was following him in. There was a commotion out in the hallway, the nurse chasing after them. Grant pointed out the door and mouthed the words "Handle it" and pushed her back out again. She went and the door closed.

The privacy curtain curved around the foot of the bed, making Grant go further in the room. He could see his reflection in the window, but there wasn't enough of an angle to see to the right. He stepped back and put his back against the wall and slid towards the glass. Gradually his line of sight improved and he could see her standing over the bed. The image wasn't clear enough to see if she had a gun. He stepped around the edge of the curtain with his .45 up. She sensed his presence and lifted her head, but didn't look at him. There was a small caliber pistol on the bed, inches away from her hand.

"Step back from the bed, Mary Magdalene. It's all over now."

She looked back down at Price. "I didn't mean to hurt him. All I wanted to do was send a warning. Nobody needed to know, but he saw the radio. I didn't have a choice. I've never had to hurt anyone before." Grant could see her look at the pistol. He took a step towards her, hoping she wouldn't make him shoot her. God only knew where the 230 grain slug would go after it passed through her slender body.

"I know about your brother, Mary Magdalene. I know why you did all this. Let it end now. There's nothing more you can do."

She grabbed for the gun, but didn't point it at him. Grant didn't understand why he didn't shoot her. "He told me my brother had one chance to live. All I had to do was come here and catch Major Bonneville and bring her to him. Then he told me what he was going to do to her. I told him he was a sick evil man." Her knuckles were turning white; she was squeezing the gun so hard, but she kept it pointed down. "That did something to him. I've never seen anyone lose control like that before. He started to beat me. That got him more excited. Then he did all those terrible things he said he was going to do to Major Bonneville. The other man just watched. They talked back and forth in Arabic while he was hurting me. They didn't know I understood them. He told the other man my brother was already dead." There were tears streaming down her face now and she was starting to shake.

Grant took another step forward. He felt a gust of air as the door opened again. He wondered who was coming in the room. Sylvia Carson? He spoke softly to Connaught trying to calm her down. "Give me the gun and we can get you some medical attention. You're not doing yourself any good just standing here. We can come back and see Price after you're taken care of." His words didn't seem to have any effect. She looked back down at Price. "He probably doesn't want to see me now."

"You don't know Jonah. I think he'd understand." There was no response. Her shaking was getting worse. "Where were you supposed to take Major Bonneville?"

She started speaking, more to Price than to him. "I knew her entire file. I knew all of your files, every little thing about you. Did you now Major Bonneville has a sister who doesn't live too far from here? It's a nice house. Too nice for what he did to me."

She brought the gun up suddenly to her chin. She tried to pull the trigger but the safety was on. She looked down at the pistol as Grant lunged. Carson stepped around the far end of the privacy curtain with her revolver leveled. Grant got a grip on the small pistol in Connaught's hand and pulled it away as she pulled the trigger. He felt the impact of the bullet on his upper arm. He heard another roar as Carson shot her in the back. Connaught gave a little gasp as she slid to the floor. She died with a little smile on her lips.

Carson stepped around the bed to Grant's side. The door burst in as a nurse appeared, her face twisted in shock and surprise. Carson told her to get a crash cart and started to check Grant's arm. There were more footsteps and loud voices in the hall as the nurse directed more armed men to Price's room. They swarmed in, and after identifying Grant and Carson as not being threats, one of them stepped over Connaught's body and checked her for a pulse. Then he secured her weapon. It was a Hungarian made .32 automatic. Grant looked at it in disgust. It was another one of those small caliber hand guns that he despised so much. They never did the job when the chips were down.

The nurses wheeled Price's bed out to another room while Carson shepherded Grant to a quiet spot. "It's a good thing she wasn't using hollow points, or you'd need a new bicep" she said as she opened up a suture kit a nurse had brought. Vaughn had appeared from somewhere and was standing in front of them. "Which one of you geniuses shot her?" he asked.

Carson held up her hand. "That would be me with my little silver gun."

"Don't get smart with me, Major. She was an asset, and she had information we could use. We may never catch up with those other two now. I hope you're happy with yourself!"

Carson ignored him for the moment and finished the stitch on Grant's exit wound. She asked the nurse to put a bandage on it and stood up her full length in front of Vaughn. "I am, General. Now why don't you go fuck yourself and give us a little peace. All your asset seems to have done is hurt people. Can't you see he's been wounded?"

"Grant's been wounded before, Major. I'm certain with your tender ministrations he'll be fine in no time." He roughly pushed her aside and spoke to Grant. "Did Connaught give you any information before your little sweetheart here shot her?" Grant thought a few moments. Connaught had said something just before she tried to shoot herself. His head was a little fuzzy from the combination of everything that had happened. He closed his eyes and tried to picture the scene. "She said something about Major Bonneville. Give me a second."

Carson put her hand on his chest. "She said the Major's sister had a nice house. Too nice for what he did to her."

Grant suddenly saw the scene in all its clarity. "Where's Major Bonneville right now?"

"She got a call from her sister. I figured the situation was under control and I let her go to be with her kids. What's the problem?"

"The Arabs are at Linda's sister's house." He grabbed Carson's hand and started dragging her down the hall. He shouted over his shoulder for Vaughn to get a team there right away. He called out a half remembered address, then corrected himself. They raced down the stairs and out to his truck. Carson got in beside him and he sped out of the parking lot the wrong way. "Do you know where you're going?" she asked.

Bonneville was watching the scene from the secure area the feds were keeping her in at the helipad. She thought she could see Grant's truck pull up, but her view was obscured by the reflections of so many flashing blue lights. Vaughn was standing close by speaking on a radio.

He seemed to be in control of the situation. There was a rush of armed agents to the building when her phone rang. It was her sister. Her voice sounded strained, but she ignored it, considering the emotional upset of their mother undergoing surgery. "Linda, there's a problem here. I need you to come right away!"

"What is it? Is it one of the kids?" The line was already dead. She tried to call the number, but it went right to voice mail. Not thinking, she called to Vaughn and told him she needed to get home to her kids. Vaughn, suffering from target fixation, didn't think about the overall situation and told the agents to take her to her car.

It was a short drive to her sister's home. There was a strange vehicle in the yard, but it didn't register. People had been coming and going all day. All the lights were on in the house, which was unusual, but again, she ignored it. She walked up the steps and pushed the door open. Her sister and kids were sitting on the couch at the far end of the living room. There was a hand on her upper arm and a hard object pressed into the back of her neck. There had been a man standing on either side of the door. She looked first at the one on the right. She recognized him as the man that Price had met in Afghanistan, the one whose mission was to get revenge on the 289th Engineers. The one on the left was a bigger shock. She saw the evil look in his eyes and focused on his face. It was the other image from the briefings and one she remembered from Africa.

"At long last, whore, you will pay for your impure life."

"Who are you?"

"I am Ali Alawa Sharif, and you will serve me now, and again in paradise."

The sister's house was only a matter of minutes away on the same road as the hospital. He had been there once before, for a social occasion, but it had been in the middle of the contentious family argument over Linda's divorce, and he swore never to return. He shut off his lights and coasted to a stop short of the driveway. They both eased out of the truck and walked slowly up the street. They could see all the lights on in the house through the trees. Grant told Carson to hang back a few yards and slowly approached the house. Linda Bonneville's car was parked by the side entrance. The front door to the house was wide open. There was a body on the porch, half out the door. Grant knelt besides the door out of the light and turned the head. It was the Arab who had been the object of the search that had started outside of the compound in Abbottabad. He was still alive, and still conscious. Grant pulled him to the side of the door and signaled to Carson. "See what you can do for him."

The Arab coughed and struggled to speak. "You're too late, you know. He's quite mad and they're all going to die."

"What's he going to use? Does he have more explosives?"

"I don't know what he has, but he is very determined to play this out." He looked at Grant in the dim light. "You know, my mission was to kill you."

"How did that work out for you?"

"Not very well, I'm afraid. I seem to have fallen in with bad companions."

Grant stepped over him and entered the house slowly, scanning from side to side. The first thing he saw were the two children sitting on the sofa at the far end of the room. They had their hands tied together and were gagged, but their feet were free. From the look in their eyes, Grant guessed that they recognized him. He motioned them with his hand to come to him, and put his finger to his lips for them to be very quiet. As soon as they were close enough he scooped them up and took them back to the porch. Carson was still working on the Arab. "Leave him for now. Get the kids back to the truck." There were flashing blue lights on the road now. "Have the feds come back and get this guy."

The Arab grunted. "My current name is Mehmet Atta Khan."

Grant ignored him. "I don't care," was all he said and went back in the house.

He heard some noises from down a hallway and moved towards them. He remembered a bathroom on the left. The door was open and the room was empty. Every light in the house seemed to be on. Whatever was supposed to happen here was not intended to be secret. The Arab was proud of what he was doing and wanted everyone to see. The next room he passed had the naked body of a woman on the bed. She was tied spread eagled to the four corners. He stepped in to check and stepped right back out. It was Linda's sister. She was bruised but otherwise appeared unhurt. Her eyes were wide and she tried to grunt something through her gag. Grant left it in place and again put his finger to his lips. There was a comforter on the floor that he picked up and spread over her body. He stepped back into the hallway and paused. There were more noises coming from the next room. A man's voice was repeating over and over "You are my whore and you will serve me now and in paradise!"

Grant quickly stepped into the open door and saw a man standing by the far side of the bed. His attention had been fixed on the figure tied to the bed, but some sound made him turn around. He crouched down and held a gun up, taking a shot at Grant standing in the door.

"It's over, pal. Put the gun down. You aren't getting out of here tonight."

"Ah, the big American. I wondered how long it would be before I saw you again. I plan to kill you and your whore tonight. Maybe you would like to watch me satisfy myself with her?"

"Like you did with Connaught? You're a pretty sick bastard, you know that?"

"I see she was able to deliver my message. I hope she fulfilled the other part of her errand tonight."

"If you mean she was supposed to kill Price, she got cold feet."

"A pity. I guess I will have to do it myself after I'm finished here."

Grant could see a reflection of the bed in a bureau mirror. He was trying to think of a way to get into the room and kill the Arab before he started shooting again. "Why did you shoot Khan?"

"You know his name? Did he tell you? Did you ever wonder why it takes so much effort to kill a pig?"

"I thought he was your ally." Grant lay on his stomach and crawled into the room. "What did he do?"

"In the end he lost the fire. He was upset with me for taking so much enjoyment from the *infidel* whores. He forgot that a warrior has a right to the spoils of his conquest."

"I'm coming for you now, rag head." Grant fired three evenly spaced shots under the bed. At least one shot hit his target and he heard a small cry of pain and a thud as he dropped to the floor. Grant spaced his remaining shots below the bed and instantly changed magazines. He scrambled to his feet and took several long strides to the far side of the bed. As soon as he saw the figure he fired two more shots into it. The man looked up at him with an agonized look on his face. The son of a bitch wasn't dead yet, even though he had four or five 230 grain slugs in him. Grant recognized the face from the Sudan, from Moldova, and from the briefing photos. The man was gasping for breath and trying to speak. "I have information, infidel, you can't kill me."

Grant considered that for the briefest of moments. The Arabs gun was close to his foot. He kicked it away and turned to Linda Bonneville. The Arab had started to cut her clothes off, not being particularly careful with the straight edged razor he had been using. She had some deep gashes on her chest and legs. Grant put his weapon down and started to rip sheets to fashion some quick bandages. He called out to the voices he could hear entering the house, calling for a medic. The first person through the door had been Sylvia Carson, followed by an EMT with an oversized orange aid bag. Carson looked at Bonneville's wounds and began issuing orders to the EMT. The EMT looked at the body on the floor and asked "What about him?"

"He can wait," Grant answered. Bonneville tried to sit up and look down at Ali Alawa Sharif. He had tied her up and made her watch as he raped his sister, graphically describing everything he was doing and telling her how he was going to do even more to her. The Arab was seriously wounded, but he still managed to lock onto her eyes and give her an evil grin. "I will be in your mind's eye forever!" he gasped out at her. She saw Grant's gun on the bed next to her leg. She picked it up and shot him in the face.

General Vaughn was standing in the driveway watching the procession of stretchers coming out of the house. Linda Bonneville and her sister were first, the sister being deep into shock. Linda was alert, almost hyper, as if killing Ali Alawa Sharif had liberated her spirits. Grant was walking besides her, holding her hand. Vaughn stopped him and pulled him aside.

"This is a pretty fucked up situation, Grant. We wanted both of those Arabs alive. He could have told us a lot about what's going on with al Qaeda and the other *Jihadists*."

"I don't care what you wanted, Vaughn. Be happy with one. I would think that Osama bin Laden's courier could give you even more info about his organization."

"This isn't over yet, Grant."

"It is for me." He turned and walked away. He watched Linda Bonneville and her sister being put into the same ambulance with the kids and watched it drive off. On his way back to his truck he saw that the Arab was on another gurney, waiting to be put into the second ambulance. There didn't seem to be much of a hurry to get him evacuated. Sylvia Carson was standing close by, discussing something with an EMT. Grant walked over and stood by the Arab, staring down at him. His arms were secured but he managed to shake free of his oxygen mask.

"I was supposed to kill you."

"I know. You already said that. Better luck next time."

The Arab gave a painful little laugh, and then coughed up some blood. The EMT tried to replace the mask but he turned his head away. "I think I would rather die than go to your Guantanamo Bay. If I give up all my secrets would that save me?"

Grant shook his head. "I'm the wrong guy to ask, Khan. That decision is way over my pay grade."

The Arab just nodded and allowed the mask to be placed over his face. Carson gave orders for him to be loaded, and a pair of heavily armed agents joined him in the back of the ambulance. Carson stood next to Grant as they watched the vehicle drive off with all lights flashing.

"Is it over, Luke?"

Grant looked down at her, then back at the receding lights. "It'll never be over."